Shabby Chic After All

a story of restoration and love
by *Kirsten Fullmer*

Produced by:

FriesenPress
Suite 300 – 852 Fort Street
Victoria, BC, Canada V8W 1H8

www.friesenpress.com

Distributed to the trade by The Ingram Book Company

To Bingo and Skippy, my George and Ringo

1

Cool spring air whipped across Julia's face as she cranked down her truck window. Squinting into the wind, she adjusted her grip on the steering wheel and wondered again at her decision to leave New York. As her thoughts wandered, emerald-tinted buds on the trees and smudges of pink wild flowers on the Pennsylvania hillsides sped past her window. Fumbling with the CD book on the seat next to her and keeping one eye on the road, she tugged out her favorite Beatles album, inserted it, and punched at buttons until *The Long and Winding Road* hummed across the tattered speakers in the pick-up truck's door.

Ringo pranced in circles on the seat next to her, then stood to plant his front paws on the passenger door. He barked once over his shoulder is if to say, "Hey, roll my window down too."

As Julia glanced from her little dog to the country highway and back to the dog, her voice faded from singing with the stereo and her expression softened. "Sorry buddy, I can't reach from here." As usual, the goofy mutt managed to draw her thoughts from apprehension to the task at hand.

Ringo yipped, his eyes bright and ears perked.

Julia slowed the truck and pulled onto the shoulder. "Okay okay, you win…" Unbuckling her seat belt, she leaned across the truck to tug and push awkwardly at the passenger window crank. Blond curls fell into her eyes and she blew at them in frustration. Still not limber enough to reach that far over her head, she scooted farther across the seat. It had been years since she had owned a vehicle without power windows and she hadn't thought about being able to roll down the window for the dog. She supposed she was bound to find many things she hadn't considered.

Leaning an elbow on the seat, she scratched the little white dog between the ears, taking in the music and the moment, his fur coarse and curly under her fingers. Though she was momentarily lost in thought, Ringo's squirming once again drew her full attention and she smiled.

"There you go."

He lapped a wet kiss across her cheek, then happily resumed his position at the window.

"Don't you fall out," she warned.

Quirking her brow at the dog, Julia sat up and slid back to her seat, clicked her belt, and cautiously pulled onto the highway. Ringo leaned into the wind, his ears flapping.

By the time they got to Smithville, they would both be wind-blown, she thought, but happier for it. Winter had been far too long and bitter. A spring breeze was exactly what they needed.

★★★

Slowing as they pulled into town, Julia felt concern pluck at her brow. The flaws and imperfections of the old buildings along Main Street, even the cracks in the blacktop of the road, stood out sharply in the bright morning sun. The bulky clay pots on street corners stood empty, and sandy gravel lay in the gutters. Both were a testament to the fact that spring was tentative. She'd been told no one here planted flowers or cleaned the debris and salt left by snow plows until Mother's Day, which was still a week away.

Kirsten Fullmer

Julia's lips moved as she read the names of business that lined the two short blocks of downtown Smithville. There was a real estate office in a beautiful old Victorian home, and a café, as well as a repurposed furniture boutique. An old gas station converted to a delivery service was the last business on the street. Recognizing the name of the service as the company delivering her furniture, she paused at the four-way stop for a closer look.

A tall, dark-haired man stepped from the building wearing jeans and a tee-shirt with the company logo on the back. He was grinning as he pulled the door closed behind him and he whistled a tune as he walked. His gaze met Julia's as he reached for his truck door and he paused, then his eyes opened wide in apparent recognition.

For a split second Julia saw herself as she had been, sitting at the stop sign in her glossy black BMW wearing a prim suit, her hair short and stiff, with designer sunglasses covering her eyes.

Ringo barked, bound across her lap, and pushed his head past her to hang out the window and bark happily at the man. Julia flinched as her world tilted sideways, and she returned to the present, sitting back in the old pickup truck, her loose curls tossed by the wind, with the dog jumping on her worn jeans. Her mind went blank and the now familiar chasm opened beneath her. Grasping for reality, she squirmed in her seat.

She hated the vacuum moments that followed her flashbacks. She felt as if they swallowed her whole. She couldn't think – couldn't remember why she was there, or where she'd been going. Her face burned with embarrassment.

Ringo's paws scrambled on her lap as he put his front paws on her chest. His stubby back legs danced on her lap and his tail wagged as he looked into her eyes, as if to say, "Mom, there's a man, there's a man." The little dog bounded back to the window, his ears flopping and tongue lolling.

The man paused next to his truck, perplexed by Julia's vacant stare. His dark hair shone in the sun as time slowed, then he lifted his hand from the door handle of his truck and walked across the parking lot toward her.

When he reached Julia's truck, he patted Ringo's head and scratched behind his ears. "Hey little fella." His gaze lifted to Julia and he smiled, his blue eyes crinkling at the edges. "You must be Julia, welcome to town."

Feeling confused as to how the man could possibly know her name, she managed a weak smile. "—Do I know you?"

"Oh sorry, I'm Chad Howard, I'll be delivering your furniture. We don't get many people here from New York, so I figured it must be you."

Her expression darkened. She had come here to find a place where no one knew her or anything about her. "—I…"

He pointed to the back of her truck. "You have New York plates…"

Her mouth snapped closed and she nodded, relieved, then extended her hand around the wiggling dog. "Oh, right. I'm Julia Arnold."

He shook her hand then stepped back from the truck. "Well I guess I'll see you in the next few days…"

She lifted her hand to say goodbye and Ringo barked. Driving through the intersection, she sighed and pushed the dog from her lap, determined not to berate herself. They'd warned her that the flashbacks and blank moments would continue to happen but she was okay. She did have New York plates, so people would know she was from out of town. Apprehension and despondent gloom filled her heart, but she pushed them back. She could do this.

★★★

Kirsten Fullmer

Chad stood rubbing the dark stubble on his jaw as he watched the pickup truck move down the street. Julia had been a surprise. Something about her wide dark eyes had moved him in an unfamiliar way. Unsure what exactly had struck him, besides her delicate features, soft curls, and silken voice; he shrugged and turned back to his truck. She wasn't really his type.

He'd see her again on Thursday. His delivery business contracted to various moving companies who used the large modular style containers, picking them up in Pittsburgh to drive them to local destinations, but rarely did one come to Smithville.

Walking back to his truck, he considered the address for the delivery. He'd grown up in Smithville and knew pretty much every person and address in town.

Like most of his friends, he'd left for college at eighteen, then had lived in Philly for five years managing a hub for United Package Service but he'd returned to Smithville last year to start his own delivery company.

Julia's delivery would be going to an old Victorian mansion farther down the highway. The house was on the verge of falling down, if he remembered correctly, and it would take a wealth of both endurance and funding to make the place livable. Come to think of it, he'd seen Mac the plumber at the house last month. Steve, his contractor buddy, had also mentioned he was replacing a wood shingle roof on a Victorian. He'd have to ask the guys if they'd been working on Julia's place.

He climbed into his pickup truck and backed from the lot. Heading down the highway, he rolled down the window to savor the cool breeze and wondered why someone from New York City would want to move to Smithville. He loved the old town but then he'd been compelled to seek the peace and quiet that was impossible to find in Philly. His folks were getting older, rarely leaving the house these days, snarled traffic drove him insane, and since the accident…city life had lost its charm. Come to find out he was just plain wired for small town life. Besides that, he had to be there for Bobby's family. Maybe he was just the type of guy who liked waving at his neighbors when they passed, wide-open spaces, and listening to crickets at night.

Julia hadn't been dressed like a typical city lady, he reflected. His lip quirked. Since when had he evaluated what a woman wore? Unless it was short or tight or…he shifted in his seat and punched at the radio buttons. Whoever she was, she was none of his business. She had looked a bit lost though.

Maybe he'd drive by and make sure she'd found the place okay. Scoffing at his thoughts, he acknowledged that the house was only two blocks away and if she'd found Smithville, she could undoubtedly find the house. But he'd drive by anyway. Something about her had hinted at vulnerability and he wanted to be sure she was okay.

★★★

As Julia pulled into the driveway of her new home, she closed the small notebook containing the address and directions and tucked it back into her purse. Ringo barked happily and dropped from the window to prance circles on the seat. "Calm down…" she muttered, craning her neck to take in the house and yard. She turned off the ignition and sat with her hands in her lap, feeling the weight of her choices heavy in her chest. The house had been purchased for cash, sight unseen, and she wondered now if she'd made a wise choice. It's not like she'd had a lot of options in the city but coming here had been a radical plan – an escape.

Pulling the keys from the ignition, she swung open the truck door with a creak and stepped onto the weed-choked gravel driveway. The old house loomed before her, the windows dark.

Kirsten Fullmer

Shadows cast by clouds blotted away the sunbeams dancing across the new wood shingles on the roof.

Absently, she reached for Ringo and tucked him under her arm. She'd been desperate to get away from the city and now she was here. Disappointment and fatigue caused her eyes to burn with tears. Evidently a new location didn't offer a different life. She was still herself, still overwhelmed, and still alone; just in a strange place. Carefully placing one foot in front of the other, she straightened her shoulders, blinked back the useless tears, and approached the house.

The two-story home spoke of grandeur long past. A rounded turret formed one corner of the home and the other end of the wraparound porch echoed back with a pointed turret roof. Dormer attic windows poked through the roof like unseeing eyes. The house was built of ancient red brick and the trim had been painted so many times, or so few times, that no paint scheme was obvious, just a hodgepodge of grayed peeling paint and weathered wood. The double front doors were missing window glass; plywood covered the openings, and a rusty awning protruded over the porch from the second story. Julia tilted her head to see if the awning had indeed once hung over the second story windows, instead of sagging onto the porch roof.

Picking her way through knee-deep weeds in the yard with birds singing riotously in the trees, she stepped onto the porch and the boards creaked in welcome. Sure enough, the crew she'd hired over the phone had replaced the rotting deck boards, leaving the porch floor looking yellow compared to the rest of the house. A new lock and handle shone on one door and Julia bent with a groan to lift the welcome mat and find the key.

Taking a deep breath, she straightened, pressed her lips into a thin line and stepped across the threshold. The smell of sawdust and new wood filled her first breath. Rays of sun streamed into the room through the dirty windows, lighting dust motes

Shabby Chic After All

that fluttered in the air like pixies. The room felt hopeful, an emotion she no longer allowed. Hope only meant reality wasn't good enough.

Ringo squirmed under her arm and she let him down to run circles, sniffing all along the floor of the room.

Smoothing her hand along the replaced parts of the wood doorjamb, the wood creamy and pale, she took in the various patched floorboards, as well as several windowsills the carpenters had repaired. They'd been told to only improve the inside to a livable point and not to paint or finish the wood. Electricians and a plumber had also been there to make sure the place was manageable, but just barely. She wanted to do all the finishes because she desperately needed a project but she also knew she'd need help with the repairs. Her construction skills were minimal to nonexistent.

Kinking her head back, she took in the stamped tin ceiling, still perfectly intact. Her eyes fell to the wall where an elaborately scrolled wood mantle, over a tarnished brass insert fireplace filled nearly half the wall. On the other side of the room, ornate wooden built-in cabinets and columns opened into the formal dining room. A smaller version of the living room fireplace was on the far wall, and the rounded turret formed a lovely bay window in one corner.

Ringo scampered through an open door off the living room and Julia followed, her footsteps echoing through the empty room. Her fingers lingered on the dark wood doorjamb, and her eyes cast upward to the dusty open transom over the door. Glancing back down, she found herself in the den, the walls lined with ancient wood shelves and grimy dark solid wood paneling. Limp velvet curtains covered the windows, blocking the sun.

"It's so dark in here," she commented, wandering to the window to tug open the drapes. Sunshine spilled onto the floor as the antique fabric tore across the seam at the top and fell at her feet with a poof of dust. Sputtering, she waved at the grimy cloud.

"I guess I won't be making a gown from those…" she mumbled, pushing at the filthy rags with her foot.

Smiling lamely at her little joke, Julia headed back to the living room. Curious, she glanced through the rooms, amazed that this was her home. Her heart beat in her ears, causing her to feel as if she were on a precipice of some kind. Pausing for a moment longer, she took a deep breath, pulling the unusual sensation of home into her lungs. Any type of excitement that bubbled up from the depths she hurriedly tamped back down because if Julia knew anything, she was certain that what felt good now would only cause her pain later.

An ornate wooden staircase led upward in the opposite corner of the living room with a landing in the corner but she chose to investigate a doorway toward the back of the house. A narrow, paneled hall led her past a powder room, obviously not original to the house, but functional, then on to the butler pantry and the back of the kitchen.

Pausing in the pantry door, she took a moment to admire the floor to ceiling cupboards; the bottom cupboard doors with peeling paint and missing hardware, the uppers with wavy glass doors. She loved to cook, and this pantry would be fantastic.

She frowned and withdrew her hand from the pantry door. She *had* loved to cook, she reminded herself. She had no idea if she could now. It might be too difficult for her to follow a recipe. Besides, she didn't have a reason to cook anyway.

Stepping inside the pantry, she reached down to open a cabinet door but instead of swinging open, the door leaned out toward her. Charmed by what must have been a flour bin, Julia wished the house could tell her all it had seen through the years. Surely it had seen happiness, drama, and tragedy in its long lifetime.

Closing the bin and laying her hand on the scarred wood counter, she decided maybe she'd been wrong about this just being a different place. She'd been inside for only a few moments and already the old home was weaving its way into her heart.

She frowned. Even the thought of liking her house brought a lump to her throat. It didn't seem right that she could come here and be happy – that's not why she'd come. Happiness didn't last; she had to be practical.

Barking and the clatter of nails on the wood floor overhead interrupted her thoughts and she walked out of the pantry. "Ringo, where are you boy?" she called into the vast empty space of the house.

There was no response and she worried distractedly about the dog as she surveyed the kitchen. The room was large enough but desperately in need of help. Filth and grease covered the walls, and the floor was stained and dirty. Only a sink sitting on cracked cupboards and a mustard-yellow fridge revealed the room had been a kitchen. The broken-down look of this room fit her expectations.

The plumber had assured her she'd have running water but had also advised her that the plumbing would need to be updated right away. Even though the crew she'd hired had swept up and taken out various kinds of trash, the room still smelled of ancient dust, grime, and neglect.

This would be her first project she decided quickly, before she could change her mind. Cleanliness came first and she could lose herself for weeks just working on the kitchen. Meals were a requirement, that was just fact. More barking and scuffling overhead forced Julia to turn back toward the living room and the steps.

Kirsten Fullmer

"Ringo?" she called, but the dog didn't reply with a yip or a whine. At the bottom of the stairs Julia stopped to touch a curve of the ornate banister before biting her bottom lip and painstakingly lifting her foot to the first step. One step at a time, she made her way to the top, her fingers white on the worn rail and sweat beading her brow.

The second floor of the house was dark and dismal with old paint and cracked peeling wallpaper. Discouraged, she paused at the top of the stairs to catch her breath and regroup. The agonizingly slow healing process never seemed to end. She'd learned to walk again fairly quickly but stairs were another story altogether.

Had she ever been agile? Had she even given it a second thought – appreciated it? She blew out a huffing breath, causing her bangs to stand up from her forehead.

Ringo trotted happily out of a bedroom to circle her feet. Julia's frustration melted away as she bent to scoop up the little dog and held him up to face her. "You naughty boy, why didn't you come when I called?" She touched the dog's forehead to hers, melting into laughter when he lapped at her face with his wide wet tongue. Cradling the dog in her arms, she smiled down at him. "Oh Ringo dog, who rescued who, huh?"

He yipped, his tongue hanging as he smiled back.

Placing the wiggling dog back on the floor, she followed him slowly through the second floor of the old home, finding four sizeable bedrooms with filthy, old fashioned, nine-pane windows. Each room contained a fireplace and there was another outdated bathroom. It was far more room than she and Ringo required. Empty space full of nothing.

Another flight of steps behind a hallway door led to the attic but she wasn't up for that just yet. Heading back down the stairs, grasping the rails with both hands, she decided that she would set up her bedroom in the main floor den for a while, at least until she could manage the stairs better.

Shabby Chic After All

Sitting on the bottom step to rest, Julia tried to imagine the home filled with furniture but no visions materialized. Rays of sun streamed across the dusty floor and her thoughts wandered.

Her things would never fill this space. She didn't own much now but a mattress and box spring, a small folding table with two chairs, a few boxes of clothing, and her basic kitchen pans and dishes. She couldn't fit much into her room at the rehab center, besides, she wanted nothing of her past. Her things would only have reminded her of what she'd lost. Memories attached to the city and the people and things she'd cared about were far too painful and confusing to face on a daily basis.

She stood to meander across the living room, Ringo by her side, his nails clattering and echoing in the empty room. Perching on the built-in seat under the front windows, Julia stared across the overgrown, weed-riddled yard. Ringo jumped into her lap and licked her hand. Absently petting the dog, Julia resolved that this was where she belonged. No one here knew anything about her, the house needed her, and she could finally get on with her sorry life.

That deliveryman, Chad, crossed her mind, but she immediately turned her thoughts away. She didn't want or need any kind of romance. The scars slashed across her heart were far from healed and if she were honest with herself, she didn't know if she was even capable of managing a relationship. She was no Snow White, and she certainly didn't deserve a Prince Charming.

Shrugging off the dismal thought of men, she headed toward the back of the house. The realtor had said there was a mower in the garage and she'd need all her strength and determination to mow the front yard. She couldn't have Ringo running around up to his eyeballs in weeds.

At the back of the house, Julia found a neglected, weather-worn, detached garage. She circled it once, her mouth tugged into a grim slash, trying to decide if the decrepit building would

Kirsten Fullmer

stay standing long enough to even open the door. The filthy windows were dark and the wood shingles on the old building were grey with age, but somehow managed to cling to the bowed roof.

Ringo barked from inside the house as Julia tugged at one of the sagging double doors of the garage. The door should have rolled on casters overhead but even without a ladder she could see that the track was rusted and leaves and debris clogged the wheels. She wasn't strong by any means but she was determined and was finally rewarded by the door skidding open wide enough to walk through.

Patting her back pocket, groping for her ever-present notebook, Julia realized she'd left it in her purse. She could have started a mental checklist of things to do and add cleaning the tracks over the garage door to the many things already piling up in her mind, but she knew that she'd never remember the list and only be frustrated that she'd forgotten the whole thing. She'd have to walk around the property later with her notebook and take notes.

With the door was finally open, Julia stood scrutinizing the dark interior of the garage. Cobwebs hung like fairy wings from the open rafters, the air was heavy with dust, and a streak of dim sunlight gleamed weakly through the cracked window on the back wall to land on the dirt floor. A grey wood ladder lay tucked amount the rafters, alongside various warped boards and an old toboggan.

As promised, a relatively new lawnmower sat near the front. Evidently the real estate firm had been sending someone to mow but once the house had been purchased they hadn't come back.

Tugging the mower out into sunlight, Julia paused to catch her breath. Why were everyday tasks still so hard? Bending to put her hands on her knees, her head hanging, for the first time she seriously doubted her choice to move to Smithville. If she couldn't do something as simple as open the garage, let alone cut the grass, how could she manage to take care of a home?

Desperate and angry, she stood upright and kicked the mower, then perversely watched for a response. Nothing happened of course, her hopelessness never seemed to change anything, so she reached for the pull handle. Remembering her father starting his lawn mower back in her childhood, which seemed five lifetimes ago, she gave the handle a sharp tug, nearly unhinging her shoulder. Luckily the mower started with the first yank and she turned to bump the noisy machine down the strip of grass beside the house leading to the front lawn.

***

An hour later, Julia put all her weight into pushing the garage door closed and flopped against it, gasping for breath. Sunbeams sliced through the naked tree branches, casting stripes across her face. Goosebumps rose along her arms as she brushed dust and dead grass from her shirt. The temperature was dropping as the spring day drew to a close and even though she was overheated, a chill rose across her skin.

Limping up the step to the kitchen, Julia turned the handle and braced herself for Ringo to vault into her arms. As expected, the little dog jumped into her waiting hands, lapping at her face as if she'd been gone for weeks. Inhaling the mingled scent of frantic dog and cut grass, she walked inside and leaned against the wall to rest.

"Come on boy, come see what Mom did," she finally mumbled to the wiggling dog, straining her neck to evade his kisses as she plodded forward. The old house echoed Ringo's whimpers and Julia's sighs as she wandered through the living room to the front window. She held up the little dog to see out. "See? There it is," she whispered to the dog. "Your bathroom."

Kirsten Fullmer

Dropping into the window seat, Julia stared blankly toward the fresh lines in the newly cut yard, now dappled with shadow. Patches of sky past the yard were streaked with pink and orange, warming her weary heart.

She had no idea what would happen to her now but she was away from the city, the past, and the pain. Loneliness she could handle. She knew that for a fact. Her expression darkened. Chad would be delivering her furniture soon. Turning away from the window, she cuddled Ringo and stubbornly decided that she would be just fine there alone and she did *not* need anyone to come over – especially not Chad.

2

In the truck hauling the moving container, Chad and his helper, Bobby, lumbered to a halting stop in front of Julia's house. Tooting the horn to announce their arrival, Chad huffed out a sigh, turned to Bobby, and grinned. "Let's get this unloaded, shall we?"

The short thin man in the passenger seat pushed his thick glasses up on the bridge of his nose, nodded, and reached for the door handle. "No problem, it can't hold much, as light as it is."

A tingle of anticipation surged momentarily under Chad's skin and he wondered at the sensation as he tugged on his work gloves. It was uncharacteristic of him to be intrigued by Julia, let alone care why she was here or what she would do next. He usually didn't think about women until work was finished, his day was winding down, and he was ready to relax.

The men jumped down from the truck and walked across the lawn. Chad cupped his hand over his eyes to get a better look at the old house. The place looked much better than he remembered, with the windows sparkling, the grass cut and fresh, and comfortable wicker chairs on the porch. The roof and porch rails had also been repaired recently. Distractedly, his head nodded in approval.

As they crossed the yard, Chad could hear bits and pieces of the Beatles song, *Here Comes the Sun*, filtering from the house, causing him to smile. The gingerbread-trimmed screen door creaked open and Julia ambled onto the porch. She was wearing jeans and a sweatshirt, and her loose blond curls ruffled in the breeze.

The sun indeed, he acknowledged.

A shy smile flickered across her face, then disappeared as she glanced over their heads toward the truck. She bit the inside of her cheek and shoved her hands into her front pockets, murmured something to the little white dog, and let the door bang closed. Behind her, the dog stood inside with his front paws on the screen, his tail wagging.

Chad glanced back at the truck and wondered momentarily what had made Julia apprehensive. Then, taking the lead, he stepped up to her and extended his hand. "Morning ma'am, nice to see you again. This is my helper, Bobby."

Ringo barked twice in greeting. Julia shook Chad's hand with a head bob and glanced toward Bobby, who pushed up his glasses and dipped his head in greeting. Releasing Chad's hand she stepped forward, her hand out to Bobby. "I'm Julia. Nice to meet you."

The little man cleared his throat, leaned forward, and pumped her hand determinedly, his eyes large behind the thick lenses of his glasses. "Mighty nice to meet you as well, ma'am. Me and Chad, we got this handled for you. That's our specialty you know, moving, deliveries, and such."

Julia retrieved her hand and absently massaged the edge of her palm with her other hand. "I don't have much, this shouldn't take long."

Chad watched as a multitude of expressions fluttered across Julia's face. He noted apprehension, embarrassment, and maybe sadness but she had a way of quickly arranging herself back to dignified before he could put a finger on how she was feeling.

Kirsten Fullmer

Julia turned toward the front doors. "Come into the house and I'll show you where I'd like things to go." She waved at them to follow.

As he stepped onto the porch, Chad watched Julia's retreating back, noticing how petite she was. Her steps were slow and measured, with the music. Her hand movements, even the way she spoke, appeared as if she had calculated every word and motion. She reminded him of a delicate bird; plucky and sensitive. Again he marveled that she was different than the brash women he spent time with. Not only did she have the most haunting dark eyes but her voice was deep and silky, like a river. She made him feel restless and contented, both at the same time, and she had a tangible quality he couldn't label. Usually he noticed women's physical assets more so than enigmatic feminine mysteries.

She opened the screen door, turned, and he was caught staring like a schoolboy. He cleared his throat, feeling awkward and off-kilter. "You wanted to show us where to put things…"

Tilting her head, she gazed at him, her strange eyes piercing his thoughts and derailing his mindless question. She said nothing, just continued to search his face. One delicate brow arched as if she knew what he was thinking and had come to the conclusion it wasn't good.

Bobby clomped up the steps, breaking the tension, and the men followed Julia into the living room where Chad immediately saw more improvements. Two plastic lawn chairs were the only furniture in the room but the house was clean and bright with the smell of lemon-oil soap radiating through the space. Repairs to the woodwork around windows and doors were evident.

Bobby sniffed and glanced around the room. "Ma'am, this place looks mighty nice. It surely does," he said, his thin face full of admiration.

Julia smiled warily, wringing her hands.

The slight man pushed up his glasses, strode to the stairs and glanced up. Ringo jumped around Bobby's work boots, sniffing his pants leg.

Bobby scooted nervously away from the dog and pointed up the steps. "Do you want a bunch of stuff upstairs?" he asked, dancing to avoid the dog. "Because we charge extra for that, you know. More effort and manpower and all. It's in the contract."

Julia patted her leg and called to Ringo. "That won't be necessary. I'm going to use the first floor while I'm..." She paused, her face fell and she went pale. "—working—upstairs." A slight blush crept up her cheeks and she clasped her hands in front of her.

Sidestepping the little dog, Bobby pushed him away with his boot. Julia bent and scooped Ringo up, tucking him squirming and bucking under her arm.

Chad nudged Bobby with his elbow and headed toward the door. "You go ahead and stand right there, Julia," he said, pushing open the screen. "As we come through, you just say where you want us to put things." He grinned over his shoulder, then headed toward the truck.

★★★

As soon as the men stepped off the porch, Julia turned away and let Ringo down to bark at the door. The room narrowed as her vision fogged. Her breath caught and she pressed her cold fingers to her cheeks.

Even the most casual conversation was difficult. Small hesitations, like just now when she had forgotten the word "renovate," caused her heart to seize in her chest.

Wandering across the room, she rubbed the side of her hand. Thoughts still came to her as quickly as they ever had but since her illness, the words got lost and disappeared somewhere between her brain and her mouth. It seemed like once she lost a

Kirsten Fullmer

word, she got flustered and struggled to maintain her emotions. She would never adjust to being so slow – never.

Feeling light-headed, she balanced on the edge of the window seat, angry that when she least expected it, she'd struggle to speak and be tossed into a panic, ever-fearful that once again she'd be trapped in a world she could only watch pass her by. Tamping down the ever-present panic, Julia tried to banish the memories of waking to find she had lost the ability to speak.

★★★

Back at the truck, Chad tugged on the latch, opened the back door of the shipping container, and surveyed the contents. Surprised that Julia had brought so little, he shrugged and glanced to Bobby.

The slender man pushed up his glasses and leaned on the bumper of the truck. "She's a looker ain't she? Holy smokes. And she has done some work on that house, I'll tell you what." His brow creased as he looked into the container. "She travels light though, don't she?" he added with concern and confusion.

Nodding his head, Chad reached toward a stack of boxes and pulled it toward the edge of the truck. For some inexplicable reason, he was irritated. He definitely didn't like Bobby talking about Julia's looks, which was odd, because they talked about handsome women fairly often. He didn't know Julia, but he got the feeling that she cherished her solitude.

The boxes were all the same size and type from a storage facility in New York, and each was marked with a black marker. Exactly what he would have expected from Julia. Shrugging off the contradicting thoughts, he tugged the boxes into his arms. "That's no concern of ours, let's get this unloaded."

Bobby scrambled into the container to reach more boxes. "I'm just sayin', she's got a great big house and precious little stuff…"

Julia held open the screen door for Chad to pass through with the boxes. Apparently unable to resist the temptation to gab, he balanced them on the window seat and turned to look down the hall where Ringo was crying and scratching from behind the powder room door. "You don't have to lock him up on our account. What's his name?"

Standoffish, Julia raised her chin a notch. "He's fine, this won't take long. His name is Ringo."

Chad wiped his forehead on his shoulder, a disarming grim spreading across his face. "You a Beatles fan?" He motioned toward the boom box on the floor.

She smiled weakly, a spark returning to her eyes. "How did you know?"

He laughed, soaking up the first scrap of friendliness she'd shown. "These boxes say clothes, where would you like me to put them?"

Julia pointed toward the den and as soon as he turned away with the boxes, a long breath escaped her lips. Bobby followed with three more boxes and she pointed toward Chad's back.

The men carried in four boxes of kitchen items and the small folding table. The mattress and box springs were placed on the den floor and soon, the guys stood back at the truck, closing the container. Chad dusted his hands on his jeans, pulled folded forms from his back pocket, and turned to Bobby. "I'll be right back, go ahead and get in the truck."

The little man tugged off his work gloves and squinted up at Chad through the smudges on his glasses. "I'll come with you."

Sighing inwardly, Chad headed back across the yard, his brow knit, wishing he could have a moment alone with Julia. He lifted his hand to knock on the screen and he could see her standing in the empty living room, looking forlorn. His knock sounded loud in the naked space and she jumped, her hand coming to her chest. Ringo barked and scampered to the screen.

Kirsten Fullmer

Julia turned toward the door and pushed open the screen, her expression once again composed. The little dog clambered around Chad's boots, and he bent to pat him. "Hey Ringo, I gotta admit, the name fits you."

Julia's expression softened. Apparently she was pleased to see the dog respond to him. Bobby on the other hand, backed away to stand in the yard.

Chad stood and Julia glanced up, her smile evaporating as she raised a brow in question.

"I wanted to leave a copy of the paperwork with you."

She nodded and he handed her the forms. She seemed contented enough now, he thought, but for some odd reason he had the desire to take her in his arms and reassure her that everything would be okay. He glanced back down at the dog pawing at his leg.

For all he knew, things weren't okay for Julia. She certainly appeared to be very much alone and she didn't have much in the way of worldly goods. The only thing he'd seen in the house when they arrived, besides the plastic chairs, was a sleeping bag and a small suitcase in the den. Suddenly he realized he was worrying about a client, not a friend. He flinched. Usually he didn't concern himself with clients, their personal lives were none of his business. He was all about the delivery but...maybe she needed a friend...

Bobby clomped back onto the porch, hesitant to get close to the playful dog. Chad looked up to meet Julia's eye. "Well, I guess that's all then."

She smiled politely and took a step back to close the screen.

"Wait—" Chad sputtered, shocked at his own outburst.

"Yes?" Julia paused and peered up at him in question.

"I was just wondering—if you needed somebody to show you around. We don't have much here in town but we have a grocery store and you probably saw the café. The boutique has furniture for good prices."

Julia hesitated, her head tilted to one side. "That's very nice of you, but I'm sure I'll be fine."

Feeling foolish, like his feet were four sizes too big, Chad edged back. "Okay then, I'm sure I'll see you around—"

Julia nodded and called to Ringo. When the little dog scurried past her, she closed the screen, lifting her hand in farewell.

Bobby got to the truck first. Adjusting the seat belt, he turned to Chad as he started the truck. "What was all that about? We don't usually show folks around after we move them."

Chad slammed his seat belt into the latch and scowled through the windshield. He may not have had a date in a while but there were plenty of women around. He certainly didn't need the attention of this one. And besides, he'd been busy starting his business and taking care of Bobby's family. So why did this woman get to him? And why *had* he asked her out?

"Just shut up," he growled. "Let's get this container back."

★★★

That afternoon Julia bent, bracing herself with her arms, to crouch at the flowerbed in front of the porch. Having cleared the dead weeds the day before, she was surprised to see tiny new weeds already breaking the surface. "I guess that means things grow good here…"

Ringo stepped over dirt clods in the flowerbed to sniff at a snail, his tail pausing between wags.

"Where do we start, buddy? I'm not even sure what I should plant here."

Noticing movement to her left, Julia glanced toward the edge of the house, surprised to see a large, fluffy, black and white cat sauntering sinuously toward them. His head was low; shoulders undulating, rolling up and down with each step; his tail high, swishing from side to side.

Julia glanced at Ringo, unsure how he would react to a cat. Oblivious, the dog continued to sniff around the snail, his tail wagging, and then he noticed the cat. His small body froze and his eyes widened, riveted on the feline still moving toward them. Thinking he was just going to stare, Julia jumped when a loud bark burst from him, followed by multiple warning barks.

The cat continued its careless approach, not even blinking an eye as Ringo got more and more riled. When the little dog pounced forward a few steps, the cat stopped and stared at him with the same unblinking gaze. Ringo bounded ahead and as he neared the cat, its back arched and its hair stood on end. Julia tilted back on her heels, struggling to stand but unable to push herself up quickly.

Knowing what was about to happen, she gave up hope of standing and lunged forward, trying to reach Ringo's back feet to pull him away from the cat. She was too slow however and to her horror, Ringo neared the feline. With one lightning-quick move, the cat's claw swiped out, tearing a long scratch across Ringo's nose. The little dog yelped in pain and surprise, and ran to where Julia lay sprawled in the damp grass. Reaching out, she collected the little dog and pulled him close, his little heart pounding under her fingers. She leaned up on her elbows to watch the cat, who was rapidly shrinking back to normal size.

Unsure what to do next, having little experience with dogs and even less with cats, she murmured endearments and patted the shaking dog. "It's okay Ringo, calm down, that kitty doesn't want to play."

The cat, now apparently unperturbed, sat and calmly licked its paw. Julia and Ringo stared at it, both unsure of what it would do next. Knowing it would take her a minute or two, Julia wondered how she would let go of the dog and stand, without World

War Three breaking loose; but to her surprise, the cat lowered its paw and blinked his yellow eyes at her, as if to say, "Truce, yes?"

Before she could respond, the creature stood and sashayed up into the porch, then bound gracefully into a wicker chair, where it lay down, curling its tail around it. Ringo bolted from Julia's arms and stood with his front paws on the edge of the porch, his torn nose twitching, and his tail low. The cat lifted its head and the little dog scurried back to hide behind Julia as she stiffly rose from the grass.

She stood cautiously, wiped her palms across the seat of her jeans, glanced between the cat and Ringo, then bent to scoop up the quivering little dog. "Let's give the kitty some space, shall we?"

Edging across the porch toward the door, both Julia and Ringo kept their eyes on the cat, who appeared to be sleeping. They crept into the house and eased the screen closed. Julia set Ringo on the floor and glanced out the front window toward the wicker chair. "Well!" she huffed, "What do you make of that?"

The little dog didn't answer, just gazed at her with liquid brown eyes.

"What do we do now?" she asked him.

As if in response to her question, he padded to the door, peered through the screen toward the chair, then trotted back to stand behind her.

Julia laughed, her amusement ringing through the empty room.

"We still need to work on the yard, shall we go look for some ideas?" Ringo jumped and yipped, then ran several circles around the room. "Okay, let me get my purse..."

★★★

Kirsten Fullmer

Thirty minutes later, Julia pulled into a parking spot in front of the nursery at the edge of town. Three long greenhouses were nearly hidden from view by a multitude of plants, ranging from trees and shrubs, their root balls wrapped in canvas, to rows and rows of potted flowers on pallets.

As she absently shushed Ringo and told him to wait in the truck, her eyes roamed over the multiple colors and textures of the blossoms. Tall, short, large, small, green, red, blue, purple, brown, every color and size imaginable spread before her like a smorgasbord. The smell of dirt and fertilizer, flowers and grass filled her senses.

With halting steps she approached the lineup of flowers, her eyes large, a smile trembling at the corner of her lips. Never had she imagined so many options. Caressing a blossom with her fingertips, she wondered if the plants needed sun or shade, water daily or weekly, and how large they would grow. The dirt in the plastic pot contained small white globules that she didn't recognize and she drew her hand back, overwhelmed by the realization that once again she was completely out of her element.

The horrific feeling was her constant companion now, reminding her that she wasn't capable, deserving, knowledgeable, or able to do things she'd taken for granted. The self-confidence and power she'd once wielded were long gone.

She'd just wanted to plant a few flowers but not only was bending difficult, she had no idea where to start, how to dig, or even what to plant. Her eyes burned with tears as she turned from the plants.

"Can I help you?" asked a trembling voice, causing Julia to pause.

She considered hurrying to her truck as if she hadn't heard but the beauty of the plants called to her on a deeper level. She turned slowly, her eyes on the ground, where they traveled across the dirt and gravel to find ancient curled boots with no laces. Following the boots up dusty, blue-striped coveralls and a muddy apron, her gaze finally met faded twinkling eyes peering at her curiously from a wrinkled face.

"I saw you admiring the flowers, would ya like to take some home today?"

Julia shrugged. No words came to her and her mouth opened and closed like a fish. A blush crept up her neck as she wrung her hands. Wanting nothing more than to run to the truck and drive away, she was surprised when the old man stepped forward and took her elbow.

"You must be the lady from New York. I imagine this may seem a bit overwhelming if you've never had a large yard." He smiled up at her, his hunched back forcing him to crane his neck to meet her gaze. "Look here…"

His crooked fingers pressed into her arm, gently moving her hesitant feet toward the plants. "These would be lovely along your front porch."

Astonishment once again forced away the clouds from her mind and words sprang to Julia's lips. "My porch?"

He cackled and nodded. "Yes ma'am, I noticed when I drove past, that you'd cleared them flowerbeds and was fixin' up the house. I was glad to see it, I can tell you."

She shook her head. "Of course…"

He continued, unaware or unconcerned with her discomfort. "These roses would be perfect for them beds, just the right amount a shade and sun, and these are a miniature variety, so they won't get too big…"

She nodded, warming to the idea of the blossoms along her porch. "They are a classic aren't they…?"

"They sure are, what color strikes your fancy?" He pressed her forward. "I have yellow, red, pink…"

Her lips pursed as her interest grew. "I—I'm not sure. What do you think?"

Kirsten Fullmer

The old man tilted his head to one side. "I like to mix it up a bit myself."

The idea of multiple colors blooming along her porch rail through the summer appealed to her. Maybe she could manage a few roses. "I like that too. How many will I need?"

The old man dropped her arm to dig through the plants, rearranging and sorting the cardboard and plastic containers, and muttering under his breath. "Let's see, I'd think three or four of the red, I'd do five of the yellow, and several pink to round out the bunch."

As he spoke, he arranged the plants in a line on the ground, turning the buckets to place the blossoms at the best angle.

Julia's heart swelled in her chest. The blooms were lovely and as the old man adjusted them, their scent wafted toward her. She'd received roses several times, delivered to her door in a box, but she'd never seen them growing like this, sweet and tender on a bush. Something about the thorns, wicked and sharp among the beauty appealed to her – it made them feel as if they contained enough pain to be part of her life.

"Do you want to plant the entire length of the porch today?" the old man asked.

She nodded, her mind spinning with possibilities. The man plucked up a bucket containing a rose bush and plopped it into Julia's arms. Surprised by the weight, she staggered slightly, wondering how the poor old guy managed.

The man tilted his head to one side and watched as she adjusted her grip on the pot. "I'll tell you what, I have Chad delivering several trees this evening, I could have him bring these by for you."

Apprehension tickled along Julia's spine at the thought of seeing Chad and she immediately forced it down. He was obviously an integral part of town and she'd have to live with seeing him from time to time. As she pushed away thoughts of Chad, she glanced from the many pots of bushes to her truck and back, realizing it would exhaust her to load and unload the flowers, leaving her no energy to plant them.

"That would be fine, thank you. What do I owe you for these?"

The man took the flowerpot from her arms and set it on the ground with the others, then tottered toward the shack of an office, motioning for her to follow. At the office, Julia paid for the flowers and then returned to her truck, her mind spinning.

Traffic sped past, one car at a time, as she watched for an opportunity to pull onto the highway, headed for Uniontown and the bookstore. She'd need to learn more about roses and gardening in general, if she planned to keep the flowers alive.

★★★

An hour later, she was headed back toward Smithville with Ringo's ears flapping in the wind and a pile of new books in a bag on the seat next to her. She'd selected one book about rose gardens, and one about yard care and gardening, as well as one about a country flower shop.

She didn't remember a lot from her past but she was fairly certain she'd never considered where the flowers that had been delivered to her door had come from, other than a vague concept of a florist shop. But the book about the florist had a romantic flair, with pages of color photos displaying seasons of flowers being wrapped for smiling customers. Something about the idea of handling flowers had lit a tiny spark in her heart. It was a glimmer of hope and brightness that hadn't scared her, or felt overwhelming, so she'd bought the book, looking forward to curling up with it on the porch that evening.

★★★

Kirsten Fullmer

Julia hadn't been home long when Chad's delivery truck rumbled to a stop in front of her house. She stood and the song she'd been humming faded forgotten into the yard as she glanced at the cat sleeping in the other porch chair. She laid the rose garden book face down on her chair and ambled to the front of the porch. Her heart skipped a beat when she heard the door of the truck slam closed but disappointment collapsed hard in her stomach as Bobby rounded the truck, lifting a hand in greeting.

Determined that she hadn't wanted to see Chad, Julia pasted a smile on her face and stepped off the porch.

Bobby pulled open the back door of the truck and scooped up armfuls of rose bushes. "Where do you want these, Miss Julia?"

"You can just put them on the porch out of the sun for now," she replied, irritated with her discontent and determined not to let it show in her voice. She'd finally found something she felt like she could manage with the roses and some ridiculous part of her was thinking of a man.

Bobby bent and placed the pots on the porch, glancing at her nervously, his eyes large and speculative behind his glasses. A long scratch appeared on his cheek and a drop of blood formed to run down his face. He swiped at it distractedly with the back of his dirty glove.

"Oh Bobby, a thorn got you, come in the house—"

Julia hurried to the door, gesturing for him to follow. He glanced at his glove and touched it to the scratch again, smearing dirt and blood across his face.

Leading him to the powder room, Julia clucked like a mother hen. "Sit here on the toilet seat and let me have a look at that scrape," she instructed.

Bobby froze in the bathroom doorway, his eyes darting around the small room as if it were a trap.

To put him at ease, Julia asked where he lived as she took his arm and led him to sit down.

"Me and my momma live on the other side of town," he mumbled, his eyes never leaving Julia's face.

Thanks to her many tumbles and awkwardness, cuts and bruises were common, so the cabinet over the sink contained gauze pads and hydrogen peroxide, which she daubed on his cheek while he blinked at her myopically through his thick lenses.

"Have you lived there a long time?" she continued, to keep his mind off the sting.

He flinched and replied distractedly. "Momma was born there and she's lived in that house her whole life."

"That's amazing," Julia commented.

He nodded, causing her to fumble and drop the gauze pad she held to his cheek. He blushed and squirmed on the toilet seat.

"Do you think you'll live in that house your whole life too?" she asked, ignoring the pad on the floor and applying a clean one to his cheek.

He paused and his lip quirked. "Well I did, but some fellers been houndin' Momma to sell."

The bleeding stopped so Julia applied a bit of antibiotic ointment on the deep scrape and stepped back to survey her handiwork. "Do you think your mother will sell?"

Bobby shrugged and Julia bent to collect the wrappers and used gauze. "You keep your dirty glove off that okay?" she said.

His Adam's apple bounced up and down a few times, then he nodded.

Chattering about roses and thorns, Julia led him back through the living room, then sat on the step of the porch to watch as he unloaded the rest of the pots from the truck. Each time he'd place the buckets on the porch, his gaze would dart to Julia, then back to the plants.

Kirsten Fullmer

When he deposited the last pots on the porch, Julia smiled and pulled herself up to stand next to the porch rail. "What do I owe you for delivering these?" she asked.

Bobby shuffled his feet, his face flaming. "Nothin' ma'am. We make odd deliveries for old Fergus from time to time and he and Chad work it out."

"You're certain?" she asked, concerned about Bobby's uncharacteristic hesitation.

"Yes'm," he replied as he turned toward the truck, stumbling on his own boots and nearly sprawling across the lawn.

Her hand came out but he waved her off and sprinted for the truck, calling goodbye over his shoulder.

Julia glanced down at Ringo and shrugged. "Do you think he's okay?"

Ringo's eyebrows lifted a few times and his head tilted to one side, then he turned to watch the delivery truck drive away, Chad's company logo blurring as it departed.

As she ambled back toward the house, the tune she'd been humming once again came to mind, and the last few bars of *I Want to Hold Your Hand* followed her and Ringo across the porch.

★★★

Chad glanced up as Bobby backed the delivery truck into the parking spot beside the office. Glaring back at the computer screen, he sighed and rubbed his fingers along his jaw. He always worried when Bobby was on a delivery. He supposed that was natural after what had happened to Bobby's brother but he'd thought the wrench in his gut would have lessened more with the passing of years.

Sighing long and loud into the room, he shoved his fingers through his hair. It had been a long day, and the spreadsheet displayed one set of numbers while the calculator on the desktop showed another.

Shabby Chic After All

"Where is my formula off?" he grumbled, shuffling through the pile of receipts on his desk, looking for his pen. He'd been working on the spreadsheets for over a week to tweak it the way he wanted it, and the columns of numbers weren't totaling correctly.

Bells over the door jangled as Bobby sauntered into the office. Chad glanced up then did a double take, watching the little man as he swaggered across the room to hang the clipboard on the wall hook over the desk.

"How'd the deliveries go?" Chad asked, still holding a spreadsheet formula on the back burner of his mind.

Bobby leaned his hip on the corner of the desk and sniffed, pushing up his glasses with a knuckle. "I'd say they went surprisingly well."

Uneasy with Bobby's demeanor, Chad leaned back in his chair, crossing one boot over the other knee. "What was surprising?" he said, almost afraid to ask.

Bobby examined the cuticles of his left hand, his lip quirked. "I delivered rose bushes to Miss Julia—"

"Right—"

The little man scoffed. "Let's just say the little lady apparently has a thing for me—" A knowing grin spread across his thin face.

Chad's head jerked back and his jaw fell slack. "What do you mean, 'a thing'?"

Lifting off the desk, Bobby strutted across the office, then turned and crammed his hands in his pockets and rocked back on his heels. "She took me in her house and—"

Chad's foot dropped to the floor and he leaned forward in his chair. Julia had shut him down cold and come onto Bobby? No, that was—would she have—? He needed more info. "And…"

Wandering to the wall, Bobby scratched at an imaginary speck on the paint, and snorted. "She has a really tender touch, yes she does."

Kirsten Fullmer

Chad's chair rolled back and slammed into the wall, shocking them both. He'd never known Bobby to act this way and certainly not over a woman *he* was interested in—in—helping. "What are you talking about?"

Bobby floundered momentarily, alerted to Chad's shock. "I—she—"

Crossing the room toward Bobby, his expression grim and concerned, Chad stared down at the little man. "She what?"

Bobby's hand flickered to his face. "She nursed my scratch."

A pause hung in the air between the two men as Chad's eyes darted from the scratch to Bobby's eyes and back.

Chad swung away, all the air escaping from his lungs in one long breath. The woman was no business of his, he reminded himself. She wasn't interested in dating him, obviously, and he had his hands full with work, but messing with Bobby was another matter altogether.

Bobby hung back, entirely stumped by Chad's behavior. "She done a nice job Chad. She has real soft hands…"

The muscles in Chad's back sagged as he rubbed his hands down his face, Bobby's sentence hanging unfinished in space.

3

Julia yawned and stretched, dropped one foot from her warm bed onto the cold hardwood floor, and then the other. Ringo scratched at the bedroom door, anxious to go out.

She pulled on a robe and padded across the bedroom and through the living room, with Ringo clicking his nails on the floor beside her. The screen door screeched as she pushed it open for the little dog to trot out into the morning sun. The cat strolled in through the open door, as if he had every right to be in the house and tiptoed around her feet, rubbing against her shin, his tail swishing languidly around her knee.

Leery of upsetting the cat, Julia froze and leaned against the doorjamb, first staring down at the cat, then lifting her gaze to survey the bare living room. It looked like she felt – empty. Her stomach grumbled, evidently in agreement. She'd walked Ringo to the café each morning for coffee and she'd survived on sandwiches the last few days but it was time to get on with what was left of her life. The only question was, where should she start?

The rose bushes blooming cheerfully across the front of the porch had been a pleasure she'd allowed herself to enjoy. She'd been craving something meaningful to do for months but now, standing alone in her empty broken house, she was once again overwhelmed.

Ringo whined at the screen and she let him in, cautiously scooting the black and white cat back onto the porch with her foot as she closed the door. With his paws on her knees, Ringo regarded Julia through dark liquid eyes. She bent to pick him up but instead decided to lower awkwardly to the floor and tugged her knees up to sit cross-legged. Ringo climbed into her lap and put his front paws on her chest, his gaze searching hers. He yapped.

"You're right little guy," she hummed, ruffling his ears. "You need a bed. Let's go see what we can find, shall we?"

Ringo jumped from her lap and ran circles around her, barking happily as she struggled to rise stiffly from the floor.

★★★

Thirty minutes later, Julia grabbed her purse from the window seat, checked to be sure her notebook was tucked inside, then opened the screen door with a creak, waiting for Ringo to pass. As she stepped off the porch, the cat in the wicker chair lifted his head, then gracefully leapt down to stretch, his hinny in the air and front paws with claws extended as far in front as he could reach. About the time Julia opened the passenger door for Ringo to jump into the truck, the cat trotted past, and with one effortless motion bound up onto the truck seat.

Ringo and Julia glanced at each other in shock.

"No kitty, get out of the truck," Julia instructed, shooing at it with her hand.

Unperturbed, the cat blinked at her one time and remained sitting calmly in the center of the seat.

She reached for the cat, then remembered his claws swiping Ringo's still swollen nose and reconsidered. Evidently the cat intended to go with them.

She shrugged. "Come on Ringo, get in the truck."

Kirsten Fullmer

The little dog circled her foot whining and sat on the gravel drive, his chin pointed up to her face, eyes imploring, clearly not pleased that the cat was in the truck.

Frustrated, Julia glanced from the cat to the dog. "Ringo, I didn't know cats like to ride in trucks either and I don't know why he chooses to ride in ours but apparently he does, so get in."

Ringo didn't move.

Julia scooped him up, deposited him on the seat, and closed the door. Ringo and the cat regarded each other solemnly, neither moving.

Julia rounded the front of the truck, muttering about animals, and climbed in the driver seat. Plopping her purse on the floor in front of the cat, she stared at him in confusion. "Seriously? You really want to ride in the truck?"

The cat blinked once in response.

In spite of her concern that the cat would flip out and turn into a spitting, clawing missile, Julia started the truck and put it in reverse. To her surprise, the cat bound into her lap to watch out the window, with one paw on the armrest. Ringo protested with a whine and Julia was apt to agree but the cat seemed ready to roll and she was fearful enough of those long claws to let him be. If he was happy she was happy.

Julia parked in front of the furniture boutique and pulled the keys from the ignition. The cat jumped from her lap and Ringo scrambled to the far side of the cab. "You guys have to wait here, I'm not sure they want you in there." The little dog whined, glanced at the cat now curled on the passenger seat, and implored Julia with his shining brown eyes as she closed the truck door.

"I won't be long," she promised. "Be nice to the kitty."

Stopping at the door of the shop to touch a garden bench made from an old headboard, she made a mental note to consider it as an option. Bells jingled as she pushed opened the door, and a pretty, middle-aged woman smiled and stepped from behind the counter. Her hair was swooped into a huge loose bun with several pencils poked through it and her jewelry sparkled and jingled on the ample breast of her loose caftan. She stopped in front of Julia and grinned broadly. "Well hello! I was wondering when you were going to stop by. I was beginning to think I'd have to come drag you in here."

Confused, Julia glanced behind her, unsure the woman was speaking to her.

"I'm Becky," the woman continued. "I heard we had a little blond beauty in town with no furniture. You must be Julia." Her hand shot out, bracelets tinkling, and she waited for Julia to respond.

Still hesitant, Julia took Becky's hand. Instantly she was pulled close and enveloped into a hug.

"My but you are a tiny little thing!" Becky stepped back and surveyed Julia from head to foot. "I'm so glad you came by."

Wobbling back a step in shock, Julia regrouped. "—Why?"

Laughter burst from Becky's bounteous chest, causing her many necklaces to glitter and bounce. "Oh honey, this is a small town. I forget you're not used to us. I wanted to say hello, that's all."

"Oh—Hello," Julia offered a weak smile. Greetings in this place were definitely different than any she had ever known. In the city, she could walk out in public and be anonymous – that would obviously be more difficult here.

"So now you need furniture, am I right?" Becky asked, her eyes shining.

Julia nodded with a lump in her throat as she struggled to think and form words. She hated being put on the spot and meeting people one-on-one was the most challenging time for her to be calm.

Kirsten Fullmer

"Do you see anything you like?" Becky asked, motioning toward the spread of furniture.

For the first time, Julia's eyes wandered over the profusion of items crammed into the small store. Bright colors and an odd mixture of old and new assailed her senses. She had never seen anything quite like it. Distracted from the stress of talking to Becky, she swallowed hard, her expression warming.

Becky scrutinized her, her head tilted to one side. "Do you have a style in mind for that wonderful old house of yours?"

Julia's head lurched back to Becky, her eyes wide. How did Becky know her house?

Placing a hand on Julia's shoulder, the older woman laughed again. "I know where you live from the gossip chain, dear. Don't worry, you'll get used to it."

Julia had nothing to say. Once again she felt as if her secrets had been revealed and she wasn't prepared. Her safety bubble of anonymity was shattered and she felt vulnerable, a feeling she had come to despise. Where had her power gone? She no longer had control over anything. What other things did these people know about her?

Concern marked Becky's brow. "Come and sit down for a minute, sweetie. You look a bit peaked." Taking Julia's arm, Becky led her to a stool near the counter.

Julia's head spun. She'd come all this way to find solitude; a place she could be alone and not be judged by who she had once been, and the whole town already knew her!

Becky pulled up a chair next to Julia, her colorful jewelry clinking and jangling. "Would you like a drink of water? Soda maybe?"

No answer came to Julia. Struggling to find footing, she turned to gaze at Becky. The older woman truly appeared to be concerned. Thinking back through the conversation, she realized that all Becky had said was that Julia was blond, new in town, lived in an old house, and had no furniture. That information must have come from the mover, Chad, and that disappointed her on a deeper level than she would have expected. She hadn't told him to keep her arrival quiet, but...

Julia cleared her throat. "Who gave you all this info about me, may I ask?"

Tapping her finger to her lips, Becky's eyes roamed along the ceiling. "Well let's see, I was at the café... and Marge said she'd seen you and she'd been talking to Bobby, so it must be him. Didn't he and Chad deliver your things?"

Warm relief flowed though Julia. That type of small town gossip didn't bother her. If all they knew of her was limited to her arrival in Smithville, she could deal with that. She didn't know why exactly but she'd hoped Chad hadn't been the one telling tales about her. She'd felt that he understood her enough to see that she wanted to be left alone.

No, that couldn't be it, she reminded herself. She didn't need or want him to identify with her, she was just glad he was professional, or more tactful.

Realizing Becky was speaking, Julia gave herself a mental shake. "I'm sorry, what?"

Smiling, Becky patted Julia's knee. "I was just saying you look a bit better now."

Julia stood and glanced through the shop window. She noticed Ringo in the truck, his front paws on the steering wheel and the cat beside him with his paws on the dash, both peering into the store. As always, Ringo's tongue hung from one side of his mouth, his ears were perked, and he seemed to be oblivious to the large cat perched next to him. Her spirits lifted and she suppressed a giggle, then turned her attention back to the various furniture spread before her. "I heard you have furniture, and you certainly do."

Kirsten Fullmer

Grinning, obviously relieved, Becky agreed, her gaze following Julia's out the window. "Oh! Your cat rides in the truck with you?"

Picking up on Becky's shock, Julia nodded and bit her bottom lip. "Yeah, he's not really my cat; he showed up yesterday and slept on the porch last night. When we got in the truck he just jumped in. Is that normal?"

Becky shook her head and chuckled – even her jewelry seemed amused. "Not that I've ever heard of. Most cats dislike cars as far as I know."

Julia shrugged. "Well I guess he likes it, he sat on my lap and watched out the window as I drove here."

"No kidding?"

"Serious," Julia replied, wandering toward a painted dresser to smooth her hand across the top. "Maybe he's been trained or something by his owner."

Continuing to watch the cat, Becky nodded, then followed Julia, unable to resist one more glance over her shoulder at the truck. "Are you going to live in the house as is, or are you going to remodel?"

Julia muttered vaguely as she wandered. "I need everything but...I don't know what my style is..." Turning to Becky she spoke louder, straightening her spine, willing herself to be confident. "I'm definitely going to update things and modernize the plumbing, but...I already— I don't think I could put modern furniture in it, it wouldn't feel right."

Becky nodded. "I agree. I don't suppose you've met Tara yet, or been to the real estate office have you?"

Julia shook her head. "No, why?"

"This is her shop and she remodeled the real estate office; the old house. I was just thinking that she would be able to give you all sorts of helpful tips and ideas. But for now, let's see what appeals to you, shall we?"

Julia nodded, following the older woman as she led the way through the tangle of furnishings to stop in front of a painted iron bed frame. "Since you like the feel of that beautiful old house, let's look at some period pieces that would be true to the Victorian era, shall we?"

Julia reached out to touch the old bedframe. The swirled iron was cold to the touch with a heavy substantial feel. The paint was missing in places, giving the piece an aura of wisdom, and the effect was charming. She was more than a little amazed that something so old and worn would appeal to her but the missing paint and dents spoke to her of hard times past, that rang true. But did she deserve something so pretty?

The bed was set up with a mock mattress, covered in a vintage quilt with pastel blues and pinks, and heaped with tattered, ruffled pillows. Delicate nightstands with twisted wood legs and matching scuffed and cracked paint stood on each side of the bed, complete with tarnished brass lamps and old books as well as a vase of roses. A braided rug on the floor added warmth to the collection.

Julia sighed, her eyes soft. "This feels so…romantic, doesn't it?"

"That's what we call this style," Becky replied. "Romantic shabby chic."

"It would be perfect for my house, don't you think?" Julia asked doubtfully but with a spark of hope. The beautiful pieces felt good to her and that alone was enough to make her walk away.

Becky nodded. "Let's look some more but you keep this in mind." Taking Julia's hand, Becky moved on through the shop to stop in front of a blue and white china hutch. "This piece is extra special because we have two the same. Have you given thought to your kitchen yet?"

Julia shrugged. "Not much beyond knowing that it needs help."

Nodding, Becky ran her hand along the side of the hutch. "I've always thought that these two old hutches would be beautiful on either side of a wide farm sink."

Pausing to see her kitchen in her mind's eye, Julia tried to imagine the hutch in the room. Function was all she had considered up to this point, could she accept this shabby romantic style? Her brow crinkled in thought. "What's a farm sink?"

"Come over here, I'll show you." Becky returned to the counter and pulled out several magazines. "You tell me what you like, okay?"

Julia nodded and found a comfortable spot to look over Becky's shoulder.

Flipping pages, Becky paused at a full-page spread of a bedroom. "This is the romantic look I was talking about. See the delicate prints of the fabrics and linens? It softens the edges and gives a room a fragile feel."

Julia leaned over the magazine, biting the edge of her bottom lip.

"Men tend to hate it." Becky smiled then continued. "Also in the Romantic style, the paint on wood furnishings is crackled and looks time-worn."

"This type of table is also popular in the cottage style," Becky pointed to the picture. "But in cottages, the fabrics and other touches are different. See here?" Becky flipped open another magazine.

Julia nodded and pointed. "Oh, I see, the fabrics are bolder, more solid colors."

"You have a great eye," Becky encouraged. "You're going to be good at this, I can tell. What kind of place did you have before you came here?"

Her face falling, Julia moved back, as if to distance herself from the discomfort of the question. "I…it was modern, sleek. I want to try something different…" That was the understatement of the century. She'd never even stepped foot into a shop with secondhand furniture until today. She'd surrounded herself with only the newest, best, and brightest. But that was then…and she didn't feel like she should have new things any longer.

Sensing her uneasiness with the past, Becky moved forward. "Well, romantic shabby is your thing then. Oh, see here, this is a farm sink."

Julia stepped back up and bent over the magazine. "I have one of those!"

Laughing Becky patted the petite woman on the back. "This is going to be fun for you. Let's go back and look at that hutch."

★★★

Ringo's barking brought Julia from the kitchen. "What is it, boy? Is the shop delivering our things?"

Wiping her hands on a dishtowel, she opened the front door and stood at the screen, breathing in the fresh spring breeze as she watched Chad and Bobby open the back of the box truck and begin removing the items she and Becky had selected. The men laughed, the sound bringing a smile to her own lips.

Unfamiliar excitement over the delivery flowed along her spine. When was the last time she'd been eager about something, she wondered. She honestly couldn't remember. Fearful of the warm sensations filling her soul, wary and confused, Julia clamped down the locks in her mind, battened down the hatches against the storm assailing her senses.

Crouching painstakingly by the dog, she patted his head. "Look Ringo, they've got your new doggie bed." He barked happily, tail wagging, his front paws on the screen. Julia did allow leeway in her heart for Ringo to be excited.

Chad stepped onto the porch carrying the miniature, four-poster dog bed in one hand and the cushion in the other. "Afternoon ma'am."

Kirsten Fullmer

His smile felt warm and authentic as it beamed down on Julia but she didn't allow it to affect her. Keeping her distance was her first and foremost important rule.

The man was everything a woman could want, she acknowledged, blinking up at him, but she was not a regular woman any more. He might be staggeringly handsome as well as charming, even irritatingly engaging, but she didn't care. She didn't date, she didn't flirt, she didn't play games, and she didn't allow emotion of any kind to break her resolve. Not that she'd ever been the least bit flighty, but all that male-female mumbo-jumbo was behind her.

The cat jumped from his perch on the wicker chair and wove around Chad's pant leg.

"Hello," Julia replied, polite but curt, grabbing the doorjamb for support as she stood. She bobbed her head, local fashion, as she opened the door.

"You got a cat," Chad commented, edging sideways to untangle the cat from his pant leg. The little animal trotted into the house through the open door.

"Is he still here?" Julia asked, biting her bottom lip and thankful for the distraction so she could distance herself from Chad. She might not be interested but evidently nothing was wrong with her hormones, because the hair on the back of her neck was standing on end.

The fluffy black and white kitty circled the room inquisitively. "I wonder if he's lost. He's been here since yesterday," she muttered. "He must be hungry."

"Well if you feed him, he's yours."

"Really, why?" she asked, her dark eyes connecting with Chad's, causing her pulse to jump. How did he manage to pierce her defenses? She took a step back, rubbing one side of her hand with the other.

Ringo yipped and trotted to the cat, touching his nose to the feline's.

Chad laughed warm and bright, causing Julia to flinch. "They say once you feed them, they won't ever leave."

"I hate to think of him being hungry," she worried, her attention finally on the cat, not the man.

"Then I guess you own a cat. Where would you like this?" he asked, lifting the dog bed to eye height.

Julia chewed on her lip as she watched the cat and Ringo. "You can put that right through the door there." She pointed absently toward the den, now her bedroom.

Chad glanced to the door, then back into the living room, his gaze roaming over the length of Julia. When his eyes met hers, she quirked her brow, irritated and indifferent.

"I'm happy to see that the boutique fixed you up with furniture," he said, sounding genuine even though it was a back pedal from getting caught checking her out.

Relenting to his friendliness, her shoulders came down a notch. "Becky was great. She even let Ringo and the cat come into the shop and she gave them a treat."

"The cat?" he said, confused.

"Yeah he went with us."

"He rode in your truck?" he asked, amusement and surprise causing him to grin.

Julia nodded, her eyes gleaming at the memory. "He wanted to go. I thought it was kind of weird too."

Pleased to see unguarded amusement radiate in Julia's face for the first time, Chad nodded, soaking her up like sunshine on a cold day. "Becky is a case. We couldn't do without her around here."

Bobby clomped up to the door, his arms full of boxes, interrupting the current of the conversation. Julia turned to open the door, leaving Chad to carry the dog bed into the den.

Kirsten Fullmer

"These here boxes say china, ma'am. You want them in the kitchen?"

"Yes, thank you," she answered, following him down the hall, and relaxing in spite of herself. Her thoughts flitted to the china she'd bought, none of which matched. That had seemed odd and vaguely uncomfortable, but sweet somehow.

Ringo trotted curiously around their feet and Julia bent to scoop him up.

Placing the boxes on the narrow countertop by the sink, Bobby turned to her, his jaw working. Finally he cleared his throat and spoke, his voice cracking. "You plan to redo this kitchen? It's pretty old fashioned."

Realizing that Bobby was one of those people with no social filter, she smiled. It felt good to understand the situation for a change and be able to function. "That's right," she offered good-naturedly, "What do you think I should do with it?"

He pushed his glasses up and planted a boney hand on his hip, his eyes darting from one wall to the other. "Well, my momma always says the sink should be under the window..."

She nodded for him to continue, intrigued by not only moving the sink but by what made the little man tick. It wasn't often she lost herself enough to focus on another person.

"And I see you have a big pantry, so you won't need a whole bunch of cupboards in here. Are you one of them people that like wood floors, or do you plan to tear them up?"

Ringo jumped from her arms and she sidestepped and glanced down. "I like them but I don't know how to fix them," she commented, biting her lip as she ran one toe along a crack in the scratched and stained floor.

Bobby stared at her, his eyes large behind his glasses. "Me and Chad know how. We did it for my momma in her house."

Her brow rose – what did she see in his eyes? "How long have you been working with Chad?"

He sniffed and his chest puffed out. "Oh, me and Chad grew up together. He used to pal around with my big brother William. They went off to school together…" His expression darkened momentarily but he continued. "When Chad come back from Philly, he asked me if I'd help him with his new business." Collecting his thoughts, he appeared to regroup, straightening his thin shoulders, and his lip quirked as he brushed his finger under his nose. "I told him I supposed I could give up my job at the grocery store to help a friend."

Julia wondered briefly when William would turn up and what his story was but she grinned inwardly over Bobby's confidence that he'd done Chad a favor. From what she'd seen of Chad and Bobby, she had a pretty good idea how the situation had developed. She'd been taught to read people and that part of her mind was still sharp. "I see…"

Hearing chairs scuffle on the floor in the dining room, they headed across the kitchen. Chad was setting four painted wood chairs around a battered thick-leg table. Julia watched as he adjusted the chair, then she sidled up to the table and ran her hand across the scarred top. "How did you get this in here alone?" she asked, glancing up to meet Chad's eye.

He shrugged with mock modesty, then a cocky grin spread across his whisker-stubbled face. "Raw muscle power ma'am," he replied, flexing one arm and pointing to the bulging muscle.

Tremors of exhilaration, pleasure, and alarm ran across Julia's skin as she watched Chad flex. Mixed parts of humor and horror flickered across her face. She hadn't had a man tease or flirt with her for over a year and the fluid warmth flowing through her system left her feeling exposed, off balance, and raw. Unsure how to respond, unfamiliar with her body, her appearance, and even her awkward reaction; and determined not to feel anything, she turned away to hide her confusion.

Kirsten Fullmer

Chad's smile withered and he frowned at her back. Turning to Bobby, he cleared his throat. "You ready to help with those hutches?" he asked, sounding embarrassed and annoyed.

Bobby nodded and they headed through the living room, Ringo at their heels.

Julia reached down to snag up the dog as he trotted past. "You can't help – you come with me." Burying her face in the dog's warm musky fur, she longed to disappear, or at least to rewind the moment and try again. The man hadn't meant anything and she'd been rude but it couldn't be helped now, she supposed. Maybe he finally understood that she wasn't like other women; that she had no sense of humor and he would keep his distance.

She crossed the room to stand at the screen, watching the men lift the heavy wooden hutch from the truck. Concern knotted in her stomach as Bobby bent under the weight of the top of the piece. Turning from the door, she cuddled Ringo and tried not to think about the movers being injured.

Footsteps alerted her when they reached the door and she hurried to stand on the porch, her head turned, flattened against the wall, the little dog tucked in one arm, and holding the screen with her fingertips as the men maneuvered the large cupboard past her. She couldn't bear to watch but couldn't help but notice the muscles in Chad's arms and back bunch and ripple as he moved past her to angled the hutch to fit under the doorjamb. The movement of skin under fabric sent a fissure of electricity down Julia's back.

Tearing her gaze away, she searched the yard, her mind spinning. This was all too new. She'd been around men since her illness but none had sparked her interest – not like this. Of course, the men she'd seen doing any kind of physical activity were lifting patients or pushing beds.

All pleasant sensations related to men had been lost to her for what felt like forever. Since her illness, the part of herself that was fascinated with the male physique had just been gone. Over time, she'd come to the conclusion that she would never again experience sexual desire. Hearing blood rush past her ears, she dropped the screen closed with a bang behind the men and plopped into a wicker chair to think, completely forgetting about the guys holding the heavy hutch in her living room.

Ringo squirmed on her lap unnoticed as she sorted through the emotions tumbling in her mind. She remembered sexual attraction like most people remembered how to ride a bike. But recently, overwhelming failure had taught her that thinking you understood something, and actually being able to do it, were worlds apart. Through painful clarity, she had learned to doubt her abilities and face the fact that she couldn't do most of the million things she used to do on a daily basis. Hell, she'd been lucky to respond to a direct question by a man, let alone experience a hormonal rush.

Frowning, she ran her fingers through her hair. Once again, just when she felt safe, her body had turned on her, forcing her into unwelcome territory.

She sighed, confident that Chad would head for the hills anyway, once he knew her a little better. Besides, she remembered enough to know that she had been attracted to spotless, highly-educated, well-spoken, expensively dressed men; the type of man who expected a high maintenance stylish woman to pose regally beside him, enhancing his overall look. There would be sharp and witty banter, competition to see who could catch the other at a loss, all of which would culminate with either the man slinking away embarrassed, or convincing her he was worth her time.

Her husband had been like that she remembered unexpectedly, with a sharp pang of regret. They had shared a cerebral relationship with physical attraction attached on the far side. It had all been measured and calculated, she remembered. Sex, like

Kirsten Fullmer

cooking or portfolio size, was just another measure of a man's talent and stamina.

She'd been a real cold-hearted bitch, she acknowledged for the hundredth time.

One thing was for sure. She was certainly not accustomed to being drawn to a man's warm smile or being aroused by his flexing arms. The notion seemed...simple. Un-evolved. Backward somehow.

"Julia, where do you want this?" Chad called from inside the house, his voice strained.

Nudging Ringo off her lap, she stood and sighed. Opening the old screen door with a long creak, she resolved that she could not allow herself any stray emotions for Chad. It felt—off, and she couldn't cope with where that might lead.

4

Chad and Bobby stood in the living room, each holding one end of the china hutch. "I should have asked you where to put this before we came in," Chad grunted. "Where do you want it?"

Trying to ignore the sheer amount of testosterone filling the room and concerned for the men's backs, Julia tapped her finger against her lips. Wandering into the dining room, she glanced toward the kitchen. "Well I want them both in the kitchen but I need to redo the floor first..."

Chad shifted his grip and winced. "So where do you want it then?"

Taking pity on the guys, she shrugged. "I don't know, you can just leave it in there I guess."

Ordering Bobby to move toward the wall, Chad set his end of the heavy hutch down and eased it into standing position. "This thing weighs a ton," he groaned, rubbing his back.

Bobby flopped back against the wall, his chest heaving and eyes bugging.

Glancing back and forth between the kitchen and the hutch, Julia frowned. "Do you think this will work?"

Chad brushed his hands together. "Will what work?"

Reluctant but with no on else to ask, Julia waved for him to follow and wandered into the kitchen, Ringo at her feet. "I bought those two hutches to put on either side of the sink," she said over her shoulder, "but the sink needs to be moved under the window."

Trailing behind her, Chad stopped in the center of the kitchen. She continued toward the old sink and ratty broken cabinets. He glanced from the sink to the window. "You're not going to put in new cabinets and counter tops?"

"I don't think so…" Julia answered, deep in thought, purposely keeping her gaze from Chad as much as possible.

He walked in a circle, critically surveying the sink, then stared at the wall with a window. "I'm not sure the sink and both those hutches will fit along this wall."

Julia winced, her eyes finally settling on his face. "Yeah, I should have measured before I bought them…"

"Don't panic yet," Chad muttered as he unclipped the tape measure off his belt. With an efficient whir and a click, the tape spread along the floor from wall to wall. "Let's see, looks like twelve-foot, one and a half clearance from base board to base board," he mumbled, rewinding half the tape.

He moved to the sink and Julia scuttled out of his way, as if to avoid the masculine force field he emanated into the room. He stretched the tape across the length of the ancient piece of porcelain and bent to get a closer look. "Almost thirty-six inches."

The tape retracted with a snap. He crossed his arms across his chest and stared at the stained grooves of the drain board. One calloused hand reached out to test the old fashioned hot and cold taps with X-shaped handles. "You really want to keep this dirty old thing? I'm sure you could get a good deal on a nice new one…"

Julia wandered back to the sink, her eyes riveted on Chad's hand, but she ran her fingers along the curved front edge. "Well, not the broken cupboards but I'm keeping the sink. Becky says it will clean up and I like it; it fits the house."

Kirsten Fullmer

His brows rose. "Okay then," he said with a shrug, "let's see how wide that hutch is." He turned and strode back to the living room, Ringo following at his heels.

Her steps dragging, enjoying the help far more than she should and lost in confusing notions about Chad, Julia followed behind him. Giving herself a mental shake, she told herself to pull it together because she required his strength, knowledge, and no-nonsense approach to the project. After all, she certainly had no idea where to start the kitchen reno.

Pulling out the tape, Chad measured across the width then the height of the hutch, then walked past Julia toward the kitchen. She followed, forcing herself to focus only on the furniture.

When she got back to the kitchen, Chad held the tape propped in front of him at hip level with one hand, the yellow steel kinked out and extended to measure along the wall.

His stance was purely male, bringing a completely different visual to Julia's mind, and it didn't involve a tape measure.

He glanced up at her then did a double take at her expression. His eyebrows rose a fraction of an inch in question, as if he could hear her hormones screaming.

Embarrassed to be caught with her hand in the proverbial cookie jar, Julia straightened her spine and met his gaze, her chin high, her eyes cool.

As if slapped, the tape measure crinkled to the floor with a clatter and Chad tore his bewildered gaze away from Julia. Shifting his feet to get back on track, he gave the tape a few expert flips and kinks and measured from floor to ceiling and then from the corner of the room to the center of the window.

Feeling surprisingly wretched over dousing the warmth in his eyes when he was just trying to help, Julia retreated a step, rubbing her forehead with her fingertips.

Holding the tape in place again with his hip cocked, trying to explain further, Chad turned to Julia. "As you can see, it's five-foot six to the center of the window and the sink is thirty-six inches wide. If you divide the sink by half, then the hutch can't be wider than forty-eight inches or your sink won't be centered under the window. Problem is, that hutch is just over four foot four." He gazed at her expectantly, waiting, the tape extending from his hip to the wall, twitching slightly, his expression one of concentration.

Silence filled the room as Julia struggled to focus on Chad's words, not the stiff steel tape extending across the room from his crotch.

Embarrassed and flustered, Julia licked her lips, then shook her head, once again reining herself in.

His brow lifted, as if he knew she was sexually addled, but had no idea what her problem was.

Awkwardly, she glanced toward the window, then back to Chad. Withdrawing mentally and scolding herself, she attempting to break the spell, but failed miserably. A spark of surprised interest glittered in his eye when their gaze clashed, and that catalyst pushed Julia over the edge. She raised her chin, shuttering her expression once again.

Chad's presence darkened at her blatant dismissal and the tape measure whirred and clattered back up into the roll in his hand; the connection between them abruptly severed.

Julia's head swam. She knew she should say something, collect her wits and get past the fact that he was a man. Mostly she knew she should be able to do the simple math to see if the hutch was too wide but the digits wouldn't line up in her mind. Some were blurry and others disappeared completely. She couldn't add or divide in her head anymore, even when she wasn't horribly distracted and muddled.

Annoyed, Chad appeared to have no idea of the visual journey he'd swept Julia into as he waited for her to respond to his comments.

Kirsten Fullmer

Retreating a step, Julia floundered. She was used to being self-possessed as well as good at math, but nowadays she needed a pencil, paper, and a calculator. Maybe even a cold shower.

She rubbed at the side of her hand. This was exactly the reason she wanted to hide away from people for the rest of her life. How was she supposed to respond? Tell him to back off because she couldn't do elementary math, let alone string two words together to form coherent conversation while he was in the room?

Sensing Julia's distress, unease flickered across Chad's face. "It's okay, you don't have to center the sink, or maybe you could take off a base board or something to try and even it up. It's only a few inches."

Obviously unsure of what was going on in her mind, only aware of her paling complexion, Chad glanced down to clip the tape back on his belt. "Are you okay?" he asked, one brow up.

Julia realized that he assumed she was upset about the hutch fitting but she had no idea how many inches it was off. Attempting to laugh, she shrugged. "You're right. What's a few inches?" But her voice was a bit thin and shaky.

Julia grappled to focus and regain some sense of where she stood. The room felt too tight and Chad was definitely too close, invading her personal space. Once again her throat closed and her vision blurred at the edges as sadness and humiliation overwhelmed her.

A small part of her wanted Chad to reach for her, hold her, and tell her it was fine to be turned on and assure her that it didn't matter if she couldn't do math in her head, that she was still a whole person, a vital woman. But a far larger and more insistent voice in her head screamed, *Stay back, don't trust, protect yourself!* Desperate for somewhere to run, she stepped to the window as if to gauge the space, but grabbed the sill for balance.

Both turned as Bobby clomped into the kitchen, the cat at his heels. "What's going on? Are we going to move stuff or not?"

★★★

Hesitating for a moment longer, Chad searched Julia's face, desperate for a clue as to what she was thinking. The woman was one overwhelming, undulating riddle, ice cold with red hot undercurrents, harsh and haughty but with sadness and heartbreak in her eyes.

Bobby glanced between Julia and Chad, then bent to pick up the cat and run his grubby glove along its back as it nuzzled his cheek.

Seemingly shocked by the cat's uncharacteristic affection for the thin nervous man, Julia stood silent like a statue, watching.

Chad grunted, then turned and motioned for Bobby to follow. Striding to the truck without looking back and mumbling under his breath, Chad was beyond irritated that Julia got so far under his skin. Usually distant with women, he was uncharacteristically picking up vibes of emotion from her, strong and distinct sensations, but then she reacted opposite to his expectations.

Most of the women he'd found appealing were motivated by fashion, fun, or money, and were emotionally volatile. There was never a question of what they were thinking or feeling. He was able to read what they wanted from him and he responded in kind.

Julia, on the other hand, liked dirty old sinks and ancient china hutches, and she managed to remain a blank to him ninety-nine percent of the time. Her dark luminous eyes were larger and deeper than most and her thoughts were a mystery to him. Just when he thought he was getting something from her, she made sure he knew he was way off base.

Kirsten Fullmer

In the kitchen a moment ago, he'd felt the strongest need to take her in his arms and assure her that the sink would turn out fine, yet that appeared to be the last thing she wanted. Why was he so far off the mark? She was feeling one thing and his gut response was completely opposite. When had his woman-reading skills got so far off track? Had he spent too much time out of commission, fighting his own demons?

He scoffed under his breath. Either way, he'd keep his distance. He didn't need the frustration. Besides, he'd always gone for more flashy women; the kind that made his pulse speed up at first sight, not the kind that rolled around in the back of his mind and kept him awake at night trying to figure them out. The deep ones were complicated. He'd had enough hurdles in the last few years; he didn't need more.

Interrupting his thoughts, Bobby shuffled up next to Chad. "What do you wanna take next?"

Chad stared blankly into the truck.

Knocking his elbow into Chad's side, Bobby tried again. "Hey, what's up with you?"

Shrugging him off, Chad scowled. "I'm thinking. We can't take a bunch of stuff into the kitchen because she wants to finish the floors and move plumbing."

The little man's chest puffed out and he sniffed and quirked his lip. "Yeah, I told her the sink should go under the window. I told you she likes me. She knows good advice when she hears it. And I told her we knew how to redo her floors too."

"You did, huh?"

Bobby nodded confidently and pushed up the corner of his glasses with his knuckle. "She don't seem to like you much though. I'll try to help you get on her good side if I can."

Chad smiled but it didn't reach his eyes. As a matter of fact, it looked more like a grimace. "Let's get this other hutch carried in. We'll leave it in the living room next to the other one for now."

Bobby nodded and they tugged the heavy furniture from the truck.

★★★

An hour later, the truck was empty and the house looked much closer to a home. The men had placed the big iron bed in the bedroom, a steamer trunk at the foot. A dresser with a mirror on top graced the far wall and Ringo's bed was nestled in the corner. The dining room contained the farm table and chairs and the living room had the two hutches and large, scarred butcher block that would all go to the kitchen. The lone, broken-down counter in the kitchen was stacked with boxes of china, and the garden bench rested under a tree in the front yard.

Julia stood on the porch watching Chad sit on the bench, testing its stability. He stood and adjusted it to one side and tried it again. He barely fit on the small piece, his broad shoulders taking up most of the sitting space. As he laughed with Bobby, dappled sun spotted his dark hair and tee-shirt through the budding tree. The sound of the men bantering, the very essence of merriment flowing across the empty yard, felt alien and delicious. Abruptly, Julia turned, not willing to be drawn into the warmth, and dropped the screen behind her with a bang.

Chad knocked on the door a moment later.

Vigilantly withdrawn, she pushed open the screen.

"Hey, I have a few forms here for you to sign." He smiled down at her, his gaze falling over her as he handed over the paperwork on a clipboard.

Her gaze flickered to his through her lashes and then she concentrated on signing the paperwork. For a moment she stared at her signature. The name scrawled on the paper still didn't look like right to her. Her handwriting had not yet regained the confident fluid lines it'd had before. They'd warned her that it probably never would.

Kirsten Fullmer

Chad interrupted her thoughts. "Bobby tells me you could use some help with your floors."

Jolted from her musing, Julia's cool gaze lifted to his. His smile faltered but held, and he waited for her to reply.

She had no idea what was involved in refinishing a floor but she assumed it must require strength and bending, neither of which she did well. Like most things in her life now, she would need help but did she want to be vulnerable and awkward in front of this man?

"Well, I—yes I suppose I do…" She sighed.

He tipped his head, trying to read her expression. "I'm not trying to crowd you, just wanted to offer a hand…"

"No, that's very nice of you," she said, "but I'm not sure how to approach this. I need to talk to Mac about the plumbing and— can I get back to you?" She hoped her expression revealed gratitude without showing any questionable interest.

He stuffed the clipboard under his arm and stepped back. "Sure, you know where to find me."

She smiled evenly, disappointed that she'd botched accepting his offer, and lifted her hand as he turned away. Sighing, she let the old door spring closed with a soft thump as she watched Chad walk across the yard and round the front of the truck. She'd been forced to accept help with practically every part of her life and her desire to be independent, to live where others wouldn't see her daily struggle, was proving more difficult than she'd imagined.

Turning to glance across the living room, Julia felt her heart calm, ruffle, then calm and fill with contentment at the sight of the old furniture. Ambling to the hutches, she smoothed her hand along the front of the upper glass doors. They were beautiful, old, heavy pieces, deeper at the base with lower panel-front cabinet doors, a drawer over each, and a butcher-block counter between the top and bottom cupboards. They were charmingly ancient, yet spotless and fresh, ready for dishes and food. The faded blue of the drawer fronts had a mellow, greenish tint that went well with the mint hue of the white milky paint covering the rest of the piece.

As she turned to the heavily scarred and slightly lopsided butcher block standing on thick legs by the hutches, her lips gently curved. Who knew where it had come from or the life it had had?

Having had only modern shiny appliances and furnishings in the past, the idea of obtaining pieces with a story to tell was new and appealing to her. This was good. Everything was different here, nothing familiar. She didn't feel as if she had to remember because she knew for a fact she'd never loved an old butcher block.

Collecting the magazines Becky had given her the day before; she wandered to the porch, holding the screen open for Ringo. She settled into a wicker chair, opened a magazine, then let it drop to her lap as she gazed across her yard to the bench under the tree. Ringo lay at the edge of the porch, his brows lifting; one, then the other, as he watched her. Birds sang in the trees and a train horn blew in the distance. A light breeze lifted and teased Julia's blond curls. Drawing in a deep breath, she smiled. She was home, and with a little commitment, the place was starting to take shape.

Chad wove into her thought and her brow creased. He was definitely handsome and sexy, and he seemed considerate and polite enough – maybe too much. She needed the help but should she spend a day, or however long it took to refinish a floor, working beside him? She wasn't limber or agile in any way and she was bound to do something stupid and embarrassing in front of Chad. Sanding must be involved and no matter how it was accomplished, she'd have to see the man's arms and chest tense and flex as he worked. He'd smile at her with his

Kirsten Fullmer

warm crinkly eyes and rub his chin…offer his thoughts, and undoubtedly draw her in like the tide under the moon.

Pushing the unsettling thoughts aside, she shook out the magazine and turned her attention to the pictures of kitchens.

★★★

Chad backed the truck into the parking spot beside the old gas station office and Bobby jumped out and headed toward the building. As Chad collected the clipboard and locked the truck, thoughts of Julia poured through his mind. Her voice, her jeans across her slim behind, her hands, her hair. Her smell.

He slammed the truck door, banishing her from further consideration. He'd help her where he could, he thought, as he strode toward the office. After all, she was a woman alone and his momma had raised him right but he'd be damned if he'd allow her to get him all twisted up.

The way she'd stared at the receipt back there, like she doubted he'd delivered everything, got on his last nerve. Did she not trust him? Shrugging off his irritation, he pulled the mail from the box on the front of the shop and sorted through it absently. Opening the door, he tossed the mail on the counter and decided he was hungry. He waited for Bobby to grab his keys, then locked the door behind them and headed for the cafe.

Walking the two blocks to Marge's place, Chad whistled a tune as the warm spring sunshine gleamed across his dark hair. He'd done it, he'd pushed that woman from his mind. He was going to have some good food and then maybe he'd call up Gloria and see if she wanted to head to Uniontown tonight for a movie.

Bells jingled over the door as he entered the café, interrupting the instrumental rendition of *Norwegian Wood* pumping from the jukebox. The smell of cooking grease and Pine-Sol filled his nostrils as he sucked in a deep breath of hometown memories.

Marge, who'd looked the same for as long as he could remember, glanced up from behind the chrome-rimmed counter and nodded a greeting, her bouffant hair bobbing. He lifted a hand to reply, heading for a red vinyl and chrome stool, then noticed Gloria sitting at a booth. "Speak of the devil…" he muttered.

Smoothly, he dropped into the booth across from her. "Hey beautiful, what's up?"

Gloria giggled and tucked a strand of red hair behind her ear, her eyes flashing as she batted her lashes. "Nothin', what's up with you, handsome?"

"Just here for some lunch," he replied, reaching for a menu. "How's your grand-dad?"

Her expression darkened. "He stays busy with the nursery but that guy keeps comin' around. You know, the one who wants to buy his place?"

Chad froze, his hand holding the menu in mid-air over the salt and peppershakers. "He's been there again? I wonder if he's been back to bother Bobby's momma too…"

She shrugged. "I'll tell Pa-Pa you asked after him."

Marge paced to the table and cocked a hip, her pencil hovering over her note pad. "What'll you have, sugar?"

Tucking the menu back behind the ketchup bottle, Chad looked up. "Hey Marge, how's the meat loaf today?"

With her lip curled, Marge glanced down to brush imaginary dust off her pristine, pink, 'fifties-style uniform.

Chad's brows went up and he laughed. "Okay then, I guess a tuna melt would be good."

She nodded and scribbled on the pad. "And a coke?"

He nodded and the older woman headed back behind the counter. Gloria reached across the table and took Chad's hand in hers. He couldn't help but notice that her long, red, square-tipped nails were the same color as her lips. Had he liked long nails and dark red lips? Compared to Julia's petite hands and pale

Kirsten Fullmer

translucent complexion, Gloria seemed made up and overblown. Even her hands resembled claws. He shook his head to clear it and withdrew his hand.

Gloria's brows rose. She pulled her hands into her lap and squirmed on the booth bench, causing her perfume to waft across the table. Regrouping, she smoothed her hand over the back of her hair. "I hear you've been moving our newest resident the last few days…"

He frowned. Could he not get away from that woman? "Yeah, she's from New York City."

Gloria sipped her Coke, her red lips pursed around the straw, glancing at him through her lashes. After several sips, she leaned back into the bench. "Becky says she's a short little thing, and shy."

Chad nodded.

"Bobby told me she had almost no furniture." Her hands clasped on the tabletop. "I wonder what her story is…" Her eyes were large and her expression animated.

He wanted to squirm but didn't. "I don't know…"

Her eyes flashed. "I wonder if she's running from something, you know, like an abusive husband or something…"

The hairs on the back of Chad's neck stood up. "She didn't say anything…"

Gloria giggled and tossed her long hair over her shoulder, one hand spreading in front of her like a vista. "Just think, one day, after an extensive Internet search and hiring three private detectives, he'll find her and drive into town and we'll finally have some excitement around here."

Chad's spine stiffened and he glared across the table. "I don't think we need that kind of excitement."

She scoffed and flounced. "Sorry, don't get your knickers in a snit, I'm just sayin', who knows what her story is. Could be anything."

Struggling to remain calm, Chad slouched in the booth. "Yeah—"

She regarded him over the table for a moment, then changed her tack. "Hey, you wanna go see a movie tonight? I bought a new sundress I'm dying to break in." Her lashes fluttered again.

He could visualize a low-cut dress, fitting taut around her ample curves and his fingers itched. He and Gloria had dated on and off, but…

Gloria leaned across the booth to reach for a napkin, pressing her generous cleavage onto the table for him to enjoy.

His stomach turned. "I don't think I can tonight…I have some paperwork to finish."

She shrugged and glanced down, her brow puckered in thought. "Okay, just thought we could have some fun. It's been a while…" She shrugged one shoulder.

Marge placed a sandwich and fries in front of Chad, the glass plate clattering and breaking the tension at the table. Glancing between them, she tapped her toe and her left eyebrow went up.

No one said a word as Chad lifted the sandwich and took a huge bite like a starving man, oblivious to the steam rising off it.

Marge glanced out the front window then stared hard at Chad as he chewed, her mind clearly spinning. She didn't know everything about everybody in town for no reason. She picked up signals, and Chad being unaffected by Gloria was definitely new.

Searching his face and finding him lost in thought, Marge had warning bells clanging loudly in her mind and her expression made it clear. Could it be that something, or someone, was finally going to pierce the facade he'd hidden behind the last few years? Marge's eyes met Gloria's and the younger woman's confusion was apparent.

The redhead turned back to stare at Chad through narrowed eyes.

Kirsten Fullmer

Marge paused, as if she were thumbing through lists and catalogs of where Chad might have been the last day or two; deliveries she'd heard about, people who had mentioned him. Her eyes widened as a few distinct impressions formed in the back of her mind. Finally, she slapped the check on the table with a grin. "Let me know if you need anything else," she stated.

Chad nodded, his mouth full, while Gloria pouted.

5

Julia held up the magazine, her gaze moving from the glossy double-page spread to the empty wall of her kitchen. Becky had been right, the hutches would be perfect and the magazine gave her ideas for all the finishing touches that would make her house feel like a home. Wanting to surround herself with softness and comfort, she was excited to get started. Working on the house had been accepted as…work, and therefore something she could allow herself to focus on.

"What do you think, Ringo?" she asked the little dog at her feet. He lifted his brows in question, forcing Julia to bend with a grunt and scoop him into her arms for a hug.

The day ahead twisted through her mind in a confusing mix of places and people. Padding back to her bedroom, Julia let Ringo down and opened the steamer chest to remove a stack of notebooks. Sorting through the pile, she stopped at a pink one and placed the rest back into the chest.

Sitting on the chest, she flipped through the pages of the notebook, stopping on the last filled page. Frowning at her uneven scrawled writing, she reviewed her notes on appointments and things she had needed to do the day before. She'd forgotten a few minor items because she hadn't reviewed the notebook before she went to bed.

She stood and plodded back to the kitchen, flipping pages and mumbling as she walked. She lifted the pencil from the narrow counter by the sink and tapped it against her lips as she read, then, in hesitating scribbles, she began to make notes for the day.

Mac, the plumber, would be stopping by that afternoon to discuss moving the sink. She glanced up. The other side of the room was a mess as well, and she needed to decide what to do about a stove so Mac could move the gas line.

Bending to scratch Ringo around the ears as she thought, she glanced at the glossy magazine on the counter. The back pages were full of replica, turn-of-the-century stoves, their look true to the time period the home was built but for some reason, Julia was partial to the elegant enamel ovens from the thirties. Something about the chrome trim and long delicate curved legs appealed to her.

The cat wandered from the mud room off the back of the kitchen, where Julia assumed he'd used his new litter box, and ambled languidly past her to the new food and water dish on the far side of the room. He'd made himself at home so she supposed she should give him a name.

Ringo's sharp bark made her jump, her hand on her chest. The little dog bounded toward the front door, his rear end sliding as he careened around corners, his barks echoing through the house.

She laid the notebook on the counter. "Who could that be?" she muttered. She didn't know anybody but the movers and Becky.

As she emerged from the hall, Julia could see a tall slim woman through the screen door. She had beautiful, hip-length dark hair that lifted in the breeze. An old woman stood smiling as well, a large leather purse gripped to her chest.

Kirsten Fullmer

Crossing the living room, Julia worked to compose herself. Meeting new people was still difficult and stressful. The women smiled through the screen and Julia relaxed a bit as she pushed open the door. Ringo bolted through the opening and scampered around the women's feet, leaping with joy.

The tall woman bent and scooped him into her arms, laughing as the little dog nuzzled her neck. "Well hello little guy. Aren't you the sweetest thing?"

"Sorry," Julia apologized, reaching for Ringo.

The women stepped into the house and the one holding the squirming dog waved Julia off with a grin. "He's fine. I'm Tara and this is Winnie, I hope this isn't a bad time to come by."

Julia wrung her hands and forced a smile. "Not at all. Please come in. I don't have anywhere to sit but around the table, is that okay?"

Tara nodded, set Ringo on the floor, and followed the old woman into the dining room. Julia pulled out a chair for Winnie and Tara sat in the one opposite.

"This table is perfect for this room, isn't it?" Winnie commented, smoothing her gnarled hand across the scarred top. "Becky told me you'd found some pretty pieces."

Concentrating on remaining calm, Julia clasped her hands in her lap. "Yes, she was very helpful." Then to Tara, "She also told me you remodeled the house with the real estate office, I hope you're willing to offer advice..."

"Of course I will," Tara smiled, "but we just came by to say hello and introduce ourselves." She tugged her hair over her shoulder to smooth the tangles left by the breeze. "Sorry it took us a few days, things have been a little crazy."

Julia nodded. "No problem, I was getting settled in. So, you run the real estate office?"

"Oh I don't really," Tara said, flipping her hair back over her shoulder, then gesturing to the old lady. "Winnie handles things there. I've actually been losing my mind opening our bed and breakfast inn, and I just got engaged, so now I'm planning a wedding too."

A stab of regret pierced Julia's heart but she managed to glance at Winnie with a slight nod to acknowledge her job at the real estate office, then dragged her gaze to Tara's hand and the glittering diamond. "How exciting. Your ring is gorgeous." The words were correct, but they sounded stilted to Julia's ears and she felt guilty for being so selfish.

Shrugging at the compliment, Tara blushed. "Thanks. We – me and my fiancé Justin, our inn is just up the road. That's where the ceremony will be and it just seems like everything is piling up on me with inn guests, not to mention we still have construction going on—."

The thought of a wedding at a bed and breakfast sounded so romantic to Julia. "Where did you say the B&B is?" she managed to ask through her ragged and torn thoughts.

Tara leaned to her left and pointed out the window. "The turnoff is right there, that gravel road, see the sign? Oh, I guess that bush is in the way, anyway, you just turn there and it's about a quarter of a mile up the road."

Julia got up and walked to the window, her back to the visitors, welcoming the chance to regroup. "I need to trim that bush," she mumbled as she turned back to Tara. "I'd love to see it someday. The inn I mean…" Immediately she regretted her words, knowing she'd volunteered to meet even more people.

A warm smile burst across Tara face. "Oh, please, come by any time."

Julia returned to the table, feeling awkward and self-conscious.

"Your roses are beautiful," Winnie commented, her eyes twinkling. "I'd heard about them from everyone in town but I had to come see them for myself."

Kirsten Fullmer

Julia blushed, once again overwhelmed that people talked about her. "I can't take much credit, the old man at the nursery suggested them."

Winnie nodded. "Fergus does have a way of connecting people with plants but not everyone can manage miniature roses, they are delicate and moody. Yours look very contented to be here."

Cupping her hand around her mouth as if to tell a secret Julia whispered, "I bought a book."

The women laughed. "Well you've done a wonderful job, I can't wait to see what you do with the rest of the yard," Winnie said, her watery eyes dancing around the room, taking in every detail. "I've always loved this old house."

Julia wanted to ask them if they'd like to see her the place, give her suggestions, but she'd have to walk up the stairs. "Would you like to see what I plan to do with the kitchen, give me advice?" she offered instead.

"We'd love to," Tara answered. Winnie nodded.

The women clattered chairs momentarily then wandered into the kitchen and Julia picked up the discarded magazine. "Becky gave me the idea and you saw the hutches in the living room." She handed the magazine to Tara, pointing out the picture that had inspired her.

Glancing from photo to the sink to the window, Tara smiled and sighed.

Winnie grasped her hands in front of her purse, her head cocked to one side. "Oh that will be perfect. Becky has such a feel for design. She really loves the sleek, mid-century stuff, but she can handle any style. When Tara brought in those hutches, Becky's eyes lit up and she immediately claimed them. You are making her vision a reality, I hope you know."

Julia approached the sink. "Becky said this would clean up but I don't know where to start."

"I have some solvents that will help," Tara assured. "What are your plans for the floor?"

All three sets of eyes fell to the dull, stained hardwood. Julia bit her bottom lip. "I want to keep them, refinish them, but I have no idea what to do. Chad, the mover, offered to help, but..."

Winnie interrupted. "Oh he'd be perfect for the job. I've seen some of his work and he knows what he's doing."

Tara's eyes widened at the comment and darted to Winnie, a question in her gaze, but Julia didn't notice. Her eyes were on Ringo, weaving circles around her ankles.

Tara tossed Winnie another concerned glance, causing Winnie to purse her lips and give a slight, almost imperceptible shake of her head, indicating not to say anything. Quirking her lips, Tara turned her attention back to Julia, her brow crinkled in question. "Are you worried about the floors?"

Giving herself a mental shake, Julia flashed an embarrassed smile to the ladies that didn't quite reach her eyes. "No, I'll take him up on the offer, I just wanted to hear what Mac had to say about the plumbing first."

Winnie smiled but Tara's lips pursed in concern as she spoke distractedly. "Hmmm, that's a good idea, Mac will do a good job..."

Finally hearing speculation in the young woman's reply, Julia glanced at Tara in question.

Shrugging off Julia's unease, Tara wandered to the window and glanced from wall to wall. "It'll be a tight fit for the hutches won't it?"

Relieved to move the conversation away from Chad, Julia joined Tara in the puddle of sun on the worn floor by the sink. "Yes, the sink won't be quite centered, but I don't think it will matter much."

Winnie agreed. "Definitely not. I can't wait to see it when you're finished."

"I should ask you about a stove," Julia flipped through the magazine, stopped at a dog-eared page and handed it over. "What do you think of something like this?" She pointed at the white stove in the photo.

Winnie looked past Tara's shoulder to see the magazine and Tara gasped. "Oh, it's perfect. As a matter of fact, I have one of these. It's not exactly the same but pretty close. I'm not sure what shape it's in but I have a guy I use for appliances. Want me to have him take a look at it?"

This time the smile glowed in Julia's eyes. "That would be great! Thank you."

Tara shrugged. "No problem. Hey, we gotta run." She motioned to Winnie and headed down the hall toward the living room. "But please, come out to the B&B, I'll be there all day tomorrow..."

As the women wandered through the front room, their footsteps echoing through the nearly empty room, Julia observed her visitors. Tara looked exactly like a best friend would in a movie; someone beautiful and confident, open and fun. And Winnie, shuffling along in her sensible grey shoes, her dress freshly ironed and a lace hankie tucked under her gold stretchy watchband, was the epitome of the grandmother she'd always longed for.

These were women she could befriend if she chose to, people she could include in her life. And people she would ultimately lose. The question was, would reaching out to them be worth the joy they could bring her, or would she only suffer far worse heartache when they were wrenched away?

At the front door, Julia hesitated, the thought of meeting more people at the inn the next day settling heavy on her mind. She'd come to Smithville to regroup and heal, away from judgmental prying eyes. She didn't feel at all ready for all the new experiences being pushed on her. Questions rang through her mind. How many people would be at the bed and breakfast? What would they be like? Would there be stairs?

She pushed open the creaking screen door and the cat trotted in.

"Oh my! What a pretty cat," Winnie gushed.

Distracted, Julia nodded. "That's George, he claimed us a few days ago." The name was perfect, she thought to herself.

Winnie grinned down at the fluffy, black and white kitty weaving between her feet.

"I'll tell you what." Tara interrupted their conversation, touching Julia's arm. "You come by the inn around two and we'll have some lemonade on the porch and chat. I don't have a lot of time, but I'd love to see you…"

Understanding that Tara saw her reluctance and was offering easy options, Julia smiled, relief flowing through her system. "That sounds nice. Lemonade at two."

Tara regarded Julia's face thoughtfully and squeezed her arm, her eyes bright with questions and mystery. "I'm so glad, I'll see you then."

Standing at the open door watching Winnie and Tara wave as they climbed into their car, Julia sighed. "There is no hiding from the world here after all, is there? Come on guys." Ringo trotted inside and she closed the screen. The cat jumped into the window seat and curled up, the little dog ran in a circle then put his paws on her knees, his eyes imploring her for attention. She laughed.

"Want to go for a walk?" she asked, ruffling his ears.

He yipped and jumped.

"Okay, let's go get your leash."

Moments later, they stepped through the front door and Julia locked it behind her. The cat had no inclination to follow them

Kirsten Fullmer

this trip, but Ringo pranced in place eagerly as she stepped carefully off the porch. Finally, Julia crossed the lawn and headed toward town, Ringo strutting beside her with his tail in the air.

A few months back, the physical therapist had suggested that she get a dog to walk. At first, she had balked at the idea. She'd never been a pet kind of person. They left hair everywhere and needed tending, and her schedule had always been far too busy for the fuss. But learning to walk again after the illness had been tedious, requiring hours of practice, and after exhausting months of walking the hospital halls gripping the handrails, then teetering around the yard of the care center alone, the thought of a companion had sounded better and better.

She'd found Ringo on adoption day at the pet supply store. He was a nebulous breed, a rescue dog; his legs too short and his head too big, his fur scruffy, but he was a charmer, and she'd fallen for him immediately.

Since that day, her walks had been far more pleasurable. Ringo had been patient when she needed to rest and didn't complain on days she couldn't go far. His companionship had been priceless and now that she had her own place, she couldn't imagine her life without him. He was truly the most patient, least judgmental friend she could have hoped to find.

Early afternoon sun dappled the sidewalk and birds chirped noisily in the trees. The old homes along the street were well cared for, and Julia realized that her house must have been the eyesore of the neighborhood for some time. Trees all along the walk were filled with blooms; pink, white, and yellow, open and fragrant. Digging through her few hazy memories, she wondered if she'd ever experienced so much pleasure from spring. It had come each year in the city, obviously, but without trees crowding the streets and lawns and shrubs blooming, it had been easier to miss.

A few blocks from the house, Ringo's ears perked and he tugged at the leash. "Whoa boy, what's got you all excited?" she asked. Glancing ahead, she could see Chad mowing the strip of grass in front of the delivery service.

He reached the end of the grass, turned the mower to head back for one last pass, and halfway, he spotted Julia and Ringo. Raising a hand, he continued to the end of the grass where they stood. When he released the mower handle, the machine sputtered and died and he wiped his forehead with his shoulder.

"Hi Julia." He bent to one knee and ruffled Ringo's ears. "How are you, buddy?"

Once again, Julia was touched at the time Chad took to play with Ringo and she realized his masculine tussles with the dog were very different than her more cuddly approach. Ringo obviously loved it.

The little dog danced and yipped then, distracted, paused to sniff clumps of damp grass as they dropped from the mower. Chad watched the dog, his grin authentic and his manner relaxed. Straightening, he gazed at Julia, and she shifted her weight from one foot to the other, squinting and blinking up at him into the sun.

"What can I do for you two today?" he asked.

She smiled tentatively, winding the leash around her awkward fingers, unsure where to begin. Should she chitchat, or get right to the point? Not wanting to give Chad the wrong idea, and feeling more than ready to have the meeting behind her, she decided to get right to the point. "I wanted to accept your kind offer to help with the floors."

His brows rose. "Okay, when were you thinking of doing them?"

She shrugged, glancing down the street. "Mac comes this afternoon to work on the plumbing, then I'll have a better idea." She turned back to make eye contact.

Kirsten Fullmer

Once again, his friendly, open manner touched her on a deeper level. Used to being around professional healthcare staff, social niceties without professional boundaries felt odd and stressful. If that had been the only draw Chad exuded, she could have managed but her traitorous body responded to the man on planes way beyond her control. "I…I don't know anything about floors. What all is involved?"

Chad rubbed his jaw, his countenance serious as he considered hardwood floors as well as the expressions flittering across her face. "Well, I'd need to take a better look at them to know. Do you want to do all of them or just the kitchen?"

Her eyes widened. "Oh…I don't know…"

He nodded. "Do you want all your floors messed up at the same time, or do you want to leave a room to live in?"

"Good point." She shifted from one foot to the other and fingered the end of the leash nervously. "How long will I have to stay off them?"

"That depends on how much work they need and what you want to do with them."

She nodded, completely unsure about the floors and distracted by the way the sun glistened across his blue-black hair. He smiled reassuringly and her heart did a little flip-flop, causing panic and bewilderment to surge in her chest.

Silence stretched between them and Julia swallowed the growing lump in her throat, the sun turning uncomfortably warm on her shoulders. Chad appeared to be content to stand and stare at her, watching her fall to pieces. Sweat beaded on her brow and she didn't know if it was because of the sun or Chad's scrutiny.

Chad's voice, deep and smooth, interrupted her misery. "How about I come by tonight and take a look at them, and we'll come up with a plan?"

Holding up a hand to block the sun, Julia searched his eyes and found glimmers of interest and hunger. Tingles ran along her spine and she stepped back, dropping her hand to rub her upper arm, her eyes on Ringo. Firmly tamping down any natural response, she quickly cleared and shuttered her expression, then looked back up to stare slightly over his left shoulder. "That would be fine. What time?"

He paused, a muscle working in his jaw, disappointment stamped across his face. Finally he spoke, his voice crisp and clipped. "I could be there at eight."

She nodded. "Fine, eight o'clock then." Turning to go, she had to tug the leash as Ringo pawed at Chad's jeans. "Come along Ringo."

★★★

A scowl creasing his brow, Chad stepped back to discourage the dog and watched as Julia crossed the street. The woman drove him insane. What was it about her that made him want to scoop her up and kiss her senseless?

He'd sworn to stay away from her but when she'd asked him about the floors, her eyes dark with questions, her curls dancing in the breeze, he'd jumped at the chance to run right back to her house. Yet the second the words were out of his mouth, she'd turned ice cold.

He yanked the mower around and pushed it stubbornly across the gravel parking lot, grumbling under his breath. He should stick with girls like Gloria who were easy to read, easy to understand, just…easy.

Tonight he'd go over there, and he'd look at Julia's floors but that was it. He'd had enough.

★★★

Kirsten Fullmer

Checking her phone to see the time, Julia grimaced. It had been two minutes since the last time she checked. Tucking the phone back into her pocket, she shifted in the wicker porch chair and lifted her book to read the same paragraph for the third time.

The sun was beginning to dim, bringing the day to a close. Julia's all-time favorite Beatles song played on the boom box in the house, bleeding strains of *Something In the Way She Moves* across the porch. George lifted his head in the chair next to her and regarded her thoughtfully with his unblinking yellow cat eyes, then settled back into his nap.

Ringo barked and Julia glanced up expecting to see Chad but the dog was barking at a bird hopping across the shadow-filled lawn. "Shush boy..." she mumbled, returning to her book. Reading was still a chore some days and evidently, today was one of those days.

Closing her book with a thump, she rested her head on the back of the chair and stared at the porch ceiling, willing the music to relax her.

"Another thing that needs paint," she noted with a sigh. The list was endless. She'd spent the afternoon with Mac as he explained her options and costs for moving the plumbing. Her notebook was full of household problems that needed attention.

He'd listened as she described the oven she wanted then he'd called Tara, asking about the measurements of the stove so he could run the gas line.

He'd also worked downstairs laying out a plan for the new plumbing and put together a bid list and sketches for the city to approve. Work could begin in a few days. In the meantime, he'd go measure the stove and she needed to agree to the kitchen layout so Steve, the electrician and all around handyman, could place the new electrical plugs to meet code. She hated the thought of cutting holes in the back of the hutches for outlets but code stated specific requirements for electrical and she didn't have many options.

The costs he had quoted weren't astronomical but she wouldn't be able to keep spending money on the needy house without careful planning. She needed to supplement her income and she needed it soon. Feelings of inadequacy flooded her system, choking any glimmer of self-confidence she may have nurtured. How could she work when half the time she couldn't remember what she was saying, let alone have enough stamina to get to a job on a daily basis.

Ringo barked and ran across the lawn to meet Chad, chasing circles around the man's feet and leaping in the air. The dog was obviously happy to see him. Chad must have walked over because his truck was nowhere in sight.

Julia stood and laid her book in the chair. Chad was wearing his usual jeans but tonight he had on a short sleeve, button up shirt and he'd shaved. He bent to play with Ringo, ruffling his ears. Then he stood, raising his arms, encouraging the little dog to leap high into the air. He laughed and the dog barked happily, the sight and sound filling an unknown void in Julia's chest.

The man looked good, Julia had to admit, fighting hard to push back a grin. Something about the way he strode across the lawn was purely masculine, predatory. Her senses on alert, as if she were in danger, she watched him approach.

As he got closer, she could smell his aftershave wafting on the breeze. The scent immediately took her back and she was standing before him in a Prada dress and two hundred-dollar heels, her makeup flawless, with her Gucci bag clutched in one hand.

"Hi…" Chad said, his head tilting at her odd expression. "You okay?"

Slammed back into real time, her head spinning, Julia reached for the porch column to steady herself. Her hand missed the column and she lurched toward Chad, her eyes huge and vacant.

Kirsten Fullmer

He reached for her, circling her with his arms as she sagged against him, her face buried in his chest. "Julia? Julia?" Grappling for a handhold on her back as she sagged against him, he tried again. "Are you okay?" he asked over the top of her head.

Julia's world slowly stopped spinning, and the soft cotton of Chad's shirt against her cheek was the first thing she comprehended. He smelled so good. She could feel his powerful arms around her, creating a sensation she'd not experienced in…ever.

She was safe, finally safe, and relief poured through her system, bottomless and sweet. For a long moment she drowned in the sensation, reveling in the warmth and softness of it.

Chad loosened his grip as she curled into him, her hands grasping at his shirt. He spread his hands across her back, one sliding up to the back of her neck and into the curls at her nape.

How had she forgotten what the human touch felt like? Julia wondered hazily. Not the touch of a healthcare professional but a touch of a person reaching out to pull her close. Had she ever enjoyed the feel of a man's fingers on the sensitive skin at the base of her neck? Surely she must have but she couldn't remember it, nor could she remember ever drowning in the need to be wanted, cared for, like she did now.

She comprehended enough of her old self to know that other people's needs had not particularly concerned her and to suddenly understand how much a person could long for human contact was a crushing and eye-opening realization. How had she moved blindly through the world with no idea how people felt? How she felt?

As rushing, tumbling emotions evolved into actual thoughts and reality focused in her mind, unrelenting fear surged back to the surface and rolled down her throat, thick and dark. The only way she knew to gain control of her dread was to make all feeling stop and it must stop now. She couldn't take any more.

"Julia? Julia! Talk to me please," Chad gasped.

Struggling for some semblance of sanity, Julia shuffled her rubberized feet on the porch and attempted to stand.

Chad relaxed his grip, his fingers barely in contact with her skin, one hand still cupping the back of her neck.

She tipped her chin up and as Chad's gaze searched her face, Julia was surprised to see concern etched across his features.

His expression softened and his hands tightened around her back. The apprehension surging through Julia's system hit a boiling point. Tension liquefied into sexual heat, draining her mind of coherent thought, causing her knees to go weak all over again.

She moaned, suspended in the moment, then gasped raggedly as reality finally clanged through her skull. This was Chad, the man she *didn't* want close! As she stiffened and jerked back, pushing at his chest, she felt him reel in shock as he released her.

Staring at him, her eyes large and deep, her chest heaving, she grasped for words. "Wha…." she muttered, her lips trembling.

His eyes searched hers. "Are you okay? I thought you were going to pass out for a second."

She stumbled back, her hands batting frantically at his, desperate to be away from him and reestablish her equilibrium. Ringo pranced around her feet, whining in concern.

It had finally happened, she'd lost it completely in front of someone. Someone who didn't understand, who had no idea what was wrong with her. What must he think?

★★★

Chad stared at Julia, one hand still hovering in the air toward her, in case she was unsteady. Her face showed no emotion but only moments ago he'd been stricken to see every expression in the book cross her face; confusion, longing, fear, warmth, revelation, anger. Now, however, she stood breathless in front of him, wearing only the closed, cool expression she always wore.

Kirsten Fullmer

Was he crazy, or had she just been nuzzled against his chest, moaning as he ran his fingers through her hair?

He'd known she was petite, but in his grasp she'd been positively tiny, delicate and fragile. She was so small she fit under his chin, and he had felt each vertebra in her back.

He frowned and shuffled his feet, staring at her. The second she'd softened in his arms, he'd gone from zero to oil well explosion, in fractions of a second, and he worked now to battle the blaze.

Searching her eyes for an explanation of her behavior, he checked down the mental list of all he knew about her. She came from New York, lived here alone; she had a dog, a cat... that was it. Was she diabetic?

"Are you still dizzy? Do you need sugar or something?" he asked.

Her blocked and vacant expression didn't falter. "No, I'm fine now, thank you. Shall we look at the floors?"

Wanting only to sweep her up and drag her into the house, he felt disappointment roaring through his system. Had she really been in his arms? She certainly showed no sign of wanting him now. Was he losing his mind? He shook his head. "Sure..."

She opened the screen and stepped gracefully, with those measured steps of hers, into the house. He followed, nearly tripping on George as the cat trotted through the door.

★★★

Julia led the way down the narrow hall to the kitchen, Ringo beside her. Her hands were shaking and her knees weak. She could still feel Chad's hands warm on her back and she knew the sensation would stay on her mind for days. The only people to touch her, for almost a year, had offered a hand to steady her, or examine her but no one had held her like that, felt the shape of her body against his, or run his fingers through her hair. How had she forgotten the intensity, the power, of a man?

Thinking back, she recalled that Brad had sat by her hospital bed and held her hand, speaking in a low voice. She could remember some of his words and a few sensations but the memory was distant, patchy and vague, like a dream the next morning. Not remembering his goodbye was most likely a blessing. She had no recollection of sex with her husband beyond impressions and hazy snapshots – nothing like this.

In the kitchen, Julia stared out the window for a long moment, willing her heart to stop pounding in her ears. She glanced down and realized she was rubbing the side of her left hand. Taking a deep breath, she shoved her hands in the back pockets of her jeans and turned to face Chad.

He stood in the doorway with one hand on the doorjamb, watching her, the cat winding around his ankle. Shocked that her first impulse was to cross the room to him and touch the buttons on his shirt, and then smooth her hands across his chest and up to his jaw, her eyes widened. Then just as quickly she tore her gaze away and glanced at the floor. "Where do we start?"

One eyebrow rose, but Chad didn't say anything about the scene on the porch. He wandered to one corner of the room, his gaze finally breaking from her to crouch and inspect the floor, George at his side. "I see you've had someone replace floor boards. It looks like they did a good job but it may be a little tricky to match the stain perfectly between the new wood and the old." His hand absently scratched George's head as he spoke.

She shrugged.

"You really don't know what you want to do, do you?"

"I know I want them to look better than this…"

"Right, right," he said touching a gap between the old boards.

She didn't know what to say so she remained silent.

Kirsten Fullmer

He glanced up at her. "How do you want them to *look* when they're finished?"

Her eyes darted from him to the floor and back. "...I don't know."

He stood and brushed his hands together, then crossed the room to stand in front of her. His eyes searched hers.

She kinked her head back, both hands still tucked in her back pockets, her gaze glued to his. Heat rolled off his body, dousing her, soaking her to the skin. Her knees went soft and rage over her weakness blossomed in the back of her heart. For some incomprehensible reason, her eyes burned and she wanted to cry.

Wordlessly, he asked her why he was there, what it was she really wanted.

How could she tell him she wanted only to hide from the world and never feel anything, ever again. But it was already too late.

Cramming his hands in his pockets, Chad watched through falling shadows as Julia closed up tight. He'd resolved to help her and he would be true to his word. But even through the dimming light and sexual frustration, he knew that thinking he just wanted to help her was a lie. He might not understand anything about the woman standing before him but God help him, he couldn't stay away from her, and he wasn't thinking about charity.

"So you think we can stain it?" Julia asked. "The floor...?"

Searching her cool features and jutting chin, he sighed. "Yeah...they'll be fine."

With her carefully constructed expression firmly in place, Julia heaved an inner sigh of relief. "I appreciate that. So...what do we do first?"

Shabby Chic After All

6

Chad stalked through the dark toward the delivery service. Julia hadn't had any idea what she wanted done with her floors but after he'd explained her options, she'd decided to just sand and stain them. She evidently liked imperfection. In her floors anyway.

Grumbling, he unlocked the office door, stepped in and flipped the dead bolt behind him. Striding across the room, he headed up the back stairs to his apartment. The door at the top of the stairs closed with a bang as he tossed his keys on the wobbly end table, and ten steps later yanked open his fridge door.

Two beers in the cardboard carton, a bottle of mustard, and two old takeout boxes glowed naked on the rusty fridge shelves. With a beer in his hand, he slammed the fridge closed, and on the edge of the chipped, laminate counter, popped the bottle top off with his fist.

Drops of condensation appeared and rolled down the bottle as he tipped it up once, then twice. Leaning his hip against the counter, he stared through the dark and out the curtain-less window into the moonlit night.

Julia had ruled his thoughts for days but now that he'd touched her, held her, it was a hundred times worse. He should have taken the clues she'd been tossing him all along and stayed away from her but no, he'd had to grab her. Snorting, he lifted the bottle and drank deep, then lowered it and frowned. Okay, he hadn't technically *had* to catch her before she fell but…yeah he pretty much had been forced to catch her…but that wasn't the point…

The empty beer bottle thumped onto the counter and he stalked across the room to toss the sofa cushions onto a chair and tug open the sofa bed. Irritation radiated off him in waves as he surveyed his sorry sleeping situation. Julia's old bed stacked high with ruffled white pillows came to mind and in response, he yanked his shirt over his head with a huff, tearing off two buttons that spun and rolled across the cracked and curling green linoleum floor.

He'd never been so torn up over a woman – what was his problem? He'd dated, had a few laughs and whatever else he'd needed, then moved on. Not that he treated women badly, he assured himself. He opened doors, bought dinner, and was considerate. He'd certainly never pressured a woman to give anything she didn't offer willingly. So what was up now? Why did Julia have him stepping all over himself to be close to her when she wanted no part of it?

He hadn't always been cavalier about women. As a kid, running wild through Smithville with his partner in crime, William, he'd experienced the deep and passionate pangs of puppy love. Even in college he figured someday he'd get married and have a family of his own. But since the accident, all that had changed. He no longer wanted anyone in his personal space.

Falling in love would mean opening himself up, sharing everything. It would mean responsibility and he had enough of that now, taking care of Bobby and his mother. He didn't want anything to do with a woman who wanted babies and houses and minivans and…him.

The bathroom door squeaked in defiance as he pushed it open. Leaning over the dingy sink, he loaded toothpaste onto

Kirsten Fullmer

his toothbrush and glanced up. The mottled bathroom mirror reflected a man in torment. In public, he wore the face of a confident, happy man but here, alone in the glaring white light of the lone bulb over the bathroom sink, he saw a reflection of what he truly was.

His hands planted on either side of the sink, head hanging, toothbrush forgotten, Chad brooded over the evening with Julia. He could still feel her curled against his chest. She had trembled with what? Fear? Longing? Whatever it had been, he hadn't been able to pinpoint what was happening, or what she needed. He was way out of his element with her and his pride stung from her rejection. For some unfathomable reason, he cared about this woman and her refusal to open up to him made him furious.

Meeting his own bloodshot gaze in the mirror, he knew why Julia made him crazy. She was just like him. She wanted no part of a real relationship, nothing that involved heart and soul anyway. Well Karma was a bitch and this was his just reward for how he'd treated everyone in his life lately.

Angrily he stomped back to the sofa. White moonlight streamed in the one window and across the end of his makeshift bed. His eyes darted around the apartment and he knew that his situation, his entire life, was devoid of anything substantial. And he'd created it that way on purpose.

Yanking open the buttons of his jeans, he dropped to sit on the bed, then angrily kicked his feet free, and watched the jeans slide down the wall into a heap on the floor. The remote on the end table offered a distraction, so he snatched it up to slump in the dim, blue and grey, flickering light, surfing blindly through channels of sit coms and infomercials.

Why now? Why did he have to choose the one woman within fifty miles who didn't want him? And one who evidently made him face his demons?

Shabby Chic After All

He clicked off the TV and flopped back onto the thin, lumpy mattress, the center support bar rigid against his spine. Tossing onto his side, he tugged at the crumpled sheet and scowled into the dark room, knowing he was screwed and not in a good way.

★★★

Julia opened the alarm on her cell phone and set it for the next morning, then placed it on the nightstand and flopped back in her bed to stare at the coffered ceiling of the den. George was curled snugly on the corner of her quilt, his delicate feet tucked neatly under him, and light snoring noises came from Ringo's miniature bed. Moonbeams splashed across the floor, scratched and broken by tree branches, and softly lighting the room.

The old house creaked and spoke around Julia, reliving lives past.

She wondered what Chad was thinking or if he was asleep. Huffing with irritation, she flopped onto her side and tugged the quilt up over her shoulder.

She'd spent months wondering where Brad was, and what he was thinking, and it had done nothing but bring her more wretchedness. Her husband had walked away when she was sick, helpless, and vulnerable and never again would she open herself to such pain. Once Brad had been told that her recovery would be painfully slow and that she may never be able to return to work or even talk again, he couldn't pack his bags fast enough. She'd learned her lessons about love the hard way.

Her future was unstable enough without inviting in the opportunity for more pain. She had a little dog who would never leave her, a fluffy cat of questionable origins, and a wonderful old house...and she would manage. She was finding her own way and that was far more than some had in life.

Pressing her face to the pillow to hold back tears, she breathed in the smell of the line-dried pillowcase. She was fairly

Kirsten Fullmer

certain she'd never hung clothes outside until she tried the line in the back yard. Even though her sheets and towels had been surprisingly stiff, they felt fresh, renewed by nature.

Coming to Smithville had been a good choice. She had purposeful things to do here. Not like her old life, which had been filled with clients, appointments, shopping and entertainment, but she could be someone else here. She wasn't sure who she would become, she only knew she couldn't go back. Losing everything and everyone she loved, losing herself, had not been her choice, but she would survive. At least for now.

★★★

A warm spring breeze lifted the flap of the bandana holding Julia's curls as she spread musty-smelling mulch in the flowerbed with her gloved hands. Leaning back on her heels, she surveyed the arrangement. The bush had been trimmed back so the sign for Tara's bed and breakfast could be seen from the road, and multi-colored flowers now bloomed all along the base of the shrub, trailing out in mellow curves to frame the corner of Julia's yard. Day lilies and snapdragons bloomed in shades of purple along the base of the bush, with vivid orange poppies intermingled and shorter blooms, including golden mums and deep-blue pansies blossomed along the front.

Before she'd come to Smithville, Julia hadn't tried her hand at gardening and much to her surprise, the smell and feel of fresh-turned soil felt elementally a part of her. There must have been a farmer somewhere in her line of ancestors, who had passed along a green thumb.

She'd pored over her gardening books and spent hours looking up plants and their needs on her laptop, making detailed notes but she was still a little shocked when she'd stood in front of the selection of plants at the nursery that morning and instead of feeling overwhelmed, ideas for grouping of blooms had poured through her mind, as if the plants themselves spoke to her.

Old Fergus had fussed and clucked over her selections, offering input and advice as well as raving about her choices. He was the sweetest old man, and Julia had felt an affinity and closeness to him. It was not something she had planned to do or even felt comfortable with but his passion for flowers and the way the old man tottered between plant stands, clutched at her heart. She understood forcing an unwilling body to take you where you needed to go, no matter the pain and time involved.

Ringo tore around the corner of the house, George at his heels, bringing Julia's thoughts back to the present. The little dog pivoted in a tight circle, coming up behind the cat, who jumped in mid-air and landed gracefully nearby to roll onto his back and take a playful swipe at Ringo.

Julia straightened, her hands on her knees for support, and she smiled at her animal family. Those two never stopped playing for long and she offered up a silent thanks for whoever had sent the cat to them. Her head tilted to one side as she noted that George had a glow to his coat. He was gaining weight, and was truly a fat and sassy kitty now.

The front screen screeched open and Mac stuck his head out. "Hey Julia, come check this out."

She patted the ground around her, searching for her digging tools then counted them carefully, knowing she had three and not wanting to lose one. She turned toward the porch, calling Ringo over her shoulder as she followed the older man. Julia paused, smiling up into the sun as she neared the house. Steve had pulled down the rusted and broken metal awning over the porch, as well as replaced the glass in her front doors.

Ringo trotted underfoot as Julia entered the living room. She lingered at the front doors, holding the screen open for the cat as she touched the new, etched, white-crystal glass panels, then glanced behind her to see that George had chosen to curl up on a porch chair.

Julia headed for the kitchen, tugging off her flowered gardening gloves and smoothed one hand over her bandana in a nervous gesture. Mac had moved the sink this morning and Steve was in the kitchen now, patching the wall. This would be her first glimpse of the sink under the window.

Steve glanced up as she walked into the kitchen. Mac gestured toward the sink and shoved tools into his toolbox. "Wha-do-ya think?"

Steve squatted back on his heels to watch, rubbing his hands across the ample stomach of his dirty blue overalls.

Her eyes glowing, Julia circled the sink, one hand caressing the porcelain as if it were a baby. "Oh, it's perfect, isn't it?" she asked, looking to the men for their agreement.

Both nodded.

"Will we be able to move in the hutches today?" she asked, her excitement contagious.

Steve stood and crossed the room. "Well the outlets are wired but you'll want to redo the floor first."

With her hand on her bandana, Julia nodded. "Right, right, Chad is coming over tonight to get started. I'm just so ready to have a kitchen again."

A look passed between the men and Julia quirked a brow. "What?"

"Chad said he'd help you?" Steve asked.

"Yeah, why?"

Both men shook their heads but neither would meet her eye as they quickly returned to their previous tasks. Slightly crestfallen and unsure what she was missing, Julia stared at the sink.

Mac's red toolbox banged closed and he hefted it to stand next to her. He stroked one hand down the length of his drooping, grey-streaked mustache and harrumphed. "This will look just the way you want it to Julia, don't you worry for a minute. Chad knows what he's doing and Becky has you covered."

Biting the inside of her cheek, she considered him through narrowed eyes. Had Chad said something to them about her?

Mac turned to go and Steve followed, his arms full of leftover wiring and tools. Julia followed them to the front door and held open the screen. "Thanks guys, get me a bill and I'll write you a check."

"Will do," Steve called over his shoulder, nodding his head in farewell as the men reached their trucks. Once again, she wondered if somehow, someone knew that she was battling feelings for Chad and it was news all across town. She shuddered. There was nothing she could do about it, so she shrugged it off and closed her newly finished front doors.

Returning to the kitchen, Julia cocked one hip against the doorjamb and imagined the kitchen completed, with glowing floors and the walls lined with shelves of dishes. Humming distractedly, she turned to go to her room and collect clothes for a shower.

★★★

At two p.m. sharp, Julia rounded the last curve in the long driveway of Tara's B&B and pulled to a stop in the shade of a tree. Afternoon sunbeams played across the roof of the long front porch, puffy white clouds floated in the deep blue sky, and a breeze ruffled the baby leaves of the willow tree between the house and the barn. Tara waved through the screen door as Julia slowly climbed the steps to the porch.

"I'm so glad you came to visit," Tara said as she gave Julia a brief hug at the top step.

Shocked by the effusive greeting, as if she were a long-time friend, Julia stood immobile.

"Come and sit down, I'll go get the lemonade."

Kirsten Fullmer

Finding her feet, Julia moved toward the wicker patio chairs with blue and white striped cushions. While she waited for Tara to return, the breeze whispered across the porch, carrying the scent of spring flowers and ruffling the sheer curtains at each column.

Tara returned, carrying a tray of glasses and a pitcher clinking with ice cubes and lemonade. She perched on the edge of a chair to pour them each a glass, then settled back into the cushions and tucked her feet under her. "So, tell me about your house and your beautiful yard," she said, her eyes bright.

A warm glow sparked in Julia's chest, not only from the open offer of friendship but from the compliment. "Well, I trimmed that bush by your sign and planted flowers around it this morning."

Tara reached out and laid cool fingers on Julia's arm. "I know, I heard they are absolutely amazing."

Julia's eyes widened but she laughed. "You'd think I'd be used to how fast news travels around here, but I'm not."

"Oh that's nothing," Tara assured her, catching a drop of condensation that slipped down her glass. "I also heard you have a crazy cat that likes to ride in your truck." She looked up, her eyes sparkling.

Almost spitting lemonade across the porch, Julia choked and coughed and set her glass on the side table to wipe at her chin. "Seriously?" She shook her head. "I'm the crazy cat lady?"

Tara waved her off and sipped from her glass, then laughed. "No, the cat is crazy, not you."

"I suppose that's a little better—"

"So how is your kitchen coming along?" Tara asked.

Julia's eyes lit up. "Mac moved the sink this morning and Steve wired the outlets. Chad is coming tonight to start on the floors."

"What are you going to do with the floors and how many are you doing?"

Julia shrugged. "We are just doing the kitchen for now, until I see what all is involved and how they look. I want something rustic— like they've never been ruined or refinished."

Nodding, Tara sipped from her glass, deep in thought. Finally she answered. "It can be tricky to work on something for hours and leave it looking as if you didn't touch it. That's one of my favorite parts of the whole shabby movement. Do you do furniture?"

Retrieving her glass from the side table, Julia shook her head. "I've never tried, wouldn't really know where to start. It sounds complicated."

"Nah," Tara assured, "It's not hard. I'll invite you to the warehouse one of these days and you can pick out a piece to redo. I'll help you get started."

"Really?" Julia asked, her eyes wide. "I have no skills with tools."

"I have a hunch you're a quick learner."

Julia frowned into her glass. She had been quick to pick up just about anything she tried until the last year. She hated the well-earned doubts that now lived under her skin.

Picking up on Julia's discomfort, Tara changed the subject. "So Chad is going to help you with the floors. What do you think of him?" she asked, studying Julia from the corner of her eye.

Caught off guard, Julia glanced up, her face draining of color. Had the whole town been talking about her? "What do you mean?"

Tara shrugged. "Oh I don't know, do you think he's handsome?" she questioned cautiously.

Julia scoffed. "Is there a woman who doesn't?"

A giggle slipped from Tara's lips and she glanced from side to side. "I'm not supposed to notice."

Julia chuckled. "Since you brought him up, I don't really know him. What's he like?"

Jiggling her glass to watch the ice cube swirl, Tara paused to think, then glanced up. "He's...he's a good guy. He was always great looking, even as a kid, but he always seemed oblivious to it and acted like a normal kid." Her brow knit as she continued. "He came back from Philly almost two years ago."

"What did he do there?" Julia asked, sensing a story in the comment.

Tara hesitated. "College, then he managed a United Package Service hub."

Her eyebrows up, Julia was surprised. "Sounds exciting. He didn't like that? Why did he come back?"

Shifting in her seat, Tara stared into her drink. "He and William, Bobby's brother, both worked there. Chad was William's boss."

Julia nodded. "Where is William now?"

Tara gazed across the yard for a long moment, her eyes sad. "He died in a traffic accident." She glanced back to Julia, paused, then continued. "Chad...he was so upset he...came back," she finished lamely.

In shock, Julia sat staring blankly. "Poor Bobby..."

Tara took a long drink of lemonade then continued. "Yeah... Anyway, Chad was always a nice kid." She stared off into the yard for a moment before she continued. "I was awkward, and he never made fun of me like the other kids did."

Her mouth open in surprise, Julia shifted gears and gaped. "How could you have been awkward? You are gorgeous."

Tara shifted in her chair to stretch one long tan leg in front of her. "No seriously, they called me hedgehog. We were poor and I was painfully withdrawn."

"We? Your family?"

"Winnie is my family," Tara answered solemnly, her foot dropping. "But the whole town watched out for us."

Julia nodded, sensing there was much more to the story of this town and its people but not wanting to dig for info.

Silence settled over the porch as the women sipped lemonade and settled into the easy camaraderie flowing between them.

Julia spoke first. "I really am excited about my kitchen but I'm not sure I can make it look the way I envision it in my head."

"I love renovating," Tara said dreamily. "It's so exciting to have a vision and make it happen. You'll do great, don't worry."

"Did you rehab this house?" Julia asked, her hand motioning over her shoulder.

Tara nodded. "Yeah, the house and the barn. Justin is building a spa now. You can't see it from here, it's around the corner of the house." She pointed past the willow tree.

"Wow, a spa?"

Shrugging, Tara laughed. "It was already in the plans for this place before we bought it."

Julia drank from for her glass, savoring the sweet smell of lemons. Her forehead wrinkled. "I don't understand, I thought you rehabbed the house…"

Waving one hand as she drank, Tara finished her glass and set it on the tray with a snort. "Oh girl, that is a long, long story."

Her interest piqued, Julia leaned back in her chair. "Give me a teaser then."

Tara looked off in space for a moment, a smile on her lips. "Let's just say this was a crazy project and Justin wasn't my favorite person when he came to town."

Julia's brows rose. "Your fiancé? Why? I don't understand."

"Well I was a mess for one thing, but he was—such a city boy. Drove me nuts."

"I'm a city girl, is that a problem?" Julia asked hesitantly.

Kirsten Fullmer

Tara laughed. "Justin and I were competing to build this place and I couldn't stand him. I don't think you need to worry."

Confused Julia lowered her glass. "Sounds complicated. How long has it been a B&B?"

Tara counted on her fingers then glanced up. "Three months. We pretty much only fill up on the weekends so far. We have a few weddings coming up in the summer, including ours, which is in…" She counted on her fingers. "Six weeks, holy cow. I'm never going to be ready."

"I'm sure you'll figure it all out. You'll have to give me the whole story some time, I'm not in the gossip network you know. You must be very excited for your wedding."

Her expression softening, Tara looked down at her hands in her lap and twisted her engagement ring. "I am, I'm just nervous. If you'd told me a year ago that I'd be getting married I have said you were nuts."

"Because you couldn't stand your fiancé?" Julia laughed. "Or some other reason?"

Tara shrugged. "It was a lot of things. I didn't want my life to change, I didn't want Justin messing in my business, I was— closed, if you know what I mean."

Julia sobered. "I understand completely," she muttered, feeling uncomfortable for the first time since her arrival. Reality slammed down hard on her heart, nearly taking her breath away. What was she doing, sitting here pretending she was normal? She stood and placed her glass on the tray. "Well, I better get going. Thank you for the lemonade."

Tara looked up with surprise and sadness in her eyes and bit her bottom lip.

Immediately sorry for her unwanted turn of mood and her complete lack of social grace, Julia hesitated. "Want to come by and see how the kitchen is going?"

Tara's expression relaxed and she stood. "I'd like that."

"Come by when you have time to talk. I want to hear the long story about you and Justin…"

Standing and smoothing her skirt, Tara reached for Julia's arm. "I'll be there."

Tara's tentative smile and simple touch on the arm made Julia pause. The dank fear that had prompted her to run flipped over and now felt like a tiny glowing spark deep in her soul. Shocked by the sensation, she took a moment to consider and accept the friendship Tara offered. A smile played at the corner of her lips and crinkles formed at the corners of her eyes as she allowed the spark to ignite and warm her heart, finally bursting into a smile that transformed her expression from hesitant to radiant.

She placed her hand over Tara's, welcoming the new bond of understanding between them. "I look forward to seeing you."

★★★

"Ringo, George, stop it!" Julia fussed. The cat and dog froze in mid-wrestle at Julia's feet and Ringo's ears dropped. Gingerly, he stepped away from George and trotted across the porch to jump into Julia's lap to lick her hand. George, unruffled as always, calmly licked his paw and smoothed it across his head, as if to comb his hair.

Immediately Julia felt contrite for snapping at her pets. They had only been playing – she was just tense and edgy as she waited for Chad to arrive. Scowling, she petted Ringo and wondered why Chad got her so riled. She didn't have many distinct memories but she was sure she'd been around handsome, well-built men and had successfully dealt with them. How had she ended up so tangled over this one?

A pickup truck rumbled to a stop in front of the house and Julia lurched to her feet, dumping Ringo on top of the surprised cat. George yowled and jumped into a chair.

Kirsten Fullmer

Chad climbed from his truck and lifted a hand in greeting, then circled around the back to lift out a large machine and head toward the house.

Julia scrambled to open the screen door as he stepped onto the porch and they clambered into the living room. Chad set down the red and silver machine with a huff. He brushed his hands together and bent to pick up the cord that was falling off the handle of the dusty thing.

The song *Penny Lane* lofted through the room, stretching out the awkward moments. Ringo sniffed around the contraption and Julia bent her head to one side, taking in the odd piece of equipment. Silence hung heavy in the air as the song ended.

"What is it?" Julia finally asked, careful not to make eye contact with Chad.

He chuckled. "It's a sander."

"Oh." Awkwardly, Julia scratched the back on her calf with her other foot. "How does it work?"

"Nice to see you too," Chad replied, waiting for some response from her.

A blush crept up Julia's neck and she blinked up at him nervously. "Sorry, thanks for coming over to help me."

"Not a problem," he said, shuffling awkwardly. "Really, I'm glad to help."

Her smile was apprehensive.

"So Steve and Mac were here today?" Chad asked.

Julia nodded.

"I saw the front doors." He motioned over his shoulder. "May I?" he asked, moving toward the kitchen.

"Sure."

Careful to keep back enough to leave a buffer zone between them, Julia followed Chad to the kitchen. He bent to touch the patch on the wall where the sink had been and nodded. "Steve does good work doesn't he?"

She nodded, no words coming to mind.

Crossing the room, Chad's eyes darted from the edge of the sink to the edge of the window. "I guess Mac measured to be sure the hutches would fit?"

Once again, Julia nodded mutely, amazed and irritated at her fascination with the purely male way he approached the project.

Chad sighed. "Sorry I growled at you back there."

She shrugged, feeling a little guilty for asking him to come help when she wasn't interested in him the way he wanted her to be. Or so he thought. "It's okay, I was rude."

"No I was rude," Chad replied, cramming his hands in his pockets.

Ringo trotted into the room and sat at Julia's feet. Chad glanced at the dog then back to Julia. When their eyes met he caught a glimmer in her gaze and the hair on the back of his neck stood up.

He yanked his hands free and took a step forward, well within her personal space, to soak up the sparks coming off her skin. She stared at him wide eyed, almost as a challenge, her feet riveted to the floor, helpless to move or speak. He raised a hand to touch her cheek and the screen door hinge in the living room screeched as the door banged open.

"Hey, you guys in the kitchen?" Bobby called.

Wrenched from the moment, Julia staggered backwards with one hand on the wall to steady herself. Chad didn't move, his eyes boring into hers.

"Oh there you are," Bobby said, striding into the room. "How come you didn't answer? Hi Miss Julia." His head bobbed in greeting.

Julia croaked, cleared her throat and tried again. "Hi Bobby."

"You moved the sink," Bobby commented, tromping across the room. Then he turned to Julia, his chest puffed out and shoulders stiff as he adjusted his belt. "I knew you liked my idea."

Chad snorted. "Come on, let's get started," he grumbled as he headed back to the living room to get the sander. Julia waited while he carried the machine to the kitchen and unwound the cord from around the handles, once again engrossed with his every movement. The base of the sander was round and flat, with a handle extending up into a T, with grips on each side.

As Chad headed for the nearest outlet, the cord spread behind him, Bobby fiddled with the machine, flipping the switch and adjusting knobs. The machine roared to life the second Chad plugged it in, and Bobby grabbed the handles in shock.

Before anyone could react, the sanding machine whirled violently in a circular pattern across the floor, practically jerking Bobby's arms from the sockets, and drove directly across the cord. Quick as a flash the apparatus sucked up the cord, whipping it violently like a snake as it wound around and around the base of the machine. Bobby clung to the wild thing, his upper body half a rotation ahead of his lower body as the sander jumped across the room. Ringo yelped and scuttled out the door.

Chad dove for the plug and yanked it from the outlet as Julia cowered against the wall with her hand over her face and one knee up. The contraption slowed to a halt, jerking Bobby one last time behind it as he scrambled for footing.

Silence fell across the room and Bobby jumped back from the sander, rubbing his upper arm with one hand.

Chad's face was dark as night and he looked as if wanted to throttle someone, but instead he huffed out a breath. "You okay?" he asked Bobby.

The thin man nodded, his Adam's apple working and his eyes far too large behind his crooked glasses.

Julia stood gaping, her mouth open. "Is that how it's supposed to work?" she asked.

"No!" Chad bellowed, then scrubbed his hand across his scalp, composing himself. "No, it's not."

"Oh," Julia squeaked.

Ringo's head popped around the doorjamb and he trotted into the room to sniff the machine and tangled cord.

"No Ringo," Julia said, pitching toward the sander to scoop up the dog, lest it suck him up too.

Chad took a deep breath and blew it out. Muttering under his breath, he bent to untangle the cord from the base of the machine. Bobby picked up the plug end of the cord and Chad swung toward him, his index finger extended. "Drop it."

The little man dropped the cord as if it was hot and took a step back, his hands up.

Kirsten Fullmer

7

Julia stepped back from the tree in her front yard and brushed her gloved hands together to shake off the dirt. Humming *Hide Your Love Away* under her breath, she tilted her head to one side and scrutinized the flowerbed she'd built circling the tree. The retaining wall made from curved terracotta blocks, which Fergus had suggested, worked well but the arrangement of blooms she'd positioned in their temporary pots looked sparse to her newly honed gardener's eye. Walking to the back of her truck, she counted the remaining plastic pots of flowers, then counted them again. She lifted four more pots of flowers from the tailgate, two pinched between the thumb and forefinger of each hand.

Suddenly she realized that she hadn't given much thought to rising from the flowerbed, or even bending over it. She'd reached out for the flowerpots and pinched them firmly between her fingers as if she'd always been able to grasp and pull. Dumbfounded, she supposed her new flexibility must be from all the work she'd been doing on the house and the yard. Doing activities that were interesting and fulfilling were definitely more fun than repeating exercises in physical therapy over and over.

Humming once again, she headed back to the tree. A car slowed in front of the house, the driver's attention focused on her house and yard. "Excuse me, ma'am, could I ask you a question?" the driver asked.

Julia paused and placed the flowers on the grass, wiping the back of one wrist across her brow as she turned toward the street. "Sure…" She said hesitantly, nearly certain she would have no idea whatever it was they wanted to know.

The driver smiled, her eyes flashing with relief. "I'm looking for the Serendipity inn. Do you know where the turn off is?"

Julia grinned, her gloved finger pointing to the sign over her bush in the corner. "Right there."

Her eyes widening, the driver scoffed with a shake of her head. "So it is! I was so busy marveling at your yard that I didn't even see it."

Warmth and happiness glowing in her chest, Julia smiled and dipped her head. "Thank you."

The lady waved as she drove away to turn down the gravel drive to the B&B.

Julia bent and retrieved the flowers, placing them in the flowerbed; her heart lighter than it had felt in eons. Rearranging the new flowers to make room, she stepped back again, liking what she saw.

Thirty minutes later, she was spreading mulch around the fresh plants when Chad's pickup truck rolled to a stop in front of her house. Self-conscious, she tucked a wisp of damp hair behind her ear, depositing a smudge of black mud across her cheek.

Chad climbed from his truck and rounded the front, lifting a hand in greeting.

Ringo roused from his nap on the porch and trotted across the lawn to greet Chad. Bending to pat the dog's head, Chad grinned up at Julia, examining her expression for some sign of how she might feel about him today. "Your flowers look nice," he said, testing the water.

Kirsten Fullmer

Contented and happy, Julia glowed. "Thank you." Her eyes sparkled as sunlight glistened off her curls.

Silent, he stood studying her, causing her pulse to flutter and her stomach to lurch. After a long moment, Julia glanced over his shoulder to his truck. "Can I help you with something?"

Shaking himself visually, he appeared chagrinned. "Oh, right, Tara's appliance guy called me yesterday and said your new old stove was ready to deliver. I guess we need to stain your floor so you can get your kitchen put together."

Julia felt like clapping with excitement, a feeling that just weeks ago she had been certain she would never experience again. Her eyes rounded and she grasped Chad's arm, her gloves making five muddy smudges on his skin.

"Oh, sorry," she said wiping at the marks, making them bigger.

Chad laughed, taken aback by her obvious cheerfulness.

Perturbed by the muddy mess she'd made of Chad's arm, Julia tugged off her gloves. "I'll get you cleaned up, I just need to water these flowers and we can go in."

He nodded and moved back a step to watch her head for the spigot by the porch and bend to twist the tap handle. She was wearing shorts, her knees smudged with mud and dirt, and when she bent he could see a light tan line on her thigh, indicative of how much time she'd been spending on the yard.

She dragged the hose to the flowerbed and turned it on the mulch between the blossoms. "What do we still need to do on the kitchen floor?" she asked, squinting into the sun toward him.

Chad stepped up beside her, swished his fingers under the water, and then reached out to wipe at the mud on her cheek.

She swatted at his hand and rubbed her cheek with the back of her wrist. "I must look a mess..."

He grinned. "You look great. Happy."

Pleased beyond all reason but uncomfortable with the closeness, Julia scoffed and scuttled to one side. "Thanks—"

Chad wiped at his arm, cleaning off the mud and watching Julia as she returned to the spigot. She washed the mud from her knees and hands, then cranked the handle and tossed the hose in a coil and stepped up onto the porch. "Come on, I'm thirsty."

He nodded and followed, Ringo trotting by his side as they passed through the living room to the kitchen. The kitchen floor was smooth and flat, muted from the sanding, the wood bare and raw. "How dark do you want to stain this?" he asked, watching her tug open the ugly yellow fridge they'd pushed into the mud room so they could sand the floor.

Julia tossed him a can of soda, which he caught smoothly.

She cocked a hip against the doorjamb and popped open her soda. "I don't know stain colors," she commented, rubbing her toe across the floor, "I just want it to look like it goes with the house."

"Goes with the house?" he teased as he popped open his soda, cupping one hand to catch the frothy white bubbles that fizzled from the can before they hit the floor.

Still uncomfortable with his teasing and yet wanting him to feel good about helping her, she snorted. "You know what I mean."

He gulped from his soda can, flicking the bubbles from his hand into the sink, working to hide a smile as he swallowed. He lowered the can, a grin still on his face. "Yeah, I think I do. When do you want to stain it?" He waited for her answer as she drank her soda, watching her chug the cold drink.

She dropped the soda can in the trash and wiped her mouth with the back of her hand, country style. Her shoulder shrugged. "When is good for you?" she asked, her eyes darting around the room in order to avoid his.

"I could come by tonight," he offered, finishing his drink.

Tonight, she thought, *just like that, tonight.* She nodded, resolutely ignoring the currents of energy flowing between them.

Kirsten Fullmer

She needed the help and she was thankful he was willing to offer it. "Awesome, how long does it take to dry?"

"It depends," he said, rubbing his fingers along his jaw as he surveyed the floor. "Do you want polyurethane on it too?"

Her brow lowered. "Polly what?"

He laughed. "It's a sealant, makes the floor shiny and waterproof."

Julia pushed away from the wall and walked in a circle around the kitchen, gazing at the floor as if it were a fine painting. What did she want? Mostly she wanted the floors to be finished so the man dominating the room would leave. She couldn't function with him so close. "I don't think I want shiny."

Chad shrugged. "It's your call. If all you want is stain, you can walk on them the next day, depending on how many coats you need."

Her gaze flew up. "How many will I need?" she asked, wondering how many more days would drag on with the torment of him in her space. Embarrassed at her bad attitude toward someone being charitable, as well as the sexual thoughts that kept climbing under her skin, she blushed.

Thinking for a minute, he considered her expression. "Shall we try one coat and see if you like it?"

She nodded, relieved that at least the floor might be that simple. "Sounds reasonable."

"You'll have to keep the pets off it overnight," he warned.

Again she nodded. "I figured. It sure looks different now doesn't it?" she said, thinking about Bobby being jerked across the room by the sander. Her eyes sparkled with humor. "Bobby —" laughter bubbled up from deep in her gut, causing her shoulders to shake. Her hand came up to cover her mouth.

Chad shook his head, looking embarrassed. "Yeah, that was quite the show…"

For the first time since she'd come to town, Julia had the upper hand in a conversation and the sensation burst upon her, feeling as if a small part of Julia, the person, had been snapped back into the broken jigsaw puzzle of her personality. She allowed her laughter to roll into the room, sounding foreign in her own ears.

Chad's neck turned red and he ran his fingers through his hair. "That's right, laugh it up…" he chuckled, embarrassed but immediately taken with her turn of attitude.

Julia sniffed and wiped at the corner of her eye, feeling more comfortable in her own skin than she had since forever.

Silence settled back over the room and Julia sighed, reveling in the sensation of being normal. Then her eyes met Chad's across the room. He stood smiling at her, his expression soft and warm.

She swallowed once, her eyes rounding.

He sauntered across the room to toss his can in the trash. "Okay, well I guess I'll see you tonight then…" He turned from the trashcan and sauntered over to stand in front of her.

The heat in his eyes charred whatever thoughts Julia may have managed to form, turning them to sparkling shards that fell around her, melting her feet to the raw wood floor. She swallowed past the lump in her throat, forcing her feet to move. Staggering back a step, she grinned crookedly. "I appreciate your help—"

"Not a problem," he assured, his voice low and smooth.

No words came to Julia as her pulse pounded behind her ears and her palms began to sweat. She should never have invited him inside, she realized too late. She might be doing better, but his persona was just too big. She couldn't withstand the draw he had over her in such close quarters.

"I know—know that you don't do this kind of thing for everybody," she stuttered, determined to show that she really did

Kirsten Fullmer

appreciate his help but accidentally heading the conversation into dangerous territory.

One of his brows shot up. "You're right, I don't."

Julia grimaced, berating herself for being such a clod. "I meant—I—"

He stepped closer and she couldn't move, her back against the wall. Heat welled up in her stomach and puddled there briefly before spilling over into her pelvis. She bit her bottom lip, willing herself to either run or jump on him, either way just make a move and end the stand off.

His gaze roamed the length of her body sliding over her shoulders, her belly, then down her legs. Her resolve withered and pure longing swelled in her chest – longing to be held, to be caressed, to be kissed.

Her eyes grew even wider, her gaze falling to his lips then back to his eyes.

His hand came to her cheek, his fingers gently caressing the sensitive skin below her ear.

She didn't move, couldn't move. Apprehension and longing melted together to flood her heart and mind with sensation, suffocating any anger still harbored there. Confusion rained down, pelting her like hail stones, drawing her thoughts back and forth, like people running for cover in a summer storm.

Where was the wit and pre-physical banter that came before a kiss, she wondered, the confrontation and conflict she'd instigated with men? All she felt was pure desire.

Slowly Chad leaned down then paused, his lips a faction of an inch from hers, expecting her to bolt but instead, her eyes fluttered closed and she rose on tiptoe to touch her lips to his. Immediately his fingers cupped the back of her head and his other hand slid around her back and drew her to him.

The first kiss was nothing more than a tentative touch and the second was only a sweet press of lips, yet Julia trembled.

Chad's tongue stroked her upper lip and she gasped, her mouth falling open.

As if he sensed that she was pressed to her limit, his kisses remained tentative tastes, his tongue touching hers, then withdrawing, only to search again.

Her trembling grew to quaking and with questions in his eyes, he set her back on her feet, his hand still on her cheek.

She wobbled slightly, her eyes filled with tears, and her lips trembled.

"What's wrong?" he whispered.

She shook her head and pulled away. Her glistening eyes were enormous and she pressed her fingers to her lips. A moment stretched between them in silence.

Soft and feminine sensations flowed through Julia's body as she gasped for a breath. Inundated with a million tender feelings, Julia was immediately reminded of why she had vowed to never feel again. It was too sweet, too poignant, and too wonderful. She clamped her eyes closed. A woman could dive into feelings like this and swim for a week, never coming up for air. But she knew beyond doubt that when the bubble burst and the sweetness drained away, the void would be too harsh, too glaring, too horrific to face. And it *would* go away…

Her heart pounded, scolding her over and over, reminding her where she'd been, what she'd been through. *Damn! Damn! Damn!* rang her thoughts. How could she have been so stupid and careless? Had she forgotten everything? She pushed away in desperation and when she spoke, her hands lashed out with her words. "I'm not…that wasn't what you think."

He shook his head in confusion. "What do I think?"

She staggered to the window. Her back was to him, expanding and contracting as she took deep breaths. Finally she turned. "I'm sorry Chad, I— I shouldn't have kissed you."

"—Why?" His expression was deadpan with confusion.

Kirsten Fullmer

She shook her head. "I can't get involved with you, or anyone. I didn't come here for that. It's not what I want..."

He rubbed his jaw, his eyes still hot. "That's not how it felt."

Her shoulders slumped and her expression softened. "I was wrong to kiss you, I'm sorry. Please...just respect me enough to believe that I'm not looking for...anything like that."

Shifting his weight from one foot to the other, he frowned. "I want you, Julia," he stated. "Why should I turn away? You want me and you're single – that much is obvious." His brow quirked. "You are alone, aren't you?"

Her shoulders straightened and she grasped at the sink for support. "Well I—I have Ringo and George."

His eyes sliced into hers and one fist clenched in frustration. "That's not what I meant. Is there someone else?"

As he held his breath, she paused, her expression impossible to read. Then she shook her head no.

He turned and stalked across the room. "I'm not one to stand by and watch when there's something I want..." he said to the doorway. Then he turned back to her. "Can you at least tell me why?"

Her eyes closed and her lips pursed. She leaned against the windowsill, deep in thought. Finally she opened her eyes and straightened. "You know that old saying, 'you won't be tested past what you can bear'?"

He nodded slowly.

"...Well I'm proof that you can."

His eyes squinted. "What do you mean?"

She sighed, her hands falling to her sides in frustration and the shuttered expression returning to her face. "Never mind. I'm broken – let's leave it at that."

Chad didn't speak, he just regarded her solemnly, hoping for inspiration of some kind to right the situation. Finally he turned and headed for the front door.

Julia followed him, her mind spinning around the upcoming evening spent with Chad in her kitchen, staining the floor. She'd botched everything now. Hell, she'd barely managed to keep her hands to herself for five minutes, how would she manage an entire evening? *And* she'd pissed him off.

"Bring Bobby tonight," she blurted, surprising both of them.

Chad turned to her, the open screen door in his hand. He didn't say anything but his expression said, "Seriously?"

She nodded, relieved that she'd pulled the idea out of her hat.

He gazed at her, his countenance changing from surprise to resignation. Stomping through the door, he headed across the porch and down to the sidewalk then looked back. "Around seven then?"

She nodded, saddened by his expression, and then folded her arms across her chest as if to block her heart. Chad was a good man, she resolved. One who would willingly help a person just because they needed a hand, not because there was something in it for himself. She frowned, determined there would not be anything in it for Chad. But the memory of the kiss burned through her resolve, causing possibilities to dance through the back of her mind.

Chad lifted a hand as he turned away and she watched him stalk to his truck, knowing she'd disappointed him. Again.

★★★

Julia wiped her forehead on her shoulder as she struggled to close the garage door. Cut grass clung to her bare shins and clumped on her sneakers. The evenings were getting warmer and summer felt imminent. Inhaling the sweet scent of fresh mowed grass, Julia turned from the garage and ran directly into Bobby. Staggering back to catch her balance, her hand on her chest, she blinked at Bobby, who resembled a marionette puppet dangling from knotted strings as he recovered from the shock.

Kirsten Fullmer

"Sorry, Miss Julia. I called to you, but the garage door was creaking something fearful. I guess you didn't hear me." He adjusted his glasses on his nose.

"It's okay, come on inside," she said when she'd recovered her voice, leading the way to the back door where Ringo's muffled barks greeted them.

Julia opened the door and the little dog burst out, unsure whether to bound into Julia's arms, or circle around Bobby's feet.

The thin man jumped and scurried to sidestep the enthusiastic dog, obviously uncomfortable with Ringo's excitement. Julia scooped up the dog and tucked him under her arm, shushing him.

In the small mudroom, Julia leaned against the wall, pushed off one grassy sneaker and then the other, then motioned for Bobby to follow her into the kitchen. When he didn't immediately follow, she turned back to find him staring at her, his eyes wide behind his lenses, a grin lifting one corner of his mouth and his Adam's apple bobbing.

"Oh no…" she murmured, recognizing his adoring expression. When had this happened? Had she done something to encourage him?

Before she could collect her thoughts, Chad knocked on the front door. Ringo leapt from her arms to race through the living room, barking excitedly.

Eager to escape the kitchen, Julia followed the dog. As she tugged open the screen, her concern spilled out onto Chad. "I'm so glad you're here," she whispered hoarsely. "Bobby is in the kitchen and I think he likes me. What should I do?"

His expression a mix of humor and surprise, Chad stepped in with his hands behind him to keep the screen from slamming. "Hi Julia," he said in normal voice, watching Bobby walk toward them over her shoulder. Then he bent to pat Ringo and whispered gruffly. "You don't know the half of it."

Fighting panic, Julia gaped from one man to the other. One she wanted to tackle and drag into her bedroom, the other she wanted to pat on the head and wipe his nose. Worst of all, they were best friends and coworkers. She had never been part of a love triangle in her life…and it happened now? Here? When she didn't want anything to do with men?

Chad grinned and patted her shoulder. "Come on, let's look at that floor." Then he headed toward the kitchen.

Bobby followed Julia, smiling lopsidedly.

"Come on, Bobby," she muttered, turning toward the kitchen. When she entered, Chad stood with one hip cocked against the sink, watching as they came through the door.

Bobby slid around Julia to stand next to Chad, crossing his arms across his chest to mimic the larger man. Perplexed and awkward, Julia stuffed her hands in her pockets to avoid wringing them.

Finally Chad spoke, breaking the tension, of which Bobby appeared to be oblivious. "Did you bring over that stain I had you pick up yesterday?"

Bobby nodded, his gaze never leaving Julia. Chad nudged him with his elbow. "Well go get it…"

Scrambling in place, Bobby regained conscious thought and headed for the back door. As soon as the door closed, Julia sprang to stand in front of Chad. "What do you mean, 'the half of it'?" she whispered sharply, her hands gesturing wildly.

"Oh he's convinced you have a thing for him," Chad replied, concerned but with amusement hiding just behind his words.

"What?!" she gasped, rearing back a step.

"Yeah, you've got it for him bad," he added, to watch her squirm.

Her hands flew in the air. "What on earth? Why?"

Chad shrugged. "That night you nursed his cheek…"

Julia froze. "Oh no. No no no. It wasn't like that…"

Kirsten Fullmer

He pushed away from the sink and she backed away. "Hey, I know that, but he's—he's—Bobby."

The resignation at the end of Chad's sentence rang true to Julia. "What am I supposed to do now?" she asked, shifting away nervously.

Chad shrugged. "Damned if I know, this is a first."

"His first...?" Julia's voice faded into the room as Bobby returned, carrying a well-worn, five-gallon bucket with black and brown stains smeared on the side. He sat the bucket in front of Chad and glanced up expectantly, waiting for instruction.

Julia's eyes were still glued to Chad, who simply nodded once, then bent to pry the lid off the bucket with a screwdriver from his pocket. "Did you bring in the rags, Bobby?" he asked, his eyes never leaving the bucket.

"Ah shoot..." the little man replied, his head hanging. He headed back toward the door.

Chad stood and Julia jumped in front of him, desperation in her eyes. "I don't want to hurt him! He's so sweet, please tell me what I should do," she lamented.

His eyes burrowing deep into hers, his expression grim, Chad's hands rose to encircle her waist, then he paused, his hands hovering awkwardly. "I told you how I feel..."

For a moment she was lost, her head spun as her body traitorously raged to life, wanting his arms around her. But allowing herself only a brief moment to wallow in the sensation, she lurched back a step and turned to face the sink, the porcelain cold and hard under her hands.

Concerned, Chad moved to her side, bending his head in an attempt to see her face. "It's gonna be okay, Bobby will adjust."

Her eyes flashing, she met his gaze. "Adjust to what?"

Shocked at her vehemence, he stepped back, the length of the sink between them.

His arms full of frayed red rags, Bobby clomped into the room and accidentally kicked the bucket of stain. The dark fluid splashed across the white floor, flooding directly toward Julia and Chad. Quicker than she ever dreamed she could move, Julia leapt up onto Chad, her stocking feet seeking footing on his legs, his waist, her hands gasping at his shirt, shoulders and hair.

Trying to escape the deluge of stain, Chad scrambled from one foot to the other, dancing clumsily across the room with Julia on him, struggling to get a grip on her as she climbed up his chest and then around to his back.

Ringo's barks brought Julia's clamber to a halt. She was on Chad's back with one knee over his shoulder and the other in his armpit. Her chest was pressed onto the back of his head, and she had one arm around his neck, the other locked across his forehead. "Ringo no!" she shouted.

Briefly resembling the multiple-armed goddess Kali, Chad reached everywhere at once, one knee in the air, trying to regain his balance and get a grip on Julia.

Quick as a flash, Bobby dropped the rags and bent to scoop up the dog, then immediately looked as if he wished he hadn't and stood holding the squirming dog at arm's length.

Ringo stilled in Bobby's hands, his little paws dangling, apparently shocked to see Julia perched on top of Chad, his little dog eyes round with wonder.

"Toss him out and close the door," Julia demanded as she squirmed and grappled on Chad, desperate to find a way down.

Hunching in an attempt to lower her gracelessly toward the floor, Chad's hands groped for an appropriate hold as his face narrowly escaped her cleavage.

"Grab some rags," he instructed, aggravation in his voice as Julia groped his face, her hand over his right eye. One of her feet, toes pointed, tapped blindly looking for the floor, then finally made contact. "And start wiping with the grain…" he

Kirsten Fullmer

grumbled as he peeled Julia's fingers off his cheek, holding her wrist to steady her. "I hope you like this color," he added as they made eye contact, nose to nose.

Still in her stocking feet, Julia blushed bright red, then turned and inched toward the growing puddle of stain to grab a rag from the pile on the floor.

"Keep it off your hands if you can, I meant for us to use gloves," Chad commanded as he waded into the worst of the stain and began spreading it across the floor, pushing puddles toward Julia and Bobby.

The three of them worked quickly to even the stain across the wood, adjusting and turning rags in an attempt to keep it off their hands, knees and feet. Julia's white socks turned shades of black as they worked, but within twenty minutes the entire kitchen floor was an even deep brown.

Bobby stood in the hall doorway, a limp, filthy rag in each hand. Chad glared critically at the floor from the door into the mudroom, and Julia stood breathless in the dining room door, unsure what to think.

"That doesn't look half bad," Chad commented, sounding shocked and his demeanor lightening.

Bobby pushed up his glasses with his knuckle, his arms, hands, and shirt stained multiple shades of brown, his head cocked from side to side, surveying their work. Chad instructed the little man to take off his boots and go through the living room. Julia peeled off her socks and followed to tip toe through the dining room to the porch.

Ringo followed them out the door and George jumped down from a wicker chair to greet them. Chad went directly to his truck and came back with hand cleaning goop, and they all gathered around the tap in front of the porch, to lather their hands and arms in the waning sunlight.

Watching Julia as she wiped her hands on her shirt, Chad stepped back to fling water off his hands. "You'll still need a shower," he said apologetically, "but at least now you can go back in without ruining the rest of the house."

She nodded, twisting her arms in front of her. "I'll be darker in spots for a while, but the floor looks great."

Bobby stood watching, his jaw slack and his hands and face dripping. His glasses nearly slid off his nose before he shoved them back up. "Sorry about that, Miss Julia…"

Smiling warmly, Julia hugged him. Just like that – full-on hugged him without thinking. Pulling herself back, she kept one damp hand on his arm. "It all turned out great so don't worry about it. For all I know, that's how it's done."

The little man didn't look too sure. Chad's laughter rang into the night as he clapped Bobby on the back. "There you go, we have a new technique."

A shiver ran through Julia's body and she was unsure if it was sparked by Chad's laughter or the cool breeze on her damp skin but it was enough to remind her that she couldn't afford to get a chill. "I better get inside now. Thanks again guys," she said, stepping onto the porch.

"I'll come by tomorrow and get the rags and stain off your back step," Chad said as Julia opened the screen door to usher the animals inside. She lifted a hand in farewell and the men waved, both looking as if they wished they could follow her.

★★★

Opening and closing drawers in her room, Julia collected clean clothes for after her bath. On the bottom step, she paused to glance up the stairway, taking a moment to gather strength for the climb. Surprisingly however, she managed to climb three or four steps with little trouble, not feeling any extra effort until she was nearly halfway to the landing. She paused to consider

Kirsten Fullmer

her newfound strength and agility. Could working around the house and the yard really have made such a difference? She was eating healthy and drinking a lot of water. And she'd been sleeping much better.

Continuing up the steps, she thought about leaping onto Chad earlier. There had been nothing stilted about her scramble. Maybe effortless activity only worked when she wasn't paying attention because by the time she reached the top step, she was winded. As she trudged down the hall to the bathroom, she was just happy that Chad hadn't commented on her sprint up his backside, or her awkward descent.

★★★

Julia finished watering the flowers and rubbed her lower back as she coiled the hose by the front porch. A car pulled slowly into her drive, the driver intently scrutinizing the yard.

Brushing her hands together, Julia drifted into the yard. "Good morning." She greeted the visitor with a curious smile as the woman climbed from her car.

"Morning," the lady replied. "I'm staying at the bed and breakfast up the road there and I heard about your yard. I had to stop by for a peek."

Surprised and pleased but a bit apprehensive, Julia extended her hand. "Welcome, I'm Julia."

"Rachel," the woman countered absently as the handshake faded, her attention drawn to the roses blooming riotously along the porch rail. Yellows and reds mingled with pink, all backed by the dark green of the leaves and the grey porch railing. "Oh my…" she gasped in admiration.

"Do you like them?" Julia asked.

"I've driven past this house several times in the past twenty years," remarked the woman, "and never once have I given it a second glance. This is just amazing."

Julia glowed shyly under the praise. "I'm not sure I can take the credit," she shrugged. "I have a fabulous source for my plants."

Rachel turned, meeting Julia's eye. "Honey I've seen flowers at greenhouses but to see them here, blooming and thriving around this old house...it's a revelation, that's what it is."

"—Well, thank you," Julia finally offered, believing for once that she had actually accomplished something worthwhile with her own hands.

"Do you sell cuts? Or offer gardening advice?"

Shocked, Julia inched to one side, as if to avoid the question and the surprise it contained. "Oh no, no... I really don't know anything about gardening. I've just read some good books..."

"I've got a shelf full of books, I need flesh and blood to help me," Rachel assured Julia. "I have no natural aptitude. You have a gift, to accomplish this." She spread her hands to indicate the yard full of color.

Blushing and tongue-tied, Julia could only nod and smile. She had not expected to be praised for being talented. She'd been sure those years were long past.

"Well I don't want to keep you," Rachel continued. "I just had to stop and gawk." The woman turned to return to her car, then stopped and waited for Julia to follow. "I'll be staying at the inn for a few days. Do you mind if I stop by again when I have more time and you can tell me more about how often you water and what type of mulch you use?"

Julia waited for the dread and fear of strangers to fill her heart but none came. Finally she stuttered, "That would be nice." She even managed a smile. Evidently the flowers spoke for themselves, leaving her space and time to offer conversation as it came.

Rachel waved as she drove away, leaving Julia with a warm glow in her chest and gratitude in her heart.

Kirsten Fullmer

At two p.m. Chad's truck rolled to a stop in front of the house. Julia creaked open the screen door and lifted a hand in greeting.

He waved as he rounded the back of the pickup and lowered the tailgate to pull out a dolly, which for some reason caused her heart to skip a beat, then race to catch up.

As she watched from the doorway, Ringo and George at her feet, anticipation and excitement glowed in Julia's dark eyes as Chad pushed her new old stove down the sidewalk toward the porch. It was wrapped in a quilted moving blanket and lay on one side, its long curvy steel legs protruding from the blanket but already she could tell that it was perfect.

Barely containing her excitement, Julia followed Chad to the kitchen, the animals trailing after them. He stopped in front of the gas outlet and wiggled the dolly from under the edge of the stove. Julia danced from one foot to the other, circling him, as he carefully tipped the old oven to stand on its shining white enamel legs.

Chad bent to unlatch the tie-down holding the moving blanket in place. The blanket fell into a puddle on the floor. A coo escaped Julia's lips as Ringo bound back to avoid being covered by the blanket. Tenderly she smoothed her hand along the tall end of the stove.

"What are all those doors for?" Chad asked rubbing his fingers along his jaw.

"I'm not sure…" Julia murmured, caressing the high end of the appliance that stood as tall as she was. "I know it has two ovens and a warming oven. I'm not sure which is which. I'll have to look it up online and learn more about how it works. Isn't it just gorgeous?"

Tilting his head to one side to regard the antique oven, Chad remained silent. The long pause in conversation finally snagged Julia's attention and she turned to give him a "really?" expression.

Shabby Chic After All

"It's an old stove," he shrugged. "To be honest I'm not sure why you don't want a nice new one."

Julia circled the stove, her eyes dancing. "I'm not sure either to be honest. I just know I want this house to be completely different from anything I've ever had before."

Chad's eyes narrowed at her confession. "Why is that, Julia?"

The tone of his voice caught her attention and she paused, her heart dropping to her feet as her hand froze on the shining black and silver oven handle. Her gaze slid across the floor and up his body to meet his eye, then quickly scurried back as she bent to peer into the open oven door.

"I'm asking you as a friend. What happened to you?"

She probably should be able to talk to Chad about what she'd been through but for some reason, only panic came to mind. She stood, her back ramrod stiff, and the oven door slammed shut. "I don't want to talk about it," she snapped, turning to leave the kitchen. Why was he asking her this? She couldn't face the horrors of her past, let alone speak of it.

He grabbed her arm and spun her back to face him. "I mean it, what happened?"

Attempting to shrug off his hand, she tugged at her arm. He wasn't gripping her tightly, just enough that she couldn't get away. Finally her belligerent eyes met his, frustrated sparks shooting between them.

"I…I got sick," she said with her chin up in defiance, but with a wobble in her voice.

His grip loosened a notch and his eyes widened. He'd expected her say something about a divorce or a cheating lover and he wasn't prepared for the tears glowing in her eyes. Leading her to the oven he leaned her back against the heavy appliance and with one finger lifted her chin up so he could see her face. "What do you mean, 'got sick'?"

Kirsten Fullmer

Momentarily, she squirmed, attempting to bolt, but he held her arms. "Talk to me Julia, please."

Her tear-filled eyes darted around the room like she was a desperate bird searching for a safe place to land, but safety was not a possibility as long as she was forced to face what had happened and how it had changed her.

The word, change, wasn't near enough to describe the pain that had stripped her of every essence of her person, taken everything but flesh and blood, and left her to start completely over.

He waited. A tremble passed through her body, breaking loose a torrent of tears, and Chad collected her to his chest, rubbing her back gently as she sobbed.

"You let it all out, baby. It's okay," he assured as she cried like only the heartbroken do.

Never had anyone held her so tenderly, offering her reassurance and support. Her childhood had been cold and barren but nothing could prepare a person for the disaster her existence had become. She'd lain in a cold bed for months longing to be held, comforted, loved...but no one had come. She had finally absorbed, on a bone-deep level, the fact that she was truly alone and hope had faded and died.

Chad couldn't possibly understand that she wasn't the person he believed her to be. That she was different now. She didn't know who she was, or even what exactly what had happened.

Ultimately, her weeping mellowed into sniffles and she pulled away from his chest to stare at his boots. He stood silent and strong, waiting for her to speak, his hands warm and firm on her hips.

That fact alone; his hands on her, broke all the rules she'd come to live by. His comfort was like a drug, worming through her system, warming her ice-cold blood, surging through her veins.

"Start at the beginning," he prompted. "Where were you when you got sick?"

Sniffling, her shoulders still wracked with hiccups, she wiped her nose with the back of her hand. "I was in bed asleep. I woke up with a fever."

He waited, his face a blank, as if he were expecting a more dramatic story. "And?"

She shrugged. "That's all I remember."

Shaking his head in confusion, Chad shifted his weight from one foot to the other as he regrouped. "Okay, so you had a fever…"

The warmth of Chad's comfort turned into an ugly demand in Julia's mind. Just like any addiction, be it the warmth of a human touch or the gratification of a substance, there was a flipside of demand that spoiled the high, and she knew the fine she'd pay to come off the drug.

Tiring of the confrontation, Julia wrenched away from him to wander to the sink where she stared out the window into the sun-dappled afternoon. "I had a very high fever. It took me months to recover. That's it."

Puzzled and sad, Chad moved to stand behind her. "What did the doctors do? What do you remember Julia? Please, I want to understand."

The hiccups were gone and she took a deep breath before she turned back to him. A long sigh escaped her lips but she straightened her shoulders and met his eye. All she had now was the emptiness of a story she'd heard others tell in hushed tones behind her back. "I remember bits of my husband telling me he was moving on. He said I wasn't the woman he'd married any more." She shrugged. "The divorce was fair enough. He sold everything and deposited half in my bank account. I never saw him again."

Shock and horror crashed through Chad's mind, leaving him speechless.

"By the time I woke up enough to understand how much time had passed, I'd lost my job. It had been six months since I got sick. For a long time, I didn't really understand what had happened." Her lip curled in a sneer, as if she were telling a story of someone she didn't like. "I'm still not sure, to be honest. Even my so-called *friends* gave up on me. I guess I wasn't any fun." The ugliness of the feelings that rose in her chest threatened to choke her.

Reaching for her hand, his heart in his throat, Chad struggled for something to say.

Julia avoided his grasp, moving toward the door to the hall. "I got better. That's it," she finished, resolute that she was not going to talk or think about the horrible fractured story for another moment. If she could slam the door now, she might escape the horror of reliving it all in broken pieces.

8

Once Chad recovered enough to move his feet, he lurched to follow Julia down the hall. "Julia, wait. What did your family do? What made you decide to come here?"

With her back still to him she plodded ahead. "My dad died when I was in college and my mom is in a nursing home in Jersey." She waited for him at the door, ready to usher him out. Ringo and George stood in the hall watching the sad scene with large eyes.

Stopping in front of her as she held open the screen, Chad tenderly took her hand in his and searched her eyes. "I won't ask you anything else. I'm sorry I pushed you, hell... I'm sorry you got sick."

She gazed over his left shoulder, her chin a notch too high and her chin wobbling.

"Julia..." he begged.

"Thanks for bringing my stove," she said, her voice clipped. "I told you I wasn't interested in a relationship. I told you...I'm not..." Her eyes filled with tears again, and she gave up trying to talk as she blinked them back, her throat clogged with emotion.

He waited a moment longer, hoping she'd respond to him in some way, but finally he dropped her hand and headed out to the porch. As she closed the screen he turned. "Steve will be by around five to connect the stove...and get my dolly."

She nodded once then closed the front door with a forceful bang. The door slamming jarred Julia to the bone as she ran headlong to her bedroom. Desperation pounded through her system and she threw herself onto her bed, tears flowing, and bottomless sadness choking the breath from her.

She'd been horrible to Chad but how could she ever explain how her life had been torn to shreds, everything she'd worked to build— destroyed. Her entire self-concept obliterated.

Rolling onto her back, she gasped for a breath that didn't burn, a thought that didn't cause her chest to seize but it was too late. The cavern had been opened and the familiar miasma of pain engulfed her. Her clenched fists came to her chest and her knees came up to push her arms tighter to her core for protection. She would never recover. This torment would follow her and haunt her forever.

Desperation came next from the knowledge that even if she did build a new life, the same thing would happen. Her own body would turn on her, dragging her away from everyone she knew and loved, everything she cherished. How could a person live with a monster inside them? She didn't know, couldn't fathom ever feeling normal again.

How had she ever walked through life so blasé, believing that she was in control of her destiny? That cocksure notion that she could do anything she wanted, live how she wanted, be who she wanted, was gone – so far gone she didn't even want to believe it again. She'd even come to scoff at others who lived under the delusion that they were in control of their lives.

She would be safer, realistic, if she believed that she could be destroyed at any moment – believed that with one blinding twist, her life would once again be thrust into darkness and loss.

Barely registering the touch, Julia felt George's fur against her arm as the cat curled up against the top of her head. Her fists had moved to cover her eyes. George's warm body only brought

Kirsten Fullmer

one more sensation in an existence where she wanted to feel nothing. She couldn't move to push him away; she was curled tight in an effort to keep reality at bay, so George lay warm against her forehead. Gradually, Julia became aware that the rhythmic hum in her mind was the cat purring. The tumbling growl from the little animal wove into her thoughts, a calm and steady thrum.

A cool nose nudged at Julia's arm, working its way for Ringo's small head to intrude into her cocoon. The dog wiggled his way to her chest and she allowed him to curl against her, his warmth bleeding into her heart. Gripping him in near desperation, breathing in the scent of his musty fur, Julia struggled to pull herself from the darkness and back to the daylight.

When she could breathe and the pain was just a horror, no longer a voracious beast, she slept.

★★★

The spreadsheet scrolled up and down, then up again as Chad stared blindly at the computer monitor. His finger on the mouse roller twitched with frustration as thoughts of Julia poured through his mind. What on earth had happened to her? A high fever? Had he ever heard of anyone waking up with a fever and losing consciousness for months?

Dropping his head to his hands, his elbows on the desk, fingers threaded through his hair, he moaned. Business planning was not going well today, he was too distracted.

He'd spent the morning looking for a way to expand his delivery service. Not a huge amount of work, just enough to add a boost and give Bobby a few more hours. Then maybe Chad would feel like he was stable enough to move out of the nasty upstairs apartment. He snorted at himself in disgust.

The business was doing well and he'd already met his financial goals for a down payment on a house twice but when it came to house hunting, he always backed out. He'd about decided he'd be fine living above the office forever.

In his defense, the business could always do better and he'd opted out of buying a house or moving on with his life, in order to work longer hours and save even more money.

He already made a run to Pittsburgh once a week. If he could find one more customer to add to the trip, the entire addition would be clear profit. It would have to be a local shop or vender though, so it didn't take up too much time…

Dropping his hands and pushing the mouse away with a grunt of defeat, he flopped backward in his chair, causing it to roll back against the wall. Threading his fingers behind his head, his legs stretched out under the desk, one boot crossed over the other, his gaze traveled along the office ceiling looking in vain for a way to calm his mind and understand what was happening to him. But no matter how he twisted the situation with Julia around in his mind, he could find no way to help her.

He understood better than most, that recovery from a traumatic illness or injury involved much more than just physical recuperation. Emotional scars ran far deeper and healed slower than flesh and blood. So how *could* he help her? He wasn't a therapist or a doctor, he was just a regular guy – a guy with his own complicated issues. He should probably just back off and let her find her way.

Even as the thought to walk away came to him, he knew he wouldn't heed his own advice. Something about Julia called to him. Bound him.

Here he'd thought he could handle people – that he was a master charmer and everyone liked him. He pretended that no one really knew why he'd come back to Smithville, broken and resolute…but everyone knew. And it was becoming clear that he would not be able to keep blindly waltzing his way through life without getting close to anyone.

Kirsten Fullmer

Snorting, he stood and stomped across the office to the window. Cramming his hands in his pockets, he glared out to the parking lot. He hated feeling helpless. He'd hadn't felt this gut-wrenched since the night he'd sent William out to check on that delivery back in Philly. The weather had been bad and one of their trucks had slid off the road, leaving a delivery stranded. Why hadn't he gone to check on the mess himself instead of sending William?

And now, years later, he was trapped in hopelessness again. He'd tried to stay detached with Julia but he was obviously too far-gone for that now. He couldn't get her out of his head.

As he turned back to stare across the dusty little office, he realized that there was only one answer. He'd have to find out more about what had happened and try to help her.

He didn't know if he was up for the job, but the only real question left in his mind was, would she let him help?

★★★

The old man at the corner raised his hand to wave, a grin spreading across his wrinkled face. Julia waved back, almost used to people pointing and smiling at George as she drove. Even though she was emotionally exhausted from her run-in with Chad, she had squeezed in a trip to the grocery store so she would be able to cook dinner on her new stove once Steve hooked it up.

The man pointed to George and gave Julia the thumbs up. Her shoulders relaxed into the truck seat and she smiled tiredly, petting George's back. She wasn't fixated on getting where she was going nowadays, because she had nothing but time.

Pulling into the driveway, she reflected that before her illness she hadn't noticed people when she drove; at least not unless they ran in front of her car or drove carelessly. Pausing longer than necessary at a stop sign, like she'd just done, was something other people did and an annoyance of the worst sort. She'd had places to go and people to see.

Now she noticed individuals and trees and signs and…the world around her. The song *Nowhere Man* came to mind.

Shade dappled her gravel driveway with shifting patterns and shadows as she pulled to a stop. The truck door squeaked when she pushed it open and George jumped from her lap to land gracefully on the ground but Ringo wiggled excitedly in the seat, waiting to be lifted down. It was a longer drop from the seat than his stubby legs wanted to take, she supposed.

Dropping Ringo to the ground, she reached back into the truck to tug the grocery bags out, contentedly remembering the ingredients she'd bought to cook on her new stove.

It had been a rough day, she thought, trudging up to the porch. Her meltdown in front of Chad had been a harsh prompt to face reality but she had felt a little better after her nap and was ready for the distraction of putting her kitchen together.

When Chad had been in front of her, his persona larger than life, she'd been tempted to give up the battle and melt into the man, soak him up, like dry, cracked dirt in a summer thunderstorm.

Well it served her right, she supposed, juggling grocery bags to unlock the door. She'd been on dangerous ground and she'd needed to be brought back to earth, back to her reality. It hurt but it was what it was. She'd known that when she pulled into town and she knew it now.

Glancing back at the truck to make sure she'd actually closed the door and not just thought about it, she remembered the day she'd bought the aging truck. She'd needed a vehicle to leave New York, and she wanted something different than the high-end BMW that had been sold while she was sick. Something she could pay for outright.

Kirsten Fullmer

When she'd walked onto the used car lot with cash in hand, the old truck had caught her eye and spoken to her inner redneck, and it had been a done deal. She hadn't regretted the purchase for a minute.

Still having no cupboards in the kitchen, Julia plopped the grocery bags on the hutches standing in the living room and took a moment to allow the blood to flow back into her fingers. Ringo sat at her feet regarding her with shining brown dog eyes, his brows lifting one after the other.

Squatting to pat his head, she smiled. "Can you hear all the crap in my head, boy? Huh?"

The dog placed his front legs on her makeshift lap so she could rub his belly. As she scratched Ringo's neck, Julia came to the conclusion that she had had a tough day and she should just lighten up. She really needed to concentrate on moving forward and to stop looking back. It was far too easy to feel like crap about who she had been instead of who she was today.

She smiled, miserable but determined. "We're going to cook dinner tonight, isn't that exciting?" she asked the little dog, ruffling his ears. His tongue lolled from one side of his mouth.

"We will finally have a kitchen," she continued.

Ringo barked twice to show he was indeed happy about the kitchen. A knock at the screen door made them both turn and Julia stood, surprised and pleased to see Tara smiling through the screen. Julia motioned for her to come in.

"I hope I didn't interrupt a moment," Tara laughed, bending to pat Ringo as he greeted her.

"Not at all, I just got home from the grocery store," Julia replied, lifting grocery bags to show Tara. "Want to help me get these to the kitchen?"

Nodding, Tara collected the rest of the bags to follow Julia. "Oh, the floor turned out so pretty!" she gushed as she wandered around the room, her eyes on the floor.

"It did, didn't it?" Julia replied as she bent to reach into the ugly yellow fridge and rearrange the contents to make more room. Turning back to the kitchen, she propped one hand on her hip to watch Tara. "Did you hear what happened?"

"When?" Tara asked, stopping at the fridge to set the grocery bags on the floor.

"The night we did the floors. Don't tell me it hasn't been all over town by now…"

Tara's forehead wrinkled in thought. "No…I didn't hear anything."

Scoffing, Julia began emptying the contents of the grocery bags into the fridge. "Maybe Chad didn't want to embarrass Bobby. Or me."

"Why, what happened?" Tara asked, stepping back to lean against the sink.

Julia stood and glanced from the bags to the fridge. Satisfied that all the required items were in the fridge, she bent to collect the remaining bags from the floor and headed toward the pantry. "Let's just say that Bobby had a little mishap and the stain bucket got knocked over."

Her eyes large, Tara followed Julia toward the door of the butler's pantry. "On the floor in here?" she questioned, glancing along the kitchen floor. "You can't even tell. Did it ruin anything?"

"I didn't have shoes on," Julia replied, loading cans onto the shelves. "I pretty much climbed straight up Chad to get out of the mess."

Tara gasped, her head pivoting back toward the pantry, her hand covering her mouth. "You didn't!"

Finished loading the shelves, Julia gathered the empty grocery bags, bent and tugged open a drawer. "Oh, I did."

Her eyes glowing, Tara laughed out loud. "What did he say? How…?"

Kirsten Fullmer

Julia shook her head and stuffed the empty bags into the drawer. "It was ridiculous. Bobby was trying to keep Ringo out of the stain and Chad was worried about the floor. I just climbed off him and we all started wiping up."

"I can almost see it!" Tara chuckled and moved aside so Julia could exit the pantry.

"It was lovely. I had a knee over his shoulder at one point, and one arm locked under his chin..."

"No..."

Julia nodded. "And I'm pretty sure he got a face full of cleavage as I climbed off."

"And he didn't say a word about this, to anyone?" Tara asked indignantly, eyes wide.

"Maybe he doesn't want to brag about his floor-staining abilities," Julia said, shrugging one shoulder.

Both women laughed.

"That is awesome..." Tara blurted, amusement still glowing in her eyes.

Julia's head jerked back in surprise.

"I mean, I thought only I did stuff like that," Tara assured, one hand out. "Seriously, you wouldn't believe some of the crap that happened to Justin and I."

"I've been waiting to hear all about it..." Julia admitted with a smile. "Come sit down and tell me all the juicy parts."

★★★

Thirty minutes later, Ringo's barking announced Steve's arrival, tearing Julia's attention away from the conversation. "Come in," she called over Tara's head.

"Ladies—" Steve said as he entered, bobbing his head, his hands full of tools. "Mind if I get started?"

Both women rose and Julia put out an arm to indicate for him to proceed.

Shabby Chic After All

"Well don't this floor look nice!" Steve commented, putting down his toolbox next to the oven. "And this thing is a gem, ain't it?" His large mitt of a hand caressed the edge of the stove.

"I'm so glad it found a good home," Tara said.

Julia grinned and crossed her arms over her chest. "I love it," she replied, her eyes shining.

"Well let's get her hooked up then, shall we?" Steve said, unloading tools from his box.

"I'm going to cook tonight," Julia said to Tara, but doubt crept into her words.

Her head tilted to one side, Tara's brow quirked as she evaluated Julia's face. "You okay?"

Turning to gaze out the window to cover her discomfort, Julia nodded. "Yeah, it's just been a while. I'm probably...rusty."

Tara harrumphed and waved her off. "It's like riding a bike, I'm sure you'll do great. I'll warn you though, these old ovens can be temperamental. It may have hot spots."

Julia nodded. "I figured. We'll have to get to know each other, won't we old girl?"

"Old girl?" Steve scoffed, his voice muffled and his arms hidden behind the stove.

"Yup. As a matter of fact, I think I'll call her Bessy," Julia declared, surprising herself more than a little. She'd never named an inanimate object before.

"Bessy..." Tara laughed, cocking her head to contemplate the oven. "It fits."

Steve stood, dropped his wrench in the toolbox and brushed his hands on the stomach of his overalls. "Okay then, I'll turn on the gas to ol' "Bessy" and we can test the connection."

The women nodded.

No gas leaked from the wall connection, so Steve showed Julia how to light the burners with a long match.

Kirsten Fullmer

"I brought you a box of these," Steve said handing her the package of matches. "They aren't easy to find nowadays, but you can get them at the hardware store."

Julia nodded, watching the ring of blue flame dance on the stovetop. Memories blurred through the back of her mind, drawing her from the room through a long dark tunnel and into a hazy past. She stood in a sleek white kitchen, holding the handle of a frying pan over a gas burner. A voice drew her attention to her left where a blond man laughed, a wine glass in his hand. Brad.

Tara's voice splintered the memory, yanking away the fragments of Julia's vision.

"Julia, oh my God! Steve help me!" Tara cried as her friend fell limply to the floor.

★★★

The room spun as things came back into focus. Two concerned faces came into view above Julia, leaning over her, pressing her shoulders down as she struggled to sit up.

"Are you feeling better now?" Tara asked, concern and fear resonating in her tone.

"Should I call 911?" Steve asked.

Tara shook her head. "Let's give her a minute." Slipping her arm behind Julia, Tara helped her sit up and lean against the wall. "Julia?"

Her hand to her forehead, Julia flinched at the light pouring through the window. Her stomach churned and the floor was hard and cold. Embarrassed at the attention, she felt a blush burn up her neck to her face. "I'm okay. This happens sometimes."

Tara struggled to stay calm. "You fainted, flat out. Are you diabetic? Should I find you something to eat?"

"No..." Julia pressed her fingertips into her eyes and pushed away from the wall. "It's nothing like that. I just get kind of—blank—sometimes."

"Should...should I stay or go?" Steve asked, turning off the burner on the stove.

"I'm fine. You can go," Julia muttered, struggling to her feet, searching for a scrap of self-respect. "Sorry I'm—just—Sorry."

"It's no problem..." Steve said, glancing from Tara to Julia and back. "Can I bring you anything?"

Julia shook her head and pulled a mantle of calm back around herself. "Really, I'm okay now. Thanks so much for hooking up the stove. I should cook for you sometime..." The offer was heartfelt, but the confidence that she could do any such thing was missing from her words.

"Okay, I'll call in a few days and see if you're having any trouble with it..." Steve offered, still obviously unsure what he should do.

Tara nodded to him, offering reassurance. "I'll stay for a bit, you go ahead."

The big man collected his tools and nodded his farewell.

"Shall we go sit down?" Tara asked.

"No, I don't want to sit," Julia said, irritated that she'd looked like a fool. Again.

Tara shrugged. "Okay, what would you like to do?"

A long sigh emanated from Julia as she glanced around the room. Her gaze paused at the oven and a tiny smile glowed in her tired eyes. She turned to Tara. "Think you could help me drag those hutches in here?"

Excitement clear in her face, Tara clapped happily. "Yes! I can't wait to see how they will look!"

The women pushed and groaned, shoved and shimmied, the two sizeable hutches into the kitchen and into position on either side of the sink, then stepped back to scrutinize their work.

Kirsten Fullmer

"It's just like I envisioned…" Julia whispered, her chest heaving from the effort.

"It's perfect," Tara agreed, still watching Julia from the corner of her eye, alert for any signs of distress.

Julia leaned over the sink to look behind a hutch. "I should have asked Steve about the outlets…"

"Let's see—" Tara offered, leaning across the sink to look behind the other hutch. "It looks like you can cut holes in the hutches, or we can run some power strips from the outlets." She stepped back. "I have some nice ones that you can mount under the top shelves if you'd like so you won't see them."

Finally able to relax and enjoy having a friend offering ideas, Julia smiled, her eyes bright with tears. Blinking rapidly, she cleared her throat. "That sounds perfect."

Tara nodded, ignoring the tears. "I can bring them by tomorrow and help you get them mounted. Sound good?"

Relieved and content, Julia agreed with a nod. "You're the best…"

Shrugging, Tara turned toward the door to the hall and grinned over her shoulder. "I know…"

On the porch, Tara paused to stroll along the porch rail, admiring the roses.

"Wait here a minute…" Julia said, hurrying back into the house. She returned carrying a pair of shears and a crinkled sheet of tissue paper. Bending over the rail, she snipped off several branches of roses in various colors and wrapped them in the tissue paper.

"For your inn…" she said with a wide smile, handing the roses to Tara.

Accepting the flowers with a reverent sniff, Tara glowed. "Thanks! Your yard is already the talk of the inn, now we can enjoy your flowers in person."

With a foreign sensation blazing in her chest, Julia waved as Tara backed out of the drive, then she squatted to pet George as he wound around her ankle. He was getting chubby, she noticed. Was she putting out too much food for him? She shrugged and decided to ask Bobby. He seemed to know about cats.

Taking a last glance across the cheerful yard, she stood. "Come on Ringo, it's time to cook dinner," she called, then waited as the little dog trotted across the porch and into the house. Both creatures followed her to the kitchen.

★★★

Using the old, four-legged butcher block that she'd dragged up next to the stove as a prep surface; Julia retrieved mixing bowls and pans. Then taking her recipe book with her, she collected ingredients from the fridge and pantry.

Having never cooked as a pet owner, Julia was amused to find that Ringo sat patiently at her feet, his eyes never leaving the counter above as she chopped vegetables, trimmed cuts of chicken, and grated cheese. The scents of herbs rose from the cutting board, and Ringo's little nose twitched with interest and excitement. When a scrap or crumb escaped to fall to the floor, it was immediately lapped up and the spot on the floor licked clean.

"Yuck, don't lick the floor, boy. That's gross," she chided.

George, on the other hand, came running when the can opener broke the seal on a can of chicken broth. But after pacing for several minutes, his tail swishing back and forth over his back, he lost interest and left the room.

Much to Julia's surprise, she remembered parts of how to cook – things like how to shake the pan to sauté items, when to turn the meat, or add the vegetables. But sadly lost to her was the list of ingredients. Checking the recipe in the cookbook over and over again, she struggled to remember if she'd

Kirsten Fullmer

added the item from the list on the page, or if she'd just thought about it.

Deciding she had to come up with a way to cope before she started the next dish, she placed all the ingredients on her left-hand side. Then, as she added the item, she placed the container on her right. Creating coping skills was nothing new but sometimes the need to stop and reorganize simple tasks to make them manageable still stung.

All in all, the cooking experience was a good one, and as Julia sat down at the dining room table to enjoy her dinner, pride and joy filled her heart.

Glancing around the table at the empty chairs, however, dulled the satisfaction a bit. She had loved cooking for friends, that much she remembered. Invitations to her dinner parties had been coveted, as only the best and brightest attended, and they'd been all about expensive food, fine wine, and networking. Her get-togethers were an opportunity to sharpen her wit and further her social status. None of it had been a heartfelt matter; it was about power and strength and ego.

Considering the fleeting bits of faded memories, twisting and turning them in her mind, she realized it hadn't been about the food or the friends at all. Frowning down at her food, she wondered if she'd ever really had a friend.

Steam, fragrant and spicy, rose from her plate and she shrugged off the sad thought like Ringo shook after a bath. Picking up her fork, she huffed out a deep breath and dug into her salad, pointedly savoring the flavor of a cherry tomato as it burst in her mouth.

9

Julia scooted George off her lap, checked again to be sure her notebook was in her purse, and pulled the keys from the ignition. "You wait here," she instructed the two small animals who observed her seriously. "I don't want you running off."

After one last gentle push to make sure George wouldn't leap from the truck, Julia pushed the truck door closed and turned toward the rows of plants at Fergus' green house. Wandering past a few plant stands, she saw the old man at the end of the aisle talking to an angry looking man. Fergus had his feet planted in the gravel and his skinny arms crossed over his chest. The other man spoke with his hands, clearly frustrated and making slashing motions in the air. Neither noticed her.

Julia scanned the rows of flowers, her mind flitting among the possibilities and ideas for where she would plant them. The smell of soil and fertilizer filled her nostrils, reminding her that she lived closer to the earth now.

Annoyed voices brought her attention back to Fergus, where the strange man now yelled at the little old man outright. Fergus took a step back and for the first time, Julia felt a frisson of alarm run down her spine. Glancing around the property, Julia didn't see anyone else, so she stepped behind a tall stand of plants, adjusted her purse on her shoulder, and called out.

"Fergus? Fergus…Rob and I could use some help over here…"

Peering between the hanging ferns, Julia saw the angry man's gaze lurch toward her, then toward her truck. He made a final comment to Fergus, his glower dark and voice deep, then turned and stalked away. Fergus watched as the man climbed in his truck and slammed the door before revving his engine and driving away, his tires spitting up gravel behind him.

Julia waited where she was until the man was out of sight, and then stepped from behind the ferns to greet Fergus. The old man appeared shaken, one gnarled hand rubbing up and down his other arm as he walked.

Taking in his muddy apron and ancient, lace-less boots, Julia wondered if the old guy was okay out here alone. "Fergus? Are you okay?" she asked, her hand on his shoulder.

He shook his head. "I suppose I'm all right." Then he seemed to shake off his concern, his beady crow eyes rising to meet Julia's concerned gaze. "How are you, Miss Julia?"

She smiled. "I'm fine, thanks." Her eyes followed the back of the other man's truck as it rounded the curve. "Who was that?"

Fergus shrugged. "Some feller from DC. He's been after me to buy a chunk of my back property."

"Back property?" Julia asked.

He nodded. "Yeah, down yonder, behind the greenhouses. He's been botherin' the folks behind me as well." The old man pointed over his shoulder. "You know Bobby. His momma told me that feller has been around her place, harpin' at her."

Tara pointed in the direction he indicated, her eyes narrowing in concern. "Bobby and his mother live back there?"

Fergus nodded. "Their people have lived there for generations and my family has been on this spread for nigh on seventy years."

"I take it you don't want to sell?"

Kirsten Fullmer

He scoffed. "Not in this lifetime…Now what can I help you with today?"

With long-forgotten sensations tingling down her spine, Julia tossed one final glance down the highway and turned her attention back to the rows of flowers, then to Fergus. Her face fell. "I was…" the moment hung in the air, collecting dust, then Julia shook herself and reached into her purse for her notebook. Flipping through dog-ear pages with a frown, she finally found the one she was looking for and her shoulders relaxed. Her gaze met the old man's and she forced a smile. "I was thinking about planting shrubs along the far side of the driveway."

He nodded once and turned to shuffle toward the tall line of trees and shrubs. "Lots of folks think that looks good…" he said, ignoring her obvious discomfort, then turned back to face her. "But truth is, shrubs grow fast and before you know it, they crowd the driveway."

Julia's brow furrowed as she struggled to regain her thought process. "Really? I hadn't thought about that…"

"May I suggest hastas? They come up each year and grow in real nice. Low maintenance…" He blinked up at her, his neck twisted to compensate for the hunch in his back.

She smiled. "Show me…"

The old man shuffled ahead, his twisted fingers reaching out to pluck off a dried leaf or blossom as they filed through the long rows of plants. "I heard all about them roses you sent up to the inn…" he called over his shoulder.

Stunned, Julia paused. "You did?"

"Yup, seems they was a big hit," he chuckled.

"Well you should get the credit," she assured him.

His grizzled head shook, his jowls swinging. "Nope nope, you've grown them real nice…"

Embarrassed but pleased, Julia stopped next to Fergus. "Thank you so much for your help."

His dark eyes glittered among the wrinkles, revealing a tooth-less grin. "My pleasure ma'am."

★★★

Fifteen minutes later, when Julia and Fergus reached the front of the greenhouse, Tara's truck pulled up next to Julia's, a billow of dust rolling up from behind the truck as it clicked and cooled. Tara stepped out, a hand raised in greeting as she neared them.

Julia waved back.

"Hello Miss Tara. Can't recall the last time I was surrounded by such loveliness—" The old man grinned, one arm around each woman. "What can I do for ya?" he asked.

Tara's expression grew serious. "I'm having trouble planning flowers for the wedding. There just aren't any good florists around here. I was hoping you'd have some ideas," she told the man, her countenance hopeful.

He cackled. "Seems as how you came along at the right time."

Tara's brow rose in question.

The man's gnarled finger nudged the purse hanging at Julia's side and Julia glanced from Tara to Fergus in question.

"This lady here…" he continued. "She should do your flowers."

Julia stepped back, shock and horror in her face. "Oh no no, I'm not a florist—"

The old man held up both hands, palms forward, as if to hold off her response. "Now… just give the thought a minute to roll around in yer head." He turned to Tara. "I'm tellin' ya, this here gal has a head fer flowers and a knack fer color and texture. She's a natural."

Tara tilted her head to one side, watching her new friend choke and struggle against Fergus's comments. "Maybe he's right."

Julia shook her head, her eyes large.

Kirsten Fullmer

"Hold on, don't panic, let's just talk about it over coffee… What do you say?" Tara asked.

Coffee did sound good, Julia thought.

Fergus gave the girls a push toward their trucks. "You two ladies go talk this out and let me know how I can help."

Tara laughed. "Follow me to the café?" she asked Julia.

Julia was still not quite sure what had just happened and her head swam. "I… I guess so…" As she opened her truck door, George leapt back to give her room to sit down and Ringo barked happily. She muttered a goodbye to Fergus, her hand raised in a wave, and she climbed into the truck.

"I'll send them hastas around to you…" the old man hollered to Julia as the women started their trucks. Grinning ear to ear, he watched them back out and drive away.

★★★

Marge smiled up at the women as they entered the café. "I'll be right there, sit wherever you'd like," she called as she finished wiping off the counter. Julia inhaled the now familiar café scents of bleach and bacon grease as *Octopus's Garden* rang from the jukebox.

"This okay?" Tara asked as she paused by a table.

Julia nodded.

Tara pulled out a chair, laughing as she caught sight of George and Ringo both gazing out the windshield of Julia's truck. "Your cat kills me," she said, her head shaking.

Flopping her purse on an empty chair, Julia nodded. "He's a case all right."

"Ladies," Marge greeted them as she made her way to the table, her hand on one hip. "What can I get for you today?"

Julia tugged the menu from behind the salt and peppershakers, and then glanced at Marge. "What's the special today?"

"Cabbage rolls, and they're surprisingly eatable," Marge replied with a grin.

Tara laughed. "I'll be brave. Bring me an order and some coffee please."

Marge turned to Julia.

Her expression one of concern, Julia hesitated. Flipping over the menu she glanced quickly down the list of sandwiches. "I'll just have a tuna melt with fries and coffee please."

"You bet…" Marge said as she turned away. Then she paused and turned back to the table. "Your roses are the prettiest things in town," she said solemnly.

Clearly shocked, all Julia could do was nod and mutter, "Thank you."

Tara smiled at Marge's retreating back, then adjusted her chair and placed both palms on the table. "So…flowers."

"I don't know what Fergus is thinking," Julia said miserably.

"He thinks you have a gift," Tara replied.

Feeling crowded and awkward, Julia glowered down at the tabletop. Couldn't she go even one day without someone pushing her to think or feel things she didn't want to face? She'd come here to get away from the pressure and expectations, not take on a load of new ones.

"Just let me tell you what I'm thinking, then you can tell me to go blow," Tara said, her expression hopeful.

Puffing out a long breath, Julia's gaze rose to meet Tara's. The warmth and hope flowing from her new friend's face broke her heart. How could she explain that she wasn't dependable? She had no solid future in which to make her own plans, let alone be a crucial part of something as special as a wedding. Besides that, Tara didn't even know her. Not the real her.

Continuing on, Tara said, "It will be a small wedding on the deck of the inn. There are already potted plants, I'll just need some color and a bouquet and flowers for the dining room,

Kirsten Fullmer

living areas, and guestrooms. Nothing fancy, I want them to feel informal, homey."

Still quiet, Julia considered Tara's words.

"When we had the grand opening of the inn, I had to get up at the crack of dawn and drive clear to Uniontown to get flowers," Tara continued. "I don't want my wedding day to be like that. I just want bunches of fresh, local flowers around me, without the hassle and worry of doing them myself."

"There is no florist in town?" Julia asked with one last hopeful rebuff.

Tara snorted. "Hello?"

"Someone who delivers?" Julia floundered.

"Sure, if I want some canned, out of a box arrangements," Tara said.

"Come on, it can't be that bad…"

Tara shrugged and glanced toward Marge who stepped up to the table with coffee cups on saucers and a steaming pot, all on a tray.

"What do you think?" Tara asked the waitress.

"Me?" the older woman said, her hand on her chest.

"Yes you," Tara laughed.

Julia shrugged miserably into her chair.

The coffee cups clinked as Marge set them in front of the girls. "About what?" she drawled, squaring her shoulders.

"Do you think Julia could do flowers for my wedding?"

The coffee pot clunked onto the table, coffee nearly sloshing out the top, as Marge yanked up a chair from the next table and plopped into it, the tray tucked under one arm. "Oh heavens yes!" she exclaimed.

Silent and withdrawn, Julia didn't respond.

Concerned, Marge placed a hand on Julia's shoulder. "What is it, honey?"

Julia sat sullen.

"Sweetie, I've watched you come in here nearly every day and I've kept to myself…"

"That's a miracle," muttered Tara, pouring herself a cup of coffee.

Flashing Tara a glare, Marge continued. "You're part of this town now and we all adore you. Please talk to us."

Surprised, Julia's gaze flashed to Marge then Tara. "Adore me?"

They both nodded vigorously.

"You don't even know me…" Julia argued.

Marge chuckled. "We know enough. You walk that cute little dog every evening and your crazy cat rides on your lap when you drive. Flowers bloom when you look at them, and your old house is coming alive."

Numb with the fatigue of aloneness, Julia stared at the table. Silence lay between them as the women waited for her to respond. Finally she took a deep breath. "You don't know what I was like before I came here…" she started.

Tara sipped at her coffee, her eyes large and expectant. Marge waited, her gaze never leaving Julia's face.

Realizing she'd have to say something more or sprint from the café, Julia continued. "I was…not very nice."

"That's hard to believe. Like how?" Tara asked, her eyes narrowed in confusion, her coffee cup poised halfway to her mouth.

Julia shrugged guiltily. "I was judgmental and uptight. No… mean. I was flat-out mean."

Tara's cup lowered to the saucer and Marge squirmed, glancing at Tara, then back to Julia.

A long breath escaped Julia. "There, it's out! I was a horrible person." She flopped back in her chair, resignation and sadness clear on her face.

Tara leaned slightly over the table, both hands around her coffee cup, her expression unguarded and concerned. "Not that

Kirsten Fullmer

I can believe that but…what changed? Because you're very nice now…"

Julia massaged her forehead, then swept her hand across the top of her head, ruffling her blond curls. Finally, she looked up to make eye contact with Marge and Tara. Both women appeared to be completely open and willing to listen. She sighed. "I had everything. The high-paying job, the expensive car, the handsome husband, the beautiful condo, glamorous clothes. I judged people who didn't live like I did. I used my power and connections to get anything I wanted. I was…horrible."

Even though both Tara and Marge seemed speechless, Julia felt as if a ton of weight had been lifted from her shoulders. Admitting the disgust she felt for what she remembered of her past self had somehow freed the weight of the guilt a little bit. Her back straightened and she took a deep breath. Her eyes flitted from the table to Tara and Marge, waiting for their disapproval and rejection. But both women just shrugged.

Marge stood and lifted the chair she'd swiped earlier. "Well, I for one don't give a fig who you were back then. You're here now and your food is most likely melting under the heat lamp. I'll be right back." She turned and hurried away.

Julia watched Marge's retreating back and couldn't meet Tara's eye. She stared miserably at the table waiting for the sting of rejection that she rightly deserved. The lengthening silence finally forced her eyes up to meet Tara's.

Reaching across the table, Tara took one of Julia's hands in hers. "Do you know what I was like last year?" she asked.

Stunned by the response, Julia mutely shook her head.

"Do you know how I treated Justin back then?"

Again Julia shook her head.

"Do you know who my parents are, or where I grew up, or went to school?"

Julia shifted in her seat. "That's not the same."

"Why?" Tara asked, her face determined.

"You don't understand," Julia huffed. "I'm not who I used to be."

"Exactly," Tara said crisply, letting go of Julia's hand to sit up stiff in her seat. "It just doesn't matter who you were, you are here and I like you now."

Julia shrugged, trying to get her head around the thought.

"On second thought..." Tara said, "what happened? I mean, if you were so mean and now you're awesome?"

Once again the continuous tedium of dealing with her past illness rose to the surface, swamping Julia's heart. "It's a long story..."

Tara leaned back so Marge could place the plates on the table. "I'm not going anywhere..."

Julia unwrapped the paper napkin from around her silverware, and then adjusted it by her plate, even though she wouldn't be using it.

Marge interrupted. "Look ladies, I've got a big group coming in for dinner and I have to get some work done." She laid her hand once again on Julia's shoulder. "Honey, I like you and I want you to know that I'm your friend, okay?"

Looking up at the older woman, Julia's eyes glistened with tears and a lump formed in her throat as she nodded. Marge gave her a businesslike confirmation nod, and then glanced over the table one more time to be sure they were set and hurried away.

Julia took a moment to regroup, knowing that Tara was waiting for an explanation. Her sandwich no longer held any appeal as her heart sank further into her stomach. Finally she spoke, her words stilted and odd-sounding to her ears. "Do you know what encephalitis is?"

Tara paused from adjusting her plate and looked up. "No...I don't think so."

Kirsten Fullmer

Watching her new friend carefully, Julia continued. "It's an infection of the brain. I had it. And now I'm different."

Blinking in confusion, Tara seemed to struggle to appear calm and intelligent. "I...I'm sorry..."

Julia waved her off, amazed that the floor hadn't opened up and swallowed her whole. Until yesterday, she'd never told anyone about her illness, fearing that somehow they would be afraid of her, or judge her, or...she wasn't sure what she'd thought they would do.

Tara shifted in her chair, her mind apparently working. "How long were you sick?"

Still feeling her way through the conversation, Julia glanced up, seeing only concern in Tara's gaze.

"I was unconscious for months. And it took a long time afterwards, to really understand much of what had happened."

Her face contorted into horror, Tara blurted, "But...that must have left you so weak...and you must have...I don't even know what all that would mean."

Julia watched Tara struggle with her response. The conversation had at some point become surreal, as if she had removed herself and they were discussing a different person altogether. She hadn't been able to face what had happened to her because the pain had been so intense. The idea of waking up unable to speak, paralyzed, and alone, even though she remembered parts of it, was still hazy and felt oddly gruesome.

"Yeah, I had to relearn a lot of things..." Suddenly Julia realized that in the long tedious, lonely months of recovery that had followed her coma, she had learned to disassociate herself from that sick person. She'd had only enough strength to face one moment at a time, one battle at a time. Not until this instant had she been strong enough to piece the whole event together into a long line and look at it as a whole. She'd been well, gotten sick, laid in a coma, awoken, then spent almost a year trying to recover.

When Chad had asked her about her illness, she hadn't been able to answer. Just segments of her past that were swathed in overbearing pain would come to the surface – pinpoint pricks of horror. She hadn't been able to tap into that part of her mind that could lay the events in order without layering on the pain as well.

Or maybe she had felt as if Chad were …off-limits. Like she couldn't have him, love him or need him, get close to him, because of her illness, and that had made her angry and unwilling to communicate.

Whatever the reason, she was amazed that just a day later she was able to speak of what had happened without falling to pieces. Now she just felt numb.

Tara shook her head and cleared her throat, then collecting her thoughts, gazed hard at Julia. "I don't know what to say. That must have been horrible for you. You are full of surprises…" She glanced down at her cabbage roll for a long moment and then back up. "We have so many things to talk about. I'd like to know more about what happened." She let out a long breath. "Seems we both have a past that we fight. But for now, this minute, let's just relax and eat our lunch. Sound good?"

Seeing no derision in Tara's comment or her body language, Julia relaxed. She felt like a rag doll or a deflated pool toy. But Tara was right. There was no way to change anything that had happened, and it had actually felt …almost good… to get a few things off her chest. Breathing long slow breaths for a moment to assure herself all was well, she finally nodded.

Kirsten Fullmer

10

Hand over hand, Chad pulled another long piece of lumber from his truck and tossed it on the growing pile. Pausing to wipe the back of his wrist across his forehead and adjust his leather glove, he scowled across the yard between the inn and the construction site where his friend Justin was building a spa.

"You look ornery as hell," Justin said as he bent to heft three long, two by sixes to his shoulder. "What's eating you?"

"Nothing," Chad grumbled, grabbing two more boards and heaving them toward the pile.

Both men turned to watch Tara's old pick-up truck bump up the driveway toward the house, a cloud of dust billowing behind it. Justin continued to carry his boards toward the open pit of the finished foundation and Chad pulled out two more pieces of lumber before Tara's truck rolled to a stop next to his.

"Hi Chad," she called as she climbed from the pick-up. "I didn't know they were ready to start framing yet."

He slid two more boards from the truck and tossed them onto the pile with a clatter. "The lumber was ready and Justin said to go ahead and bring it out, so I did."

"Okay…" she replied, her head cocked at an angle.

Justin joined them, pulling Tara to him for a quick kiss.

Leaning into the kiss, Tara smiled as she admired Justin's good looks. "What's got him all puffed up?" she asked, pointing her elbow toward Chad. "He looks like a thundercloud."

Justin shrugged. "He told me it was nothing but my bet is that nothing has blond curls."

Two more boards clattered to the pile. "That's fine, talk about me like I'm not here…" Chad grumbled.

"I just had lunch with Julia…" Tara offered, watching Chad for a response.

"Oh yeah?" Chad growled as another piece of lumber was hurled to the pile.

"Holy crap, don't take out your problems on my lumber," Justin laughed.

Chad stopped and stared at his boot, then looked up, squinting into the afternoon sun. "Okay then, how is Julia today?"

Tara's face fell, diverted from teasing Chad to thinking about Julia. "Actually we had a strange conversation. Has she told you much about her past or why she came here?"

Chad yanked off his gloves and cocked one hip against the back of the truck, his brow furrowed in thought. "The woman talks in riddles."

"I've never met her but I've heard she's a sweet little thing," Justin offered.

Tara nodded. "She is, but evidently she's been through a really hard time."

His head swinging to Tara, Chad blurted. "What did she tell you?"

Taken aback, Tara paused. "Why? What has she told you?"

Wondering if Tara knew about their kisses and their stilted relationship, Chad was unsure what to say. "You tell me first…"

"Oh for heaven sakes," Justin scoffed. "Would you two just spill it? What happened at lunch and what is going on with you two?"

Kirsten Fullmer

Chad stared toward the construction site and Tara toward the house, both silent.

"Okay, I'll tell you then…" Justin prompted as he pointed at Chad. "You have the hots for Julia and don't know why because she's not your type." He turned to Tara. "And she finally opened up to you about something and you're not sure if you should tell Chad because you know she likes him."

Neither Tara nor Chad offered any disagreement. As a matter of fact, neither said a word or could meet the other's eye.

"Do I have to carry the whole conversation here?" Justin responded in frustration.

Chad shrugged a shoulder. "You're right, you're right… she's…on my mind, and yeah, she's not my type."

Tara laughed. "Or maybe she is exactly your type and you just didn't know it."

"What does that mean?" Chad snapped defensively.

"I've know you since we were kids," Tara said. "And since you came home, I've never understood why you only chased the flashy girls."

Justin laughed, his voice ringing across the yard and past the barn. "Honey, isn't that obvious?" he said, siding with his friend.

Exasperated, Tara continued. "You're horrible." She shoved at Justin's shoulder. "No, I mean, you have a heart of gold, yet you never offered it to anyone," she lamented to Chad. "Is that because of what happened to William? You don't want to be close to anyone?"

Obviously uncomfortable, Chad shuffled from one boot to the other, then finally glared at Tara. "Don't go there…" he warned, his voice cracking.

Her hands raised as if she were innocent, Tara backed up a step.

Staring at his boots, Chad cleared his throat and struggled to regroup.

Tara's head tilted to one side. "You feel different about Julia don't you?" she prodded, not one to let it go.

Chad turned away to gaze across the property.

"Ah-oh..." Justin muttered, rubbing his hand across the top of his head.

His fingers massaging his jaw in thought, Chad put one boot on the bumper of the truck.

"What has she told you?" Tara asked gently, maneuvering to Chad's side.

His eyes desolate, Chad sighed and turned to Tara. He paused, glancing over Tara's shoulder to Justin, who nodded for him to continue. His foot dropped from the back of the truck and he twisted his gloves in his hands. "She said she doesn't want to get involved with me or anybody, and somehow it has to do with her being sick before she came here."

Tara nodded. "I knew it."

"Knew what?" Justin asked, turning to Chad. "I'm confused. I thought you and Julia had a thing going...You told me she was a good kisser..."

Tara's head pivoted to Justin and then back to Chad. "Really? She didn't tell *me* that!"

Chad grimaced and Justin hooted.

"I didn't mean it like that," Tara stammered. "I know you're a good kisser, I just meant..."

"Oh really?" Justin teased, nudging Tara with his elbow in mock horror.

Bumping the butt of her hand on her forehead, Tara moaned.

"Okay look," Chad blurted, "I made a move because I thought she was interested and she said she wasn't but I swear to God, she seems interested." He turned to stare back across the yard. "I don't know..."

"What did she tell you about being sick?" Tara asked, shrugging off Justin and placing her hand on Chad's arm.

Kirsten Fullmer

He scowled in thought before he answered. "She said she had a high fever and was unconscious for months."

Tara nodded. "She told me she had encephalitis."

"What is that?" Chad asked, his eyes bright with concern. "What else did she tell you?"

"Not much, but I Googled it on the way home."

Justin threw his hands in the air. "You told me you don't get online when you drive any more."

"I pulled over," Tara retorted with a condescending grimace.

"Never mind that," Chad interrupted, "What is it? What did it say?"

Tara turned back to Chad. "An infection of the brain. It hits fast and can leave people brain damaged or even kill them. There are several types."

"Well her bastard of a husband divorced her at some point," Chad growled. "Of all the nerve. What ever happened to 'in sickness and in health'?"

"She was married?!" Tara gasped. "Oh my gosh…"

Justin stood looking helpless, wanting to offer support to both Tara and Chad but having no grounds to comment. "She must be traumatized…" he finally offered.

"She told me she lost her job too," Chad said, rubbing the back of his wrist across his forehead.

"Poor girl," Tara muttered.

"What are you going to do now?" Justin asked Chad.

He shrugged.

"You can't just give up," Tara insisted, her voice cracking with emotion.

Both men turned to her. "Who in this town decided that men have to pursue impossible relationships?" Justin mumbled.

Chad glowered at him.

Tara's eyes flitted between the two men. "Well…you're happy enough aren't you?" she asked Justin, challenging him to disagree.

He snorted. "I'm fine now, but…"

"Fine? …Fine?" she inquired in a huff.

"Could we get back on topic here, please?" Chad interrupted.

Both turned back to Chad, Justin eager to change the subject and Tara still ruffled.

"I don't even know what to say to her," Chad continued sadly, looking to his friends for some type of solution.

"Don't treat her any different," Tara assured him. "She's worried about how different she is, she thinks she's a pariah. She probably doesn't tell people because they treat her weird."

"Am I just supposed to ignore what she's been through?" Chad asked. "That seems pretty cold and unfeeling. She obviously isn't okay with things the way things are now."

"I'm no psychiatrist," Justin interjected, "But it seems to me that you like her the way she is now. Isn't that the point?"

Chad stared at Justin. Through him. Finally he shook his head in confusion. "What are you going to do, Tara?"

She shrugged. "I'll read everything I can about it and move forward with our friendship. I'll try to be sensitive, but…"

"Right, see?" Chad interjected. "I'm afraid I'll say the wrong thing. Hell, all I did was ask what happened and she threw me out of her house…"

"I'd like to have seen *that*…" Justin muttered under his breath.

Both Tara and Chad scowled at him.

Justin raised his hands in surrender and took a step back.

Tara frowned. "Just promise me you won't give up on her. Please?"

Chad shrugged and tugged his gloves on, then reached for another board.

Kirsten Fullmer

Julia turned from the dish drainer to glance down at George. He'd been in and out of the mudroom all afternoon, pacing and meowing. "What's up little man?" she asked, crouching to scratch between his ears. The cat uncharacteristically moved away and headed back to the mudroom. Julia shrugged and washed her hands.

Dishtowel in hand, she contemplated the wall of her kitchen. Tara had helped her tack the power strips to the underside of the top cabinets on the hutches and she'd placed her mother's china, as well as the mismatched pieces she'd bought at the boutique, in the upper shelves behind the wavy glass doors, where they sparkled in the evening sun. What she really needed, she decided, was a set of antique canisters on the countertop of the hutches and maybe a colander full of leafy greens.

Tilting her head to one side, she envisioned a curtain along the bottom of the sink to hide the pipes; one that matched a lace valance. The magazine picture that had been her inspiration, showed a wood shelf across the center of the window, piled with colored glass. She'd have to stop at the boutique in the next few days to look for treasures that would complete the room.

George once again emerged from the mudroom, yowling and fussing. Julia glanced at him from time to time as she finished the dishes, unsure what he wanted. When the last plate was set in the wood drying rack on the sloped draining board of the sink, she wandered to her room in search of a good book.

Bending, she creaked open the trunk at the foot of the bed and surveyed the contents. A stack of dog-eared notebooks, as well as gardening books, took up one end of the truck but she shuffled through the books on the other end. The second one from the top was the flower shop book she'd bought on her first trip to the Uniontown bookstore. Pausing in contemplation, she stared at the cover, Tara's words replaying in her mind.

She lifted the book from the chest to brush at the dust jacket, longingly smiling at the picture of the shop on the cover and its rows of flowerpots and buckets of cut flowers in front of the plate-glass windows.

She tucked the book under her arm and closed the chest. The front porch was her favorite reading spot and it was the perfect evening to curl up in the big wicker chair with a book.

She padded through the living room with the book tucked under arm and opened the door for Ringo but he hung back. Julia shrugged and wandered onto the porch. Tucking her feet under her in the wicker chair, Julia took a moment to gaze across the yard and admire her flowers. The mums and pansies under the tree bloomed in riotous reds and yellows, mirroring the day lilies across the yard. The new hastas were planted along the side of the driveway, nearly hiding the ancient, chain-link fence. The roses along the porch bloomed in soft reds and pinks and mild yellow tones, their scent wafting toward her on the breeze.

Opening the book, she flipped slowly through the pages of pictures, reading the captions. Could she really do the flowers for Tara's wedding? What had Tara said — bunches of flowers for the dining room, living areas, and guestrooms? She hadn't even been inside the inn. Maybe tomorrow she would drive up to see Tara and see what it was like inside.

Ringo barked in the living room, the noise echoing through the nearly empty room. "Come out here boy..." Julia called distractedly as she turned pages. More insistent barking drew her attention away from the book and she stood, placing the book on her chair. Drifting across the porch, she paused in front of the screen door. "What is it, dog?" she asked.

The little dog sat in the center of the room, staring into the den. At the sound of Julia's voice, he ran to the screen and barked twice, then trotted back toward the den. He stopped and looked over his shoulder at Julia and whined.

Kirsten Fullmer

"Geeze Lassie," she muttered as she creaked open the door and drifted across the empty room. "You act like little Timmy fell in the well." Following Ringo to the den, she ambled to the end of her bed, her arms spread wide and looked down at the frantic dog. "What is in here, huh? What has you all freaked out?"

Ringo trotted to his bed where to Julia's surprise, George lay panting. "George, get out of Ringo's bed, you bad kitty," she exclaimed, shooing at the cat.

Meowing loudly, more like a long, drawn-out growl, George stared up at her, then his eyes closed to slits as he panted heavily. A fissure of concern crept along Julia's scalp. Whatever was bothering the poor cat, he wasn't acting normal.

Her bedsprings creaked as she dropped to sit on the edge, her hands twisted in her lap, her gaze on George. "What's wrong buddy?" she asked, as Ringo paced in front of his bed. The cat yowled again and stretched one leg, his little body shaking.

"Did you eat something that made you sick?" she asked, hoping for some sign of what was making George act this way. Suddenly, the cat rose and hunched his back, his fur twitching in ripples across the high arch of his back as he growled. Then he flopped back into Ringo's bed, panting.

Julia rose and hurried to the kitchen where she rummaged in her purse for her cell phone. Scanning her list of contacts, she searched for someone to call. Tara didn't answer, so she tried Chad, biting the inside of her cheek and pacing at the foot of her bed as it rang on the other end.

"Hello?" A high-pitched male voice answered.

Surprised, Julia yanked the phone away from her ear to see if she'd called the right number. It said Chad's office, but she'd never called him before.

"Hello?" the voice said again.

"Chad?" she replied hopefully.

"Miss Julia? Is that you?"

"Bobby?" she cried into the phone. "Oh Bobby, where is Chad? Never mind—Can you come right over? George is sick."

"Chad had to go to Pittsburgh and he told me to mind the phone. What did you say about George?"

"I think he ate something bad, I'm worried about him." Julia stopped pacing to watch George hunch again. "Will you come look at him and tell me what you think?" she asked, running her hand through her hair. "You know about cats, right?" Desperation was creeping into her voice.

"My momma has lots of cats…I know a bit," Bobby drawled.

"Are you at the office?"

"Yeah…"

"Well come right over, I'm really worried." Julia said, glancing down at the yowling cat.

A long pause filled the line.

"Hello? Bobby? Are you there?"

She heard a throat clear and the sound of a chair scrape across the floor.

"You want me to come to your house?" Bobby asked in amazement.

George rose up again, his back arched and his eyes clamped closed.

"Yes! Come now!" she almost shouted into the phone, causing Ringo to run in circles around her feet.

"Oh…okay…I'll lock up and drive over. To your house, right?"

Irritation was running rampant through Julia's body at this point. "Yes Bobby, please come to my house now!" In an attempt to keep from completely losing it, Julia forced herself to sit on her bed and take a deep breath.

As the line went dead, George hunched again and cried as if in pain. Julia hit 'end' and tossed her phone on her bed to crouch on the floor, unsure whether she should pet the cat or

Kirsten Fullmer

not. Chad's office was only two blocks away, so hopefully Bobby would arrive soon.

"Hang in there little guy…" she murmured soothingly to George.

Ringo trotted to her side, his tail down, his little body shaking. Julia pulled him onto her lap, caressing him gently in an attempt to calm them both.

As he panted heavily, George's yellow eyes thinned to slits and Julia felt panic rising in her chest. He might only be a cat, but to her he was family. She couldn't imagine riding in the truck or sitting on the porch without him.

A clatter on the porch announced Bobby's arrival and a bit shaky but without much thought, Julia rose from the floor to hurry to the door.

"Come in, I'm so glad you're here…" Julia gushed as she dragged Bobby by the arm through the living room. Nearly shoving him into her bedroom, she pointed to Ringo's bed. "There he is, what do you think is wrong with him?"

Blinking behind his lenses, Bobby's eyes scanned Julia's room, pausing at the bed, then glancing to her face. A deep blush crept up his neck but she nudged him toward the cat. He bent to kneel and run his hand along George's back. The fluffy cat panted, his eyes clamped shut.

Seemingly confused, Bobby's knobby fingers roved over the cat's legs and head, then to his stomach, where he paused, his hand very still and light on George's heaving abdomen.

"Well?" Julia sputtered, wringing her hands. "What do you think is wrong with him?"

Slowly, Bobby's head turned to gaze up at Julia, his hand carefully withdrawing from the cat.

Wanting to shake him until he spoke, Julia wrung her hands and shifted from one foot to the other.

Bobby's mouth fell open, then snapped shut. "Uh…Miss Julia, I think we have a problem…"

"Is it bad?" she gasped. "Just tell me! What is it?"

Straightening, Bobby rubbed his hands across his face.

Julia grabbed his upper arms, giving him one good shake. "Bobby! Talk to me!"

Gradually the little man's eyes focused on Julia's face, while the color drained from his.

She ground her teeth and gave Bobby another shake. "Speak!"

With a slight shake of his head, the man cleared his throat. "Miss Julia, I know what's wrong with George…"

"And….?" She resisted the urge to shake him again.

"He's havin' kittens ma'am."

Kirsten Fullmer

11

Julia's grip went slack on Bobby's arms, her hands falling to her sides. "Kittens?!"

He nodded.

"But...how could..." Her mind spun. Had anyone actually told her that George was a male? No, she'd just started referring to him as a him, or referring to her...as a him. "Kittens!"

A wide grin spread across her face and her eyes shone. "I'm gonna be a mother! Or a grandma..." Dropping to her knees, she stroked George's back, murmuring about babies and how sorry she was for assuming she was a male kitty.

The cat yowled and twitched and Julia pulled her hand back, her head snapping up to gaze at Bobby. "What do we do now? How do we help her?"

His eyes wide with panic, Bobby backed away. "I don't know nuthin' about birthin' cats..."

She stood, brushing her hands together. "Well...do I boil water, or get rags, or something?"

Bobby shrugged, his face turning pasty white. "I think I should go get my momma," he muttered, making a move for the door.

Julia grabbed his arm. "You can't leave us here!"

To give the man credit, he was stronger than he looked, and he made it to the bedroom door before Julia dug in her heels, and grabbed the doorjamb with her other hand. "Bobby! Stop!"

A momentary tug of war ensued but he shook off her grip and bolted across the living room as if he were running for his life. "I'll get my momma and be right back…" he called over his shoulder, the screen door banging behind him.

The sound of gravel from the driveway being tossed in the air under grinding tires met her ears as she stood blankly in the living room staring after him.

The empty room echoed, sending chills down Julia's spine. She was alone and George was in pain. An overwhelming surge of inadequacy threatened to knock her to the floor. She should have never gotten pets. She wasn't able to provide for their needs. George had been wrong to trust her to be his…her protector.

Wringing her hands, she turned back toward her bedroom where Ringo whined. What should she do?

George growled in pain, the sound tearing at Julia's heart. She had to pull it together for him. Her. The poor cat deserved that much.

Snatching up her tablet from the folding table, Julia hurried back to her bedroom. She bent down near the dog bed, the floor cool and hard, but as she booted up the tablet and pulled up Google, she managed to find a comfortable position to sit near the cat.

Her teeth nibbled at her bottom lip as she mumbled and typed. "Cat, birth, kittens…search."

As a list of options appeared on the touch screen, the sound of a truck in the driveway dragged at Julia attention. Ignoring the noise, she continued to scan down the list. "Wiki… YouTube videos…"

Boots clomped across the porch. "Julia? Are you okay?" Chad voice demanded, echoing through the empty room.

Kirsten Fullmer

"In here..." she called as she scrolled down the screen.

Chad's head poked into the bedroom, his eyes frantically scanning in search of her.

"Down here," she said, double clicking on a YouTube video.

His head swung down to her on the floor, a scowl darkening his face. "What the...Bobby said you needed help over here then hung up." He lumbered into the room. "What happened?"

Motioning for him to join her on the floor, her eyes didn't leave the screen. "Ever seen a cat give birth?" she asked, her voice flat, her eyes flitting across the screen in the dim room.

Chad flung his hands in the air. "What the hell is going on here? Cat?"

"Shush..." she instructed, her voice firm as she read through the options on her tablet screen. "Sit down and stop yelling at me."

"I'm not yelling," he roared, adrenaline and worry still surging through his system. "You scared the crap out of me..."

The one time she wanted his calm assurance and he was a wreck, Julia thought as she lowered the computer tablet to glare at Chad. "Oh for heaven's sake, sit down!" she snapped.

Startled to hear Julia mandate anything, he meekly dropped to the end of the bed. The look of focused concentration on her face was a side of her he'd never imagined she could muster. And her voice...she sounded...so... authoritative.

Watching as Chad stared at her in amazement, Julia momentarily explored an inner strength she had no idea she still possessed. The sensation both thrilled and terrified her. It felt like the old Julia, not like the person she was now. Squirming, she tamped it down.

"George is having kittens," she announced with a mixture of panic, elation, and wonder.

Chad's eyes widened and flew to the cat in Ringo's bed. "George?"

Even though she felt like giggling over his reaction, which must have mirrored her own, concern for the cat drew her focus back on track.

"Yes, and I'm trying to find out what I should do, if anything…" She replied distractedly, scowling down at the tablet. "I just found a video. Come down here and watch it with me so we can help George."

★★★

Still in shock over the confidence Julia exuded, as well as a cat he'd thought was male giving birth, Chad managed to get a grip on his panic and slid off the bed to crowd onto the floor between Julia and her bed.

The cat growled and arched her back where she lay, then partially relaxed and panted, her eyes barely open.

Chad's palms began to sweat. Glancing between George and Julia, his lips a grim line, he felt at a complete loss. He knew nothing about cats or kittens and the fact that this cat belonged to Julia added a deeper element of anxiety. From the moment they'd met, he'd wanted to comfort her and make sure she was safe. Now she appeared to have a handle on the situation and he was floundering.

His mind spinning through all the possible outcomes, he distractedly watched the video with Julia as she stroked George's back and murmured reassuringly. His masculine instincts told him to escape the feminine tension but his desire to stay near Julia held him bound to the floor.

As the video ended, Julia sighed, assured that nature would take its course and there wasn't much she could do. "So all we can really do is watch, I guess." She reached up to place the tablet on her bed, vaguely surprised she could reach so easily, then turned to Chad.

Kirsten Fullmer

The poor man resembled a cornered lion. He was far too large to be scrunched into the narrow space between her and the bed with his shoulders hunched and knees to his chest. The look on his face reflected misery, multiplied by horrified fascination, with a dash of contrition.

Her shoulders shaking with barely contained mirth, Julia climbed from the floor and motioned for Chad to stand. "I'm gonna go get a clean towel. I'll be right back," She assured him as she turned to leave the room.

"Wait—" Chad blurted, still on the floor, glancing nervously from Julia to the cat and back. "What should I do?"

She shrugged. "Exude calm..." Then she smiled as his hopeless expression.

"And just how do I do that?" he responded, irritation returning to his demeanor. But he only asked her retreating back as she hurried from the room.

Chad studied the cat with uncertainty. "Bet you wish you were a guy right now..." He muttered, rising to perch on the side of the bed.

Radiating efficiency and excitement, Julia returned carrying a white towel and she knelt by Ringo's bed. "I think it's happening!" she whispered, motioning for Chad to come down and kneel by her.

Ringo whined as George strained. The cat's eyes clamped closed, as a small blob emerged under her tail. Julia watched in fascination as George turned to sniff the blob and nose it gently.

"That doesn't look like a kitten to me..." Chad disparaged, leaning in for a closer look.

George licked the kitten, her rough tongue pushing at the sac of membrane surrounding the baby. Julia hands fluttered at her sides, straining to control the urge to help the mother cat bring her baby into the world.

His nostrils flaring with disgust, Chad leaned back on his heals, fighting the impulse to run.

Suddenly the bag of membrane gave way and a tiny damp kitten foot, complete with itty-bitty claws, emerged from the bag, followed by the accompanying leg and another foot. Soon George had the miniature creature freed from the sac and it mewed pitifully, its eyes shut tight.

Julia clucked and cooed with excitement.

Chad's eyes widened as he leaned over the dog bed, fascination chasing away his disgust. "It's so little…" he uttered in amazement.

Glancing to Julia, he saw tears tumbling down her cheeks past a tremulous smile. Her eyes met his, her dark gaze filled with emotion and wonder. She turned back to admire the kitten as it staggered and nudged its way toward George's now prominent nipples. "He's perfect…"

Chad laughed. "You better check before you start calling it a he…"

Tossing him an annoyed glance, she giggled and shrugged. "Whatever, it's so sweet. Look at its tiny little mouth looking for food."

Looking on, Chad felt an odd rush of masculine protection toward both Julia and the new baby. Julia cocked her head to one side, joy in her gleaming eyes as she watched the kitten nurse, and Chad's heart swelled. The new sensations poured through his chest, stirring up concern and confusion. He stood, feeling as if he were being pulled into a spider web of emotional attachment.

A commotion out in front of the house drew his attention. "Sounds like Bobby's back," he commented, "I'm gonna let them in."

Julia nodded, her eyes never leaving the cats.

Kirsten Fullmer

As he tromped through the living room, Chad attempted to shake off the feeling of fate that pressed in on him. When he reached the screen door, Bobby was helping his mother onto the porch. The little man's eyes were large and his entire body shook with nerves.

"How's Miss Julia and George?" Bobby croaked, his voice thin and strained.

Feeling more himself now that he had something to do, Chad took Bobby's mother's arm and led her across the living room. "They're in here and both are fine," he assured.

★★★

Julia stood when Bobby and his mother entered the room. Mrs. Middlewood huffed as she wobbled forward, the large woman's face red with exertion and eagerness.

Noticing Bobby's mother's faded muumuu and bathroom slippers, Julia cringed. "I'm sorry to make you come out so late…" she apologized.

Mrs. Middlewood waved her off. "No trouble, now where is the little mother?"

Guiding the woman to the perch on the edge of her bed, Julia pointed toward George.

The woman hummed to herself, rocking forward and back. "I see I'm a bit late…" she chortled, glancing up at Julia, who nodded silently.

Julia's heart filled with mixed emotions over sharing her precious new baby kitten as she studied Bobby's mother with wary curiosity. The woman's appearance spoke of poverty and a simple life. Her thinning hair was grey, limp, and flat in the back, as if she spent most of her time reclining. The lines on her face spoke of poor health, sorrow, and decline yet her pale eyes burned bright with pleasure as she watched the kitten lustily nurse, and her crooning voice spoke of a woman who had spent her life comforting others, with precious few to console her own moments of despair.

"Looks like we've got another one coming now don't we, little mother…" Mrs. Middlewood murmured.

Bobby reeled on his feet, his face a shade of pale green. Chad grabbed his arm, leading him to the window. "You sit here," he instructed, plopping Bobby into Julia's desk chair.

The little man nodded, his eyes huge and bloodshot behind his dirt-streaked glasses.

★★★

Three more kittens entered the world via Ringo's bed before George expelled the last of the afterbirth, tidied up, and reclined back to watch her babies nurse. Chad had wandered over to join Bobby, more than willing to distance himself from the repellent birth conversation between Julia and Bobby's mom.

Noting the glow of excitement fading from Mrs. Middlewood, to be replaced with a veil of fatigue, Julia offered to walk Bobby and his mother out.

Rising from the bed, Bobby's mother observed Julia shrewdly. "Bobby has told me a lot about you, young lady."

Glancing toward Bobby, Julia swallowed a bitter dose of self-doubt. How would Bobby describe her to his mother, she wondered. "Only good things, I hope."

Bobbing her head in the affirmative, the older woman didn't grin, yet the perception of a smile was there. Her bright eyes passed from Julia to Chad and back to Julia. "I can see for myself how things are." She paused, her expression shifting through multiple emotions. Finally she reached out to grip Julia's hand. "I'm glad you're here, Miss Julia."

The words were simple and plainly spoken, but the emotion and meaning behind them left Julia feeling as she were missing

Kirsten Fullmer

half the story. She looked to Chad for answers but he took Mrs. Middlewood's arm to help her toward the door.

Julia followed them through the dark, empty living room and to the front door. Bobby's mother turned and looked back at the room, then to Julia. "You need some furniture in here, girl," she announced frankly.

Glancing to Chad and suppressing a grin, Julia could only agree. "Yes ma'am."

"You let me know how sweet George and her babies are getting on, won't you?" Mrs. Middlewood inquired as Bobby helped her toward his shabby pickup truck.

Julia nodded and waved.

Bobby helped his mother into the truck, paused to wave and call out a good night, then climbed in and they rumbled away, leaving Chad and Julia standing on the front porch.

Rubbing her arms in the chill, Julia looked up at Chad.

His face was blank as he gazed back, cricket chirps filling the night around them. Finally he opened the screen and waited for Julia to pass into the house.

Julia closed the front door and as she wandered back through the dark living room, she laughed. "Bobby's mother was right…I do need furniture in here."

"Oh I don't know," Chad retorted, following. "It's kind of growing on me…"

Scoffing, Julia drifted through the door of her room and to the end of her bed to gaze down at the new members of her family. Chad strolled up behind her and looked over her shoulder.

"They're cuter now, aren't they?" he commented.

She nodded, certain they were beautiful, her heart already full of love for the tiny sleeping babies. Lightning bolts of fear over the force of her feeling bounced around in her mind, but she banished them in order to linger in the moment. It had been far too long since warmth and joy had filled her broken heart.

Chad's hands rose to her upper arms, his palms warm on her chilled skin. Drowning in the warmth of contentment, Julia leaned back into his chest. He brushed his hands lightly up and down her arms to warm her up, sending tingles of pleasure up her spine and along her scalp.

"Goose bumps," he said. "Are you cold?"

Drawing in a breath, inhaling the pure male scent of him, she turned, her eyes meeting his. "No, not cold…"

Checking twice to be sure he was reading her correctly, Chad finally slipped his arms around her to pull her close. He wanted to kiss her but that never ended well, and the last thing he wanted right now was to be sent away, so he simply cradled her to his chest, the fingers of one hand rising to caress the back of her head.

George began to purr, the rhythmic thrum filling the room like music, and Chad gently rocked back and forth, as if he and Julia were dancing.

Sexual tension leisurely grew and crackled through the room, building like a thunderstorm but Julia and Chad cuddled in a cocoon of simple affection. Each knew that he or she could unlock the gate and allow the persistent desire to flood upon them, but at that moment they wanted only to explore the warmth of companionship. Everything beyond that threatened unwelcome feelings and ramifications for them both.

Julia's heart swelled at the knowledge that she was surrounded by Chad and her little family, and like the Grinch in the Christmas movie, whose heart grew two sizes, she felt herself burst deep inside, unleashing a torrent of emotion she'd kept carefully contained.

As she melted into Chad's chest, her eyes filled with tears and she wept, both with joy and for the cold, heartless places she'd

Kirsten Fullmer

been keeping herself. As her mind and body overflowed with hunger and fear, hope and love, a deep trembling over took her. Unsure she could contain the reality of the moment but with no ability to hem it back, she rode the waves, peeking over crests of joy then plunging into troughs of panic and insecurity.

★★★

Disconcerted, Chad held her back to survey her face, his eyes searching for the meaning of her distress. Without asking or thinking, he gently laid her back onto the bed and climbed up beside her, then tucked her into his side, his arms encircling her to hold her close. He didn't speak or ask her what was wrong, he simply held her and wondered if he'd ever before led a woman to bed without planning to immediately undress her.

The house creaked as the wind outside picked up and one of the kittens cried. The bedsprings chirped as Ringo jumped onto the bed and curled up in the crook of Chad's bent knee. The muted sound of a car rumbled past and moonbeams danced on the floor in front of the window.

Stints of sexual interest surged and waned through Chad as Julia moved briefly against his side as she settled into sleep, her tears fading to hiccups; all the while unnerved that holding her this way, feeling her breathe, allowing her to shift and mold his thoughts and emotions, felt far too intimate.

His ears rang with warning as his actions proved he was involved on a deeper level; one that smacked of commitment beyond neighborly consideration or sexual interest. How would he untangle himself now? He couldn't get up and leave Julia this way, nor did he want to. But if he stayed, she would wake at some point and her dark eyes would blink and focus, finding him holding her, and then what?

Would she stiffen and push him away? Is that what he wanted? Or would her gaze soften, her fingers caress his cheek, and her lips find his? If she came to him willingly asking for passion, what would he do? If he allowed himself to get close to this woman, he knew he would be under her spell and his so-called 'easy and carefree life' would be lost. As would his heart.

12

The next morning, Chad awoke to the steamy smell of dog breath. Cracking one eye open, all Chad could see was blinding sun light flooding from the window and across the bed, casting a halo around Ringo's head, which was propped on his chest.

Glossy brown dog eyes peered soulfully at Chad as the man blinked and grappled through the past evening's events to recollect where he was. Then it hit him full force in the chest. Julia.

Bolting up in bed, nearly pitching Ringo onto the floor, he found Julia stretched out beside him, still asleep.

She snuffled, her dream interrupted by him jostling the bed. Lips pursed, her hand shifted under her cheek, then her deep breathing resumed.

Carefully, Chad lowered himself back down onto the bed, his gaze glued to Julia's face. With her lips slightly open and her muscles relaxed, she looked youthful and remarkably delicate. She must hold herself in a very terse manner he realized, to hide such vulnerability.

Ringo whined at his side and he reached down to pat the little dog's back. "I know, buddy," he whispered. "There is a cat in your bed and I'm in Julia's."

Calming under Chad's pats and scratches, Ringo stretched and ever so slowly, as if he thought that if he moved gradually enough no one would notice, rolled onto his back, feet up, to get his tummy rubbed.

Chad stared at the ceiling as he scratched Ringo's belly and contemplated a getaway. He was definitely at a loss as to how to handle the situation. Even though south of his belt buckle he had some interesting ideas fully formed, he pushed them away to formulate a more feasible plan.

Maybe he could get off the bed and sneak out without waking Julia but did he want to miss her waking up? Her lashes would blink as those unusual dark eyes absorbed him. What would she do, jerk back in shock? Smile languidly? Stretch and moan?

His earlier ideas came rushing back with fierce determination. Reaching down, he rearranged himself under his jeans in search of relief. Julia muttered and snuggled into his side, causing him to bite his bottom lip. *This isn't good,* he thought, as his mind wandered toward reaching for Julia and pulling her full against him. He could almost feel her breath hot on his neck, her cool fingers sliding under his shirt.

"Chad?" Julia mumbled.

Her voice jolting him from the daydream, he turned to face her, braced for just about any response she would offer.

She stretched – first her legs, then her arms, her stomach pressed into his side.

He suppressed a moan.

Julia leaned up on one elbow to cup her hand under her cheek and studied him solemnly; her hazy dark eyes reflecting his hesitation and indecision. "Should we fire up old Bessy?" she asked, rubbing one eye.

Honing in on the "fired up" part, he was all game until he realized he didn't know what she was taking about.

"Bessy?" he asked, carefully shifting to bring his hand up to rest on her hip.

Kirsten Fullmer

"Yeah," Julia grinned sleepily.

Confused and distracted, he reached up to smooth her tangled curls, watching all the time for any sign that she was not in a mood to be touched. "I don't understand."

Her eyes closing slightly under his strokes, she purred. "You know…Bessy the stove…breakfast?"

Chad's hand paused. "The stove?"

Julia giggled and rolled away to sit up. "Yeah, I named the stove Bessy."

Disappointed that she was thinking about food, he tugged at her hand. "I'm hungry, but…" She tumbled onto his chest. "Not so much for breakfast," he murmured, rolling her onto her back under him.

A myriad of expressions fluttered across her face, and in the mix he identified longing and irritation. While he waited for her to settle into one emotion, or even a few in the same general family, he smoothed one thumb along the blanket line on her cheek.

"Chad…" she whispered, her hands wriggling up between them to press on his chest.

"Wait," he insisted, his finger to her lips. "I just want a kiss, then we'll go find Betty." He leaned down to kiss along her jaw line with little nibbles. She smelled of soap and flowers and… warm sleepy woman.

Her back arched slightly and her fingers curled into his shirt. "Bessy…not Betty."

"Whatever…" he mumbled into the hair above her ear as his other hand, limited by holding his weight on that elbow, teased her upper arm. Goosebumps rose along her arm under his fingers so he kissed her cheek. "You feel so good…" he whispered, the fingers on his other hand weaving in her hair.

"So do you…" she moaned, her hands coming up to cup his jaws.

Boot steps clattered on the front porch, followed by loud banging on the front door. Ringo sprang off the bed and clattered through the living room, barking as if the world were ending.

Chad moaned, the sound coming from deep in his soul, every inch of him resisting the interruption.

Julia sighed, her eyes focused, and her expression once again registered the careful calm she wore like a mask.

"Hey, Miss Julia? Chad…" Bobby's muffled voice squawked, as he pounded on the door.

Kittens meowed and cried, awakened by the knocking and barking.

"I'm gonna choke him…" Chad muttered, rolling off Julia to stand by the bed.

Julia primly jumped up to stand beside him, her expression giving away nothing. Hurrying toward the door, straightening her shirt and smoothing her hair, she nearly tripped over Ringo as he frantically jumped and ran in circles. "Down boy," she said, pushing at the dog as she pulled open the door.

Bobby stood on the front porch, his neck craned to ogle Chad's truck pulled up beside the house. "Is Chad here?" he asked without greeting or preamble.

"Good morning Bobby," Julia welcomed calmly. "Please come in. Yes, Chad is here. He came by to check on me and the kittens."

After a slight hesitation and a dark glance through his grubby glasses, Bobby stepped into the living room. "My momma wanted me to check and see how the babies were getting along, so I stopped by on my way to the office."

"See for yourself," Julia suggested, her hand out to propose the way.

Eyeing her warily, Bobby paraded past. Julia sighed and readjusted her calm face, then followed. In her room, the bedcovers

Kirsten Fullmer

had been straightened and Chad was crouched by Ringo's bed, apparently captivated by the kittens.

With his skinny hands on his hips, Bobby scrutinized the scene, then glanced up at Julia. She smiled and threaded her fingers in front of her, the very picture of serenity. "As you can see," she said, "they are doing well. We had a quiet night." Chad didn't look up, but from her vantage point Julia could see his cheek muscles clench.

"Hmph," Bobby huffed, then shouldered past her to stomp back through the living room. The screen door slammed, followed by footsteps across the porch.

★★★

Julia's hands came up to cover her face. "This is will be all over town within minutes, won't it?" she muttered through her fingers.

Chad stood and stared down at the hungry crying kittens and frowned. "No, Bobby will see this as a betrayal and he'll be hurt. He won't say a word to anyone." With a heavy sigh he rubbed his fingers along his jaw, then his hands dropped to his sides and he turned to Julia. "He thinks I stole his girl."

"I'm not anyone's girl," she objected, her hands twisting.

He grimaced. "I know that but in his mind, you liked him and I stepped over the line."

Julia's expressed fell. "He thinks we…."

Chad nodded, silently wishing it was true and they'd had time to continue what they'd started and that Bobby didn't know.

Both stood silent and solemn, considering the situation. The kittens mewled and tumbled, jockeying for position to nurse, while Ringo sat gazing at them all with liquid brown eyes.

"What are we going to do?" Julia finally asked.

Longing to sweep her up and resume where they left off, Chad tossed his hands. "I have no idea. None of this has ever happened before." He jammed his fingers through his hair, leaving it standing on end. "I guess I'll go to the office and see if I can talk to him."

Julia dropped onto the edge of the bed, the springs squeaking in protest. "What will you say?" The question was simple enough, but the meaning behind the words was far deeper and more complicated.

Walking to the bedroom door, Chad stared across the empty living room. "Are you ever going to get furniture?" He knew his response was an obvious sidestep but he had no idea what he would tell Bobby because he hadn't a clue what the hell he was doing.

When Julia didn't respond, he turned back and cocked his hip against the doorframe. Ringo whined and wandered over to sit on his boot, his chin pointed to the ceiling as he looked up at Chad.

Her head hanging, Julia stared at her hands in her lap. "Sorry…" she muttered.

Chad pushed away from the doorframe. "You didn't do anything, don't feel bad. I'm gonna head to the office." He waited for a response but none came. "I need a shower and a shave."

Still nothing.

"Julia?" he asked, his head dipping as he tried to see her face.

She looked up, misery written across her expression. "I told you I wasn't…" She shrugged, unsure what she was trying to say.

Chad roamed to the edge of the bed and reached out to caress her cheek, searching for words that would bring back the intimacy they'd shared earlier, which in itself felt odd. "I'll call you later," he finally said, his hand dropping in resignation.

She nodded.

He turned and his footsteps echoed through the house. The screen door creaked then closed quietly, and Julia sat staring at

Kirsten Fullmer

the kittens, now happily nursing. Why had she opened her heart? One unguarded evening and somehow everything had changed.

★★★

Bending to sweep the last of the dirt and debris into the dustpan, Julia stood and turned to dump it in the trash. Plodding to the mudroom, she tucked the broom and dustpan behind the door, brushed her hands on the front of her shirt, then stood in the doorway to survey the kitchen.

Morning sunshine spilled through the window over the sink and onto the clean floor. Her mother's china glittered behind the wavy glass in the hutch cabinets and across the room, Bessy stood proudly beside the old cutting block. The only sour spot left in the room was the mustard- colored fridge. "All things in time…" she muttered, heading to the bedroom to collect her clothes for a bath.

Perching on the foot of her bed, her hands in her lap, Julia gazed lovingly down at her new kittens as they squirmed and wrestled with high squeaking mews across Ringo's bed. George was busy licking and arranging the babies, keeping a watchful eye on them as they tumbled over each other blindly. Julia grinned, realizing she could watch all day and she gave herself a mental boost to get moving as she rose off the bed.

Pausing in the living room, carrying her bathrobe and slippers, she decided to get cleaned up and go see Becky at the boutique to get some ideas for the living room. It was time. Humming a sad tune and with her mind on couches and coffee tables, she plodded up the steps not grasping the handrail,

In the old bathroom, Julia bent to turn on the hot water tap, then balanced on the edge of the tub to think, distractedly swishing her fingers under the water, waiting for it to get warm.

Paint peeling from the wainscoting drew her eye. The room needed a good scrape and sanding, including the floor, but the

Shabby Chic After All

bones were good. Her head tilted to one side. Some color on the wainscoting, teal-green maybe, and fresh paint on the outside of the tub would freshen things up, silver leaf on the claw feet... perhaps a chair in the corner and a tall glass door cabinet for towels, a braided rug... Ideas flowed and ebbed through her mind as she stood and twisted the cold handle, testing the water.

Steam wafted up from the tub and Julia dripped a dollop of bath oil into the water, filling the room with the scent of lavender.

Her clothes slipped to the floor and she stepped into the tub, flinching as her feet contacted the still-cold porcelain under the hot water. Her thoughts wandered as she eased in, steam rising around her, and she willed the deep tub to fill faster.

The kitchen was almost finished, she contemplated, minus the million little touches that would come with time, and today she would get started on the living room.

Her brow lowered as she considered a budget for the room. Her account had been comfortably full when she arrived in town, due to Brad selling their condo and all her earthly goods and depositing the funds, but she knew she couldn't spend on the house forever without an income. The checks from her long-term disability insurance were enough to pay her modest monthly bills, but her savings were waning and she needed to find an income, even if it was humble.

Twisting the taps off, Julia lolled languidly back into the hot water, murmuring thanks for the deep tub and a functional water heater. Thoughts of the upcoming day poured through her mind. The boutique, furniture, a visit to Tara to see the bed and breakfast and to talk about flowers for the wedding.

Her head rested on the curved edge of the tub and her eyes roamed along the ceiling. She'd talk to Tara about the living room; maybe even ask if she had a fridge that would go with her

Kirsten Fullmer

kitchen. Her eyes dropped closed and she drew in a deep breath of steamy lavender.

A truck rumbled past outside, interrupting her thoughts, and her eyes popped open as the memory of Bobby stomping out of her room invaded her peaceful moment. Resolutely she sat up and reached for the soap and washcloth. Maybe Tara could help her sort out the mess she'd made with Chad and Bobby.

★★★

Chad scowled as he pulled into the office parking lot. Bobby's old pick-up truck sat next to the box truck and the closed sign was in the window with the blinds still drawn. It would have been obvious to his friend that Chad hadn't been there yet that morning.

Occasionally over the past two years, Bobby would beat Chad to the office and it was understood that Chad had stayed out all night with a woman.

His heart heavy, Chad knew that Bobby had every right to assume he'd been up to his old tricks with Julia the night before. For once, however, it wasn't okay for Bobby to assume that he'd been carousing. Not only because it hurt Bobby but because no one should think that of Julia.

As he lumbered across the gravel lot, he wondered what he could say to the man that would possibly resolve the situation.

The door buzzed when Chad pushed it open, but Bobby didn't look up from the schedule he held clutched in one hand. His skinny shoulders squared a bit too stiff and his lips thinned, pursed tight, told the story.

Chad slouched to the desk, feeling like a complete heel, then irritation began to build along his spine and spike through the top of his head. He was facing the firing squad and he hadn't even committed the crime! Hitting the power button on his computer, he dropped into his chair and shuffled crossly through papers on his desk, in an attempt to fill the silence swallowing the room.

"I see Fergus has some deliveries this morning," Bobby stated. "Then Becky has some things going from the boutique to Uniontown and a load of lumber is going to Justin's spa." His voice was cold as ice.

Chad's eyes dragged across the floor and up to Bobby's face where they flinched at the little man's expression. A nod answered in the tense stillness.

Bobby slung the clipboard onto the wall hook with a violent swing of his arm, then snatched the keys to the box truck off the desk, his eye never meeting Chad's.

Standing so quickly his chair rolled into the wall, Chad lifted a hand. "Bobby…"

"I don't want to hear it," Bobby snapped, his back stiff and straight as he stomped to the door, crossed through, then slammed it with a colossal bang, rattling every windowpane in the building.

Chad sank back into his chair and rubbed his palms down his beard-stubbled face.

★★★

With her elbow cocked out the truck window and her hair blowing in the breeze, absently humming *Let it Be* along with the radio, Julia glanced toward the delivery office and thought of Bobby. Shaking her head, she wondered for the hundredth time how she had managed to hurt such a sweet guy.

Ringo barked, his paws on the base of the passenger window looking toward Chad's office, as Julia rolled to a stop at the four-way intersection.

He probably knows Chad is there, Julia thought distractedly. What was he doing right now? Sitting at a desk? Working on the computer? Taking that shower he'd mentioned? Warmth spread

Kirsten Fullmer

through her abdomen and settled into her lap as her thoughts wandered to join him under a steaming stream of water.

A horn blast jerked her attention back to the fact that she'd been sitting at the stop sign far too long, and she stomped on the gas, nearly tossing Ringo off the seat.

"Sorry boy," she offered to the dog as he crouched against the seat back, his eyes wide.

Heaving a loud sigh, Julia continued down Main Street and pulled up to the boutique. A tantalizing mix of new items crowded the sidewalk since the last time she'd been there, and she scrutinized them as she instructed Ringo to behave and closed the truck door. Several antique metal breadboxes painted with delicate flower patterns, caught her eye. They were stacked next to a lidded copper pot and she pursued the stack of goods, lifting price tags curiously. The bread boxes and the pot would look perfect on top the hutches in the kitchen, she thought, hefting the items, balancing them on top each other. She tugged open the door and wobbled precariously into the shop, causing the bells overhead to jangle merrily.

"Oh honey, let me help you with those," Becky exclaimed as she hurried around the counter. Placing the bread boxes and pot on a nearby table, Becky lifted her bejeweled glassed from the chain and settle them on her nose, cocking her head up and down to inspect Julia's selection. "Let me guess, you're going to put these on top of the hutches in the kitchen?" She turned and gazed over her glasses like a wise owl, waiting for a reply.

Julia nodded, a smile spreading across her face. "How'd you know?"

"It's a gift," Becky shrugged with a smile. "Now, what else can I get for you today?"

"I need living room furniture, as I'm sure you well know…" Julia laughed.

Becky nodded, beckoning for Julia to follow. "Bobby was in here this morning…" she mentioned casually over her shoulder as she walked, causing Julia's stomach to fall into her feet. "He said you have new kittens."

Like the sun breaking through the gloom, Julia's face lit up as she stopped beside Becky. "That's right, four. I'm not sure if they are boys or girls though."

"Oh that George is a tricky one isn't he?" Becky teased. "What color are they?"

"Two are black and white, one is kind of striped, and one is yellow. I haven't come up with names yet."

Becky grinned and patted Julia's arm. "Well I'm happy for you. Bobby said that he and his mother came to help."

Julia nodded, wondering what else Bobby had said. "How did he seem? Bobby that is…" she ended lamely, her expression turning grim.

Becky's head cocked to one side, her eyes sharp, and her hand came to her chest. "He was a bit down…"

Slinking deeper into her own skin, Julia shrugged guiltily.

Without pause, Becky took Julia's arm to lead her to a sofa, pushed her gently to sit then settled next to her, ready to hear the entire story.

When Julia remained silent, unsure if she should ask for advice or even where to start, Becky offered a jumping-off point. "He said he and his momma were more than happy to help deliver the kittens…"

Julia nodded and twisted her fingers in her lap. "Yeah, but George already had it under control. We just kind of watched. I think she'll be a good little mommy."

Becky nodded, waiting. "And…"

"Chad came too. I guess Bobby called him."

Her eyes wide and ready for the story to develop, Becky nodded.

Kirsten Fullmer

"So when all the kittens were born, Bobby took his mother home. She's very sweet by the way…"

Becky rolled her hand in the air between them in frustration, encouraging Julia to continue.

Feeling crowded, Julia jumped up from the couch. "And I need to buy some stuff for my living room." Her head turned from left to right, searching for anything living room appropriate, as if she weren't standing in the middle of an assortment of sofas.

Reaching up for Julia's hand, Becky tugged her back to sit beside her. "Did you know Bobby was sweet on you before this morning?" she asked carefully.

Julia's head swung to meet Becky's gaze. "How…did he tell you?"

Becky's expression softened. "Honey, I've known Bobby his whole life. Not much that boy does or says gets by me."

Her eyes gleaming with unwanted tears, Julia nodded, swallowing past the lump in her throat. "I wouldn't hurt him, not…I mean, I would never hurt him on purpose…"

Reaching over to squeeze Julia's fingers, Becky clucked. "Oh I know that, now tell me what happened. Maybe I can help."

Julia shook her head and one tear escaped to roll down her cheek. "I don't even know…"

"That Chad is something, isn't he?" Becky offered, causing Julia's head to whip up again.

Her eyes wide, her mouth open, Julia gaped at Becky, who sat back into the sofa cushion and waved off Julia shock. "Oh honey, come on, everybody with eyes knows you two shoot sparks off each other."

"But, we're not…we've never even been in public together…"

Becky brushed at a nonexistent piece of lint on one of her many her necklaces, then looked up. "In this town, being seen together isn't really required…"

Julia shook her head in confusion. "That's ridiculous, how could anyone possibly know anything about us if they haven't even seen us together?"

A long sigh rolled from Becky's ample chest. She fiddled with her bracelet then finally looked up to meet Julia's indignant gaze. "You really want to know the truth?"

Julia nodded.

Becky's head wobbled from side to side, her jewelry jingling. "Okay…" She took a deep breath. "Chad's truck has been seen at your house from time to time." She paused for effect. "And his best friend, Justin, *is* engaged to my boss." She watched Julia for a response. "Goodness, Chad's mother is my momma's second cousin, and Bobby tends to run on about things he shouldn't. Besides…you two are just a perfect couple."

Her mouth dropping open, Julia was speechless. She stood, her back stiff, then she seemed to crumple as she sunk limply back onto the sofa.

"Nobody is saying anything bad, mind you," Becky assured. "But I drove by your place early this morning and saw his truck there…" Her gaze skittered off to the left.

Julia shook her head and covered her face with her hands.

"There, there," Becky patted her knee, "We were all glad to see it, if that helps."

Her hands dropped from her face. "We?" Julia gasped, horrified.

"You live on the highway that runs through town, dear."

Moaning, Julia sank further into the couch.

"Chad has needed somebody like you. I'm glad to see him making a move, to be honest," Becky stated matter of factly. "So is everyone else. Well, except maybe Bobby," she admitted.

When Julia had no reply, Becky patted her knee. "Come on, let's pick you out a living room, shall we?"

Kirsten Fullmer

An hour later, Julia pulled onto the highway, her head swimming with excitement over the pieces of furniture she'd selected from the boutique. However, the sting was still on the knowledge that the entire town had concocted various ideas about her and Chad. With her thoughts bouncing between where to put her new couch and concern for Bobby, she headed up the gravel drive to the bed and breakfast.

As Julia pulled her truck up under a tree near the porch, she couldn't help but be curious about the construction site past the barn. Work trucks were parked at all angles and piles of dirt, lumber, roofing supplies, and hardware were stacked around the site. The structure was going up, with stud walls being lifted into place by work crews and a large, yellow lifting machine of some sort. Tara stood off to one side, talking with a handsome man in a hardhat.

Climbing from the truck, Julia lifted Ringo and tucked him under her arm. "Shall we go over and take a look?" she asked the little dog. He panted and squirmed as she made her way toward the busy construction site.

The man with Tara nudged her and pointed toward Julia as she approached, and Tara turned and grinned, her hand raised in greeting. Out of breath, Julia stepped up next to Tara, let Ringo down, and told him to sit.

Tara gave Julia a quick hug, then stepped back. "Julia, I'd like you to meet my fiancé Justin. Justin this is Julia."

Julia grinned and extended her hand. Justin smiled and glanced to Tara and back, a light dancing in his eyes. "I'm glad to finally meet you, I've been curious about the lady who could get Chad all tied in knots."

The smile on Julia's face faded and she withdrew her hand. One of the workmen shouted and Justin's attention was drawn away. He took one step toward the building, then turned back to Julia, awkward and unsure. "I didn't mean anything, I'm sorry."

Taking pity on the man, Julia waved him off. "It's fine."

Tara smacked Justin on the shoulder. "Go build some-thing…" she laughed, then she turned back to Julia and put her arm around her, turning her toward the main house. "We have girl talk to get to."

Justin nodded. "Have fun ladies," he called over his shoulder with a lift of his hand as he went back to work.

"Men," Tara scoffed. "They have a gift for saying the wrong thing."

Julia nodded and bent to scoop up Ringo. At the porch, Tara paused to pluck a few dead blooms from the flowerbed by the steps, giving Julia time to leisurely make her way up to the porch.

"Come inside, I've been dying to show you something," Tara said as she passed Julia to open the front door.

"Okay…" Julia replied, continually shocked by the easy way Tara drew her in, making her feel comfortable, as if she'd been dropping by the house for years.

Once in the door, Julia bent to place Ringo on the floor, then gasped and froze. "Oh Tara…this is perfect." The warm tones of the floor reflected the cool mint green of the walls. The rug centered under the white slip-covered sofa and chair softened the room, adding color and pattern to the clean lines of the furniture. The shelves and fireplace mantle sported collec-tions of interesting and homey knickknacks and framed photos.

"Thanks," Tara glowed. "This is what I wanted to show you," she said, reaching into the glass door cabinet along one wall and drawing out a large china dish with rosebuds painted along the rim. The fluted edge of the bowl was punched to create a basket-weave pattern.

Kirsten Fullmer

"Isn't that pretty," Julia whispered, her finger tracing the delicate, almost translucent edge of the dish.

Tara handed the bowl to Julia. "It's yours. It will look great in your kitchen."

Julia's mouth dropped open. "I—I don't know what to say."

Shrugging, Tara smiled. "Just say thanks. Now, come on into the kitchen, it's one of my favorite rooms." She turned, leading the way. "We don't have any guests this week because of the construction but we're full up next week for the first time." In the door to the kitchen she turned back to Julia. "I hope most of the hammering and banging will be done by then."

Julia nodded, following with the dish cradled in her hands.

"Anyway, this is the kitchen" Tara continued. "I love how it turned out."

Her eyes wide with wonder and appreciation, Julia wondered past Tara, Ringo at her feet, her gaze flitting around the room. She placed the dish on the counter, her fingers caressing the soapstone. "What is this? It's not granite..." She turned toward Tara.

Opening the upper cupboard, Tara took out two glasses and set them on the counter. "It's soapstone. It went out of style in the fifties, but it's coming back now. Pretty isn't it?"

Julia nodded, still soaking up the ambiance of the room. "What do you call this?" she asked, pointing to a set of green glass canisters on the counter. "I saw some of it in your boutique too."

"Jadeite. It was popular around World War Two," Tara said, as she carried a pitcher of ice tea from the oversized stainless steel fridge to the counter. "Is ice tea okay?" she questioned, lifting the picture.

"That would be great."

"Sweet or un-sweet?"

"Sweet please," Julia muttered, drifting toward the French doors on the far side of the kitchen. One hand came up to touch the ornate antique doorknob as she gazed out the door. Multilevel decks ascended toward a sparkling blue pool, and behind that, green lawn led to deep-green forested Pennsylvania hills that rose along the back of the property. "This is amazing…"

"Like I told you before," Tara said as she added ice from the icemaker to the glasses. "I never thought I'd end up owning this place with Justin but it feels like home now."

Julia turned back to face Tara. "It feels so welcoming, I don't know how…"

Interrupting her, Tara scoffed. "Eh, you're a natural, you're already figuring it out at your place. Come on, let's go sit on the deck."

A fresh spring breeze lifted their hair as the women stepped outside. Tara handed Julia her glass, then dragged two chaise lounges side by side to face the pool. Ringo sniffed along the edges of the deck then returned to curl up on the end of Julia's chaise, his head on his paws.

"The pool is gorgeous," Julia sighed as she sipped her drink.

"We just finished it last week," Tara replied, crossing her ankles and leaning her head back. "It's been so hectic with all the construction, and the wedding creeping up…"

Julia glanced toward the construction site where the poof poof of nail guns could be heard among distant shouts of the men and the muted roar of the equipment. "I can imagine. They're building a spa?"

Tara turned her head toward Julia, one hand shading her eyes. "Yeah, we designed this place as a company retreat and Justin already had the spa in the plans. When we bought it, we figured the spa would be a nice touch for the B&B." She laughed. "Besides that, all the women in town vowed to shoot me if we didn't go ahead with construction."

Kirsten Fullmer

Julia laughed. "What kind of amenities will you offer?"

Lowering her glass, Tara scowled. "I don't know yet, we are still working on the logistics of cost versus income for start up. Plus there's not really a glut of experienced people around here to run it."

"Right…" Julia agreed.

Silence settled around the women, interrupted only by the sounds of construction down the hill.

"Speaking of flowers…" Tara finally said, a smile playing at he corner of her lips.

Julia's head rolled on the chaise headrest to face Tara. "Were we?"

Tara shrugged and laughed. "I thought of trying a segue into the conversation but what the heck…"

Draining the last of the tea from her glass, Julia swung her feet over the edge of the chair to sit up. "I have been thinking about it actually. Can I bounce a crazy idea off you?"

Tara sat up, her eyes wide. "The crazier the better."

Julia shrugged. "Well, it started last night before the kittens came…"

"I heard about that!" Tara interrupted. "I love kittens! That sneaky George, I can't wait to see them."

Not able to withhold a smile, Julia nodded. "They're so amazing. So tiny and sweet. George doesn't want us near them yet and I'm trying to honor that but it's killing me. That's why I brought Ringo with me…"

Tara nodded and reached over to pat the little white dog. "So continue with your idea."

Julia shifted in her seat as she regrouped. "Okay, so anyway, I was on the porch reading my book about a country florist shop, and this idea came to me—"

Tara nearly jumped from her chair. "Oh my gosh, Julia! You have to open a florist shop in your house, it's perfect!"

13

Caught off guard by Tara's enthusiasm, Julia shrank back. She was unused to sharing her thoughts, let alone stray dreams. "Well...I don't, I don't...know much about it," she stammered. "It was just a wild dream that I had for a minute."

Ignoring Julia's discomfort, Tara leaped up and paced in front of her. "This is awesome! Oh my gosh, so many people will love this. You can sell cuttings from your yard and advice on how you grow such beautiful flowers. You can sell cut flowers and arrangements and do local funerals and deliveries. And weddings for us!" She stopped in front of Julia, talking excitedly with her hands. "This town has needed a flower shop forever."

Completely overwhelmed, Julia retreated into herself, the color draining from her face. Tara plopped back into her chair, continuing enthusiastically. "I can help you find stands and display cases, and you can talk to Chad about doing the deliveries..."

Already disconcerted, the idea of working with Chad caused Julia's senses to reel. Something inside her snapped as thoughts of Chad and Bobby and kittens and flowers tumbled over and over in her mind. Her chest constricted and she struggled to find right side up.

The lack of response from Julia finally soaked into Tara's consciousness. As her last sentence hung in the air over the deck, then wisped away on the breeze, Tara stuttered for a way to take back her overzealous response.

"Julia, I'm sorry, really I am. I do this…" She jumped back up to pace, then dropped onto her chaise, her hands imploring. "I hear something…and I get so excited and my mouth runs off. Oh my gosh…" She stared up at the sky, then back down to Julia's bent head.

Moving to sit beside her friend, Tara put her arm around Julia's bowed shoulders and waited for the awkwardness to pass. "Julia? I really am sorry. I'd like to hear about what you were thinking…honest…"

Julia's gaze stayed on Tara's sandals as she concentrated on breathing in and out. Ringo whined and lay at her feet. Coming to Smithville had not been the hideaway she had planned. Every day seemed to force larger and more demanding expectations onto her already weak shoulders.

Tara gave Julia a squeeze and tried again. "So…you were reading a book about a flower shop…"

Julia shrugged knowing that nothing she could say now would compare to the fabulous scheme Tara envisioned.

Shifting back to give Julia some room, Tara changed her tack. "Forget that for a minute, tell me what is going on with you and Chad."

There was no response but the breeze shuffling the plants on the deck.

Tara sighed long and twisted her hands in her lap. "Julia, please look at me."

Julia glanced up, and she was stuck by Tara's expression of misery.

Tara held her gaze. "You have no idea how much I want to be your friend do you?"

Shock registered across Julia's face.

Kirsten Fullmer

"It's true," Tara nodded. "I've been a loner my whole life. I never felt like I had a connection with a girl my age, until I met you."

"Me?" Julia croaked.

"Yeah, you." Tara pulled her hair over and shoulder and ran her fingers through it as she gazed across the pool. "I had a weird childhood and it left me feeling like no one understood me." She tossed her hair back over her shoulder and turned to face Julia. "Something about you makes me think you feel the same way...somehow."

Julia glanced back to Ringo, his head on her foot as he whined with concern. Here it is, she reflected, another defining moment when she could open up or turn away. Running her fingers across her scalp, she arched her back, struggling to find perspective and footing in the slippery emotional realm.

"I want to understand you," Tara continued. "Can you talk about it?"

Shrugging, Julia glanced away.

"I heard from Justin that Chad had kissed you..." Tara prompted.

The statement brought Julia's head up to meet Tara's gaze.

"Yup, it's true. Boy did I feel like a bad friend," Tara lamented.

Julia scoffed and sniffed. She didn't want to know how Justin found out, she just wanted to...she wasn't sure what she wanted anymore.

"I saw that he spent the night at your place," Tara continued. "Was it because the kittens were having trouble...or..."

Julia's mind ground to a halt, as if the entire world was waiting for her to either open her mouth and have a genuine conversation about her fears and hopes and relationships, or it was waiting for her to shut down and disappear all together. Unfortunately, she knew all too well that the ground wouldn't swallow her up just because she wished it would.

Shabby Chic After All

Carefully examining Tara's face, Julia saw a person who appeared to have no hidden agenda. Julia knew that nothing hinged on her response but gaining a friend, which in itself was a commitment she'd promised herself never to make again.

Relaxing her hands in her lap, Julia took a deep breath, then made the first step to a new life. Once the choice was made, the words poured from her like a flooded reservoir spilling over the sluicegates.

"We fell asleep. I was crying because of the kittens…in a good way but… that's what I do when Chad is getting too close…and he was so close…and he was…I was bawling like a baby so he held me…" She turned to Tara and grabbed her arm. "And oh God, Tara, he felt so good this morning when we woke up…and then Bobby came to check on the kittens and he thinks that we…"

Julia's hand dropped to the chaise. "But we didn't…I mean we might have if he hadn't…" She paused for a breath and her forehead wrinkled. "But no, I don't think we would have." Her hands waved in agitation. "Anyway, he likes me, Bobby that is, well Chad too…" One hand came up in explanation. "But, I didn't know about Bobby until the night we stained my floors, and I swear I wouldn't have hurt him if…" Her brow lowered in thought. "But there was already this thing with Chad…and I didn't…I wasn't…" the torrent slowed, the stream of words reducing to a trickle. "Chad is just so…and I wanted…"

Tara sat with her eyes wide, desperate to catch the words as they rushed past. When silence fell between them, her mouth moved as she struggled to form a coherent response to the deluge of emotion.

Ringo jumped to his feet and barked as Justin opened the door and stepped onto the deck with a soda in his hand. "Oh, there you are. I was looking…" His sentence faded as he noticed the tense silence and blank expression on both women's faces.

Kirsten Fullmer

He glanced over his shoulder, then across the pool, wondering where the bomb had dropped.

"Don't move," Tara said, squeezing Julia's hand. Then she jumped up and hurried to Justin's side. She leaned toward him, her back to Julia, and whispered a few adamant sentences to him, one hand gesturing.

Justin's eyes widened and he took two steps back into the house and quietly closed the door. Tara turned and hurried back to sit by her friend and took Julia's hand in hers, her face wearing a falsely serene expression.

Julia glanced toward the door, embarrassed. "What did you say to him?"

Tara shrugged. "I just told him if he trusted me, he should believe that he didn't want to be out here and to go back in the house."

"And he went? Just like that?"

"Well," Tara laughed, "We've been dating for almost a year now and I think he's learned to be afraid…"

Considering Tara's comment and Justin's response, Julia shrugged.

"So, back to what you said—" Tara redirected. "You cried and Justin held you and you slept?"

Julia nodded, still uncomfortable with vocalizing her non-relationship with Chad.

"And then you woke up…"

Standing, Julia moved to the deck rail, Ringo at her feet, to gaze across the pool toward the forest.

"Did he try anything?" Tara tried again, looking a bit cha-grinned, as if she knew it was a personal question but was dying to know.

Julia didn't answer for a long moment and then she turned to back to face Tara and leaned against the deck rail. "I don't know…he kissed me…and I liked it…then Bobby came to the door."

Spreading her hands palm up, her face to the sky, Tara closed her eyes. "Thank you! Now we are getting somewhere." She stood and meandered to the rail. "Has anyone told you about Chad?" she asked cautiously.

Julia tipped her head to one side, her brow quirking in thought. "Not really, but people act funny about him sometimes, even you."

Nodding, Tara's expression grew grim. "I'm not going to gossip, his story is his to tell but you should know that he has been through some hard times the last few years, and he sees Bobby as a little brother. Chad is devoted to taking care of William's family."

"Okay…" Julia replied, unsure what that had to do with her.

Tara struggled for words. "It's just…well… Chad hasn't allowed anyone to get close to him for years. He's a great guy, don't get me wrong, but you are the first person he has…the first woman…"

Shocked, Julia groped for understanding. "Surely he has…I mean he must date…"

"Have you met Gloria yet?" Tara interrupted.

Julia shook her head.

Tara thought for a moment, then turned back toward the chairs and bent to retrieve their glasses. "Chad has dated Gloria on and off for over a year," she stated flatly.

Shock bubbled up from Julia's toes then surged into an angry boil under her skin. "He has a girlfriend?" she sputtered.

Pausing, Tara shook her head. "No, I wouldn't say that."

"Then…then what are you saying?" Julia stammered, confused.

Returning to the rail, Tara balanced the empty glasses on the top handrail and examined Julia's face. Finally she spoke. "Like I

Kirsten Fullmer

said, he hasn't let anyone get close. Gloria is…not the marrying type per se…"

"She's a…?"

Waving her hands, Tara backed up. "No! Nothing like that, she's a nice enough girl but…I've known Chad wasn't interested in settling down with her. Do you understand any of what I'm saying? I'm not good at this…" She tugged her hair over her shoulder and ran her fingers through it again.

Julia stood, looking blankly toward the pool. "I don't think I understand…"

Tara tossed her hair back over her shoulder and grasped Julia by the shoulders. "I'm trying to say that we all adore Chad, and he's been kind of…closed down. You are the first glimmer of hope we've had for him."

Not sure whether to be flattered or overwhelmed, Julia sorted through her feelings. She'd been thinking this was all about her and her issues – her running from Chad and come to find out, everyone was worried about Chad. Already overcome by her own problems, she felt even more at a loss as to how to deal with Chad and Bobby.

As Julia visibly retreated into herself, Tara began to panic. "What is going on in that head?" she asked, leaning forward.

Stepping back, Julia wanted to run. "I'm not…I'm not the one he should…I can't…"

Regaining her grasp on Julia's arm, Tara disagreed. "Don't you see? You are drawing out Chad. Don't be afraid…"

Julia tugged at her arm. "No, I need to go now…"

Tara dropped Julia's arm to step in front of her. "Stop and listen to me for a minute. Don't run, I always run and it doesn't help. Geeze you are so much like me…" She shook her head then continued. "I promise, I didn't mean to pressure you. I know you've been through a hard time too, and all I'm saying is that maybe you two can help each other…"

Julia paused. "I don't want help…"

"You haven't done anything yet but be your charming, beautiful, alluringly distant self and Chad has been drawn to you. I guess my point is that Chad doesn't know what he's doing or what he's feeling and he's confused, so don't be surprised if he acts…stupid."

Silence hung between the women as Julia thought back on Chad's responses to her over the last week.

"Well, maybe stupid was the wrong word," Tara clarified. "'How about…cloddish?"

A giggle bubbled up Julia's throat.

"And Bobby drives him completely insane," Tara continued, rolling her eyes. "But he loves the kid."

Julia's head tilted. She couldn't have helped but notice that fact. "I'll think about what you've said. I am drawn to him… but….that's another thing, he's so not my type."

Tara laughed. "Watch out then, because those are the dangerous ones!" She collected the glasses from the deck rail and turned away. "Come on, let's go in the house and I'll show you where I want flowers for the wedding."

They stepped through the door, Julia pausing for Ringo to trot in front of her, and found Justin seated at the table, typing on his phone. He froze and looked up, his expression one of alarm and question.

"You're safe now." Tara laughed, waving one hand dismissively.

Justin sighed and stood, a grin spreading across his face as his stance relaxed. "Well, that's a relief."

"Sorry about that…" Julia said, her face turning pink.

"Hey no problem," Justin assured her. "I'm glad you two are friends. I'm thinking that you will take some of the heat off me."

Tara snorted, her eyes shooting sparks, one hand on her hip. "What does that mean?"

Kirsten Fullmer

Justin swept up to her side and scooped her into his arms, bending her back so he could nibble kisses on her neck. "That means…" he said between kisses. "That you will love having a girlfriend to tell how horrible I am."

Squirming to get away, Tara giggled and swatted at Justin. "Well I do need that…"

Enjoying the diverting and playful energy of her newfound friends, Julia noticed that her shoulders relaxed and her stress dissolved, especially when she considered that she had officially turned a corner. Resolutely, she decided to enjoy her new friendships for as long as they lasted.

★★★

As Julia wound down the long drive from the inn, the song *Imagine* came to mind. A long happy sigh escaped her lips as she hummed the tune, the lyrics flowing freely through her mind, even though they probably wouldn't have if she tried to sing them out loud. John Lennon had created one of her all-time favorite songs, and as the music reverberated through her mind and soul, Julia allowed the afternoon visit with Tara to waft through her thoughts, unfettered by fears or insecurity.

They had walked through the inn, Tara showing Julia where flowers should be placed for the wedding. The house had stunned and amazed Julia and its charm and appeal were still on her mind.

So many cold lonely days had passed since she had thoughtlessly connected with a friend, allowing conversation to flow unstinted, her own pleasure and enthusiasm obvious in her voice, gestures, and expressions.

The whole afternoon had left her feeling energized and hopeful. A few weeks ago she would never have believed she could feel this good, and even now it felt surreal. Though she was unsure that it would last, her heart grasped at each happy moment, holding it dear, as the breeze blew through her curls and song lyrics now ascended and fell intermittently and quietly through the truck cab.

Anticipation to see the kittens pulsed through Julia as she pulled into the drive. Ringo danced around her feet as she crossed the yard and juggled keys to unlock the front door, the china dish tucked carefully under her arm.

Padding across the living room, Julia placed the bowl on the folding table, then paused at the door to the den, poking her head around the doorjamb to peek at Ringo's bed. George looked up, her yellow kitty eyes bright and wide in the quiet room. The cat purred as Julia tiptoed in to kneel by Ringo's bed. One hand reached out of its own accord to caress the velvet soft back of the tiny yellow kitten where it lay curled against its mother. George continued to purr, her eyes closing briefly in a blink, as if to say, "Go ahead, I trust you to touch my babies."

Julia's heart felt as if it would burst with contentment and love.

The rumble of a truck pulling up to the house roused her from the moment and she stood to pad back across the room and step through the door, quietly closing it behind her.

Glancing through the screen door, Julia could see Bobby and Chad climbing from the moving truck. As they rolled open the back of the truck, she leaned against the doorframe, sizing up the men. Even from the house she could feel tension radiating off Bobby and tired chagrin weighing down Chad.

Only a few head bobs and minimal greetings passed between them as Julia held open the screen for the men to carry in the furniture. She unobtrusively muttered directions as to where she'd like things placed, and once all the furniture was in the house, Bobby announced he would walk back to the shop. As the screen slammed behind him, Julia's eyes met Chad's, both miserable.

Kirsten Fullmer

Julia crammed her hands into her back pockets and scuffed her toe along the faded wood floor. "I suppose we should have done these floors before I bought furniture…"

Chad shrugged.

"Did you try to talk to him?" she asked, looking up, obviously aware that even if he had spoken to Bobby, it hadn't gone well.

Rubbing his fingers along his unshaven jaw, Chad shook his head. "He won't talk to me about anything but work."

Julia nodded, biting her bottom lip.

"Becky boxed up a bunch of stuff for you, I left it by the door…"

Turning to see a pile of cardboard boxes stacked by the door, Julia nodded, then closed her eyes, trying to ignore the silence radiating between them on a current of stifled energy.

"Would you like something to drink?" she finally asked, her question hanging awkwardly in the room.

Chad nodded, but instead of heading for the kitchen, he reached for Julia and pulled her to his chest, tucking her head under his chin. For the first time, Julia became aware of the vibe of pain and uncertainty that emanated from Chad. As her arms wound around his back and his heart beat under her ear, she contemplated the man who held her. She'd been so buried in her own drama and fear that she had failed to notice, let alone feel, the depth of Chad's soul, the nuances of the person, even though she'd seen it shining through his eyes. Was that the thing that drew her to him – an agonized longing, similar to her own?

As his hand slid up her back to cradle her head, she knew it was that and yet so much more. The sexual tension radiating off him was palpable and his strength and pure masculine warmth were like a toxin snaking through her body, leaving her weak and confused, yet wholly focused. Begrudgingly, Julia had to admit that the man had a hold on her on multiple levels.

"I need to talk to you about something…" she mumbled into Chad's chest.

He leaned back to see her face, questions and trepidation in his eyes. "It's never good when a woman says that."

Stepping away from him, Julia tugged awkwardly on the bottom of her shirt, as if she could shrug off the physical impact he had on her. "It's nothing like that," she assured him. "Come sit down."

As she crossed the blue and grey, slightly tattered Turkish rug they had placed in the center of the large room's floor, Julia took a moment to survey her new furnishings, giving Chad a moment to stew.

Her white slip-covered sofa was settled onto one side of the rug, facing the fireplace. Two wrought-iron side tables flanked the sofa, each with scarred and chipped, twisted, swirly legs. The wood coffee table only held remnants of the ancient whitewash paint that had once covered it, leaving the low table charmingly decrepit. A heavy, iron fireplace screen stood on the tile hearth, its white enamel paint greyed and etched with cracks but intact, and a huge intricate and mottled, antique copper-framed mirror rested on the mantle. But her favorite piece, a faded rosebud upholstered, sweeping, curved-back chaise, had been placed in one corner in front of two tall, ancient, louvered shutters that were propped against the wall.

It took all her control to stay focused on her conversation with Chad and not to hurry over to dig through the boxes from the boutique and exclaim excitedly over the candles, bottles, printed boxes, and picture frames that would crowd the tables and mantle. She could already see the chaise and sofa piled with frilled and delicately printed pillows.

Chad passed her to perch uncomfortably on the sofa and Julia sat across from him on the coffee table, where she could read his expression.

Kirsten Fullmer

"This isn't personal…" she started, then wobbled her head and tried a different tack. "I mean, I want to talk about business."

Chad's eyebrows rose in question. "Okay…"

"I've been thinking about starting…or opening…a…well, a flower shop. Here…" She spread her arms wide to encompass the house.

Still unsure what Julia was getting at, Chad was a bit surprised that she wanted to open a business but he waited for the rest of the explanation.

Julia watched his face intently, but saw nothing. "I'm going to need some help…"

"What kind of help? I don't understand."

Shifting on the table, Julia tried again. "I'll need flowers delivered to me from Pittsburgh once a week, and of course the flowers that people order will need to be delivered…"

"Oh!" Chad exclaimed, her meaning finally breaking through the hormonal haze she cast over him. "Well…I've actually been looking to pick up another Pittsburgh run." He rubbed his jaw in thought. "How many deliveries are we talking about?"

Julia shrugged. "I'm not sure, I've only done a little cursory research, but I can't do much more until I have a delivery service on board, both so I can get flowers I don't grow and for deliveries. It will start out fairly slow, take time to get word out, and I don't plan to advertise much, you know, start out small."

Chad nodded, the idea becoming clearer. "At United Package, we did a lot of 1-800-flowers stuff, are you planning to do that?"

"I don't know." She frowned. "You will have to tell me all about how that works. I mostly want to do local, drive-by type stuff to get started. I'm not ready to face weddings and funerals and catered stuff just yet, if ever."

"Why do you say that?"

Julia shrugged. "I get overwhelmed…"

"Hell, you can do this, I have no doubt," Chad assured her. He grinned. "I bet Tara jumped all over this idea."

"It was basically her idea...her's and Fergus's anyway."

He laughed. "How did I know that?"

"So anyway, how about I do more research and explore the idea? Is it something you may want to do?"

Chad stood. "It sounds like an interesting thought. I have some room in the schedule and like I said, I was already looking for a Pittsburgh run. So yeah, I'd like to hear what you come up with."

As Chad smiled down at her, Julia suddenly wondered what she had been thinking. Opening a business? Working with Chad around all the time? What had she done?

"I have to get going." Chad interrupted her thoughts, heading for the door.

Julia stood to follow him. At the door, he turned and tugged his leather gloves from his back pocket, then paused to gaze into her eyes.

Wondering if her hair was standing on end because of the look in his eye, Julia shifted from one foot to the other. "What are we going to do about Bobby?"

Chad shook his head. "No clue."

"Right..." she mumbled. "Well thanks for bringing the furniture."

He glanced across the room. "It looks nice, old fashioned, like the kitchen."

She nodded. "That was the idea."

"I guess so." He shrugged. Then with one last warm glance, he turned and went out the door. At the foot of the porch steps he turned to pat Ringo and look up at Julia as she stood holding the screen open. "Want to grab dinner at the diner with me tonight?" He tossed out the question easily, as if it wouldn't be

Kirsten Fullmer

their first date, or an announcement to the town, as sure as if they'd printed their intent to date in the town paper.

As if she were on a game show, Julia could feel the weight of the question. Time ticked past and the studio audience stared at her. Questions whirled in her mind as the plinking, thinking music wound down. She had to decide, this was the moment—was she willing to actually date?

How many times now had Chad been over to her house? How did she really feel about him? She frowned. It was dinner not an elopement, she reminded herself. Her mind reeled back to him holding her a few moments earlier. A myriad of emotions fluttered across her face, but were quickly replaced by a timid smile. "Okay, what time?"

Chad's jaw went slack momentarily before he contained his surprise. "I'll walk down and get you around six."

She nodded and he grinned like a schoolboy, then tipped an invisible hat and strolled to his truck, whistling.

14

"Ringo honey, it's okay, I'll be back soon," Julia assured the anxious little dog as she gently pushed him inside to close the door. She locked up then turned to meet the solid wall of Chad's chest with her face.

Instead of moving back to give her space, Chad rubbed one hand up and down the back of her arm and inhaled deeply. "You always smell so good."

Nervous and jumpy, Julia pushed past him, fumbling to shove the house keys into her purse. They tromped off the porch and down the sidewalk, Chad wanting to be close to her and Julia skittering out of his reach. Finally they settled into a confortable pace as they walked toward the diner a few blocks away, and Julia could take a deep breath.

"I'm not sure this is such a great idea," she muttered, adjusting her purse strap on her shoulder.

"Sure it is," Chad reassured her, but a tiny wrinkle twitched at the corner of his eye.

"We may as well stand on the roof and yell to everyone that we're dating," Julia huffed.

"They'd already know," he replied flatly, then bit the side of his bottom lip.

Walking in silence, the late May evening radiated its charm, giving them blossoms bobbing on trees and birds singing cheerfully. At the diner, Chad stepped behind Julia and pushed open the door for her, his hand warm on her back to lead her through.

Bells chimed, announcing their arrival, and Marge glanced up from behind the counter. Her customary greeting froze on her lips as she did a double take, her conversation with a bald man seated in front of her forgotten.

The song on the jukebox ended and all the diners turned in the suddenly silent room to watch Julia and Chad walk to a table.

As Chad pulled out Julia's red vinyl and chrome chair, the jukebox clicked and clattered, changing records. The first few words of the song *P.S. I Love You*, drifted across the room, as Julia did the butt-lift and scoot maneuver so Chad could scoot up her chair. The other diners slowly returned their attention back to their plates and conversations.

"It's the Beatles," Chad commented distractedly, shifting his chair up to the table, his eyes darting nervously between Julia and the other customers.

She nodded, seemingly engrossed in digging through her purse for something. Giving up in frustration, completely forgetting what she'd been looking for, she turned to hang her purse on the back of the chair, inadvertently catching the eye of a man and woman at the next table who sat staring, with their forks still hovering in mid-air.

Chad cleared his throat and lifted two menus from behind the salt and peppershakers. "So, what do you want to eat?" he asked, his voice a bit too loud.

Jumping in her seat, Julia's gaze flew from the staring couple, back to Chad. "I—I'm not sure. What's good here?"

Pretending to glance over the menu, Chad berated himself for bringing Julia to the diner. Why hadn't her taken her to Uniontown where they could have cuddled in the corner

Kirsten Fullmer

booth of a crowded restaurant where no one would notice them? Feeling the back of his neck burn, he glanced over to see Marge's pink tennis shoes on the floor next to the table.

He sighed inwardly and followed the pink uniform up to Marge's face, which clearly but silently said, "I knew it!"

"Well," Marge stated, her tone speculative, a wide grin on her face. "What can I get for you two this fine evening?"

Chad glanced at Julia, noting the misery written across her face, and he flinched. "I'd like a Coke. Julia?"

"Water please," she muttered, not making eye contact with Marge.

Pretending to scribble on her pad, Marge sized up the couple over her reading glasses. "You got it," she finally replied, turning on her heel.

Julia adjusted the salt and peppershakers into a row with the container of sugar packets and the ketchup, then turned her attention back to her menu.

"I like the meatloaf," Chad said, glancing up.

"Hmm," she mumbled, turning the page.

"And the tuna melt."

Julia nodded.

"Sometimes I get the—"

Marge plopped two large red plastic tumblers on the table, and scooted the one full of water toward Julia. The aging waitress then tugged two paper-wrapped straws from her apron, tossed them on the table, and collected her pad and pencil. With one hip cocked and her glasses balanced on the end of her nose, she glanced between Chad and Julia.

Chad watched as Julia's neck turned red, the color flooding up over her chin, then her cheeks. "Give us a minute please," he said, his eyes never leaving Julia, angry at himself for being such a dunce.

Wishing she were invisible, Julia suffered the curious stares of the other diners. Shoving down her discomfort and battling to muster even a dab of confidence, she glanced up at Chad.

He took a long drink of soda, then set down his glass. "Sorry, we should have gone to Uniontown..." he muttered.

Julia straightened in her chair. "No, I'm fine, really." She lifted her glass. "Have you had time to think about the flower—" The tumbler in her hand shifted in her grip, then fell to the table top, the water and ice pouring across the gleaming white table and directly onto Chad's lap.

His chair screeched back as he bound to his feet. Wiping at his pants and shaking his hands, Chad danced backward in an effort to miss the torrent, barely managing not to fall into the lap of the woman seated behind him. When he looked up, all he could see was Julia's stricken expression.

"I'm so sorry," she gasped, then hurried around the table. Plucking a handful of napkins from the dispenser, she frantically wiped at Chad's crotch.

"Julia—" he stuttered, still in shock, his hands and shirt dripping into the growing puddle.

She continued to press the napkin into his jeans, desperate to help.

"Julia!" he said louder, grasping her wrist in his fist.

She stopped, frozen in horror, finally noticing that everyone in the diner sat staring at her hand pressed to Chad's crotch. She stood and her hand dropped from Chad's grip, her face turning so pale he was afraid she would faint.

Snickers passed through the crowd of diners, causing Chad to scowl darkly. "Come on," he growled, grabbing Julia's arm with one hand and her purse with the other.

Julia fumbled for footing as Chad dragged her to the door, the bell overhead dinging loudly as he yanked it open and thrust her out into the night ahead of him. Once they were farther

Kirsten Fullmer

down the sidewalk, out of the light pouring through the diner's front windows, he ground to an abrupt halt.

"Are you okay?" he asked Julia, pressing her back into the wall of the insurance office building and squinting in the dim light to see her face.

She didn't answer, just stood with her head hanging.

Chad gave her a gentle shake. "Julia? Don't you faint on me. Are you okay?"

The panic in his voice forced her chin up, her eyes glimmering. "I'm sorry," she squeaked. "Sometimes I drop things."

Once he was relieved that Julia was okay, blood could finally reach Chad's brain again. He ran his fingers through his hair, then reached down to tentatively pull at his sopping pants.

Julia slumped against the brick wall and a tear slid down her cheek. Glancing up, she could make out Chad's outline. He was so handsome, so fierce, so…soaked. She waited for him to say something…anything.

Finally, she noticed a slight tremor in his profile and he began to shake, then a loud laugh rang out over her head. She thought he was laughing at her and shame flooded her heart. She had no social graces. She was an embarrassment. Bitterly, she wished she had followed through with her plan to hide herself away forever.

With tears drying on her cheeks, she turned to run home, but Chad grabbed her arm, swinging her into his chest. The front of her shirt and skirt were immediately soaked, and she pushed against him.

"Oh Julia," he murmured, hugging her tightly.

She froze, her senses reeling. "Let me go! I want to go home!" she gasped, still trying to escape his grip.

Chad released her enough to look into her face.

Julia could see the humor gleaming in his eyes, glowing in the night. "Why are you so damn happy that I can never show my face in public again?" she sputtered, pushing and swatting at his damp chest.

"What are you talking about?" he asked, sobering. He released her enough to point back at the restaurant. "That in there...Julia, that is the first time in almost two years that people have looked at me without pity."

"Pity?" she gasped in shock. "They...I spilled my cold water in your lap! I'm a klutz! Of course they pitied you!"

He laughed out loud. "Honey, what they saw in there was a beautiful woman with her hands all over my crotch! They didn't care about or think—It finally wasn't about me and—ah hell, come on." He grabbed her arm to lead her down the sidewalk.

Numb from shock and wounded pride, Julia snatched her forgotten purse up from the sidewalk and struggled to keep up. "Where are we going?"

"To my house so I can change," he said, "Then I'm taking you to dinner somewhere that we can eat in peace."

★★★

As they marched through the night toward the delivery office, her shirt quickly drying, Julia began to understand that to Chad, the incident at the diner hadn't been about her clumsiness but about how he felt in public. She had been so consumed by shyness and then horror, she hadn't realized that Chad had his own issues with being around the people of Smithville.

Was it possible that he wasn't upset with her for spilling half of a quart of ice water in his lap? Had he been uncomfortable about everyone looking at *him* before she spilled her water? Had the town's reaction been about Chad and not about her? What had happened to him that caused people to stare? Was it really possible that she offered Chad the opportunity to move beyond his own personal torment, like Tara said?

Kirsten Fullmer

With thoughts still pinging around in Julia's head like a handball tournament, they stopped at the door of the delivery office. Chad arched his back and muttered, struggling to tug his keys from the pocket of his wet jeans.

Finally the door was unlocked and Chad slogged across the office and up the dark narrow steps, Julia behind him. The door at the top of the stairs swung inward and Chad flipped on the light and tossed his keys on an end table covered with change, crumpled receipts, torn ticket stubs, candy wrappers, and other pocket trash.

Julia glanced curiously across the room to the dingy, cluttered kitchen, then over her shoulder to the bathroom door that stood ajar. "Nice place."

Chad snorted, tugged his wallet from his back pocket and dropped it on the end table. "Right."

He stomped across the room and started digging through a laundry basket on the floor. "Sorry the place isn't clean, I wasn't planning on company," he said over his shoulder, tugging on the leg of a pair of jeans. The jeans finally came free from the basket, spilling socks, tee-shirts and boxers onto the linoleum.

He tossed the jeans onto a chair and reached for the button at the top of his jeans. He had three buttons open before Julia managed to make a choking noise.

He paused. "Oh, sorry." Snatching up the jeans from the chair, he slopped past her toward the bathroom, and she heard the door scrape closed.

Picking her way across the messy room, Julia bent to salvage the clothes that had fallen on the floor. The bathroom door scraped open and she turned to see Chad standing in the doorway staring at her as he tucked in the front pockets of his dry jeans.

Looking down, Julia realized his boxers were in his hand. Embarrassed she nearly dropped them, but then she realized he hadn't taken any in the bathroom with him... so he must be going without—unless he was still wearing the wet ones he'd had on—but that was ridiculous.

Chad smiled, knowing exactly where her thoughts were as he snatched his wallet and keys from the end table and tucked them into his pockets. "You ready?"

Julia stuffed the boxers into the basket and scuttled past him, her cheeks burning.

★★★

Two hours later, Julia lifted her coffee mug for a sip, the steamy scent comforting and familiar, as she peeked over the rim of her cup at Chad. He was turned sideways in the other side of the booth, his back leaned against the wall with one leg extended along the seat. He played with his straw, chopping at the ice in his glass as he grinned at her.

"You were hungry..." he said, with a glance at her empty plate.

Julia lowered her cup to the saucer. "It was so good, I couldn't help myself."

He smiled in response, his eyes sparkling in the dim glow of the lamp hanging low over the table.

Julia recognized that look and it spoke of speculation. Hopeful speculation. She shifted in her seat primly, more than a little amazed at her miss-ish discomfort. She'd been married for three years and had dated plenty before that, so why was she antsy?

Chad pushed away from the wall and reached for his wallet. He tucked several bills into the check folder and scooted from the booth. "Let's get out of here, shall we?"

A surge of sexual interest caught Julia by surprise as she collected her purse and scooted along the seat of the booth.

Kirsten Fullmer

She couldn't meet Chad's eye as she stepped past him toward the door.

Even though her memory wasn't great, she knew that the old Julia would have been calm cool and collected, toying with her date, teasing him into a frenzy before she decided if she would appease him. This was all new. Tonight was about Chad, not sex. It was about his fingers wound in her hair, his laugh, his breath on her neck.

Chad opened the passenger door of his truck and Julia climbed inside. As she reached for the seat belt and settled her purse on her lap, she watched him round the front of the truck, tugging the keys from his front pocket. Once again his lack of boxers came to mind, and she took a moment to consider the idea.

When he climbed into the truck and turned to her, he caught a trace of feminine interest, and his eyes glittered in the darkness. He started the truck and punched radio buttons, settling on a crooning country ballad, then backed from the parking spot.

As they sped down the highway toward Smithville, Julia studied the passing shadows as they played across Chad's face and arms. His skin took on a golden glow in the light of the dash.

Never before had she been so fascinated with the way a man's fingers gripped the steering wheel, the way they curled around the hard cool plastic, then lifted, hand over hand as he turned, then settled once again to find a comfortable groove. As if he read her thoughts, one hand loosened and slid along the wheel, his fingers skimming the curved edge in time with the music.

Goosebumps danced along Julia's arms and her scalp tingled. Lost in a sea of wonder and feminine hunger, she didn't notice that they had stopped in front of her house until Chad's hands left the steering wheel to open his door.

Before she could respond, he was at her door, tugging it open to pull her into his arms. His kiss was warm and deep, his grip tender and searching.

When he broke away and pulled back to whisper in her ear, cool air swooshed between them and she felt bereft, as if a long awaited meal had been snatched from a starving person. As they tumbled across the yard, Julia realized what he had whispered in her ear moments before and under the sexual fog, a tiny frisson of excitement and alarm ran down her spine.

Chad waited for her at the door, but she clutched at her purse in a blind stupor, struggling with the zipper. Finally, she managed to pull out the keys and Chad swept them up to unlock the door.

He handed the keys to Julia, turned the handle, and deftly scooped up the whiney little dog who bolted through the opening. "You go ahead, I'll let him do his business," Chad said to Julia over his shoulder as he stepped off the porch and lowered Ringo to the ground.

The living room full of furniture surprised Julia and she smiled as she ran her hand along the back of the sofa. Chad stepped back into the room and closed the door, locking it behind him and smiling as his eyes wandered languidly over Julia.

Taking her hand, he led her to her bedroom, pulled her inside, waited for Ringo to follow, then quietly closed the door and leaned against it.

Julia knelt by Ringo's bed counting squirming kittens, then rose to face Chad. Her knees trembled as she drifted toward him, and she wasn't sure if she were shaking from apprehension or excitement. When she reached him, she lifted a hand to trace his jaw line and his fingers circled around her wrist. His eyes burned into hers, branding a stamp across her heart, the steam rising off the sensation and evaporating the last of her resolve.

Kirsten Fullmer

★★★

Never before had Chad wanted a woman like this. He'd been hot for a woman, maybe even needed a woman, but never had he longed to climb deep into her heart and pull himself inside. Never had he wanted to completely surround himself, body and soul with a woman.

His clothing felt tight and cumbersome as he lifted Julia and placed her on the bed. Standing over her, he marveled at his desire to devour her whole, and then consume her again, over and over, tonight and tomorrow night and every night after that.

Understanding that she was hesitant, Chad tamped down his raging hunger in a concerted effort to think. He knew that he shouldn't approach her like he had other women. She seemed ready and willing, but that wasn't enough with her. He wanted her to feel the same way about him. This wasn't a night of sport, fun, or anything else frivolous. He wanted her to come to him again and again, and he was unsure how to achieve that outcome.

Should he just take her? Stun her, woo her, and engulf her? Or should he tease her, taunt her, and make her tremble with need. Should he speak? Tell her how beautiful she is? Or just show her with his fingers and his mouth?

Julia reached for him and he tumbled to her side and threaded his fingers through her hair. "Julia…" he whispered, nipping kisses along her jaw. "I want you so much." He moved over her, levering his weight on his elbows, and leaned down to taste her, long and deep.

She moaned, her back arching upward to press her body into his heat.

"Oh baby," Chad murmured. "You taste so sweet. I want you tonight and every night. I want you beside me, in my bed, in my life…" His fingers skimmed down her neck and along her collarbone, but to his surprise, she stiffened under him and her eyes popped open.

Shabby Chic After All

His mind told him to hesitate and calm her, sooth her back into the moment, but his body wasn't responding to the message. His fingers couldn't stop their downward journey of discovery and his mouth continued to suckle at Julia's neck. His hand roamed across her chest and about the time his fingertips contacted a taunt nipple, Julia bucked under him, sputtering for him to get off her, her fists flailing on his back.

Finally Julia's wide panicked eyes came into focus, and he rolled off her, dragging air and into his lung as he willed his brain to engage.

She tried to jump off the bed, but he lunged after her to grab her wrist. "Wait Julia, just stop for a minute!" he gasped.

She tugged at his grasp, her other hand trying to peel his fingers away.

"Julia! I'm not going to hurt you!"

His words finally seemed to pierce her frenzy and she stopped thrashing and pulling.

Chad changed his grip from her wrist to her hand, and patted the bed beside him, allowing her to make the choice to sit.

Eyeing him warily, Julia perched cautiously on the end of the bed. As she calmed and her breathing slowed, she appeared to be embarrassed, and wouldn't meet Chad's eye.

This is a new one, he thought, searching through his past experience with women, grappling desperately for an idea of what he should do next.

"I'm sorry," Julia muttered. "You must think I'm crazy."

Chad shook his head. "No, I think you're hot as hell."

Her head rose and her white face came into view in the dim light. "Oh…well, you kinda freaked me out back there…" Her hand waved vaguely toward the center of the bed.

Chad sat up and rubbed his hands over his face. "Look Julia, I'm sorry. I guess I read you wrong. Again."

It was her turn to shake her head. "No, you read me right."

Kirsten Fullmer

His hands dropped to his lap. "So...what happened? I'm confused."

Julia stood and paced by the bed wringing her hands. "I don't think you really know me."

Chad stared at her in shock. "What?"

She perched back on the end of the bed. "You don't know who I was before, and you don't really know much about me now. I'm not like you think."

"What do I think?"

"I was different before I got sick. Really different. You would have hated me."

Chad shook his head. "Well who cares? I don't hate you now."

"It feels weird," she argued. "I feel like a fraud."

Chad leaned across the bed to take her hand. "Julia, I like everything I have seen about you here and now. I want to know all about you. I want you in my life."

"No you don't."

"Yes I do."

Julia stood and began pacing again, her mouth working to form words. Finally she tromped to the end of the bed and bent to open the chest. Reaching inside she pulled out a stack of small notebooks with rubber bands carefully binding each one closed. Returning to the bed, she poured the stack onto Chad.

He lifted one and held it in the air. "What are these?"

"My life," she said flatly.

"I don't get it," he muttered in exasperation. "What are you talking about?"

"Open it."

"Okay..." Chad drawled, pushing the rubber band off one end of a notebook. He opened to the center page and found a date scrawled carelessly across the top of the page, and under it a hastily written list of tasks which included wash dishes, feed Ringo, water plant, eat lunch, medication. The list went on and on, filling the page, and each item had been marked off with a line through it.

"Who wrote this?" he asked, looking up at Julia.

"I did."

He scratched his head. "Were you in a hurry or something?"

She sighed, relieved that even though this was painful, the web of secrets that held her bound was beginning to unravel. "No, that's how I write."

"It is?" Chad asked, then realized he was being rude. "Sorry, I guess I pictured your writing different…"

"See?" she cried, jumping off the bed where she'd perched awkwardly, "I told you I wasn't what you thought."

"Calm down, it's just handwriting…"

"No it's not, don't you see…" She nearly screamed, reaching across the bed to grab a handful of notebooks and shake them at him. "This is my life! *This!*"

"Everybody feeds the dog and eats lunch…" he said, confused.

Julia tossed the books back onto the bed. "Not the lists, the books! Don't you see, I don't function!"

"No I don't see," he answered, anger rising below the frustration. "What am I supposed to see?"

"Chad, listen to me…I have a very limited short-term memory. I honest to God won't remember to eat lunch if I don't write it down and mark it off. I can't make coffee or start a load of laundry without having a system to get through the steps."

He still looked blank.

"I know it doesn't seem like laundry needs a system but believe me, when you have no memory you realize it does! You have to sort the clothes, then put them in the washer and add the soap and start the machine. Never mind remembering you need to go back and put them in the dryer!"

He waited for her to continue, his head beginning to spin.

Kirsten Fullmer

Pacing again, she spoke with her teeth clenched, slashing her hands in the air. "Have you ever stepped into the shower and not known what to do? Needed a drink of water and had no idea where to get one?" She stopped and leaned on the edge of the bed, her eyes bright with tears. "Have you ever had to go look at the front of your house to know your address?"

Chad shook his head. "Are you telling me that those things happen to you?"

"Every day!" she ground out, tossing her hands. She turned from the bed, the swung back around. "Now you know! I'm handicapped, disabled, broken, whatever politically correct word you want to use…"

His ears ringing, Chad scooted to the edge of the bed and dropped his feet over the edge. "Is this because of the encephalitis?" he asked.

The question seemed to deflate the anger and emotion feeding Julia's tirade and she melted onto the floor, her head in her hands.

Chad lowered himself slowly to sit beside her. "Is it, Julia? Tell me about before you got sick."

Sobs wracked Julia's shoulders but she looked up, tears streaming off her chin. "I was smart," she cried. "I graduated at the top of my class, had a fantastic job. I was…I was…" Wrenching tears took over her confession.

Gently Chad scooped her into his lap, rocking her gently as she cried.

"Julia, I'm sorry this happened to you," he murmured, smoothing his hands over her hair.

Her muffled voice continued. "They shaved my head. I was ugly—my own husband didn't want me."

"You could never be ugly," he soothed as his heart broke and fell around him. Clinging to her, Chad wished he could somehow reverse the horror that had befallen such a sweet person. "You didn't deserve this sweetheart," he whispered into her hair.

Julia lurched back, her eyes huge. "But I did! I did deserve it. I was mean and petty and judgmental. I thought I could do anything, have anything…"

Taken aback, Chad paused. "Well…nobody deserves to get sick Julia, I don't care how you were, you didn't get sick because you weren't nice. You can't think like that."

"You don't understand," she sobbed, burying her face back in his chest.

For what seemed like hours, Chad held Julia on his lap, rocking and soothing her, reassuring her that she was okay, to go ahead and cry, and that he didn't care if she had to use a notebook; but in his heart he knew that he could never have a relationship with her. Not until she could believe in her own heart that she was worth loving.

Leaning his head back against the wall to stare at the ceiling, Chad felt absolutely helpless. Holding Julia tight, he willed hope and comfort into her fragile body.

Kirsten Fullmer

15

Julia leaned one hip against the hutch in the kitchen and rubbed the back of her wrist across her forehead as she watched coffee trickle into the pot. The rich steamy smell of the brew carried a hint of normalcy to her swollen and tender heart. Tugging her bathrobe tighter across her chest, she sighed then leaned her elbows on the counter in front of the coffeemaker and dropped her forehead into her palms.

What had she done?

Bared her soul, that's what she'd done.

The last few drips of coffee dribbled into the pot, urging Julia to straighten and pull a delicate china cup from behind the wavy glass doors of the hutch. She knew the cup had been designed for tea, but this was a coffee morning, no question.

Once her cup had been enhanced with a dash of half and half and a liberal helping of sugar, Julia snatched an ornate spoon from the dish drainer on the sink, and stirred her coffee as she wondered to the living room. As she paused in the doorway to speculate on her new furniture, the sound of mewing kittens mingled with her thoughts and a weak smile tilted up one corner of her mouth. Even through her emotional fog, the simple pleasures of her new home filled her heart.

She padded to the sofa and bent to arrange a pile of rose-bud-covered pillows, then dropped down onto the cushions and snuggled her back deeper into the pillows. Sipping from her steaming cup tentatively with a flinch, she gently plopped first one slippered foot, then the other onto the coffee table. Languidly she stretched, inhaling the scent of home and coffee, the night before spinning through her mind in fragments and flashes.

Had she ever cried so much in her entire life? She wasn't sure but she didn't remember crying more than once or twice before she got sick. Then again, she didn't remember ever feeling deeply enough about anything *to* cry. She'd mandated her life like a business and thrown an angry fit when it hadn't gone as planned.

Shifting guiltily on the sofa, Julia pushed away her past. She was here now, and she had created plenty of drama keep herself busy. So much for her plan to hide away and live quietly. That option was long gone.

At some point in the night Chad had tucked her into bed and silently walked away. And she had let him. Neither of them had known what to say. He'd wanted her until she'd lost it and freaked out on him. He must think she was some kind of wacko. She'd been in fine form all right, yelling that she was disabled and tossing notebooks at him, then sobbing for an hour.

A frown fell across her face and the coffee cup lowered to rest on her stomach. Her head tipped back onto the pillows and her gaze roamed across the tin ceiling, searching for hidden clues as to what to do now, but there was nothing in the ancient pattern that gave her any ideas.

Pulling her feet from the coffee table, Julia sat up and leaned forward, placed her cup on the table, then rubbed her hands across her face, her fingertips circling to rub her still swollen eyes.

She remembered bits and pieces of her past, memories of being perky and confident. How could it be that she was even the same person? She felt like Frankenstein's monster, as if she

Kirsten Fullmer

had been completely disassembled and sewn back together haphazardly, with pieces sideways or missing completely, and with some parts not even from her own body. Surely the joints between the awkward parts were obvious, with deep uneven stitches pulled through her skin, leaving gaps and scars that could never possibly heal into one cohesive person.

Giving herself a mental shake to dislodge the horrible image from her mind, she reached for her coffee cup. Swallowing deeply, she felt the hot brew burn her tongue and the roof of her mouth, and she cussed. Finally, she pushed up from the sofa and wandered back to the kitchen to dump the coffee, rinse her cup and set it in the sink. It was time to think about moving forward. If there was one thing she knew, it was that nothing was gained from lingering in the past.

Collecting a fresh notebook, Julia climbed onto her bed to sit cross-legged and chew on the end of her pencil. Finally she balanced the notebook on one knee and scribbled Flower Shop across the top of the page, then under that, Business Plan. Balance sheets, business license, income statements, and cash flow analysis rolled around in her mind in a jumble as she struggled to list and order the things she needed to consider if she were going to open a flower shop.

★★★

Tara's horn tooted in the driveway as Julia reached for her purse and glanced into her room to check the kittens. As she hurried across the living room, she instructed Ringo under her breath. "You be good and don't bother George and the babies, okay? I will only be gone for a few hours."

The little dog whined, his brown eyes liquid and pleading to go along but Julia slipped through the door and locked it. Tara waved and grinned as Julia crossed the yard.

As Julia opened the truck door, Tara dusted at the seat of her work truck. "Sorry, it's a bit of a mess in here."

Julia clicked her seatbelt and shrugged. "No problem."

"So are you ready to create a display counter?" Tara asked, turning to watch traffic as she backed onto the street.

"Ready as I'll ever be I suppose."

Tara snorted. "Try not to sound so thrilled, I'll get a big head."

Julia shook her head. "Sorry, it's not you, I'm just…in a funk today."

"Why what happened?"

"What makes you think something happened?"

Tara's gaze darted from Julia to the highway, concern etched across her face. "Your eyes are red and you look exhausted. Is this not a good day to go to the warehouse?"

Staring out the window, Julia frowned and shook her head. "No, I'm fine."

"—Obviously," Tara replied.

Silence filled the truck as they rattled down the highway.

"Sorry the radio doesn't work," Tara offered, unsure how to reach out to her new friend.

Julia shrugged and waved one hand as if to say no big deal.

Tara stared out the windshield, her frown deepening. As they slowed to pull off the highway, she sighed and tried again. "Come on, I'm a good listener. I heard your date last night got off to a bit of a rough start. Did it get better?"

Julia's head fell back and she stared at the roof of the truck. "Of course everyone would know about that…I'd almost forgotten."

"I heard it was pretty awesome actually, you with your hand all over Chad's—Hey, it happens, okay? Do you really think anybody will judge you harshly for spilling water? That stuff happens to everyone."

"I guess," Julia muttered as she turned to stare back out the window.

Kirsten Fullmer

"Where did you go when you left the diner?"

"Uniontown, well— we went to Chad's place for him to change first."

Tara nodded and laughed. "That's a stylin' bachelor pad, isn't it?"

"Kind of horrifying actually. Why does he live there? Is it lack of money?"

Shaking her head, Tara pulled up behind the warehouse, put the truck in park and turned off the ignition. She bit her bottom lip for a moment as she gripped the wheel and stared out the windshield, and then turned to Julia. "You know, I really don't think so."

"What do you think then? I can see the wheels turning… speak," Julia demanded.

"Well—has he told you anything yet?"

"About himself?" Julia asked. "No, he's been far to busy dealing with my freak-outs."

Tara grinned briefly. "Well I need to hear that story but back to Chad, it's almost like he's been—on hold—since he came back."

Julia shifted in her seat to face Tara. "About all that, what on earth happened to him? He seems to think the whole town feels sorry for him."

Tara grimaced. "Yeah— well, they kind of do."

"What do you mean? Why?"

Tara released her grip on the steering wheel and tossed her hands in the air. "Ah what the hell, it's public knowledge."

Julia waited, unsure what was to come and wary that she wouldn't like what Tara was about to say.

★★★

The afternoon sun beat hot on Julia's back as she squatted in front of the display case, pushing the sander up and down.

Tara had dug the beautiful old oak cabinet out of her stash and they'd dragged it behind the shop, along with the armoire Tara was sanding. The display case was waist high, with a wood top and scrolled wood trim. Glass windows in the front of the case would display vases and other gifts for sale, and a cash register would sit on top.

At least that was the plan. Right now the piece was a filthy mess. Water damage marred one side and deep scratches and stains covered the top counter. Since Tara was working next to her, showing her how to sand and clean the piece, Julia was feeling more secure about her ability to restore the piece.

Tara stood and rubbed her back. "Shall we take five for a water break?" she asked.

Julia nodded and switched off the sander, then followed Tara back to her truck. Accepting the dripping bottle of cold water Tara offered, Julia leaned against the truck, her mind sifting through the story Tara had shared earlier.

Chad must have been absolutely crushed when his best friend had been killed, and to know he'd sent William on the errand that had ended his life must have made the tragedy nearly unbearable. No wonder Chad felt responsible for William's family.

According to Tara, the weather had been bad that day, a Nor'easter blowing hard with near blizzard conditions, when William's delivery truck had spun out of control on a bridge, hit the guardrail, and careened over the edge.

Julia wiped her dripping hand across the back of her neck, shaking her head over the weird twist of fate that she actually remembered seeing footage of the wreck on a morning news show before she got sick. Sadly she hadn't even flinched over the story that morning as she'd contemplated her upcoming meetings and activities.

Kirsten Fullmer

How had she been so cold and self-centered not to realize that people's lives had been shattered? The wreck had made a sensational story, not only because of the utter gore of hurling over a bridge into an icy river in a blizzard but when the truck hit the rail, the back doors had flown open, strewing packages across the highway and down the sides of the narrow ravine. Some parcels had stuck in trees and others had floated down the river.

Julia remembered now that she had paused long enough to wonder if anything she had mailed could have been lost but then she had shrugged it off to get on with her day.

A lump lodged in her throat just thinking about William, Chad, Bobby and Bobby's poor mother. Tara said it had taken almost two days for the weather to clear enough for rescue crews to retrieve William's body from the river. Had Chad and Bobby's family held out hope that William had somehow survived the fall and drifted down river?

Tara tossed her empty water bottle back into the cab of her truck. "You okay?" she asked Julia. "Do you need to stop for a while? We could finish tomorrow…"

Tipping up the bottle to get the last drop of water, Julia sighed and screwed the lid back on, then tossed the bottle into the truck with Tara's. "No, I'm fine, thanks though. I think I've about got the display case sanded. Will you check my work?"

The two women wandered back toward the furniture. Tara smoothed her hand across the bare sanded wood of the top, a gentle smile playing at her lips. "Looks much better, don't you think?" she asked.

Julia nodded.

"Do you want to stain it or paint it?"

Circling the piece with a critical eye, Julia struggled to focus her miserable thoughts back to the task at hand. "Would it be blasphemy to paint it?"

Tara laughed. "Honey, the best thing about shabby chic is that you can do what ever you please with it. And if you don't like it, just sand it down and do it again!"

The tightness in Julia's chest lightened a few notches at Tara's smile and she resolved to put aside her concern for Chad and how his past would affect their new and tentative relationship. At least until she got home and had the time and space to think it all through, that is. She did, however, finally have a grasp on why Chad felt as is everyone looked upon him with sympathy. Undoubtedly they did.

She couldn't even think about Bobby and how she had unintentionally heaped more pain upon his thin shoulders.

★★★

Later that night as she lay in bed, Julia tugged the covers up to her chin and contemplated the shadows playing across the ceiling. The narrow and spiky tree branch shadows of her first few nights had been replaced with shifting patterns of leaves in the breeze.

One of the kittens woke and mewed in the darkness, then hushed as George's purr reverberated through the room. Ringo shifted on the bed and fitted his curled body against Julia's side. The house creaked and shifted, speaking to her of its day and many others long past.

Chad wandered through her thoughts, touching tender places in her heart, and triggering apprehension in her mind. He'd been so gentle with her the night before, holding her as she cried. He hadn't responded to her revelation of memory problems. Had he decided that she was just too messed up to deal with? He already had a plate full of his own troubles.

His laughter on the sidewalk outside the café came to mind. Was she a diversion to his problems? Or maybe she offered him a chance to move past them, like Tara said?

Kirsten Fullmer

Julia frowned. She could barely manage her own baggage – she was in no position to help anyone else. What should she say to Chad now? Things would already have been awkward after her meltdown, and now that she knew about Bobby and William, she'd be even more tongue-tied than usual.

Chad had texted her earlier, asking if he could come over the next evening to talk about deliveries for the flower shop. Knowing that she'd wake up in a few hours and shower and dress with the intent to see him felt different now somehow. She'd already considered what she would wear, what she'd offer him to drink, maybe she'd make a vegetable tray, or a whole dinner? Maybe she'd try perfume again. It had been forever since she'd done much prep-work to meet with a man, and it made her feel fake. Like she was trying too hard.

Was she trying too hard? Chad had liked her in faded jeans and a sweatshirt with no makeup; maybe she should just go with the natural thing. No, absolutely no effort didn't feel right either.

Her sigh melted into the room and drifted to the ceiling. What would she say? Planning for the flower shop was moving along; they could talk business. She'd applied for a license and printed out forms as well as worked on the business plan. She'd even created a business card template. Being able to talk with him wasn't what worried her she realized, it was all the non-verbal communication that concerned her.

The way he'd look at her; his hands moving as he spoke, and his fingers rubbing his jaw. She knew his touch. Hell, just being in the room with him limited the amount of oxygen.

She clamped her eyes closed and wondered what it was about a man that did that to a woman. Was there a hormone they could capture in a test tube that made women get soft and stupid? Her eyes drifted open. She didn't think they'd found it yet, because if they had it would be packaged and sold by the gallon.

Maybe it was her. Maybe she was just needy and not capable of living on her own. Maybe she was scared and had somehow twisted her issues and confused them with feelings for Chad. Did she have feelings for Chad? Where had that come from? If she never saw him again would it really bother her?

Her fingers clenched onto the quilt. She'd resolved never to allow anyone into her life that she couldn't stand to lose. Could she lose Chad and come out the other side able to move on? What did she need him for?

Her eyes darting back and forth with her thoughts, Julia skimmed across all her encounters with Chad; his laughter, his capable attitude, his dealings with Bobby, his tenderness.

With a flash, she realized she'd been married for three years and had not felt as deeply about her husband as she did about Chad. She'd wanted Brad, respected him, sure, but he hadn't... no, it wasn't him, it was *her*. She hadn't been vulnerable enough to feel anything this deeply.

She hadn't even contemplated what it would mean to pour out her heartache and turmoil onto a man and to be held and comforted. And likewise, neither had she considered being open enough to experience a man's personal tumult, let alone want to help. None of that would have appealed to her in the least even if she had considered it.

So what had changed? Why was she so different now? What about the tragedy of her illness had altered her on such an elemental level?

★★★

Winnie waited calmly on Julia's porch and rang the bell a second time as she adjusted the loaf of foil-wrapped banana bread tucked under her arm like a football. Footsteps and rustling behind the door prompted the old lady to purse her fresh lipstick and straighten her back.

Kirsten Fullmer

The lock clicked and the door swung open. Ringo squeezed through the opening and circled Winnie's feet. Glancing up to Julia, Winnie smiled, then hesitated. "Julia, honey, are you feeling okay today?" she inquired, her forehead wrinkled in concern.

Julia smiled lamely and pushed open the screen door. "Morning Winnie, this is a nice surprise, come in."

The old woman shuffled in and placed one hand on Julia's arm, then caught sight of the living room. "Oh my!" Winnie's hand dropped and she turned to gaze into the room, her mouth falling open. "I heard you'd been shopping, but this is…why it's simply lovely!"

Julia grinned, ran her fingers through her bed-fresh curls, and tugged her bathrobe tighter across her chest. "It did turn out pretty, didn't it?"

"Has Tara seen this?" Winnie asked wandering past the window seat, taking in the soft pink cushions, crocheted throw, hand-embroidered pillows, and sheer drapes.

Shaking her head, Julia walked toward the sofa, motioning for Winnie to follow. "Not yet," she answered, allowing herself a moment to admire the way sunbeams played through the blue glass bottles in front of the mirror on the mantle.

Winnie tottered to the sofa and perched delicately on the edge, tucking one ankle under the other. For a long moment she scanned the room, her eyes softening when they settled on the soft curvy chaise in the corner. Finally she turned back to Julia. "This is for you dear," she said, holding out the banana bread.

Julia accepted the gift, momentarily startled. "Thank you but…what did I do to deserve this? It smells heavenly."

Winnie clucked and arranged her purse on her lap. "You are you, that's all." Her head tilted to one side. "Are you feeling under the weather today?"

Shrugging, Julia blushed and tugged again on her robe. "No, just slow to get moving. How about I cut this and make you a cup of tea? Can you stay for a bit?"

"That would be lovely," Winnie replied with a nod.

Julia turned toward the kitchen. "Want to see how the kitchen turned out?" she asked over her shoulder.

"Oh my, yes," Winnie huffed as she hoisted herself from the sofa to follow Julia down the hall. "But first I want to see those kittens."

Nodding, Julia motioned for the old lady to follow her into the bedroom. When Winnie stepped to her side, Julia bent down by Ringo's bed, carefully lifted a sleeping kitten, and stood, offering the kitten to Winnie.

Winnie's wrinkled cheeks trembled as she took the kitten, cupping it gently in her gnarled hands. The kitten woke and mewed loudly.

Julia bent and petted George, reassuring her all was well.

"My, but she is the sweetest little thing, isn't she?" Winnie murmured.

Julia nodded, then reached up to indicate it was time to put the kitten back. Winnie handed the tiny creature to Julia, then stood shaking her head. "No matter how many times I see it, babies are always a miracle, aren't they?" the old lady whispered.

Standing, Julia smiled and quietly placed a hand on Winnie's arm to lead her from the room, then gently closed the door behind them. When they entered the kitchen, Winnie stopped in the doorway with one hand on the jamb, her eyes darting from the butcher block to the hutches, to the sink and finally to the stove. Slowly, with her eyes bright, she moved toward the stove. "Julia, this is…why it's…" She lifted a shaking hand to caress the front edge of the old stove.

"That's Bessy, do you like her?"

Kirsten Fullmer

The old woman's head swiveled up to Julia. "Bessy?" She turned back to the oven and chuckled. "Yes, the name fits her doesn't it?"

Julia opened a drawer in one hutch, pulled out a knife and began slicing the banana bread on the butcher block; watching Winnie the from the corner of her eye. "I thought so, but I've never named an oven before."

Winnie carefully tugged open the oven and bent to peer inside. "We had one of these when I was a little girl. I remember the day my father brought it home for my mother."

Adding water to the teapot, Julia smiled, her head tipped to one side, then stepped up next to Winnie and lit a burner. "What did your mother do when she saw it?" she asked.

"Oh she sniffled and sobbed and made a show of it for my father." Winnie chortled. "But in truth she knew it was coming. She did love that oven though…"

Julia crossed the kitchen and reached for a selection of decorated tea tins. "Is chamomile okay?"

Winnie walked across the room to smooth her gnarled hand across the counter of a hutch. "Sounds wonderful dear."

Reaching into a hutch to take down two delicate china plates, Julia placed a slice of banana bread on each, then got down two matching rosebud cups with delicate, gold-leaf handles.

Winnie touched the edge of one plate. "What lovely china, where did you get it?"

Placing a tea bag into each cup, Julia sighed wistfully. "It was my mother's."

"Where is your mother dear? Has she seen what you've done with this house?"

Julia's mouth tugged into a grim line and she turned away to place the tea tin back on the hutch. "No, she's in a nursing home." She paused, then faced Winnie. "She has Alzheimer's."

Placing twisted fingers around Julia's cold hands, Winnie tilted her head to one side. "I'm so sorry, dear. How bad is it?"

The words were always hard to say because Julia didn't want to admit they were true. "It's bad. She was struggling with early onset before— before I got sick." Julia pulled her hands away and tugged on her robe, pulling it tight across her heart. "I hired a nurse to take care of her."

Winnie nodded. "That was kind of you."

Julia frowned. "No Winnie, it wasn't kind. She didn't live far from me. I could have done more. I was her only child and…" Silence filtered through the room.

After several long seconds Winnie prompted, "And…"

Releasing a heavy sigh, Julia looked up to meet Winnie's gaze. "I paid someone else to be with her because I was too busy. Too busy for my own mother."

"That is a very difficult and complicated disease, Julia, and many family members have a difficult time coping."

Julia leaned one hip against the sink and nodded weakly. "But…when I got better…it was too late. By the time I could travel and go see her, she didn't know who I was." A tear formed and rolled silently down Julia's cheek.

Without waiting for further invitation, Winnie reached out and pulled Julia into a tight embrace. Rocking back and forth she crooned, "Now, now, dear. Life is a hodgepodge of missed opportunities. Happens to the best of us. Don't beat yourself up over illnesses beyond your control."

Julia sniffed and the teapot worked up a whistle. Turning to the stove, she shrugged and reached for the teapot. "I suppose you're right, but I haven't gone to see her since I've been here, it's so hard…but I feel bad…"

"I'll go with you next time," Winnie stated matter-of-factly.

Surprise clear on her face, Julia paused with the teapot in midair. "You will?"

Kirsten Fullmer

Winnie nodded. "Of course I will dear. I'd love to meet your mother."

"But…it's a three-hour drive, and she won't—"

"Shush and pour that tea before the water cools, dear," Winnie said, as she collected the plates of bread and shuffled toward the dining room.

16

Chad paused at the edge of Julia's porch. The tune of *Love Me Do* he'd been whistling disappeared into the breeze as he studied Julia standing in the doorway holding open the screen.

She smiled, her expression speculative as she bobbed her head in greeting. "Chad."

"Julia," he returned as he scooted past her.

As the screen door banged gently shut, Julia asked if he'd like a beer. He nodded and she headed to the kitchen.

Chad wandered to the mantle to examine the various blue bottles in front of the antique mirror, distractedly scratching Ringo between the ears. Glancing from the pillow-covered sofa to the coffee table books sprawled across the low table, he nodded. "She did good in here didn't she, little guy? It looks like her."

Ringo wagged his tail in answer.

Chad looked up and Julia stood in the hallway, a beer in her hand and her worn jeans and sweatshirt appearing soft and somehow seductive. Her feet were bare and her blond curls were mussed. She looked delicious.

"I'd planned to fix some food and have paperwork ready when you got here," she said, handing him the beer, "but Winnie came by this morning and brought banana bread and…"

Chad scoffed. "Hey, her bread stops traffic, no need for explanations."

"Would you like a slice?"

He nodded and they headed toward the kitchen.

"How are the kittens?" he asked.

Julia reached for a plate and smiled. "Amazing and perfect in every way."

Chad nodded and took a long pull from his beer, noticing the way the evening sun made a long orange stripe across the dark floor they'd stained.

"One of them fell off Ringo's bed this morning," Julia said, "I was worried for a minute, but George just picked him up and put him back in the nest."

He nodded again and set down his bottle, watching the grace of Julia's movements as she sliced the bread and placed it on a plate. "Smells great…"

She handed him the dish. "Shall we talk at the dining room table?"

Already taking a bite of the bread, the plate held under his chin, Chad nodded and followed Julia as she scooped up his beer and headed from the kitchen.

As she pulled out a chair, plopped his bottle on the table and sat with one foot curled under her, she smiled privately, happy to see him scarfing up the bread. "I've got the business plan written and cards ready to print. I've requested a business license on line, and lined up a distributor; they can start with orders to be picked up on Mondays, if that works for you."

Chad daubed the last bite of bread across his plate to catch every crumb. "How big will the order be? Does it need to be refrigerated?"

"I'm not sure of all that yet," Julia muttered, rubbing her forehead. "I will know more when I'm ready to order. Is refrigeration a problem?"

He tucked the last bite of bread into his mouth and chewed. Finally he swallowed and pushed back from the table. "No, I have a cooler I can plug into the back of the truck if needed."

She nodded.

With the food gone and the conversation lagging, Chad squirmed in his chair and tipped up the last of his beer. He leaned forward and laced his fingers on the tabletop. "Hey, are you okay?"

Glancing at him through her lashes, Julia could see concern and—something else— etched across his face. "I'm okay, I just didn't sleep very well last night." She shrugged. "It happens sometimes."

He stood and moved around the back of her chair where, much to Julia's surprise, he began massaging her shoulders. His touch was sure and firm, yet tenderness underlay his movements. The conversation earlier with Winnie still reverberated through her mind and heart as his fingers worked magic on the base of her neck.

"Whoa, what is this?" Chad asked, pausing at one point between Julia's shoulder blades. "You're all tied in knots."

"Yeah…" she murmured, her head falling forward as his thumbs massaged the muscles along her spine.

After working at the tender spot for several seconds, Chad's fingers skimmed gently up Julia's neck and into her hair. Tingles and honey flowed through her veins as he massaged her scalp. Concern and trepidation melted from her body and fell to the floor forgotten. Once she was nearly numb with calm, Chad stepped in front of Julia and tugged her up to stand in front of him.

Searching her eyes, he held her firm with a big hand gripping each of her arms. "Julia, I don't care about who you were before or what you did. I didn't know you then. I know you now. Want you now, all of you, whatever is included."

Shabby Chic After All

Julia wasn't sure if currents of electricity passed from his eyes to hers, or if the power he emanated surged through his hands – either way, she couldn't move, couldn't breathe.

"Do you hear me?" he asked, waiting for her to respond.

All she could manage was a bob of her head and a giant swallow.

When Chad's lips came down on hers, perceptions had altered since their last kiss. The graze of his lips spoke of passion and tenderness, acceptance and possession, not just sexual tension.

Julia's world tipped on its axis, but for the first time ever, the sensation was filled with wonder and allure instead of disorientation and fear.

Their kisses built from tender caresses to passionate challenges, their hands roaming and searching across each other's backs. Chad finally pushed back and took Julia's hand to lead her to the bedroom. Floating above the floor, she followed, feeling shy.

Chad pulled Julia into the bedroom and leaned her against the wall by the door. A wicked smile lit his face as he bent to nibble kisses up her neck, his fingers inching up under the bottom of her sweatshirt.

Julia sighed, melting into the wall of the dimly lit room, her fingers in his hair. The sound of Ringo pacing on the wood floor, nails clicking, mixed with kittens mewing and Chad's murmured endearments.

He moved toward the bed and Julia glanced down at the kittens, surprised to see them alone in their bed, George nowhere in sight.

As Chad tugged her onto the unmade bed, her mind spun in an attempt to focus on the kittens instead of Chad's hands caressing her stomach. Lost in sensation, she left the cats to the world and fell headfirst into the sensation of his fingers on her skin. Before she could form another coherent thought, her shirt

Kirsten Fullmer

was slipped over her head and Chad rolled over, pulling her up onto his chest.

She could feel that he was hard and ready under her, and she knew it was time to make a conscious decision. They had to stop now, or not stop at all.

Leaning up to straddle Chad, Julia formed herself against him and reveled in the way their bodies fit together, her knees at his sides and her feet tucked against his hips.

He raised his hips to grind his jeans against hers.

Trying to think, she ran her hands over her face, then up into her hair, scooping it into a pile on top of her head and arching her back. "Wait a minute. Just…"

Realizing she was hesitant but willing, Chad gripped her hips in each hand and rocked her against him. "What's wrong? If you're worried about protection, I brought some."

Her stomach lurched with desire and her brow quirked, unsure if she was flattered or offended, but very sure they needed to talk for a moment. "That's…that's good I guess, but what about after?"

"After?" Chad asked as he paused, his mind unable to focus on anything but the beautiful woman on top of him.

"Yeah, you know, tomorrow, the next day, next week…" Julia pushed, her expression stolid. "What will happen if we do this? I can't just sleep with you—and then…we are supposed to be doing business together."

Chad sighed and released her hips to rub the corners of his eyes. "I hardly think making a delivery run once a week will force either of us into a bad situation."

Biting the inside of her lip, Julia pulled her thoughts away from Chad between her legs, and turned to gaze at the kittens who still mewed and tumbled around the bed, searching blindly for their mother.

"I haven't been with anybody since…" she started, but Chad cut her off.

"Are you afraid you've forgotten how?" he chuckled.

She shook her head. "It's not like that. I can't bend some ways and I don't… I have some muscle control problems, limited movement, and numbness in places. I haven't given much thought to…any of that. I may not be able to…finish it," she ended lamely.

"Really?" he asked in shock. "You haven't even…by yourself?"

Julia blushed deeply, covered her cheeks with her hands and felt the need to run. Once she'd been sophisticated, sexual, and in control. Now she was an insecure, awkward freak.

"Don't freeze up on me Julia," Chad said, his hands back on her hips. "It's good that we can talk like this, tell each other stuff, right?"

She thought for a second then her hands dropped. "I suppose so, I just hate being such a loser."

Chad grinned. "Honey, the only thing you are about to lose is your clothes, and then your mind." His fingers toyed with the button of her jeans just as one of the kittens toppled from Ringo's bed and onto the floor.

Julia glanced over and when she saw the kitten, she jumped at the chance to avoid the situation and yanked herself from Chad's grasp to leap from the bed. Gently scooping up the blind kitten, Julia lifted it to her cheek to feel its downy fur against her face. The kitten swatted at her with its tiny paws and cried for its mother.

Chad sat up and leaned over the edge of the bed for a look. "Julia, they'll be okay."

She sighed and cuddled the kitten to her chest. The baby clawed at her skin, his little claws catching on the lace of her bra. "I know, but…" She held up the kitten. "Isn't he the cutest thing?"

Kirsten Fullmer

"Are you sure it's a he?" Chad grumbled, his plans falling to ruin.

Lifting the kitten higher, Julia shot Chad a dirty look then looked at the kitten's rear. "His tail is in the way."

"Julia…" Chad disparaged, his male ego battered over her rejection, no matter the reason.

Glancing up at him, Julia realized she was avoiding the situation. "Just let me see if George is in her litter box or eating, and I'll be right back. Okay?"

★★★

A silent moment hung heavily in the air. Even though he was rattled and ready for sex, Chad recognized that Julia's hesitation had far more to do with her insecurities than it did the kittens. He knew that some people could push through emotional trauma once they were "in the mood" but others had to feel comfortable, in order to relax and get into the moment.

Julia was important to him and even though he was ready and willing to show her how to relax, and confident that he could, he wanted her to come to him willingly, as excited as he was. Determined not to pressure her, but disappointed in the extreme, he tamped down his frustration and rolled over to sit on the edge of the bed. "I'll come with you."

The smile Julia beamed on him lit the dark room.

Placing the kitten carefully back onto the dog bed, Julia padded down the hall toward the kitchen with Chad behind her, his hands around her hips as they walked in step. She glanced to George's food and water dish, no kitty, then headed for the mudroom. No George was in the litter box.

Julia twisted one of her curls. "George has never left the kittens before."

Desperate to hurry the cat hunt along, Chad tromped past Julia and into the nearly dark mudroom. He lifted coats on hooks and looked behind the door, even moved the mop bucket. Turning, he noticed that the back door was open and the screen was closed but not latched. Irritated that the cat may have gone outside, he felt his excitement begin to shrink.

He jerked open the screen door and glanced toward the garage, then behind the house. A glimpse of black and white fluffy fur disappeared around the corner of the house and into the shadows.

"Oh no you don't, George," he muttered under his breath as he hurried behind the house. Rounding the corner, he could see the cat in the deep shadows near a bush, her black and white fur barely discernable. "Your little walk-about is over, missy," he declared as he sprang forward, catching the surprised cat around the hips.

Standing and pulling the cat closer so she couldn't escape, he called to Julia. "I've got her…" but as the words left his mouth, the animal in his arms scratched and scrambled, emanating an odd noise as it struggled. A strange warm sensation hit Chad's face and arms about the time he realized that he wasn't holding a cat.

Tossing the frightened animal away from him, Chad fell against the side of the house, his hands rubbing at his face and eyes. A pungent, sickening odor rose around him, burning his senses. Blindly, he staggered back toward the corner of the house, swearing and cussing. He fell to his knees in front of the garage, misery and anger mixing with disgust, defeat, and embarrassment.

Julia hurried up beside him wearing a hastily tossed-on jacket from the mudroom. "Chad, did you get…Oh my Gawd!" Her hand flew up to pinch her nose. "What on earth?"

With his hands on his knees, his head hanging, Chad stopped cussing, to cough over and over.

Kirsten Fullmer

Julia glanced at the corner of the house and back to Chad. "What did you do?" she cried, her voice clogged and nasal. "Grab a skunk?"

★★★

In the ten minutes it took for Justin and Tara to lurch to a stop in the driveway, Julia had managed to guide Chad to the front of the house and spray him down with the garden hose. As he stood dripping, his eyes watering, Chad understood how a mating dog must feel when the hose is turned on him. Humiliated, he hunched in his skin, not looking up, as his friends jumped from Justin's truck and hurried across the lawn.

"You look like hell," Justin laughed.

"Pee-ew-ee," Tara offered, pinching her nose.

Irritated and angry, Chad's eyes flashed in the porch light. "Thanks guys. Did you drive down here to comment or help?"

Julia giggled. "He's a mess isn't he?"

"So what's the plan?" Justin asked, tucking his hands in his front pockets. "I've never been sprayed by a skunk. What do you country folk do?"

Tara cocked a hip, her head swiveling toward him. "Well we hillbillies are *usually* smart enough to stay away from skunks!" she retorted, then turned back to Chad. "I have no idea."

"Hang on," Julia said, hurrying across the porch and through the front door. Ringo trotted out past her toward Chad, but ground to a halt two feet away and backed up. Rolling in the grass, the little dog pawed at his nose and whined.

"Does it hurt?" Justin asked.

Flashing him a nasty glare, Chad flung water from his hands. "My eyes burn a little but the water helped."

"You're just painful to the rest of us," Tara laughed.

"Either help me or go away," Chad scowled.

Julia returned carrying her computer tablet. "Good news!"

Shabby Chic After All

Chad's expression showed hope. "You found a cure?"

"Oh…no, but George is back in her bed."

"Oh course she is," Chad muttered.

Julia continued. "I Googled it and there is a mix we can make from hydrogen peroxide and soda that should help you."

"What about tomato juice?" Justin asked. "I heard that you should take a bath in V8."

"That's old school," Tara scoffed. "Becky's dog got sprayed once and she washed him in tomato juice. He just smelled like skunk spaghetti afterward."

"Oh that's a lovely thought," Justin laughed.

"Excuse me?" Chad interrupted. "Can we get back on topic here?"

"I have these ingredients," Julia said, scrolling on her tablet. "But anything you touch will smell. Lucky for you I haven't decorated my bathroom yet."

Chad ran his hands across his head, flinging water, causing Justin and Tara to scuttle out of the way. "Don't worry about it, I'll just go home."

"Don't be ridiculous," Tara said. "Your truck will smell like skunk if you do that."

Grinding his teeth in frustration, still lamenting his lost plans with Julia, Justin scowled across the yard. "Fine. Whatever."

"Tell you what," Julia said, "Tara and I will be in the kitchen stirring this up," she held up the tablet, "And Justin, you help him strip and get up to the bathroom, touching as little as possible."

"Oh there will be no touching if he's stripping…" Justin scoffed.

"Knock it off will you?" Chad huffed.

Julia and Tara headed across the porch, Ringo at their feet, leaving the men to sort out Chad's problems. As Julia passed through the door, she clicked off the porch light.

"This is not what I had planned for tonight," Chad grumbled as he tugged the smelly dripping shirt over his head. "Where should I put this?"

"What did you have planned?" Justin asked, avoiding the dripping shirt, interest ripe in his question.

Chad rubbed a stinking hand across his face, his nose wrinkling. "Nothing. Forget it. What am I going to do with these clothes?"

★★★

Bobby clomped into the office the next morning wearing a scowl, as he had for the past week. When the door closed behind him, his nostrils flared. "Did a skunk get in here?"

Chad didn't look up from the computer where he was toying with adding Julia's deliveries to the schedule.

Dropping his keys on the desk, Bobby sniffed again. "Seriously, it smells in here."

Irritated, Chad rolled the office chair back from his desk and glared at Bobby. "Oh, so now you'll talk to me."

Bobby shrugged. "I'm just sayin' it smells, that's all."

"Look, we really need to talk," Chad stated. "Sit down."

With a curled lip, Bobby pointed toward the door. "Could you talk with me up-wind?"

"No."

Bobby sighed and pulled up a chair across the desk. "Okay, what."

"I'm your boss, don't 'what' me."

Leaning back in his chair, Bobby stared up at the ceiling then made eye contact. "So this is about work then."

"Bobby stop it. You know what this is about. Julia and I had a thing going since she pulled into town. This whole thing is a misunderstanding. She's not...We haven't…"

Sniffing and shifting in his chair, Bobby made it clear he didn't believe a word Chad said.

Chad shoved to his feet and paced, then turned back to face Bobby. "It's different with Julia."

"Different how?" Bobby demanded.

"I…I feel different about her," Chad started.

Bobby's head swiveled up to Chad, his eyes large behind his smudged lenses, for the first time in weeks, responding as a friend instead of an enemy. "You mean like…like…"

Chad turned away and ran his hand across the top of his head. "I don't know, I only know I want to be with her. For a long, long time."

Shifting to sit up in his chair, Bobby cleared his throat. "So you're saying this is serious. Between you two I mean."

Staring out the window, Chad was at a loss. Finally he shrugged. "Yeah, I guess it is," he confessed. "I suppose you could hate me forever but I'd really rather you didn't."

Bobby considered Chad's words, his eyes riveted to the back of Chad's desk, his hands limp in his lap. He looked up. "You're my best friend, man, more like a brother, and you…" He sighed. "How does Miss Julia feel about this?"

Chad exhaled. "She feels really bad that you are hurt."

"Not that, I mean how does she feel about you?" Bobby corrected.

"Oh," Chad returned to his chair and rolled forward, adjusting it under his desk. "Uh, she seems…I mean…she feels the same way."

Bobby's face scrunched. "You don't sound very sure."

Chad stared at the computer screen. Finally his gaze lifted to meet Bobby's. "She's scared."

Bobby jumped from his chair so fast it tipped over. "Scared!" he sputtered. "What did you do to her?"

Kirsten Fullmer

Chad rubbed his hands across his face. "It's not like that, Bobby. She's not scared of me."

Bobby leaned over the desk. "I don't get it then, what is she scared of?" he asked, his hands flinging into the air.

Once again at a loss, Chad leaned back in his chair. He laced his fingers across his stomach, pondering exactly what Julia was afraid of.

Pulling his chair upright, Bobby sat down, waiting.

"I guess she's afraid she'll be left alone again."

"What do you mean?"

Chad leaned forward. "Did you know she was married?"

Bobby jerked back. "No."

"Well, she was and she got very sick and her bastard husband divorced her and walked away."

"But that's…" Bobby's mouth hung slack. "That's just mean…and…"

Chad nodded. "I know." He rubbed his fingers along his jaw. "She came here to hide away from people so she wouldn't be hurt again."

"And *you're* not going to hurt her?" Bobby asked, sarcasm in his voice, his jaw thrust out and his eyes glimmering.

Shrugging, Chad leaned back into his chair. "I know I've been…but I'm gonna do my best, Bobby, I swear to God." Saying the words out loud made them real, causing a swell in Chad's chest that terrified him more than a little. "But I still don't know if she'll give us a chance," he continued. "I know she wants to, deep down, and so do I."

Bobby slumped staring at the floor, his hands twisting in his lap as a long moment slipped past with only the sound of occasional traffic outside the door. Chad waited, wondering which way the conversation was going to go.

Finally Bobby looked up, his eyes bright as he pushed up his glasses and his back ramrod straight. "Well, I'm not gonna let nobody hurt her again. You hear me?"

Chad nodded solemnly.

Standing, Bobby scooted his chair back against the wall. "I'm watching you…" he promised Chad.

"Understood."

Kirsten Fullmer

17

The next afternoon, Chad's box truck rumbled down the road toward Julia's house. Bobby sat with one boot propped on the dash as he sang loud and off-key with the truck stereo, utterly ruining the song, *Day Tripper*.

Chad grimaced at the noise and braced himself to see Julia, knowing that once she was near him, his blood would surge and his brain would lurch into low gear. She needed time, and that was one thing he had, so he'd give her space to figure things out. He just hoped she wouldn't need too much time because he was a patient man but he was no saint.

Thankfully, Bobby's strained singing came to a halt as they pulled up to Julia's house. Jumping from the cab, Chad and Bobby walked around to the back of the truck and Chad tugged open the rolling door to reveal the display counter Julia and Tara had refinished. From the look of the crackled paint and worn edges, the softly glowing white case looked as if it had just been pulled from a high-dollar, turn-of-the-century store.

As the men lugged the piece from the back of the truck and across the lawn, Julia and Tara appeared on the porch, each cradling a kitten to her chest.

"This is so exciting!" Tara gushed, running her fingers along the kitten's downy back.

Julia lifted her kitten away from her shirt, releasing its tiny claws from the fabric with her other hand, and turning toward the house. "I better put this little guy back and help…"

Tenderly placing the kitten back into Ringo's bed, Julia murmured to George, then snuck out quietly and closed her bedroom to keep the little monsters from escaping and getting underfoot. Since their eyes had opened, the kittens were determined to explore.

Chad instructed Bobby to ease the display case onto the porch and then he set down his end and leaned back with a huff. With one hand resting on the case he gazed at Julia. "Hey beautiful. Hey Tara…" he said in greeting, his eyes roaming over Julia like silk lingerie. "Where do you ladies want us to put this?"

Julia bit her bottom lip and glanced toward the living room. "I was thinking I could move the living room furniture around and make the space more of a parlor. I could ring up purchases there and set up a side table with tea and snacks. You know, like a tea room, where ladies can sit and chat." Her gaze darted between Tara and Justin for input.

Tara grinned. "The room would be perfect to relax in and I know every woman in town is dying to see it. I've been telling them all how romantic it is."

"Sounds like something that would attract women," Chad offered. "I guess the men who come to the shop can just stand outside under a tree…"

The girls laughed.

"Why would the men stand outside…?" Bobby asked, pushing up his glasses.

"Just grab your end there, bud," Chad chuckled as he bent to lift the display case.

It took Julia and Tara thirty minutes to decide where everything should go, both instructing the men to move the furniture and display case around the room. But finally they felt that traffic

Kirsten Fullmer

would be better between the door and the seating, as well as grant access to the tea table, if the display case were placed just inside the door by the window seat, where customers could easily check out.

Chad backed away, wiping his brow with the back of his wrist, and Bobby placed his hands on his knees, breathing heavily, his glasses nearly slipping off the end of his nose.

Tara tipped her head to one side, still cuddling the kitten. "This room looks absolutely perfect," she stated matter-of-factly.

Julia nodded in agreement. "It turned out lovely." She turned to Tara. "Thank you so much for helping me and showing me how to refinish the case."

Shrugging, Tara disengaged the kitten from the front of her shirt and smiled. "It's been fun."

"I brought the surprise," Chad said to Tara as he removed his gloves and tucked them into his back pocket.

Nearly jumping up and down, Tara hurried to return the kitten to the bedroom, then practically pushed Julia out the front door. "Come see what I found for you!"

Tara danced around Julia as they all walked out to the truck. "I couldn't believe it when I saw it, I had to get it for you," she chattered excitedly while Ringo ran circles around them, barking cheerfully.

At the back of the truck, Julia peered into the dark interior. "Lumber?" she asked in confusion.

Tara jerked her gaze from Julia's face to the back of the truck. "No, silly, not that, over there." She pointed at the other side of the truck to a lump covered in a tarp.

Bobby jumped up into the truck and carefully lifted the tarp to reveal a large, black, antique cash register, with gold-gilded number keys and a sparkling glass window at the top to display totals.

Julia gasped, her hands covering her cheeks. "Oh Tara!"

Without thinking, Julia placed one knee on the bumper and scrambled up into the truck to lovingly caress the cash register. When she turned back toward Tara and Chad, her eyes were bright with tears. "You shouldn't have, you've already done so much…" She gulped, swallowing hard.

Tara shrugged and smiled, her hands clasped in front of her chest. Chad offered a hand to help Julia down, then leapt up into the truck to help Bobby lift the cash register. Several seconds of terse instructions from Chad ensued as the men maneuvered the antique machine from the back of the truck. Then they headed toward the porch, each carrying one side.

With stars in her eyes, Julia held open the screen door for the guys, then stepped back to watch as they placed the cash register on the end of the display case.

The intimacy and emotion of the moment nearly overwhelmed Julia, and she dropped to sit on the stairs and soak up the joy radiating through her.

"That's not all," Chad said with a grin.

Julia's head swiveled to him. "What?"

Chad pulled his work gloves on. "That lumber you saw? That is a surprise from me and Bobby."

Julia stood. "I don't understand…"

"That's right, Miss Julia," Bobby babbled excitedly. "We have a surprise for you too. A flower shop gift!"

Tugging a folded paper from his pocket, Chad smoothed it open and handed it to Julia. "What do you think of this?"

Scrutinizing the detailed sketch on the paper, Julia's eyebrows flew up. "This is brilliant!" Her surprised gaze flitted between Bobby and Chad. "Who designed this?"

Chad shrugged. "I've been thinking about it for a while…"

"I suggested we use two by fours…" Bobby assured her, pushing his glasses up.

"Let's see," Tara said, looking over Julia's shoulder.

Kirsten Fullmer

Julia placed the drawing on the display case and moved aside so all of them could see.

Chad pointed to the drawing. "It's a frame to hold eight, five-gallon buckets of cut flowers, and thanks to Bobby's idea," he elbowed Bobby who grinned and tugged on his belt buckle, "it's made of two by fours."

Tara leaned in for a better look. "Look Julia, the back row is taller than the front, and they're sloped to display the flowers. You will be able to lift the buckets in and out each day so you can bring the flowers in and place the whole bucket in the cooler at night." Her gaze lifted. "Very nice Chad."

Shrugging with pleasure and embarrassment, Chad held Julia's gaze. "It's my pleasure." Then tearing his attention away from Julia and to Tara, "We have enough lumber to make two, and if we get moving we can have them done today."

"You guys are all amazing," Julia whispered, her voice choked with emotion.

"Well let's get going then," Bobby prompted, brushing his hands together.

Tara and Julia chatted happily about details for opening day of the flower shop as Bobby and Chad constructed the display stands in the front yard.

At one point, Bobby picked up a board and turned, slamming it into the back of Chad's head, Three Stooges' style but the rest of the afternoon wound down quickly and happily as the friends planned for the shop.

★★★

The next few days flew past as Julia prepared for the shop. Tara had helped paint the stands Chad built but with her wedding only a week away, the spa still under construction, and guests filling the inn, she had very little time to be involved further.

Shabby Chic After All

Winnie came and brought Becky, when Becky's schedule at the boutique would allow, and together they were at Julia's disposal to help with set-up.

To Julia's surprise and pleasure, local women began to show up at her door, a few at a time, each carrying handmade items. One brought a small basket of fragrant soaps, one came with homemade jewelry on an antique stand, one with tiny jars of homemade jelly, and one with a stack of brightly colored, vintage-style aprons she'd sewn. All the women offered their goods for sale, explaining that Winnie had told them about the shop. Becky set up a spreadsheet on the tablet to help Julia coordinate the ladies and their goods.

One woman came by with a box of vintage-style, handmade greeting cards. She knocked on the door, biting one side of her lip. Becky turned from setting up the tea table to smile toward the open screen door.

"Hi, come on in," she encouraged over her shoulder. "Look around and make yourself at home. I'll grab Julia." She smoothed her hands down her hips as she bustled toward the kitchen. The girl perched on the pink window-seat cushion, her eyes darting around the room.

"Julia," Becky huffed, twisting a necklace around her finger nervously. "You have a guest…"

Looking up from the cutting block where she was making sandwiches, Julia smiled. "Okay, who is it?"

Jerking her head toward the living room twice, her expression a little frantic, Becky didn't reply, just motioned for Julia to follow her.

Curious, Julia grabbed up the dishtowel and wiped her hands as she headed toward the front of the house.

Becky hurried toward the front door. "I'm just gonna grab that—thing—from the car…" she stuttered before escaping onto the porch, tossing a nervous glance over her shoulder.

Kirsten Fullmer

Julia scowled in confusion, then shrugged, turned to the woman, and smiled shyly. "Can I help you?" she asked, admiring the woman's long, glossy red hair.

The twenty-something girl stood and stepped hesitantly forward. "I brought cards for your shop—but I don't know if you'll want them."

A little taken back by the woman's demeanor, Julia smiled with what she hoped was a reassuring expression. "Let's take a look, shall we?" She motioned toward the display case.

The girl stepped to the counter and cautiously spread out her cards for Julia to inspect, her gaze darting back and forth between the cards and Julia.

"These are wonderful," Julia whispered in awe as she lifted an artfully created card with a bird motif and ribbon. "I hear it's fun to make these, but I don't think I could ever make something like this…"

The woman smiled weakly, shrugged one shoulder and twisted her hands in front of her, her long red nails clicking. "Oh I'm sure you could."

Hoping the girl would relax, Julia smiled and extended her hand. "I don't think we've met, I'm Julia."

The woman bobbed her head and placed her cool palm in Julia's for a handshake. "I'm Gloria."

Shock jolted through Julia as she stared into the girl's deep-green eyes and understanding and maybe even a challenge flashed in her expression.

A pink blush spread up Gloria's neck and under the sprinkle of freckles on her cheeks as she withdrew her hand. "It's nice to finally meet you. Well, I'll be going now," she announced, adjusting her purse strap on her shoulder. "Good luck with the shop."

Julia nodded, unable to find her voice until Gloria was nearly out the door. "Come again, and bring more cards," she called.

Gloria just lifted a hand in farewell and ducked out the front door.

Moments later, Becky creaked open the screen and poked her head around the doorjamb to gaze at Julia. "You okay?" she questioned, her eyes large.

Julia snorted and tucked the box of cards in the display case. "Yeah, no thanks to you." She straightened and plopped one hand on her hip. "I can't believe you jumped ship at the first sign of pirates."

Adjusting her necklaces, Becky laughed. "I figured you didn't need my help but I did stand on the porch and listen…" She grinned, her eyes twinkling.

"Oh, and I appreciate that…" Julia laughed, reclaiming the dishtowel and turning toward the kitchen.

"No problem…Captain," Becky chuckled, returning to the tea table.

★★★

By the end of the week, the display case was filled with one-of-a-kind, handmade items and the porch was brimming with flowers and houseplants, in colorful, cast-off pots of all kinds, rusted buckets, jars, and crocks, and other various vintage containers. Chad's bucket-stands stood in the yard under the shade tree, ready for buckets of flowers.

Becky tacked a frame containing the shop's business license to the wall over the cash register and brushed her hands down her flowered caftan, happy that Tara and Winnie's connections at the courthouse had pushed through the license without a hitch.

Tugging a pen from her lop-sided bun, she marked the license off her checklist, then tucked the clipboard under her arm.

She sauntered to the kitchen humming a tune, then paused in the doorway and sighed happily. "Oh Julia, this room is just like I dreamed it would be."

Kirsten Fullmer

Julia turned from arranging decorated tea tins on an antique wood tray and smiled. "I love it. I'm so glad you showed me that picture in the magazine."

"When did you get the fridge?" Becky asked. "It wasn't here last time."

Lifting the tray and heading for the living room, Julia laughed. Justin saw it at a yard sale for thirty dollars and picked it up for me. Don't you love the pump handle?"

Becky nodded. "It was the final piece to complete the room. It's perfect."

Julia laughed as she passed Becky. "Oh don't worry, I'll be collecting stuff for a while yet," she said with a wink.

"It gets in your blood, doesn't it?" Becky agreed as they moved down the hall.

Julia placed the tea tray on a side table where a hot water dispenser stood empty but ready. Stepping back to gaze around the room, she sighed. The place looked like a quaint boutique. Never had she dreamed it possible.

Becky waited at the front door and both women stepped onto the porch where Winnie rested on a wicker chair with a kitten on her lap. "This little gal is purring like a motor boat," the old lady crooned.

Julia and Becky dropped exhausted into wicker chairs, and Julia ran her hand through her curls and sighed. "Thank you so much ladies. I could never have pulled this off without you."

Becky laughed. "We would never have been able to stay away."

Crickets chirped as the day wound down, the sky glowing pink and gold.

"Chad will be delivering the first batch of cut flowers early in the morning," Julia said, rubbing one hand across her forehead. "I'm going to practice with them; see if I'm any good. You ladies are welcome to come by and offer your opinions."

"Oh nice!" Becky replied.

Winnie nodded and continued to pet the kitten. "I'd love to."

"Fergus is on stand-by with more house plants and garden flowers if needed," Julia said, mostly to reassure herself. "I think we're almost ready."

Becky sighed contentedly, and Winnie nodded again, her knobby fingers gently smoothing down the sleeping kitten. Quiet moments passed, filled with bird song and a gentle breeze.

"I don't suppose you'd consider parting with this little gem," the old woman asked Julia hopefully. "It's been pretty quiet around the house since Tara moved up to the inn."

Pain flooded Julia's heart. She had known on some level that five cats would be a bit much, but she hadn't allowed herself to think about letting any of the kittens go. Losing those she loved was still not something she could deal with. Willing her heart-rate to slow, she watched Winnie snuggle with the kitten. Undoubtedly, the little thing would be adored and pampered.

Slowly, her fear of loss ebbed into a faint glow of pleasure at the thought of Winnie spending her evenings with the kitten curled on her lap.

"Well," she started, her voice cracking, "She's still too young....but, I haven't named her yet..."

Becky absently arranged the multiple necklaces on her chest. "What did you name the others?"

Julia smiled shyly. "The tiger striped one is John and the black one is—"

Becky's hand flew up. "Let me guess, Paul?"

Winnie laughed as Julia nodded. "How did you know?"

Lifting the kitten to her cheek, Winnie chuckled. "You do know that Paul is a girl, right?"

Julia laughed out loud. "Perfect."

★★★

Kirsten Fullmer

Julia lifted a hand in farewell to Winnie and Becky as they backed from the driveway. As she turned back to the living room, Ringo trotted up to stand beside her. Julia's eyes roamed through the room and the little dog sat on her foot, evidently a little insecure from all the hustle and bustle.

She looked down at him and smiled. Bending to scoop him into her arms, Julia buried her face in his neck fur. "Sorry I've been so busy, little man," she crooned. Holding him up to gaze into his eyes, she tilted her head. "You doing okay with all this?"

Ringo panted and smiled, his tongue lolling. Julia laughed, tucked him under her arm and wandered toward the kitchen.

George lay on the kitchen floor, watching her kittens scamper and chase dust motes. Julia let Ringo down and leaned on her elbows across the butcher-block island to watch.

Things were changing – she was changing.

The kittens tumbled and tussled and she smiled. Turning to wander to her bedroom door, she stopped to stare across the room and thought of Chad. He'd called a few times, mostly just to say hi and see how she was getting along. She'd been busy, she acknowledged but she kind of missed having him pop in. Her brow rose in surprise and a slow grin spread across her face. That sneaky man was giving her the time to miss him.

★★★

The next day dawned bright with birdsong waking Julia. As she sat up and stretched, welcoming Ringo onto her lap, a gentle smile spread across her face. Normally new and unknown situations left her feeling awkward and tense but today was all about her flowers and friends. She could do this.

Hurrying through her bath and getting dressed, Julia kept an ear open for Chad's truck, but she had all the buckets lined up on the porch and half filled with cool water before he arrived.

Nearly dancing in place, she watched Chad and Bobby carry the coolers of flowers up the walk.

Chad put the first cooler down and laughed. "Could you look any happier?"

"I don't think so!" Julia exclaimed as she bent to remove the lid. "Oh Chad, look at these!" Carefully she lifted an elegant bunch of red tulips from the cooler and held them to her face to inhale the smell. "Aren't they beautiful?"

He grinned and motioned to Bobby to grab more coolers. "You sure are."

Julia blushed, her eyes shining.

When the flowers were unloaded, Chad tugged off his gloves and stood beside Julia, watching her work magic with the flowers. Julia sensed his mood shift and warmth ran down her spine like warm water. She glanced up and he shuffled his feet. "I'm gonna get out of your way now," he murmured. "You all set?"

Julia waved at Bobby as he climbed in the truck. "I think so," she answered, gazing around her at the coolers and flowers as if she were a child in a toy store. Finally she smiled up at Chad and he grinned back, lost for a moment before he shook himself and said good luck, then sauntered down the walk toward his truck.

★★★

Julia was still unpacking bundles of long-stem roses, daisies, carnations, and freesias when Winnie arrived.

"Thanks for coming," Julia called over her shoulder as she arranged purple snapdragons in a bucket. "I'm not sure how I'm going to figure all this out."

"No problem dear," Winnie commented. "Oh my lands! Just look at all this!"

Julia nodded, stepping back to take in the buckets of blooms displayed in the racks Chad had made, a rainbow of color and

Kirsten Fullmer

scent spilling from each. Her breath caught in her throat as Winnie's arm clamped around her shoulders.

"It's like a dream…" Julia whispered.

★★★

The day flew by with Julia and Winnie bustling around the house talking nonstop about complementary colors, flower arrangements, and packaging.

Julia's favorite part of the day was combining selections of cut flowers, then laying them on colorful paper and wrapping them with a big lacey ribbon. By the end of the day she felt like a pro.

Becky came by in the afternoon and all three women enjoying themselves immensely as they had a sit down session around the dining table to discuss the vases and planters Becky wanted to bring over from the boutique.

Bobby's mother arrived, ending the meeting, her chest heaving and eyes bright in her red face. "You certainly know how to get people talking," she huffed at Julia, her darting gaze missing nothing. "At least you finally got something for a body to sit on!"

Julia smiled and nodded, unsure if the woman was referring to people talking about her or the shop.

The large woman inspected the kittens one by one, and then spent almost an hour carefully scrutinizing each and every item that would be up for sale by the locals before she settled into a chair on the porch with a cup of tea.

Ringo spent the day trotting through the house sniffing around guest's ankles, and scurrying out of the way as the women tromped through the house talking and laughing.

As evening threatened, Julia tugged on the hose where she stood watering the flowers along the border of the yard. She was chatting with an inn guest who'd stopped by to ask about mums, when she noticed Fergus standing in the corner of the yard, his apron stiff with dried mud and his boots still lace-less.

Excusing herself, Julia hurried to his side. "Hi Fergus," she said, giving him a tight hug, "I'm so glad you came by, would you like some iced tea?"

The old man shook his head, his crow eyes glittering. "Nah, I just wanted to see how things were coming along."

Looking back toward the groupings of flowers all along the yard and porch, Julia shook her head. "It's surreal isn't it?"

"Oh, not to me, young lady." The old man beamed, gaps in his teeth showing. "I always knowed you was special."

Unable to stop herself, Julia reached for Fergus and hugged him hard with both arms, leaving a tear mark on one of his wrinkled cheeks. "You were my first friend here, you know," she told him as she daubed at his face.

The old man nodded, his own eyes overflowing. He sniffed and rubbed the back of his hand under his nose. "Eh, weren't nothing. You're easy to like."

★★★

The next afternoon, Winnie rested on the porch with her soon-to-be kitten on her lap and Ringo at her feet, as Becky stood in the kitchen with Julia discussing teacups; which patterns and styles should they use for the shop, how many would they need...

"I have a fabulous tea company that delivers tea right to the boutique," Becky said, shifting her necklaces to one and side and pulling her cell phone from her ample bra. "I'll write down their contact info for you."

Nodding and trying to hide her mixture of horror and amusement over Becky's phone holster, Julia grinned. "I'll also need lemons, and tea spoons, and a million other little things…" Her thoughts drifted off into the room as she glanced around her for her notebook.

Kirsten Fullmer

Becky looked up from her phone. "What did you decide about flower refrigerators?"

Motioning for Becky to follow her, Julia headed for the living room. "I found two good ones online, they'll be delivered next week." She frowned and thumbed through her notebook to scribble on a page as she walked. "I should have Tara's appliance guy check them over."

"Good idea…" Becky agreed.

"I still have a million paperwork issues to sort out," Julia worried, biting her lower lip. "I'll have invoices for the flowers and delivery costs, taxes, accounting…"

Becky pointed to her notebook. "You just write them all down and I'll help you," she reassured.

Julia smiled weakly and nodded. Becky patted her on the shoulder as they stepped through the front door and onto the porch.

Chad's truck rolled to a stop in the driveway. A happy thrill raced down Julia's spine and she cautiously allowed a tiny glow to settle in her heart as she tucked her notebook into her back pocket.

Chad joined them on the porch, leaning on the rail to survey the yard, as Julia and Becky settled into wicker chairs. Ringo got up and walked over to sit on Chad's new boot, his chin pointed up to gaze at his favorite friend.

"I hear you had a record-breaking crowd here today," Chad commented.

"And what record would that be?" Julia asked.

He shrugged. "The flower shop planning record of course."

"Of course," Julia agreed with a smile.

Winnie rose and tucked the kitten into the crook of her arm. "I should be getting home now. I'll just put this little sweetheart in her room." The old woman shuffled into the house.

Becky sniffed. "You seem to be fully recovered," she said to Chad with a smirk. "That was quite the prank, grabbing a skunk right up off the ground."

Chad tossed her a dirty look and she hooted with laughter.

"Cost me a pair of good boots," he muttered. "Couldn't stand the smell of em."

Winnie returned to the porch and Becky stood. Julia rose to hug each of the women, thanking them both over and over. Winnie kissed her on the cheek and then, with a wave, Becky led the old woman to her car.

Chad tucked his hands in his pockets and smiled down at Julia. "You have lipstick on your cheek."

Julia's fingers rose to her face, almost as if she cherished the remainder of the kiss. "Mhhm," she muttered.

"You must be exhausted," Chad said. "How about I buy you dinner?"

Julia flopped back into her chair and propped her feet on the porch rail. "I don't think I can move."

"Okay," Chad tried again, "what if I grab us a sandwich while you soak in a tub?"

Julia rolled her head on the back of the chair to look up at him. "Don't threaten me with heaven."

He laughed. "What do you think about the shop? Will you be ready to open in a few weeks as planned?"

"I don't know," she moaned. "I'm just glad the shop will only be open three days a week. I don't think I could handle more."

Chad smiled. "Everyone will be curious at first but things will settle down."

"I sure hope so," Julia replied, flopping her arm across her eyes. "The wedding rehearsal is in two days and then the wedding. I'm tired just thinking about it."

"I know the wedding flowers are a special delivery run, is all that set up for me?"

Kirsten Fullmer

Julia lowered her arm. "Yeah, it's being shipped to Uniontown though so you don't have to go clear to Pittsburgh."

Chad nodded. "Okay, well…I'll go get dinner, you get all cleaned up and then we can just relax."

Heaving herself from the chair with a whimper, Julia nodded. "Sounds good. Thanks Chad."

On a whim, he leaned down to kiss her before he stepped off the porch.

It felt like a remarkably normal thing to do.

★★★

When Chad got back with the grease-splotched paper bag, he let himself into the house and called for Julia. Hearing no reply, he walked through the dark living room to the bedroom door and peeked inside to see her lying across the bed fully clothed, sound asleep, with one hand tucked under her lipstick-marked cheek.

Sighing and resigning himself to another evening alone, Chad plodded to the kitchen and removed his dinner from the bag. He put Julia's share in her fridge and sat on the back step to eat his burger, sharing his fries with Ringo.

Once his trash was tucked in the can, he returned to Julia's room, removed her shoes, shook out a folded quilt from the foot of her bed, and spread it over her. Tenderly, he bent to kiss her cheek, patted Ringo's head, checked on George and the kittens, then backed from the room and turned out the light.

He locked the front dead bolt with a solid and depressing click, turned out all the lights, then left by the back door where he could lock the doorknob and pull the door closed.

18

Julia's eyes blinked open and she jerked to a sitting position. What time was it? What had happened? Looking down, she realized she was fully clothed. Groping around her desperately, looking for her phone, she realized that she must have fallen asleep when Chad left.

Ringo jumped on her lap, reminding her that he needed to go out, so she rubbed her hands over her face and scooted to the edge of the bed.

George stared up at Julia, the kittens nursing. "Morning," Julia mumbled.

Staggering to the kitchen, she found her phone on the counter and scooped it up on her way to let the dog out. As Ringo did his duty, she checked for missed calls. Clicking the phone off, she let Ringo back in and headed for the coffee maker.

As the machine bubbled and perked, Julia wandered to the fridge and tugged it open. Sure enough, on the top shelf sat a paper-wrapped burger in a red and white striped cardboard basket with fries on the side. The thought of cold greasy food made her empty stomach turn, so she closed the fridge.

According to her phone, she really needed to bathe and get dressed. Quickly, she poured herself a cup of coffee and headed up the stairs, stirring the coffee as she walked.

As Julia cleaned the dinner dishes, with thoughts of the shop rattling through her brain, thundering like ten lanes of traffic over a bridge, she sighed. Wide rolls of tissue paper with a dispenser and cutter, foam blocks to support arrangements, supplies of dried baby breath, ribbon, cards…

Gloria materialized out of the depths and crossed Julia's mind for the umpteenth time. Julia knew what Tara thought of Gloria, but how did Gloria feel? Did *she* see herself as the type that a guy didn't take home to mother? Gloria had seemed sweet enough, maybe even vulnerable.

Or maybe, Julia thought, she was just picking up on everyone's discomfort lately and read it as vulnerable. She wandered to the living room, her eyes roaming over all the preparations for the shop to open.

Reaching under the counter of the display case, Julia pulled out her stack of notebooks and a pen. "Come on, Ringo – let's sit on the porch," she said to the little dog.

Julia settled into a wicker chair and Ringo wandered into the yard to sniff all the people smells of the day. George pushed open the screen and wandered languidly to a chair to join them. With one deft leap, she jumped into the chair and padded around the seat for a moment, then curled into a circle on her side, her black fluffy face touching her paws.

Rolling the rubber band off the top notebook, Julia reviewed her notes for the day as she chewed on the end of her pen. This notebook was filled with personal things she needed to do. Had she eaten? Not enough. She had bathed though – check. Apologize to Chad for falling asleep and missing dinner, was next on the list. There was still time for that.

As she ticked through the list, it became clear that she had managed to get through her day without forgetting anything major. She closed the notebook and wrapped the rubber band

Kirsten Fullmer

back around it. The second notebook was shop business, which still had a long list of items to do, but she was too tired at the moment.

The third notebook was the most worn and dog-eared and contained her list of long-term goals. She hadn't opened this one for weeks but instead had carried it around with her stack of notebooks, pretending she'd get to it.

Staring down at the notebook in her lap, Julia smoothed her fingers across the cover. The book was a painful reminder of all the things she could never do. Every time she'd tried to work on it, instead of feeling hopeful and engaged in creating her future, she'd felt defeated and hopeless. Just finding things to write in it that were in any way attainable had seemed impossible. More than it was a book of goals, the book was a pathetic reminder of her limitations.

Resolutely, Julia rolled the rubber band down the cover and it twisted and dropped to lie curled in her lap. Slowly, she thumbed through the pages of jumbled handwriting to the last page she'd written just after arriving in town. Her eyes scanned down the page and with each item on the list, her eyebrows rose. The notebook dropped to her nap as she stared blankly across the yard.

Finally, after the moments of shock had ticked away, Julia lifted the book to scan the list again. Only seven items were written for the month of May; work on the yard, buy a stove, get a bed, practice going up steps, increase upper arm strength, try to cook, and find a grocery store.

Thinking back, all those items had been things she needed to do, things that were out of her comfort zone, but looking at the sad little list now, she realized that she had not only attained all those goals, but she had completely overshot them.

Her yard was the prettiest in town (well, except for maybe Winnie's.) She loved to cook on Bessy, her bed was comfortable and beautiful and…thoughts of Chad interrupted her train of thought. Shaking her head, she refocused and glanced back to the page.

Just that morning she had hurried up the steps stirring her coffee, and she'd been lifting and moving things for the shop for days. She'd found not only a grocery store but also the boutique and Fergus' greenhouse. Her house resembled something from a magazine. She snorted under her breath. Friends and a lover had been the last thing she'd have ever written down. Those had been unattainable dreams, locked away in the back of her mind.

What had happened to her in the last few weeks? Had she truly changed that much?

Chad's truck stopped in front of her house, interrupting her thoughts. He climbed from his truck and the evening sunshine sparkled across his dark hair as he smiled and lifted a hand in greeting.

Warmth spread through Julia's veins, causing her heart to melt. As he approached the porch Julia studied his walk, his hands, his dark, stubbly jaw. Everything about him was exactly what she would have chosen in a boyfriend line-up. And he was here to see her.

★★★

Stepping up onto the porch, Chad bent to plant a light kiss on Julia's cheek. "Hi beautiful, did you get some sleep?"

Julia smiled up at him, a faraway look in her eye.

"You okay?" he asked, bending to scratch Ringo between the ears, concerned that Julia, her expression dreamy, appeared to be lost in space.

"Hello? Earth to Julia?"

She jolted, almost as if his comment had knocked her back into the present.

"Huh?" she mumbled, her lashes blinking.

Kirsten Fullmer

Slowly, Chad lowered himself into a wicker chair, his wary gaze on her face. "I asked if you got enough sleep…"

Julia smiled crookedly. "Yeah. I did. Thanks."

He paused, trying to comprehend her odd behavior. "You seem kind of— out there," he stammered. He'd seen her scared, hurt, angry, embarrassed, passionate, and confused, but this was definitely new. "So—what were you doing?"

"Oh," Julia gasped, "I was just going through my notebooks." She picked up the book in her lap and waved it vaguely.

Chad relaxed a little and nodded; he knew about this. "Which one is that?"

Julia looked as if her hand had been caught in the cookie jar. "I was just—I was looking at stuff I'd written."

"Obviously. Isn't that what you do with these?" he asked, pointing to the other notebooks in her lap.

Squirming in her chair, Julia appeared to collect herself. "Yeah, I was just— this one is long-term stuff. I hadn't looked at it for a while."

Chad nodded. "Checking up on your progress?"

She nodded. "Something like that."

The conversation lagged and Chad's neck started to itch under Julia's penetrating gaze. She looked as if she were contemplating eating a tempting dessert. Wait! Could this mean…?

"What are you thinking?" he asked, hope mounting south of the border like a sunrise.

Julia smiled a warm slow smile, her eyes going soft again. "I was just thinking about how everything has changed."

Not the response Chad had been hoping for, so he tried again. "Like what?" he asked, hoping he was in there somewhere.

She glanced away and shrugged. "Oh just everything. The shop, the house, Tara." She paused and looked back, her gaze as hot and liquid as molten lava. "You…"

Chad stiffened as all the blood in his body surged to his lap. "What about me?" he almost whispered, his hopes spiraling upward, his thoughts scattering as if a tornado had hit the porch.

Julia shrugged, glancing at him shyly behind her lashes.

That's all it took and Chad was ready. He clenched his fingers into the arms of his chair, forcing himself not to jump up and scoop her into her arms, then run pell-mell into the house. This was it, the moment he'd been waiting for and trying to instigate for a week, and he didn't want to blow it.

He cleared his throat. "Julia—" His voice cracked and he tried again. "Julia, would you like to make love with me. Right now?"

She blushed and nodded.

His fingers tightened on the chair, his knuckles white. "You know that I want to be with you for as long as you'll have me, right? This isn't just a fling…"

She nodded, her expression growing serious. "I want to be with you too."

Chad jumped from his chair and it scuttled backward into the porch rail. Forcing himself to slow down, he reached out to take her hand. When she laid her palm across his, he could feel her trembling. His heart raced as he struggled to appear calm.

"Come on, Ringo," Chad called to the dog. The little dog trotted up to the porch and followed them into the house. "Dog in or out of the bedroom?" he asked Julia.

She giggled. "I don't know. Out I suppose."

"Okay," Chad said as he locked the front door. Tugging Julia gently behind him, he paced to the bedroom, concentrating on deep, even breaths. "Where is George?" he asked himself, more so than Julia, as he glanced through the dim room toward Ringo's bed. To his utter delight, George lay sleeping, curled around her kittens.

Kirsten Fullmer

"Stay right here," he said to Julia, then turned and sprinted to lock the back door and toss his cell phone on the kitchen counter.

When he returned to the bedroom, Julia had slipped off her shoes and socks and lay on the bed leaning on one elbow. She smiled and his breath caught in his throat, his pulse surging.

Carefully and quietly he shooed Ringo from the room, then closed and locked the door.

"Do you have anything you need to say…or something to tell me before…"

Julia's brow creased. "I don't think so."

He swallowed and sat on the end of the bed. "Anything you're worried about, or—or forgot?"

She giggled and shook her head. "No, I think we're good."

All the tension drained from Chad's body as he neared the bed, his entire focus caught and held in Julia's dark eyes. He went to her then, his heart open, and as he held her, touched her, kissed her – she was the only reality in his world.

She met him willingly, all warmth and womanly smells, her skin like silk under his work-hardened hands. The sounds she made, her movements under him, pushed him to a place he'd never been.

Carefully watching her every response; her gentle gasping sighs, the toss of her head, the flash in her eye, he became acquainted with all things Julia.

★★★

Julia pulled her truck up to the bed and breakfast and craned her neck, looking for a place to park. Cars and trucks were parked at all angles behind the barn, under trees, and up both sides of the driveway. People of all ages, sizes and shapes flocked across the yard and porch, some carrying covered dishes of food, others carting chairs and tables, or chasing kids and toting babies.

Shabby Chic After All

Old ladies relaxed in the shade of the porch, gabbing like hens, and old men gathered in the open door of the barn, swapping stories and fanning themselves in the summer heat.

Julia reached over to the passenger seat for the pasta salad she'd brought for the potluck and hopped from the truck. As she crossed the yard, people called to her and waved. She smiled and waved back.

On the porch, Winnie met Julia at the steps and took the salad bowl, giving her a peck on the cheek. The old woman's bright eyes twinkled as she regarded Julia thoughtfully. "You're different somehow," the woman said with a sly smile.

Julia shrugged and blushed, causing Winnie to chortle as she turned to take the salad in the house.

Following her elderly friend, Julia noticed that the inn was designed for people to gather in cozy sitting areas, and to congregate in larger groups.

The kitchen was bustling with activity, women babbling and uncovering food, clinking dishes and silverware. Children ran around their feet, chasing a dog someone had brought. Julia was glad Ringo was safe at home; he'd be terrorized by this group.

"Your shop looks like it's going to be a huge success," Becky said with a grin as she squeezed up next to Julia. "From what I hear, the town plans to buy up everything in the first week."

With a shrug, Julia blushed and laughed. "I have my work cut out for me to get all the paperwork done, that's all I know for sure."

Becky nodded. "I'll come by next week and help you with it if you'd like."

Admitting that she would appreciate that, Julia relaxed into the warmth of the gathering and gave Becky a warm hug.

Becky turned away to swat a teenage boy out of the desserts, so Julia left in search of Tara, finally finding her surrounded by women in the dining room. She gave her a hug but the craziness

Kirsten Fullmer

kept them from being able to speak more than a few words of greeting.

Joining the folks on the deck setting up tables and chairs, Julia chimed in on the conversation, laughing as she shook out a tablecloth Marge handed her, and wafting it across a table.

A warm hand on her back sent shivers down both arms and she turned to smile up at Chad. They stood quiet for a moment, the crowds and noise forgotten. Warmth spread through Julia's chest and contentment radiated around her.

The women in the kitchen called for everyone to come eat and the crowds began to move toward the open door and the mixture of tantalizing smells. Julia and Chad wandered the opposite direction, to the far side of the deck, in the shade, where she leaned against the rail, feeling suddenly feminine and a little shy.

Chad smoothed his palm across her glossy curls, pulling her to his chest and holding her to him. She sighed and closed her eyes, her arms slipping around his back.

Finally she was truly happy, and she'd enjoy it for as long as it lasted.

★★★

People lingered as the meal wound down, swapping stories of Justin and Tara, who reigned at the head of the table. Laughter rang across the yard where children ran, their hoots filling the afternoon air.

Finally, Justin stood and announced it was time to gather the folks in the wedding party and get on with the rehearsal. The women not in the ceremony began gabbing as they collected dishes and silverware from the tables and the men folded tables and moved chairs with a clatter.

Julia and Chad followed the wedding party into the living room.

Shabby Chic After All

Tara pulled Julia close with one arm around her shoulder and introduced her to the pastor, who pumped her hand up and down enthusiastically.

"My wife is so excited for your little shop to open," the man drawled. "It's all she can talk about."

Tara gave Julia's shoulder a squeeze.

The group shifted as more people shuffled into the room and Tara informed the pastor of everyone's assigned place in the wedding party. She spoke briefly about where everyone should stand, then the group headed back out to the deck where the tables had been cleared away and the chairs had been arranged into two groups with an aisle down the center.

The pastor was led to his position in front of the pool, his eyes darting through the crowd, which was clearly enjoying the festive air of the wedding rehearsal.

"Justin," Tara called over the crowd. "Grab Julia and Chad and line them up by the French doors, then get down here."

Shoving Chad to get him to stop gabbing and get in place, Justin nodded to Julia, as she stepped into position, then headed down to the pool to stand near the pastor.

"Ms. Maid of Honor…" Chad said, grinning, as he took Julia's arm.

"Mister Best Man…" she echoed back with a laugh.

Tara trotted back up toward Julia to position the flower girl and ring bearer, pausing to hug them both. Just as Tara stepped into line behind Chad, a rumble of raised voices emanated from the kitchen, causing a ripple of heads to turn toward the house.

Mac burst from the dining room, his eyes wide. "There you are!" he said, grabbing Chad by the arm. "Thank God I found you."

A hush fell over the people closest to Julia and Chad, their eyes wide, some rising to stand.

Kirsten Fullmer

"Listen, the sheriff is out at old Fergus' place," Mac exclaimed, pointing toward the hills. "And he's got some kind of papers to evict him. Bobby and his momma were headed here when the sheriff stopped them on their way past the greenhouse."

Mac gasped for a breath then continued, "Gloria is with Fergus but Chad, they're taking all their land. Bobby's and Fergus'. All of it, greenhouses, homes and all!"

The older man paused, giving his words a moment to sink in, then went on. "Bobby went at the sheriff when he heard they were takin' the house and property. Chad, they've padlocked their houses, wouldn't even let them pack their stuff."

19

A moment of silent shock hung heavy in the air around Chad and Mac, then a rumble of concern spread through the crowd as people began talking, moving, and shifting from their chairs. One person told another and a flood of apprehension swept quickly across the deck.

"Who's taking their land?" Chad asked. "Slow down Mac, start at the beginning."

Mac yanked off his worn ball cap and ran his hand across his balding head, then slammed the cap back on. "Okay, okay, Bobby called and he was hysterical. It took me a minute to even understand him."

Chad nodded as Justin elbowed his way up to stand beside Tara and Mac continued. "Bobby said he and his momma were driving here, you know how their driveway comes out right there by Fergus' greenhouses…"

Chad nodded again, anxious for Mac to get in with the story.

"Well, Bobby said the sheriff was there and he had padlocks on Fergus' gates, so they stopped and the when they got out, the sheriff pulled them aside and sent two deputies up toward their house. The sheriff told them he had papers to evict them because some big land company is taking their land."

"Land company!" Tara gasped, springing forward. "What land company?"

Julia dropped limply into a near-by chair and Justin pulled Tara back, shushing her, indicating for Mac to continue.

"I don't know! I don't know who did this but Bobby put the sheriff on the phone and he said it's true." Mac paused and nodded, his eyes big. "Evidently Bobby went berserk and took a swing at the sheriff. Somebody needs to get out there and get Bobby under control."

"Let's go!" Tara shouted, turning to push through the now moving crowd. Justin rushed after her, calling for her to calm down.

Mac and Chad moved toward the deck steps but the crowd was at a standstill as everyone bottlenecked at the stairs, so they turned back to the French doors and hurried through the house.

A flood of anxious and concerned people rushed around and through the house, toward their vehicles. Parents snatched up children and food lay forgotten, drink glasses sloshing from being tossed down.

As Chad jumped off the porch, fishing his truck keys from his front pocket as he ran, he suddenly realized that Julia was not at his side. He lurched to a stop, causing the people behind him to plow into his back, and a domino-effect of bodies crushed together as he turned. Catching people's arms and apologizing, his eyes darted through the crowd searching for Julia. Had she been ahead of him?

Excited shouts behind him mingled to cause a cacophony as car doors slammed and engines revved. Everyone who had reached their cars tried to back out at once, causing a jam of vehicles all doing multiple point turns in reverse.

Justin and Mac stood in the center of the confusion, waving their arms and issuing instructions as to who should back out first.

When the people around him were once again moving, Chad stretched his neck and jumped in place, searching every direction, trying to see Julia through the crowd. Spotting no blond curls, he turned back toward the deck and elbowed his way, moving against the flow, through the stragglers of the group to the back of the house.

When he reached the deck, he saw Julia slumped alone in a folding chair on the otherwise evacuated collection of disorganized seats, her eyes staring blankly ahead and her hands in her lap. Taking two steps at a time, he sprinted up to the deck and hurried to her side. "Julia," he gasped, "Wha—what are you doing? Aren't you going to go help Fergus and Bobby?"

Julia didn't respond, just continued to stare into space, like a statue.

Chad shook her shoulder in concern. "Julia? Hey, are you all right?" he asked, perching on the chair next to her. "Talk to me, please."

Slowly, Julia turned to him, her face white as death.

Taking her hand in his, Chad searched her eyes for an explanation. "Julia, what happened? We need to go. Will you ride with me?"

Without waiting for an answer, Chad tugged Julia to her feet, hoping she'd collect herself. With his hand under her elbow, he helped her stagger off the deck and toward his truck. By the time they reached the front yard, the last few cars were falling into the line of vehicles that rushed down the driveway, stirring up a colossal cloud of dust.

Chad yanked open the passenger door, but Julia just stared at the interior of the truck, so he picked her up and gracelessly tossed her into the cab. Checking to be sure that her hands and feet were in the truck, he slammed the door and ran around the front to climb in. As the engine roared to life, he turned to Julia. "Hey, get buckled!"

The song *My Life* wafted from the radio and Chad punched the off-button, then tossed his arm on the back of the seat, craning his neck to see out the back window as he pulled out from under the tree. Julia nearly tumbled off the seat.

Momentarily, Chad juggled the wheel and Julia to keep her upright, then in exasperation, reached across her for the seat belt and clicked it across her lap.

"Hold on," he instructed as he jammed the truck into drive and took off down the driveway.

"This must be about that guy who's been pressuring them to sell…" Chad muttered under his breath as he scowled out the windshield.

"I should have checked it out," he continued. "I just didn't figure it was a big deal!" He pounded the steering wheel with his fist, then rubbed his hand across the top of his head. "The sheriff would never do this unless his hands were tied…"

Julia shifted in her seat with her hands over her face. Broken moans muffled behind her fingers, and her shoulders slumped.

"What is up with you?" Chad demanded, his frustration level rising by the moment.

A tiny mumble came from Julia as her hands dropped to her lap and her head fell back to stare at the ceiling of the truck.

"What?" Chad asked, his eyes darting between her and the highway.

Julia shook her head, her face a sick green color. "I knew it. I knew that at some point something like this would happen."

"Talk louder," Chad demanded. "What are you talking about? What would happen?"

Not willing to answer, Julia stared out the window, muttering under her breath and moaning.

Within minutes, they neared the sprawling greenhouse that belonged to Fergus. The highway was choked with cars and trucks, all parked at crazy angles, some two and three deep, lining the sides of the highway for hundreds of yards.

Kirsten Fullmer

Ignoring the crowds, Chad wove his truck through the maze of parked vehicles and stopped directly in front of the crowd, blocking what was left of the eastbound lane. Yanking open the door, he jumped from the truck and ran around the other side. Julia had unbuckled and opened her door, and without further ado, Chad hauled her from the truck and set her on her feet.

Not waiting to ask if she could walk, he hurried forward, elbowing his way through the crowd, dragging Julia by the arm behind him.

In the center of a group of angry people, the sheriff stood toe to toe with Fergus at the gate to the greenhouse. A sheaf of papers was clenched in the lawman's hand and his face was grim. Fergus' face was bright red and his arms were crossed across his chest.

A large chain and padlock were wound through the chain-link gate, locking them from the crowd.

Next to Fergus stood Bobby, his thin face grimy with smeared tears and dust, his glasses barely hanging onto the end of his nose. He was covered in dirt and scratches and his hair stood on end. His mother sat on an old crate next to him, her face grim with worry and fear.

"What's going on here?" Chad bellowed as he broke through the crowd. Stepping up to Bobby, he surveyed the man from head to foot, then glanced over Mrs. Middlewood as well. "Are you two okay?" he asked, his manner authoritative.

Bobby stumbled toward Chad, his face a mask of fear. His mother nodded once but when she opened her mouth to speak, nothing came out but a choking sound. Bobby stood stricken and silent by Chad's side.

Chad put his arm around Bobby for a quick reassuring squeeze, then turned back to the sheriff.

"What happened? What is this all about?" he demanded.

The sheriff sighed and raised the paperwork to wave it at Chad. "I got these last night. I had no choice but to do my job."

"What is it?" Chad asked, planting his feet apart and crossing his arms over his broad chest. He looked as if the answer had better be good, or he'd tear the papers and maybe even the sheriff, to shreds.

"It's an eviction notice," the sheriff sighed. "I called the attorney's office that filed them and told them they better be out here for an explanation this morning or I wouldn't act." He waved his hand off to his left. "This fella showed up at dawn with more papers. I have no choice, I tell you…"

All heads in the crowd turned to glare at the tall, prim-looking man in an expensive suit, who stood near the fence. His hands were in his pockets and he appeared to be completely unconcerned and bored.

Chad unclenched his arms to rub one palm across the top of his head. "Can I at least see the papers?" he asked with a sigh.

The sheriff shrugged and handed them over.

Julia had been standing beside Chad but when she saw the attorney, she shrunk in her skin and shuffled behind Chad, only her eyes peeping past his arm to read the papers as he shuffled through them. Unable to read as fast as she once could, Julia scanned the papers, her eyes searching for key words and lingo.

Chad's hand dropped to his side and swiftly, Julia snatched up the papers and continued to sift through them.

The sheriff glanced at Julia, then returned his attention to Chad. "Look, I don't file this stuff, I just have to enforce it. I don't like this any better than you do."

Chad shuffled his feet, clearly grasping at straws. "I don't claim to understand that crap," he said, gesturing toward the papers. "But from what I see, somebody is forcing Mister Fergus and Mrs. Middlewood to vacate because they refused to sell their property?"

Kirsten Fullmer

The sheriff nodded. "That's right. They claim that multiple fair offers have been made on the property but according to this guy," he waved his hand toward the attorney, "they refused to sell. In the case of public works, they can take the land to build infrastructure."

"Public works? Like a highway? What are they planning to build?" Chad huffed. "I haven't heard of anything going up out here."

"Some pipeline," the sheriff replied. "Seems if it's in the public's best interest, it don't matter if the owners want to sell. And if they don't sell, they get tossed off and the property is seized."

Bobby stepped up to shout at the sheriff. "That guy didn't say nothin' to us about a pipeline!" His head swiveled to Chad. "I swear it Chad, he never said nothin' like that!"

★★★

The noise of the crowd faded to a dull roar and receded to the foggy reaches of Julia's mind. The second she'd overheard Mac tell Chad that the sheriff was evicting Bobby and Fergus, her heart had sunk to the soles of her feet.

How had she ever believed that she could put her past behind her, move forward, and be someone different? She should have known that she could not escape from who she truly was.

All the way to the greenhouse, she'd felt like an incompetent, useless shell. The people she loved were in trouble and she couldn't help. Fear and shame flooded through her veins and chilled her heart.

She'd run from the city to get away from the pressure, the loss, the vastness of her disability. Given her lack of capacity, she'd considered fading into the back of the crowd and keeping her mouth closed. Maybe she could pretend she was as shocked and upset as everyone else. Maybe she could just fake horror and confusion. Maybe…

Chad bumped Julia, nearly knocking her down, as he stepped forward to get between Bobby and the sheriff. The noise of the crowd roared in Julia's ears.

Bobby was screaming and crying, rage and fear causing his entire body to shake. "You're not gonna take my momma's house! Do you hear me?" he shouted at the sheriff. "She's lost everything in her life, everything she ever loved, and I'm not gonna let you do this!"

Chad stood in front of Bobby, trying to hold the little man back.

The sheriff took a step back and reached for his handcuffs. "Look Chad, I've tried to be realistic about this but Bobby's already come at me once."

Julia's gaze fell to Bobby's mother, who sat silently weeping, her hands covering her face. Julia had no idea the load of sorrow the woman had borne in her life but something told her that the weight of it was substantial.

And then there was Fergus. His bravado was fading, quickly being replaced by the grey, haggard look of a tired old man. Gloria stood next to him, her arm gripped tight around his shoulders, and Julia remembered that someone had told her that Fergus was Gloria's grandfather.

Tara stepped up to kneel beside Bobby's mother, placing her arm around the sobbing old woman. Julia realized that this should be the happiest time of Tara's life. It was the night before her wedding, and now the whole town was in an uproar.

And Chad. He stood next to Bobby, his expression drawn and his muscles bunched, as if he were contemplating springing forward to devour the sheriff whole. She knew Chad would do anything to save Bobby and his mother, and she couldn't take it. She knew exactly what was happening and her heart twisted in her chest, choking the very breath from her.

Kirsten Fullmer

No matter what, she knew she had to do something. She couldn't just stand by and watch Chad and her friends suffer, but her knees were shaking so hard her feet wouldn't move. Her mouth was dry and her fists would not unclench. Clamping her eyes closed, she willed her body to cooperate, and with a jolt she lurched forward, nearly falling at the sheriff's feet. Straightening, she glanced up into the lawman's eyes. His expression was forbidding as he moved toward Bobby with the handcuffs.

Some long-lost part of Julia's brain clicked into gear and she reared up, stepping directly in front of the sheriff. "Excuse me sir, may I have a word with my clients?" she stated in a loud, rock-solid, demanding voice, causing everyone to pause and heads to turn her way.

The sheriff, confused, his eyes darting to Chad, stopped and stared at Julia. "Your clients?"

With her back straight and her shoulders stiff, Julia tossed the sheriff a condescending glare and stepped toward Bobby. "That's right, Mister Bobby Middlewood and Mister Fergus—" She paused.

"Barnett," whispered Chad, his jaw slack with shock.

Julia nodded. "—Mister Barnett, have retained me as their attorney, and your treatment of them today is ungrounded and reprehensible."

The sheriff scratched his head. "I have paperwork..." At which point he realized Julia was holding the paperwork he'd given to Chad. "Give that back," he snapped, reaching for the sheaf of papers.

Julia snatched them to her chest and gave the sheriff a glare that only a fool would ignore. She calmly lifted the papers and scanned her finger down the first page. "Did I hear you say there was an attorney representing the plaintiff present?" As she spoke, her knees once again began to shake violently, and she stiffened her legs, faking confidence.

Nodding, the sheriff pointed to his left and the stunned crowd parted to allow the attorney to step forward. The man swaggered toward Julia and she gave him the evil eye. She'd met this man before, in her dealings with property law, and she knew his sort. At this point, she was desperately sure she could never compete with him given her memory problems but she had to try.

Three steps from Julia, the attorney's expression suddenly changed and his steps faltered. His hands sprung from his pockets and his eyebrows flew up as his mouth dropped open. Quickly regaining self-control, he cleared his throat and straightened his already perfect tie. "Ms. Arnold, I—We heard you were—I didn't know you were practicing out here—I didn't recognize you!"

Julia stood very still, appearing to be calm and composed, and looking down her nose at the man. She harrumphed in disgust and wrinkled her nose, as if the man smelled bad, and she glanced down at the papers. Finally she looked up, her glare icy. "What's behind this Mister—I'm sorry, what was your name?" As if remembering his name was below her.

The attorney shuffled his feet and straightened his back. He mumbled his name and reached into his jacket pocket for a business card. His eyes darted through the crowd as he extended the card but Julia simply glanced at it with distain. The attorney's hand dropped and he spoke up to defend his position with a cracking voice. "You know how this works. All the paper-work is...there."

Julia took a long moment to toss him a condescending glare, then shuffled through the paperwork again. Silence fell over the crowd, only the sound of a baby fussing hanging in the air as all eyes were on Julia.

Forcing her breathing to slow, Julia struggled to concentrate on the key points at hand. Finally she spoke. "This looks legit

Kirsten Fullmer

on the surface," she said waving the paperwork, "but something about it smells, and you know it."

The man shot his chin in the air. "I can assure you, all the facts are in order."

"Who is the buyer?" Julia demanded, her voice so harsh that Chad did a double-take.

"I don't have to disclose that and you know it."

"You know I can find out in a matter of minutes," Julia threatened.

"That's not public record," the attorney said, with his chest puffed out.

An old man pushed through the crowd. "I'm the district judge here and if this young lady is these folks' attorney, then she has a right to see the records!"

The crowd cheered. Julia glanced around her at the people she'd come to love and admire. Her back straightened and she stared the attorney down. When he glanced away, Julia motioned for Fergus and Bobby to come to her side, hoping they wouldn't notice that her hand was shaking like a leaf in the wind.

Chad and Gloria helped Bobby and Fergus step forward. Tara stayed back with Bobby's mother.

"You well know that the property owners may challenge the right to take their land if the proposed taking is not for 'public use'," Julia stated confidently, "And if it's not, the afore mentioned party is not legislatively authorized to take said property and I intend to show that whomever your client is, they have not followed the proper substantive or procedural steps required by law."

Shocked by the words flowing from her mouth, Julia resolutely held onto the persona of brazen calm that she wore. The crowd muttered, shocked and captivated by Julia's speech.

"What makes you think you can beat this?" the attorney demanded.

Julia puffed up, her eyes shooting shards of ice, and her voice dull as cold, grey steel. "Because I know you—," she growled. "And Bobby doesn't lie. Something about this stinks of a cover-up and I'll find it."

The man standing before Julia shriveled under her glare, but stood his ground.

"Furthermore," Julia continued, "we will simply drive to the courthouse and file a motion to stay the eviction and these good people will be back in their homes within the hour."

A look of relief washed over the sheriff's face. "You can do that?" he asked, his eyes darting from the judge, to Julia, to the attorney.

"Sure can!" the judge piped up with a grin.

Julia turned to the sheriff. "You can take these chains down sir, the stay will give Fergus and Mrs. Middlewood ten days for me to sort this out.

The sheriff nodded. "Ned take those chains down and stay here until —this young lady— returns with the paperwork."

The deputy nodded, unlocked the padlock and with a grumbling clank, tugged the chains from the gate of the greenhouse.

The crowd erupted into cheers and Bobby ran to Julia's side, enveloping her in a tight hug. "Oh Miss Julia, thank you!" he cried.

Julia nodded and patted Bobby's back, smiling over his shoulder at Chad, Fergus, and Tara, her heart finally slowing its staccato beating. For the first time in well over a year, she felt as if she were a competent person who could stand up for herself and stand her ground.

Thank goodness this was just a paperwork issue, she thought to herself as she was patted on the back and admired by what seemed to be the entire town, because she knew in her heart that she could never prepare a court case again, or preform in a court room. Those days were gone but when it really mattered,

Kirsten Fullmer

she'd found courage and dug up some attitude and helped her friends. And Chad.

A small part of her heart shriveled, however, at the knowledge that they all admired her because they thought she was a competent land acquisition attorney, not just a broken-down bit of bravado.

★★★

Morning sun poured through Julia's window and across her face. Chad watched as her lips smacked and her nose wrinkled, then one eye opened. She blinked up at him, a slow languid smile spreading across her face.

"Hi," he said, smoothing the hair back from her cheek. "I'm glad you got some sleep."

Julia moaned and cuddled into his side, her arms pinned between them.

Running his fingers through her mussed curls, Chad stared into the room over her head, his heart tight in his chest. Julia had grown to be such a huge part of him, he felt as if his past life was all pushed off-kilter, and his footing was on loose rock.

Julia mumbled and ran her fingers up his chest, causing a million thoughts and emotions to flash through his mind but his mood remained pensive. Today was Justin and Tara's wedding, and he'd stand beside Julia watching, wondering if she was dreaming of her own wedding, and what that would mean to him.

As he'd sat with her at the courthouse half the night, searching through computer records and microfiche, he'd contemplated the fact that she had been a high-powered land attorney. Julia had told him that he wouldn't have liked her, and he had to admit that when she'd stood toe to toe with that attorney, Chad hadn't known her at all. The things he loved about Julia had been completely missing. Her deep, dark, shining eyes, her tenderness, the sweet vulnerability she usually radiated had been banished behind the face of that vicious, powerful woman.

She really was completely different since her illness. The trauma had irrevocably changed everything about her. And thank goodness, because he didn't know what he'd do if that scary woman showed up again.

Insecurity swamped his soul, throwing a damper on the relief he felt over Julia's ability to help William's family. He'd experienced a horrible crushing sensation yesterday at Fergus' place, knowing that once again he'd failed William.

The fact that Julia could fix the situation, and come to find out, save William's family in a far more effective manner than he had, bit at his pride. He'd sworn to be there for Bobby and his mother, to make sure they were safe and cared for, and now Julia had overstepped him in a magnificent and astounding way.

As Julia's fingers roamed up his neck and she fit her body to his, Chad wrestled with ferocious inner demons. He loved the woman in his arms fiercely, yet feared her and resented her at the same time. Never had he imagined that love could be so complicated.

Carefully releasing Julia's grip, Chad kissed the top of her head. "I better be going. That wedding delivery will be in Uniontown by now and you'll be fussing for it soon."

Julia rolled onto her back. "I'm glad you didn't have to go clear to Pittsburgh today."

"Me too," he said as he collected his clothes, feeling guilty for his relief at the excuse to leave.

Kirsten Fullmer

20

Julia arrived at the inn just after nine o'clock, ready to help prepare for the two o'clock wedding. She'd been delayed leaving the house because she'd had to track down a wayward kitten. Paul had wandered out of the bedroom while Julia was in the bath, and she'd spent frantic moments searching under furniture until the little kitty had been discovered curled up asleep between two pillows on the sofa. How she'd gotten on the sofa was beyond Julia's imagination, the little minx.

Ringo had whined and followed her through the house all morning, as if he knew something big was cooking and he wanted to be part of it. She'd taken an extra moment to play with him in the yard before she'd loaded up the ribbons and supplies and headed out.

Tara had picked up all the flower arrangements for the guest rooms before the wedding rehearsal the day before. Julia had been so pleased with them, she'd barely been able to let them go. Roses in pink and soft yellow, and puffy white mums spilled from blue crocks and jars, adorned with ribbons and scraps of lace, with leafless branches painted white, or stems of baby's breath filling out the arrangements. If Julia thought she was excited about the flower arrangements for the guest rooms, she was breathless to dig into the fresh delivery that Chad had just unloaded and get started setting up the flowers on the deck for the services.

Each post along the sides of the deck would be topped with a salvage-wood box, overflowing with antique roses in white and pale pink.

As a surprise for Tara, Julia planned to string a chain of flowers and pearls that matched the mixed arrangements, along the deck rails and down the aisle. Placing the last cooler on the deck, she counted carefully, then double-checked the numbers in her notebook. It appeared that the flowers were ready to thread through the vine and ribbon, triggering Julia to smile and hum under her breath as she tucked her notebook into her back pocket.

Becky bustled up to Julia's side, sidestepping around the men on ladders hanging wire over the deck. She huffing slightly, her hand on her chest. "I just heard, and I can't believe it!"

Julia smiled. "It was a bit of a shock, wasn't it?"

"I just can't get over how you handled that snooty attorney!" Becky gushed, fiddling with one of her necklaces.

Shrugging, Julia reached for a cooler of flowers.

"How did you find out that other man had been bilking people out of their property?" Becky asked.

Julia tugged vines gently from the cooler. "Well, it's pretty common for the gas companies to have a dummy buyer acquire land for them when they want to build a pipeline but the gas company didn't know this guy was pressuring people to sell their land to his shell company without disclosing that it was for a pipeline." She scratched her head, trying to focus on flowers and law at the same time. "Anyway, turns out he was basically embezzling from the gas company that hired him to buy land for them, by buying it for himself and then hiking up the price."

Becky's brow puckered. "How did he manage to get papers to evict them?"

Working her fingers tenderly through a knot in the vine, Julia scoffed. "That's where he messed up. He tried to use the power of the gas company to acquire land through eminent domain laws, and he'd have gotten away with it if I hadn't spotted his bogus company from a mile away."

A glazed look fell across Becky's face.

Julia tried again. "The guy made his company look like a smaller company buying the gas."

Becky nodded, her eyes darting to the pool and back. "Right...so anyway, now the gas company wants their land for the pipeline and that's a good thing? I'm confused."

Julia laughed. "They just want to lease part of it," she explained. "Basically, Fergus and Bobby's mom will be getting a hefty check in the mailbox each month from now on."

"Well isn't that something!" Becky smiled, finally understanding the meaning behind yesterday's debacle. "Need a hand here?"

"That would be great," Julia replied with a smile as she handed Becky a roll of ribbon.

***

An hour later, Julia and Becky pulled the last of the ribbon from the roll. "Do we have more of this?" Julia asked as she turned to dig through her boxes.

"I thought I saw another one but maybe we used it," Becky said, rubbing her lower back and glancing back at the rail.

Shuffling through now empty cardboard boxes, Julia tossed paper and empty cardboard rolls behind her like a boat wake. "This isn't good, I've only got ten feet left to finish the aisle."

"Don't panic," Becky reassured, "I'm sure we can figure something out."

Julia dropped into a chair and huffed out a breath. "Sorry, I didn't get much sleep..."

Shabby Chic After All

Becky sat next to her and patted her hand. "I know, but you're the town hero."

Shaking her head, Julia's face scrunched into a frown. "No I'm not, I'm just…"

"How can you not feel fabulous about saving Fergus and Bobby's family?" Becky asked, in shock.

Julia stared across the beautifully decorated deck to the shimmering pool. "I'm not really…I mean, it wasn't…"

"Oh honey, you are exhausted. What are you trying to say?"

Turning sad eyes to Becky, Julia swallowed hard. "I used to be that person. That lawyer. But I'm not now. I could barely remember all that law lingo. Now I'm just…"

"Just our friend and flower shop owner?" Becky asked, her eyes glowing. "Don't you see? We all love you. All the parts of you."

Julia shook her head.

"Look at me, Julia," Becky demanded, waiting for Julia to make eye contact.

Finally, Julia shrugged, tipped her head back, and made a dubious face, but looked at Becky.

"Listen to me, you are who you are, honey. You are Julia. The girl who was a sassy lawyer and now you're a sweetheart with a flower shop. We're all good with that."

Julia's gaze fell to her hands in her lap. "I get the feeling Chad isn't."

Becky's brows slammed down. "What do you mean?"

"I don't know," Julia lamented, "He just felt kind of weird to me this morning."

Becky stood and began collecting paper wrappers and ribbon rolls. "His best friend is getting married today, maybe he's just feeling out of sorts," she said confidently, but one brow quirked. "Want me to talk to him?"

Kirsten Fullmer

"No," Julia said stacking up the empty coolers. "It's not a big deal, he's busy helping to put the arbor together, it's fine," she said, but her voice was heavy with concern. "Anyway, I have plenty of time, I'm going to run to Uniontown and grab some more ribbon."

Frowning, Becky gave Julia a hard stare. "Are you sure you're okay?"

Julia nodded and bent to pick up the coolers. "I'm good, I'll be back in a bit," she called over her shoulder.

Becky watched her walk across the deck carrying the stack of coolers. Julia reached her foot out, tapping as she inched forward, to find the top step. A cool breeze whipped across the deck and goosebumps rose along Becky's spine. "Oh I will talk to Chad all right,…" she muttered under her breath.

★★★

Julia hurried from the store in Uniontown, and a strong wind whipped at her hair and the bag of ribbon in her hand. She glanced to the west where billowing black clouds were rising swiftly overhead.

"Oh no, not rain on Tara's wedding day!" she cried. She unlocked her truck and jumped inside just as the first fat rain drop splashed on her windshield. "Maybe it will blow over quickly," she worried, thinking about all the flowers on the deck at the bed and breakfast.

Julia chewed on her bottom lip and checked her watch for the time. The wedding was still almost two hours away, she had plenty of time to get home, grab her dress, and get back to the inn. If the flowers were mussed she'd have time to fix them, she assured herself.

About the time Julia pulled onto the highway, the first bolts of lightening streaked across the sky. Before she could utter a curse, thunder rumbled past, un-nerving her even more.

The storm was violent and fast moving. The road quickly became covered in water as rain fell in sheets, limiting Julia's vision and slowing traffic. With her windshield wipers slapping back and forth, Julia's tension level rose. Would she be late getting back? Would the storm let up in time for the wedding? Would the flowers all be ruined? She shouldn't have left! If only she'd been more prepared, she would have been there to bring the flowers in and help clean up after the storm.

Minutes ticked past as traffic crept along the highway, many cars pulling off to one side to wait out the downpour. Resolutely, Julia pushed forward, creeping ahead with only the taillights of the car ahead to lead her way.

Sweat beaded across her upper lip as she gripped the wheel with white knuckles. The old truck didn't have a stellar defroster and the windows fogged around the edges. Even though the truck had decent tires, the water on the road was six inches deep in places, and the truck lost traction a few times but Julia managed to get the fishtails under control and keep going. The farther she got from Uniontown, the more traffic would thin and she could pick up speed.

A few miles from Smithville, Julia rolled her shoulders and concentrated on relaxing. By the time she got to the wedding she'd be a sweaty mess if she didn't calm down. Heaving a sigh of relief, knowing that around the next curve she would be able to see town, Julia was caught off guard when the truck hit a puddle of water and hydroplaned straight through the curve.

Before she could even hit the brake, the truck careened off the side of the road and down an embankment. Julia slammed on the brakes, jerked the wheel hard, and managed to miss hitting a tree head-on, but the truck slid sideways, pushing through the deep wet mud and weeds on the slope. Unable to slow its sideways momentum, the truck lurched heavily to one side.

Kirsten Fullmer

Julia felt the driver-side wheels lift from the mud as the truck began to roll.

★★★

Chad climbed the steps to the deck, his thoughts heavy with the upcoming wedding and concerns about Julia. At some point, he'd evidently turned into a real wimp, because he had to admit he was intimidated. Everyone was talking about how amazing Julia was and what a changed life Bobby's family and Fergus would now lead.

Of course he was relieved that money was no longer a concern for his adopted family but it was almost as if the two years he'd spent supporting Bobby, fixing leaky shingles, and working on their cars had been forgotten. Had he done such a poor job of caring for them?

He'd also watched Justin struggle through the morning with pre-wedding jitters.

Chad knew that Justin loved Tara and he'd be devastated without her but why did people have to get married anyway? Wasn't it enough to be devoted to a woman you loved without leaving your home and giving up your plans and signing your life away?

Hating himself, he knew he was being an idiot but he couldn't help it. He kept picturing his inevitable first quarrel with Julia and in his mind, she'd turn back into the horrible, manipulative woman he'd seen the day before. What would happen if she wanted an expensive car or a fancy house someday? She could be so…demanding.

Glancing up, Chad realized the deck was empty and that Julia was nowhere in sight. Even the coolers and boxes of supplies she'd brought were gone. A cool breeze ruffled his hair and he turned to the east where dark clouds lined the horizon. He frowned and shrugged. Maybe she'd gone home to change.

The wedding was in less than an hour, she was probably doing her hair.

Bobby hurried across the deck toward Chad, one shirttail flapping out of his overlong khaki pants and a tie in his hand. "Will you help me with this?" the little man asked, extending the orange-striped tie toward Chad.

Nodding, Chad kinked up Bobby's collar, wove the length of the tie around the little man's neck and tossed one end over the other to form a Windsor knot, all the while his mind a thousand miles away.

"...Are you, huh?" Bobby asked, forcing Chad to realize he'd been ignoring his friend's rambling questions.

"Am I what?" Chad muttered as he finished the knot.

"Gonna marry Miss Julia..." Bobby replied, his eyes huge and expectant behind his lenses.

Chad slid the Windsor knot upward with a jerk, nearly choking Bobby half to death. "That's none of your business, is it!" he ground out, pushing the little man away.

Bobby staggered backwards pulling at the tie. "No...sorry," he muttered, surprised and concerned.

Chad sighed and ran his palm across the top of his head, mumbled an apology, then turned and wandered into the kitchen. He wove through the gaggle of chattering women, who clattered dishes and waved, calling out to him as he headed for the home gym. He'd hung his rented tux there earlier, thinking he could shower and slip into it after helping set up.

With a sigh, he lugged his shaving kit and tux into the shower room and locked the door. What was wrong with him? Most men would be thrilled that they were no longer responsible for the monetary needs of an entire family, and they'd be happy to have a hot, sassy girl friend. As he stepped into the steaming water of the shower, he wondered if he was losing his mind.

Kirsten Fullmer

★★★

Julia held onto the wheel with all her strength as the old pickup truck rolled onto the passenger side with a bone-jarring crash, slamming her head into the driver-side window. Then it flew into the air, continuing to roll, making another ear-splitting, rib-breaking crash as it landed on the passenger side roof. On impact, glass shattered and flew through the cab of the truck, spewing sparkling glass in a surreal slow-motion. Julia clenched her eyes closed and clung to the steering wheel.

The vehicle became airborne once again, doing almost an entire revolution in the air as it flew down the incline, finally landing with a horrendous crack on two wheels, smashing Julia back into the door. The truck hung there momentarily as its momentum slowed.

Rocking violently, the truck was not quite able to roll all the way back up to all four wheels, and with one more shuddering slam, fell back onto its roof, leaving Julia hanging upside down in her seatbelt.

The moment froze in time as Julia hung, clenching the steering wheel. Glass continued to shift and tinkle through the wreckage and the engine revved, spinning the tires in space. Rain poured in through the broken windows and soaked Julia to the skin. She opened her eyes, blinking as a twisted and unrecognizable, upside-down horizon came into view.

Disoriented and shaking, she turned her head, shocked and terrified to see the roof of the truck smashed in on the passenger side. "Ringo!" she screamed, her heart seizing in her chest until she remembered Ringo hadn't been with her.

The seat belt dug into her chest, shoulder and hips, and her entire body felt painful and numb at the same time. Fighting the urge to scream again, Julia twisted slightly, struggling to gain a sense of up from down.

With one hand, she groped blindly over her head along the roof of the truck and realized it too had been smashed in. But luckily, it had not taken a direct impact of the roll, leaving her just enough headroom. Bracing herself with one elbow, she released the seat belt with the other hand, falling directly onto her head and shoulder. Her knees slammed into the steering wheel then fell into the twisted wreckage of the passenger side.

Painfully, Julia shifted and turned, trying to find an upright position. Broken glass dug into her palms, arms, knees, and back but she hardly felt the cuts springing up all along her exposed skin. Once she crouched on her hands and knees, shivering in the wind, she realized blood was running into her face. Wiping at it distractedly with the inside of her elbow, she inched toward the smashed-out side window, crunching broken glass with each move.

When her head emerged from the truck, Julia was shocked at the downpour of rain and she flinched, blinking painfully up toward the road. Through a terror-induced fog, she called out for help, her voice weak and lost in the storm. Choking on the pounding rain, she painfully inched back into the cab of the truck and was overcome with shivers. Shaking violently from head to foot, Julia realized that no one would be able to see her truck from the highway.

★★★

Chad frowned at his reflection in the steamy mirror and tugged once more on the bow tie that had a strangle hold on his throat. With a huff, he turned and collected his dirty clothes and towel and left the shower room. With his arms full of dirty clothes and the tux bag, he lumbered down the hall. When he reached the living room, he turned to head for the front door, intent on taking the armload to his truck.

Kirsten Fullmer

In his peripheral vision, Chad noted a cluster of people in the kitchen, their heads together in serious conversation. He paused, the vibe in the air pricking goose bumps along his scalp. Becky raised her head from the group, her eyes large and solemn, her mouth a tight, thin line. The blood froze in Chad's veins as he registered the look in her eye.

"What is it?" he asked, his voice flat and cold with trepidation.

Becky left the group to walk toward Chad, her journey of ten feet taking years as he waited, his arms clenched around the garment bag.

"Julia hasn't come back," Becky said, tangling and twisting one of her necklaces in her fingers as she spoke.

Chad's stomach fell to his knees, even though he wasn't sure where Julia should have been. "Come back from where?"

"She ran to Uniontown to get a few more rolls of ribbon. But that was hours ago and no one has seen her since," Becky replied, her eyes large with concern.

Turning to dump his load onto the back of the sofa, Chad swung back and grabbed Becky's arm. "When did she leave? Where was she going?"

Shaking her head, Becky chewed at her bottom lip. "I'm not sure. We finished decorating about eleven-thirty and she said she had plenty of time to go get more ribbon…"

"Did you call her? Check her house?"

Becky nodded. "I just came from there. Her dress is still hanging there in her room, ready, like she would have left it this morning. I don't think she went back there."

The floor fell away under Chad's feet. "I don't understand, where would she be?"

"We don't know…" Becky began, carefully choosing her words, with one hand on Chad's arm. "Marge says that a nasty thunderstorm rolled through the east side of town about an hour ago, and folks at the diner said it was much worse in Uniontown."

All the blood drained from Chad's face and time screeched to a halt. This could not be happening again.

"Chad? Chad, do you want to sit down?" Becky fussed, motioning Mac to come from the kitchen. The older man took Chad's arm and led him into the kitchen, then pulled out a chair for him.

Plopping into the chair, Chad's mind spun back to the day William had died. It was the same – the same confusion, the same lack of information. Part of his brain screamed to just tell him that Julia was gone, let it be done with no long, drawn-out hope but another part of him fought violently against the idea. She couldn't be gone. Or hurt. She couldn't. This couldn't happen to him twice.

He lurched from the chair, his arms swinging to clear the people gathering around him. "I'm going to find her!" he yelled, his voice tight and strained with emotion.

Mac grabbed his arm, pulling him back. "Just wait a minute, boy, listen to me!"

Desperate to do something, anything, Chad flailed to get past the older man.

"Chad, Justin, and Steve are already out looking, just stop for a minute and listen to where they went."

Breaking away from the crowd, Chad stomped through the living room. "Talk while we walk," he demanded. "I'm leaving. No one is going to make me sit here and wait this time!"

Mac hurried along Chad's side as they crossed the yard, explaining that Justin was driving around town and Steve was checking the highway between Smithville and Uniontown. He also explained that Tara had called the store and the clerk remembered Julia buying ribbon and hurrying out before the

Kirsten Fullmer

storm hit. "Let me go with you," Mac urged, concern for Chad piling on top of his worry for Julia.

Chad shook the man off and climbed into his truck, causing Mac to jump out of the way as the engine roared and the truck slammed into drive, its tires throwing up gravel and dirt as he sped down the driveway.

★★★

Julia wrapped her arms tighter around her stomach as she huddled, shivering, in the wreckage of the truck. Soaked from the rain and in shock, she could hear traffic passing up on the road, yet the sounds were disconnected from reality. She'd tried to find her purse and her phone but the cab of the truck was twisted and smashed beyond recognition and glass was everywhere. Unsure whether her purse lay on the smashed side of the truck or had been tossed free in the roll, Julia had given up searching and resolved to give the rain a few moments to pass.

She shifted painfully and dabbed at the sticky blood on her forehead with her fingertips. Hours crept by but it was actually only minutes. Time inched and crawled, glass continued to tinkle through the wreckage and she finally realized she should turn off the truck.

Unhinged thoughts tumbled through Julia's mind. Where was she exactly? Was the truck in danger of rolling more if she moved? She assured herself over and over that Ringo was safe at home and had not been with her. For one panicked moment, she thought she might lose it altogether and scream in fear and pain. But she'd been through far worse, she reassured herself sadly, controlling her breathing as best she could. When the rain finally seemed manageable, she once again shuffled toward the window.

The task of pulling her battered body from the wreckage seemed insurmountable. The window glass lay sharp every place

Shabby Chic After All

she tried to place her knees or hands, and the ground outside the truck was slick with mud and scattered with rocks and weeds, which were also covered with broken glass.

One of Julia's arms hurt horribly and a bruise was quickly darkening just below her elbow, but with one last herculean effort, she tugged her legs from the cab of the truck and into the sodden weeds and mud. As her knee made contact with the ground, Julia cried out in pain. Glancing down she could see that her ankle was swollen and already turning blue and purple.

Wanting only to curl up in the mud and sob, Julia dug deep, searching for the strength to climb up the incline to the road. Why did these things happen to her? Hadn't she been through enough? And then, as if to make her situation absolutely unbearable, Julia remembered that she was missing Tara's wedding. Once again she was on the outside, hurting and alone, as the rest of the world went merrily on with life.

She pushed up to her knees in outrage but the pain was unbearable.

Sobs wracked through her chest and she fell back into the weeds, her clothes soaked with mud, rain, and blood, her heart broken. She couldn't take any more – she was finally destroyed.

Tears mingled with the rain and blood on her cheeks as thoughts of Tara's wedding flashed through her mind. A beautiful outdoor ceremony, with the people Julia had grown to love, all laughing and smiling. Without her.

Thoughts of Chad poured through her entire battered body, causing her to cry out with the tremendous yearning for him to be there with her. She should have never let herself need another person. It always ended this way for her. But she needed him nonetheless. He'd know what to do.

Painfully, she pictured Chad enjoying the wedding; handsome and sparkling in her vision, resplendent in his rented tux. But slowly, like snow melting in the rain, the picture of him

Kirsten Fullmer

laughing with his friends melted and was replaced by a vision of his face when he realized she was missing. No matter how hard she tried, she could not imagine him anything but frantic.

Julia frowned and hugged herself tighter, lingering raindrops mingled with the tears on her face, and her heart ached anew. Chad's experience with William's death could not be repeated – Chad had just began to open up to her and get on with his life.

Drawing on an inner strength she had only recently come to recognize, Julia rose to her knees, then to her feet. Her ankle throbbed wildly, making it impossible to put weight on it, but she limped on her toes, her sandals long gone and her feet bare, clutching at weeds and rocks to crawl and claw her way up the slope to the road.

21

Chad's fingers were white on the steering wheel as he drove out of town. Steve had called to say that he'd seen no accidents on the highway to Uniontown, so Chad slowed, his mind spinning with visions of Tara's old truck spinning out of control from a bridge and hurling into a ravine. Watching for anything out of the ordinary along the sides of the highway, like smashed weeds or tire tracks, he struggled to remain calm.

What had he been thinking, resenting Julia for helping Bobby? He'd been such an idiot! She'd changed everything for him, giving him a reason to look to the future and once again believe he was capable of more than coasting through life, living in a broken-down hole and never feeling anything for anyone. It had been weeks since anyone had looked upon him with pity, probably because he no longer pitied himself. Julia was smart and funny and strong and wonderful and he'd been stupid enough to fear her.

Uttering a silent prayer, Chad willed Julia to draw upon the toughness she'd shown in front of the greenhouse, and hang on until he could find her. He realized now that not only did he love her soft and tender side but he also admired the core of steel she'd drawn upon to survive her illness and begin a new life. She'd been fierce all along, but vicious only in her desire to live and be whole.

His eyes fogging with tears that he determinedly blinked back, Chad frantically hoped Julia could continue to pull from the force of strength that had brought her to him. His eyes darted from one side of the rain-soaked road to the other, his mind spinning back to the day William had died and the horrific hours spent pacing and waiting for news of finding his body. The desperation in his heart was a repeat of that day but today he wasn't waiting, he was searching.

So many times this feeling of helplessness had strangled his heart, rising in the back of his throat until he couldn't breathe, and here he was again. What was it about fate that was so cruel? Whatever brutal thing had taken William was once again clawing into Chad's chest and he gasped for air, the truck swerving on the wet road. Then quietly, warmth settled through the truck and a reassuring voice in Chad's mind hummed that he'd find Julia.

Shocked and caught off-guard, Chad didn't know how or why, nor did he question, he only knew that William was with him, solid and true as he'd always been, and with that added boost, Chad found the strength to choke down his fear and continue to search the sides of the road as he drove.

About the time Chad saw the deep tire marks leading off the highway at the curve, he saw the small figure of a person emerge from the weeds and mud at the side of the road and wobble to a standing position. At first he couldn't make out the mud-covered form as Julia, but his heart jumped in his chest, elation and joy surging through him, and he knew it was her.

Veering to the side of the road, he slammed the truck into park and jumped out, leaving the engine running and the door hanging wide open. Stumbling blindly through his tears and deep puddles, Justin ground to a stop in from of Julia, hesitant to touch her.

Kirsten Fullmer

"Oh my God, baby, you're okay! You're hurt!" he screamed, his hands flailing as he searched her head to foot for a fraction of a second, then scooped her into his arms and held her to his chest.

"Chad..." Julia sobbed, wrapping her arms around his waist.

Relief emanated from Julia as the sentiment of safety and warmth overflowed her numbed senses. Chad held her tighter.

"I'm okay Chad, I knew you'd come for me," Julia sobbed into his chest as her knees buckled.

Bundling her into his arms, trying to be careful of the cuts and bruises already covering her body, Chad glanced over the edge of the curve to the wrecked underside of Julia's truck, and then he spun on his heel and hurried to his truck.

Tenderly, he placed Julia in the passenger seat, his gaze settling on her forehead, then her ankle. Yanking open the glove compartment, he pulled out two napkins and carefully folded them in half and placed them over the bleeding, three-inch cut on her forehead. "Can you hold this?" he asked.

She nodded, her shaking hand rising to hold the napkins in place.

"Where else do you hurt?" he asked, trying to help her settle her swollen foot into a comfortable position, pushing down panic at the sight of blood smeared from a mass of small gouges all across her body.

Julia didn't answer, she only gazed at Chad with tear-filled eyes, her heart in her throat.

"God Julia, I was so scared, I thought..."

"I'm okay," Julia assured him again, a weak smile crossing her face.

Emotions he couldn't name filled Chad's chest, and he nearly staggered under the potency of his relief. "I'm gonna get you to a hospital," he finally said, cautiously clicking the seatbelt around her.

She began to protest and Chad closed the truck door, took two steps, then turned back, yanked it open and leaned in to kiss Julia. "I love you," he whispered as he stepped back, wiping gently at the blood and mud on her cheek. Then he slammed the door and ran around the front to get in.

★★★

Julia protested heavily all the way to the hospital. She wanted to get back to what was left of the wedding, make sure the flowers had been okay, and congratulate Tara before they left on their honeymoon but Chad wouldn't have it.

Once Julia was in the hands of doctors in Uniontown, Chad stepped away to call Justin, still wearing his now blood-spattered tux jacket. He quickly conveyed what had happened, then returned to stay by Julia's side.

All through X-rays, Julia fussed about getting back to Smithville. Then, as they casted her broken ankle and bandaged her head, she fretted over missing Tara's big day and causing her friend concern.

Finally they were headed back toward Smithville. Julia sat silently, wearing a ratty pair of sweat pants and a paint splattered shirt Chad had found behind the seat of his truck. The pants wadded at her ankles and the shirtsleeves were rolled up multiple times, but the outfit was far better than the ruined one she'd been wearing. The nurses at the hospital had washed her up but her head was spinning, not only with pain and distresses over the wedding, but with worries over her truck, her lost purse and phone, even her pets at home.

To ease the tension and attempt to comfort her, Chad put in a CD and pushed buttons, pausing to grin at Julia as the notes of the song *Blackbird* filled his truck.

Julia unclenched her fists and relaxed into the seat as the familiar melody wafted over her battered body, the sweet words

Kirsten Fullmer

leading her thoughts to a more thankful place. She had survived the crash with only a sprained arm, a broken ankle, and a minor concussion. She could easily have been killed or hurt far worse, been unable to climb up to the road to be rescued, lying there for hours, in pain and fear until someone stumbled across her. Thankfulness finally established itself into a small corner of her heart and began to grow.

Sure enough, like the song said, she'd had broken wings when she arrived in town, but she'd learned to fly, and not only fly, but soar to heights she'd not imagined. She was battered once again, but her wings were intact and she'd fly once more.

Her eyes had been sunken but as the tune implied, she'd learned to see. She now experienced life through an altered filter, with new and strangely brilliant emotions coloring her view. She'd come through the darkest of dark nights and continued through life with her face to the sun. And now, in this moment, she realized she *had* been waiting. Waiting to understand how odd and unforeseen life could be, yet how vivid and hopeful and surprisingly superb each day truly was. In a dark and terrifying moment, when all seemed lost, not only had she been strong, but she'd drawn upon her love for Chad to give her that strength.

Rolling her head on the headrest to face him, Julia realized he was gazing at her, his eyes darting back to the windshield, then to her again, as they wound up the driveway to the bed and breakfast.

He reached over and squeezed her hand. "Are you sure you're up for this? You're still covered in blood and dried mud," he asked, concern ringing in his tone.

She nodded and extended her hand to him as they pulled up to the old house. "I really want to see Tara before they leave."

Chad looked dubious but parked the truck. Cars were still pulled up hither dither all around the yard, and Julia was relieved and hopeful that they'd arrived before the festivities were completely over.

"Thanks for finding me," she whispered, tears gathering in her bright dark eyes. "I knew you would be there for me." She sniffed and blinked, wiping her other wrist across her nose. "And I love you too."

Chad's eyes softened and a slow, heart-melting smile warmed his face as he squeezed her fingers, the lines of concern around his eyes easing. Her words had been simple but he knew that from Julia they were nothing short of a miracle. Her concept of love and people in general had been devastated, and the simple phrase she'd uttered meant she had confidence in him and believed in him to be there for her, which spoke volumes about her belief in herself.

"I'll always be there for you," he whispered back.

Before he could say another word, people began spilling from the inn to pour across the yard toward them. Leading the pack was Tara, her wedding dress grasped in both hands and hiked to her knees so she could run through the grass, tears streaming down her face.

Quickly Chad ran around the truck and opened Julia's door to help her out, her feet touching the ground just as Tara reached her.

Without a word, Tara grabbed Julia to her chest, crying and sobbing words of relief and concern.

Shocked and worried about mussing Tara's dress, Julia struggled in her friend's grip.

"Tara, honey I'm fine, you'll ruin your dress," Julia mumbled into the flounces of Tara's veil. But Tara continued to rock back and forth, her grip tight on Julia as she sobbed.

"Julia, oh Julia, I was so afraid I'd lost you. I was so scared."

Finally Tara relaxed her grip enough to hold Julia at arm's length, her eyes scanning the bandage on her forehead, her

Kirsten Fullmer

muddy hair, borrowed clothes, and casted foot. "Oh my God, Julia, come in and sit down. Are you sure you're okay? You don't look okay."

Tara moved to Julia's side, still gripping her good arm, and Chad moved to her other side, his arm around her waist, allowing her to put her bandaged arm around his shoulder for support. Becky hurried to help Tara lift her wedding dress and they stepped around the truck.

Julia paused, faltering in shock, at what appeared to be the entire town parting, to allow them to pass, hands reaching out to pat and grasp at her as people uttered concern, their voices mingling into a jumble of warmth and kindness.

"Everybody get back and give the girl some room," Becky demanded, waving her arm for them to move.

Winnie's wrinkled smiling face appeared, then Fergus' and Bobby's. Gloria stepped up to grip Julia's hand briefly, the girl's brilliant green eyes bright with emotion, then she ducked back into the crowd. Bobby's mother waved from the porch, tears on her overwrought red cheeks. Marge shooed children from the steps to give the group room to pass, and Steve and Mac scuffled briefly over who would open the front door.

When Julia was inside, the crowd pressed closer as Becky and Tara blocked the injured girl with their bodies and babbled instructions, pointing all directions. The coffee table was cleared, a pillow was plopped on it, and Chad instructed Julia to sit in the overstuffed chair and prop up her foot.

Julia was silent with shock as a glass of water was pressed into her hand. Pillows were fluffed behind her back by unseen hands as the voices of her friends filled the room with questions about what had happened.

Tara grabbed up bunches of her dress and shoed people away from Julia's chair. Kneeling by the coffee table, the bride took Julia's hand. "Are you comfortable? What can I get you?"

Blushing, Julia could only nod, overcome by the attention and kindness pressed upon her. Grasping for words, she gazed into the faces all staring at her, the members of the crowd still muttering and their expressions bright with worry and relief.

"Shouldn't you be leaving for your honeymoon?" she finally asked Tara, her voice thick with emotion.

Justin laughed and shouldered past Chad to stand handsome in his tux at Tara's side. "Don't you think we should get married first?" the groom asked, his eyes twinkling.

Julia's eyes widened. "What do you mean? Aren't you... the wedding?"

Tara laughed and squeezed Julia's cold fingers. "Honey, I couldn't get married without my best friend."

The room spun as Julia grappled with her friend's words. "You mean...you didn't have the wedding?"

Tara stood and put her arm around Justin, her eyes bright. "Julia," she said, "Everyone was out looking for you. Besides, we *wanted* to wait for you." She looked up to Justin. "Didn't we, babe?"

Justin nodded, his expression serious. "We couldn't have got married when everyone was freaking out and I was out driving around looking for you. Hell, as soon as Chad heard you were missing, he took off at a dead run."

Tara's brow furrowed. "Of course, if you're not up to it, we can postpone..."

Realization dawned on Julia. Life had not danced cheerfully past as she lay alone in pain and fear. Not this time. These people, her friends and neighbors, had put everything on hold to search for her, find her, and care for her.

The crowd faded as tears filled her eyes and the glass of water nearly slipped from her shaking fingers before Chad knelt by her side and caught it, handing it off to Becky. Muttering voices rose around her in concern.

Kirsten Fullmer

Julia's heart burst with a sweetness she had never imagined. So this was what it felt like to be secure. It didn't mean power or money – it meant love, both given and returned. Never had she imagined that her chest could hold so much happiness. With her breath coming in gasps and tears spilling down her cheeks, Julia's hands shook as Chad took them in his.

At Julia's first gasp, Becky spread her arms wide. "Everybody back up!" she bellowed.

Chad flinched and Julia giggled, her emotions now too all-consuming to be contained. She hiccupped with an uncontrollable mixture of delight and surprise, looking for all the world as if she couldn't breathe.

"Julia?" Chad worried. "Do you want to have them reschedule the wedding, honey? Are you hurting?" He stood in preparation to get her out of the room.

Julia raised her good hand, a smile lighting her face through her wracking hiccups. Finally managing to choke out that she was okay, she sniffed and accepted Winnie's delicate hanky, which had been shoved into her hand. "No, no, please, I want…" She blew her nose and tried again. The crowded room pressed closer, waiting silently for her to continue. "Let's have a wedding!" she finally sputtered happily.

A cheer of approval rippled through the room as everyone issued orders and people moved away to resume their seats and positions for the wedding. The sound of Bobby's mother's voice boomed over the hubbub. "What did she say? What did the girl say?"

Julia giggled again, her tears drying on her cheeks as Chad knelt back by her side. "Are you sure? You don't have to go through with this you know…"

"I wouldn't miss this—for anything," Julia stuttered, a catch in her voice and a smile bright in her eyes.

Shabby Chic After All

Much commotion ensued as the wedding got back on track. Women trooped to the kitchen to pull the giant lace and flower-trimmed cake from the fridge and Tara was whisked away to her bedroom to freshen up. The men retreated to the safety of the deck to shuffle the chairs into order, and Julia was taken to the shower room where Becky helped her clean up.

"You'll look as pretty as a picture once we have you all dolled up," she assured Julia.

Regarding her reflection in the mirror, Julia was dubious. "Were the flowers ruined in the storm?"

Becky shook her head and helped Julia drop stiffly into a folding chair. "No honey, the storm didn't come through here, we didn't get a drop of rain."

Flinching as Becky began to comb through her ratted and matted curls, Julia was astonished. "Not a drop?"

"Nope," Becky replied, her brow wrinkled in concentration as she used a wet cloth to remove dried blood from the hair at Julia's scalp.

A knock sounded on the door and it opened a crack with Marge's head popping around. "Are these the flowers you wanted?" she asked Becky.

"Perfect." Becky nodded, motioning to put them on the counter with her elbow. "Thanks!"

Marge smiled and patted Julia on the shoulder, then quietly retreated.

Working carefully and quickly, Becky wove and pinned the remaining vines with tiny white flowers around Julia's head and through her hair. The large bandage still stood out like a patch of snow on Julia's tan forehead, but her face glowed with anticipation, completing the picture of a bruised but contented woman.

Moments of awkward finagling crept past as Becky helped Julia slip into her high waisted, form-fitting gown. "Want a few

Kirsten Fullmer

squirts of perfume?" Becky asked as Julia stood to turn and twist in front of the mirror.

"You are a miracle worker!" Julia gushed as Becky sprayed a dab of warm musky scent in front of her and Julia leaned into it with a smile. "I'm ready!"

As Julia limped down the hall toward the kitchen on crutches that had magically appeared, her sore arm awkward and painful, happiness and anticipation radiated around her like beams off the sun.

Tara stood in front of Chad, straightening his bow tie. The best man's tux jacket and shirt were damp in several places from spot cleaning and both turned as Becky said, "Ta-da!" her arm extended as if to introduce Julia. Chad turned and a smile lit his handsome, clean-shaven face.

"You look beautiful!" both Julia and Tara gasped at the same time, then giggled and shrugged, hugging each other around the crutches. "Are you ready to do this?" Julia asked in a whisper.

Tara beamed. "Very ready," she whispered back. "I'm so glad you're here!"

"Me too," Julia confirmed.

Winnie brushed at the skirt of Tara's dress one more time, then reached up to place her wrinkled hands on Tara's cheeks. "I'm so happy for you, dear," she murmured against Tara's face as she planted a light kiss, careful not to leave a lipstick mark.

Tara smiled and swept Winnie into a hug. "I love you, Winnie," she whispered into the old woman's ear, then steadied the shocked old lady back on her feet. Winnie tugged her hanky from under her watchband and dabbed at her watery eyes as she teetered out the door and toward the front of the deck to her seat.

Tara smoothed her palms down the bodice of her dress and grinned. "Let's do this!"

With a nod and a smile for luck, Becky handed her a bouquet of pale pink roses, then bustled to the door and motioned for the music to start.

Julia could see Justin over the heads of the guests, standing next to the pastor down by the pool, his eyes bright in the evening shadows that fell across the gathering. Patterns of dancing sunlight played through the twisted branch arbor over his head and the pink and white roses and draped pearls covering the arbor swayed lightly in the breeze. Justin rocked on his heels and smiled across the deck toward the open French doors.

As the first notes of *Till There was You* filled the air, the flower girl pranced across the deck in her pink lace frock, tossing rose petals, followed closely by the solemn little ring bearer wearing dark trousers and striped suspenders over a crisp white shirt, his eyes riveted to the pillow carrying the rings tied in white and gold ribbon. Lanterns twinkled merrily throughout the wedding party, their tiny fires bobbing and dancing in dimming light as the children shuffled down the aisle.

Julia nodded once more to Tara, then began to shuffle through the door next to Chad. Feeling cumbersome, she managed a few lurching steps down the aisle before Chad stepped in front of her, took the crutches, handed them to a nearby wedding guest and swept her up into her arms.

A rumble of laughter passed through the crowd and Bobby jumped to his feet, hooting in approval.

Contentment glowed in Chad's eyes as Julia's arm wound around his neck and laughter burst from her to float across the deck. He knew he had beaten the odds this time and found himself the most amazing girl on the planet, and he planned to keep her close and enjoy every day they were given.

As he carried Julia down the aisle, both their faces overflowing with joy, her gold antique-lace dress swished in the breeze against his black tux. Chad laughed, then kissed her cheek. "Let's you and me do this soon, what do you say?" he whispered in her ear.

The sky burst into hues of pink and purple as she nodded, too overcome with happiness to speak.

"Did the best man just carry that girl down the aisle?" Bobby's mother inquired loudly over the music. A mumble of amusement spread through the crowd and Chad carefully lowered Julia onto the folding chair that had been hastily brought to the front.

As Chad stepped up next to Justin, the best man nudged the groom with his shoulder and tossed him a grin.

The music changed to the wedding march and all heads turned to gaze back up the aisle. Several wires had been strung over the deck and delicate strips of trailing tulle had been draped over them to form an elegant path for the bride.

Tara came through the French doors. Her white gossamer gown had a hand-embroidered, form-fitting bodice that laced up the front. The skirt was draped in handkerchief flounces of ruffles and just brushed the deck as she moved. The bride floated down the aisle, her face covered with a delicate, frothy veil. The dress, bustled in the back, finished with a flounce of ruffles trailing behind her like a princess. She reached the altar and the music faded as Justin reached for her hand.

The couple stood gazing into each other's eyes, barely hearing the pastor's words. Finally, it was time to repeat their vows and their voices blended into the violet sunset, wafting on the warm summer breeze, across the pool and into the deep-green, Pennsylvania forest.

As Justin lifted Tara's veil to kiss his bride, a cheer erupted from friends and family in the crowd, and Winnie dabbed at her tears with her hankie. His hands behind his back, Chad rocked on his heels and winked at Julia.

Music rang out and waving happily, Tara and Justin headed back up the aisle, across the deck toward the house.

22

Three weeks later, Julia trudged up onto the porch of Winnie's house, her foot encased in a black Velcro walking cast and her arms full. For a moment, she juggled the items she'd tucked under one arm, and then finally rang the bell with her elbow. As she waited, she glanced back to the driveway and her light-blue, 1957 Chevy truck, a grin crossing her face at the painted logo of the flower shop on the passenger door.

Winnie answered the door and a wide smile spread across her wrinkled face. "Oh my, Julia, come in!"

Julia grinned and wobbled carefully through the door, twisting and turning to fit her load between the jambs.

"What all have you got there?" Winnie asked, wringing her hand in her apron, her eyes bright with excitement.

Laughing, Julia dropped a large fluffy pillow and a bag of kitten chow onto the couch. "Like you don't know…" she teased.

Winnie stepped up to Julia's side and put out her hands. "Come here sweetheart, I've been waiting for you," the old woman cooed.

Julia paused, not yet willing to give up the little yellow kitten she grasped carefully in the crook of her arm. She raised the tiger-striped kitten to her cheek, brushing the soft yellow fur down her face, past the scar on her forehead, now only a faded red line. The kitty mewed and grabbed onto her shirt with its sharp little claws, as if to never let go, and Julia's heart twisted in her chest.

Slowly she lowered the little cat and disengaged her tiny claws, gazing into the animal's petite face. "You will be good for Winnie, won't you pretty girl?" she crooned. The kitten answered with a loud raspy mew and the women laughed.

Justin and Tara emerged from around the corner. "Oh, the kitten is here!" Tara declared, prancing up to Winnie's side. Justin leaned against the doorjamb and grinned, a steaming coffee cup in his hand.

"I can't believe the babies are already six weeks old," Julia mumbled, her eyes still locked on the kitten.

"It seemed like eons to me," Winnie said, stepping closer to Julia.

A clatter on the porch announced Chad's arrival. "Sorry I'm late, did I miss Winnie's pancakes?" he asked, strolling through the door with Ringo trotting happily at his heels.

"No, young man, you haven't missed a thing," Winnie assured him, her hands still out to receive the kitten, her knobby fingers wiggling. "Hand that darling over now, or I'll burn your breakfast."

Ringo trotted to Justin for a pat on the head, then sat on his friend's boot, panting happily.

Julia swallowed hard and Chad placed his hand on the small of her back. Her gaze swung up to his handsome, beard-stubbled face, then back to the kitten. Slowly and with a shaky smile, Julia extended the kitten toward Winnie.

The old woman murmured endearments to the baby as she wrapped her gnarled fingers around it and lifted it to her wrinkled cheek. "Aren't you the sweetest little thing," she hummed.

The kitten cried, clutching at the front of Winnie's ruffled apron, and Julia leaned into Chad.

Kirsten Fullmer

A long moment passed and Justin finally cleared his throat. "Were we going to eat or stare at that kitten all morning?" he asked with a chuckle.

Julia laughed with a choke in her voice. "I'm so glad you're all here," she said, her hand slipping into Chad's.

The group turned to head for the kitchen, Ringo leading the way. "We wouldn't miss this, or Winnie's pancakes," Tara laughed. "I was thinking we could do this again next weekend up at the inn when you bring us our kitten."

Justin halted abruptly, his coffee sloshing over the top of his cup. "Excuse me?" he said as Chad and Julia laughed.

"Sounds good to me," Chad chuckled. "How about it babe?" he asked down to Julia.

All heads turned to Julia as she contemplated the thought. "I think that would be great," she finally said with happy tears bright in her eyes.

Chad gave her a squeeze. "I think it's settled then."

"It's not settled," Justin muttered as he wiped dripping coffee from the edge of his cup and followed the group toward the kitchen.

Tara happily clattered plates from the cupboard onto the kitchen island. Winnie tucked the kitten into the crook of her arm and settled onto a stool. Justin placed forks by each plate and everyone pulled up a stool. Ringo trotted across the kitchen, turned around three times on the hooked rug in front of the sink and flopped down for a nap.

Julia glanced around the sunny kitchen, thinking of her own house and that day at the boutique when she'd first heard that Tara had remodeled this place. Never had she dreamed that she would be able to fill her own home with flowers and treasures of all kinds, including love and friendship.

Laughter bounced through the room as the plate of pancakes was passed around the gathering, warming Julia's heart to the point of bursting.

Pausing to watch the tiny kitten nuzzle into Winnie's lap, Julia realized Chad's hand was hanging in mid-air with the syrup bottle. Jolted back to the task at hand, Julia took the bottle, her gaze warm on Chad as he smiled down at her, understanding where her thoughts lay.

He cleared his throat and turned his attention to Winnie, who sat contentedly stroking her new kitten. "So what do you plan to name her?" he asked the old woman.

Winnie lifted the kitten to eye level and smiled at her tiny face. "I was thinking maybe Elvis…"

Kirsten Fullmer

If you or someone you know or love has suffered from encephalitis, or if you'd like more information about the disease, you can go to:

http://www.encephalitisglobal.org

If you'd like to know more about how you can help, support groups and a global network of friends who understand, go to:

http://www.inspire.com/groups/encephalitis-global

Lightning Source UK Ltd.
Milton Keynes UK
UKOW04n1144040915

258044UK00004B/23/P

9 781460 245385